ADVANCE P

"*Centerline* is a great novel . . . captures the story of what many Americans fail to appreciate — the sacrifices of our armed forces and the families who support them. The tactical flight operations and ground combat scenes are real—not Hollywood, and the stories of wounded warriors and the military medical teams that care for them are unforgettable."
—GENERAL BILL BEGERT, USAF (RET),
Former Commander, Pacific Air Forces

"*Centerline* captures the passion, dedication, heartbreak and triumph of combat medicine and aeromedical evacuation in a way no reader can forget. Not every hero is at the front. Not every act of valor takes place under fire. This is an important story. I am glad to see it told right."
—LIEUTENANT GENERAL (DR.) PAUL K. CARLTON JR., USAF (RET), Former Surgeon General of the Air Force

"*Centerline* is the realistic and compelling story of the 'battle' after the fight is over. . . . Military members, some injured and some not, yet all having to deal with the issues of career, family, health, recovery and frequent exposure to the trauma of combat. An excellent story highlighting aspects of sacrifice that are frequently hidden from public view."
—GENERAL WILLIAM S. WALLACE, US ARMY (RET),
Former Commander, United States Army Training and Doctrine Command, Former Commander, US Army V Corps, during the ground invasion of Iraq

"*Centerline* is a superb, fast-paced novel that realistically captures the spirit and emotion of Americans involved in seeing that our wounded warriors are professionally cared for. The artful description of a C130 flying low level brought back many memories . . . of bouncing around in a darkened cargo hold, tethered to the floor by a sling rope, as we approached an unlit airfield. The story of how our wounded return to their loved ones is told in a very powerful way . . . *Centerline* is an awesome read."
—COMMAND SERGEANT MAJOR MICHAEL A. KELSO, USA (RET), Ranger Hall of Fame, 2010

"I was a combat medic on the front end of the global military medical system that McIntyre describes—until an RPG made me a critical care patient. As someone who has experienced an arduous medical journey through this system—from serving in Afghanistan to treatment at Walter Reed (40 operations), and finally, back home to Mississippi, I learned a great deal of all the processes unseen to me as a casualty."
—C. J. (DOC) STEWART, Former Medic in 101st Airborne Division, Wounded in Afghanistan, June 15, 2010

"Not since the early works of Tom Clancy has an author so superbly captured the drama, detail, and personal experience of soldiers and airmen at war—except these scenes are real. Do you want to know what it is like to fly a four-engine airplane, in bad weather, with a serious emergency? Read *Centerline*."
—HOWARD PUTNAM, Former CEO Southwest Airlines

"The flying scenes in *Centerline* are detailed, realistic and thrilling. You smell the jet fuel and sweaty flight suits. You feel the enormous strain we've placed on our crews and airframes during the past decade. Brilliantly written . . . unforgettable."
—ROBERT F. DORR, Author of 72 books on military aviation including *Mission to Berlin* and *Mission to Tokyo*

"I read *Centerline* one night on an airliner flying through stormy weather. I got so engrossed in the story and narrative that when we touched down at each stop, my mind and body were in the seat of a C-130. I honestly thought we'd touched down, in a Herc, at that "air base outside Baghdad" . . . with all the adrenalin and reactions that might've entailed. It was that real!"
—GENERAL CHARLES T. (TONY) ROBERTSON, USAF (RET), Former Commander USTRANSCOM and Air Mobility Command

"As a military spouse and new mom, with a pilot husband on his second tour to a combat zone, I understand the hardships and sacrifices that go along with the constant cycle of separation that families endure. Gone to war—gone to training—gone to war. I am thankful somebody finally told this part of our story."
—KELLI FARGASON, Army Spouse, Illesheim, Germany

"If you've flown over Iraq at night, cringed at incoming rockets in the Green Zone, dined with the Combat Support Hospital staff with their ears cocked for in-bound choppers, held the hands of our young soldiers, dazed and freshly admitted from an IED ambush that devastated their unit, and then participated in the honor, recognition, and rehabilitation of our returned wounded warriors—then you will recognize the scenes in this book. *Centerline* brings it home, often with a tear, for those who sacrificed, physically/mentally/financially, more than most Americans will ever appreciate. Dave—THANKS!"
—CHRIS NORTH, Counterinsurgency and Counterterrorism Advisor, Iraq 2007, 2009-11, Advisor to Afghan Army, 2012

"*Centerline* captures not only the intensity of aeromedical evacuation but accurately depicts the tremendous advances made in keeping our wounded warriors alive. It is a fitting tribute to the dedication and expertise of the medical teams and the bravery and sacrifice of our wounded warriors. It is an inspirational story for all."
        —COLONEL (DR.) ROBERT P. KADLEC, USAF (RET),
    Former Special Forces Flight Surgeon

"As a young copilot flying in the middle of the night across the north Atlantic, I remember the feelings I had while reading Ernest Gann's *Fate is the Hunter* for the first time. It was a story written by a pilot, about being a pilot. But it was much more than that. Now comes a story for this generation. Life and leadership boiled down to its essence. How the seemingly random turns out to be amazingly perfect . . . like it was meant to be. How your past is always preparation for your future. Ever wondered what that might be like? Read *Centerline* and find out how it feels."
        —MAJOR GENERAL RANDAL D. FULLHART, USAF
    (RET), Commandant of Cadets, Virginia Tech

"Riveting! I couldn't put it down. I believe *Centerline* should be required reading for every spouse of a member of the United States Military. I gained more insight into what my husband does from reading this book than from any military spouses' workshop I've attended over the last 29 years."
    —KATY KANE, Air Force Spouse

NOT EVERY HERO IS AT THE FRONT

CENTERLINE

A NOVEL ABOUT WOUNDED WARRIORS COMING HOME

To Walter
Gig-Um?

DAVE McINTYRE

Dave McIntyre

GoodBlood

This book is a work of fiction. Names, characters, businesses, organizations, places, events, and incidents are either a product of the author's imagination or are used fictitiously. Any resemblance to actual persons, living or dead, events, or locales is entirely coincidental.

Published by Narrative LLC in partnership with GoodBlood
P.O. Box 11968
College Station, TX 77845

Copyright ©2012 Narrative LLC
All rights reserved.

No part of this book may be reproduced, stored in a retrieval system, or transmitted by any means, electronic, mechanical, photocopying, recording, or otherwise, without written permission from the copyright holder.

For ordering information, please contact:
Narrative LLC or order online at CenterlineTheBook.com or amazon.com.

Design and composition by Greenleaf Book Group LLC
Cover design by Megan Van Wagoner and Christa Albano
Map by Christa Albano
GoodBlood is a trademark of NSPYR LLC

"Rock Around the Clock," written by Max C. Freedman and James E. Myers, performed by Bill Haley and His Comets, Decca Records 1954.
Hooters is a trademark of Hooters of America LLC

Publisher's Cataloging-In-Publication Data
(Prepared by The Donohue Group, Inc.)

McIntyre, Dave.
 Centerline : A novel about wounded warriors coming home / Dave McIntyre. -- 2nd ed.

 p. ; cm.

 Issued also as an ebook.
 ISBN: 978-0-9857929-0-9

 1. Soldiers--Wounds and injuries--Psychological aspects--Fiction. 2. Homecoming--Psychological aspects--Fiction. 3. Airplanes, Military--United States--Fiction. 4. Military personnel--Psychology--Fiction. 5. War--Psychological aspects--Fiction. 6. Christmas stories, American. 7. War stories, American. I. Title.

PS3613.C56 C46 2012
813/.6   2012943118

ISBN: 978-0-9857929-0-9

Second Edition

This book is dedicated to my heroes:

COL Nick Rowe
United States Military Academy, West Point, Class of 1960
Murdered by Communist Guerrillas, Philippines

LT William Ericson
United States Military Academy, West Point, Class of 1968
Killed in Action, Vietnam

LT George Bass
United States Military Academy, West Point, Class of 1969
Killed in Action, Vietnam

LT Ken Gillihan
United States Military Academy, West Point, Class of 1970
Died in Training, Ranger School, Ft. Benning, GA

COL Jerry Thompson
United States Military Academy, West Point, Class of 1971
Killed by Friendly Fire, Iraq

LTC Dave Pickett
United States Military Academy, West Point, Class of 1973
Murdered by Communist Guerrillas, El Salvador

*Let it be said "Well Done;
Be Thou at Peace."*

—Paul S. Reinecke
from *Alma Mater*
United States Military Academy

CONTENTS

Acknowledgments xi
Foreword xiii
The Herc xvii
Map: Wolf 41/Air Evac 1492 Airports xx
Prologue: IFE
    1230 hours 22 December 2007: SR219, Arkansas 1
Chapter 1: Storm Warning
    1930 hours 22 December: Little Rock Air Force Base (AFB), Arkansas 26
Chapter 2: Lucky Few
    0500 hours 23 December: Little Rock AFB to Scott AFB, Illinois 37
Chapter 3: Nothing to Report
    0955 hours 23 December: Scott AFB to El Paso International Airport, Texas 61
Chapter 4: Broken
    1305 hours 23 December: El Paso, Texas 95
Chapter 5: Fixed
    1320 hours 23 December: El Paso, Texas 117
Chapter 6: Quick Turn
    1440 hours 23 December: El Paso, Texas, to Garden City, Kansas 138
Chapter 7: Evasive Maneuvers
    1620 hours 23 December: Lubbock, Texas, to Garden City, Kansas 164

Chapter 8: Comfort and Joy
 1700 hours 23 December: En Route Garden City, Kansas   187
Chapter 9: "I'll Be Home for Christmas"
 1120 hours 24 December: Scott AFB to Randolph AFB, San Antonio, Texas   212
Chapter 10: Into the Darkness
 1745 hours 24 December: Randolph AFB to Home   227
Chapter 11: Centerline
 0100 hours 25 December: Little Rock AFB   260
Epilogue: En Route
 1600 hours 22 December 2011: Somewhere else   274
About the Author   277

ACKNOWLEDGMENTS

No author writes a book like this alone. It is impossible to name all those who have inspired and helped me to tell this real story as a composite fiction.

But I will begin with those in my family who lived *CENTERLINE* and proved invaluable in its telling. My younger son, Captain Sam McIntyre, USAF—recently returned from his eleventh deployment—flew these missions in combat and at home. His encyclopedic knowledge of flying and his professional attention to detail made the book possible.

My older son, former Captain Roy McIntyre, USA, helped me get the details right of a new fight and a new Army I do not entirely recognize after leaving it a decade ago.

My daughters-in-law provided a unique and essential woman's perspective. Former Captain Cheryl McIntyre, USAF, helped me understand life in the Green Zone. And—critical to this story—dedicated military wife Carolyn McIntyre (also in the Air Force, as every military wife understands) inspired me with the way she has handled her own war and her own little platoon while her husband deployed over and over and over.

Many military members advised me on details for this book, but two military nurses stand out for telling their emotional stories in a dispassionate way. Lieutenant Colonel Cheryl Brown, USA (Retired), helped me capture the remarkable details of emergency medicine at war. Lieutenant Colonel Beverly Thornberg, USAF, helped me understand the special challenges of serving our wounded—and saving them—in the back of an aircraft in flight.

The family team of Tracy and Colonel Bentley Nettles, Texas Army National Guard, shared two inspiring personal perspectives on the disorienting challenge of recovering from a grievous wound. Other vets and wounded contributed to my understanding as well. Professional advice from author Jay Lavender made the book better in every way.

I could not and would not have written this book without the help, guidance, encouragement, and assistance of Colonel Randall Larsen, USAF (Retired). Our fifteen year friendship, began on the faculty of the National War College, fused by our joint experience on 9/11, and growing still as we work together on Homeland Security issues on a daily basis, has been a highpoint of my professional life.

Finally, I must acknowledge my debt to the real soldier in the family, my wife Cathy—born into the Army in the building that became the Infantry Museum in Ft. Benning, Georgia—who moved twelve times in our first twenty years of marriage, who bore lightly all the rigors of military family life, who stayed after me until I wrote something I really wanted to write, and who looked up from an early draft of this book and said "Hey! That's my kitchen! Don't I have copyright on this dialogue?" Thanks, Cat.

And to all those deployed around the world, living *CENTERLINE* today—Godspeed.

Dave McIntyre
College Station, Texas

FOREWORD

On 18 December 2011, the last American soldier in the last American vehicle crossed the border from Iraq into Kuwait. This was the end of the American combat mission—the trail element of thousands of military vehicles and personnel who moved in single file along Main Supply Route TAMPA, retracing the hard-packed desert highway that had brought America into the war nearly nine years earlier. The columns heading south that cold December day were, of course, from the same Army that had once thundered north along this very road, smashing Saddam Hussein's armored forces as it went.

And yet in many ways it was not the same force and would never be the same force again. In the first place, these columns were smaller than those of the invasion because some of their once-proud members had now joined their defeated enemies as rusting hulks in nameless side streets among the dusty villages south of Baghdad. The columns were slower, too, than those that had "shocked and awed" the world in March 2003. Many of the vehicles making this trip south had left the best years of their working lives behind them in Iraq. They rolled now with mismatched wheels, engine parts scored by sand, and pieces salvaged from vehicles that were not making the trip home. All of them bore, in some way, the marks of their long, hard service in that terribly inhospitable environment, and many of them were headed for long months in maintenance depots and repair shops. Even with those attentions, few would ever recover to run again the way they had the day they first rolled off the ships so many years before, loaded for bear and eager for contact.

However, despite the damage, the years of war, and the wreckage left behind (and make no mistake, war wrecks even the victors), one thing still linked these columns unmistakably with their former selves: their military bearing. The jutting angles of their armor, the alert gunners manning turrets dotting roof lines, the clipped radio directions of a hundred vehicle commanders, and the ordered actions of their soldiers at rest halts . . . for all their scars and reduced size—in fact, perhaps *because* of them—these columns bore the unmistakable look of a battle-hardened military force executing a military maneuver.

But who tells the story of those maneuvers when they lead to the maintenance bays rather than the battlefield? Who photographs the columns at the repair depots? Who writes about the parking lots at the port of embarkation and departure for home?

And what about the men and women who rode in those vehicles? Those who slept on them, hid behind them, killed from them, and bled in them? They, after all, are the beating heart and quivering muscles of the military machine. What of the damage they sustained? Who tells about the hospitals, the psych wards, and the VA centers that are now guaranteed a generation of customers who left their best years in the sand and rubble? Who immortalizes those who will be paying the price of that great adventure for the rest of their lives, with every foot-fall on a titanium rod, every painful stretch of burned skin, and every memory that forces its way to the fore in the middle of the night? And who tells of the heroes who evacuated the wounded—nursed their bodies and repaired their spirits—along their own lonely and difficult Main Supply Route to home? Who remembers them?

We do. Those of us who traveled MSR TAMPA and lived the story of America's war in Iraq, as well as the return home. And we are grateful that someone has told an important and otherwise invisible part of that story in this book.

Roy McIntyre
Former Captain of Cavalry
United States Army

THE HERC

Some aircraft have become icons for their age. For World War II in Europe, that icon was the B-17. For the War in the Pacific, and its end over Hiroshima and Nagasaki, it was the B-29. For the Cold War, it was the means-business image of a B-52.

And since 1956 the image over foreign lands that meant the United States of America had arrived was the C-130 transport. Not a fighter jet that flashed in and flashed out. Not a bomber that came with its load of destruction or threatened that trip to promote deterrence. Not even the nimble helicopter with its agility but short range. As important as these aircraft and their crews have been, it was the arrival of the humble cargo plane – the global workhorse of the United States Air Force—that meant America was in for the long haul. And for six decades that workhorse has been the venerable C-130 Hercules—"The Herc" as its crews and passengers know it.

Need paratroopers in the Dominican Republic or Grenada or Iraq (or Little Rock, Arkansas)? Call the Herc. Need supplies to lands torn by earthquake or tsunami? Call the Herc. Need ammunition delivered to remote dirt airstrips, or by low level parachute drop over inhospitable terrain? Call the Herc. Need to know what's happening in the center of a hurricane, or critical parts carried to a base at the South Pole? Call the Herc. Need our troops extracted from the hell of combat and a flying hospital to save their lives on the way home? Call the Herc.

Part of the reason for this extraordinary success, is the aircraft's remarkable cargo-carrying capacity, with a bay that can be quickly reconfigured to hold anything from combat paratroopers, to light tanks, to fire fighters or civilian evacuees, or racks of stretchers and highly skilled medical teams. Part of the success comes from an excellent aerodynamic design and rugged construction that has made it a highly prized purchase for many foreign air forces as well. Another advantage is a modular concept that has allowed new engines, new avionics, new communications (and for some models, new weapons) to be added regularly, so an airplane conceived in the mid 20th century can now employ cutting edge technology from the 21st.

And part of the reason for 60 years of American success in this aircraft is 60 years of crews, on the ground and in the air, in the front and in the back, who have put duty above family, and service above self, day after day and night after night, in every kind of weather, doing every kind of mission, in almost every airspace over almost every country in the world.

Like the crews who fly the aircraft and the nation it represents, the Herc gains strength from its ability to renew itself over time. The C-130A model that first carried the American flag on its tail in 1956 has given way to successive models leading to the C-130J today—an astonishing monument to American engineering and American aviation. But wars are wearing, and sometimes aircraft become tired before they are replaced. As do their crews, and the medical and other teams performing duties inside, and the troops depending on their presence. And the families waiting at home.

The C-130E that plays a stoic lead role in this book is a great aircraft that has grown weary in the service of its country. The first C-130E, tail number 61-2358, entered service in 1962. That aircraft retired from

Little Rock Air Force Base in 2012, headed for display at Edwards Air Force Base in California.

If it could talk, it would tell a story like *CENTERLINE*.

WOLF 41/AIR EVAC 1492 AIRPORTS

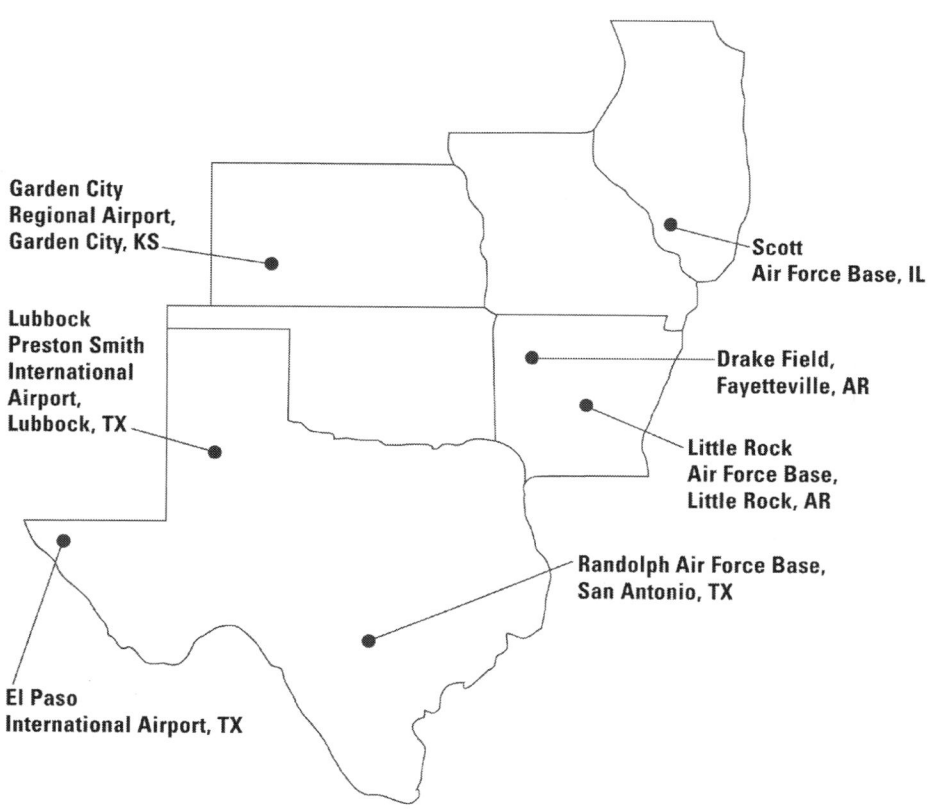

PROLOGUE

IFE

1230 hours 22 December 2007: SR219, Arkansas

Across open sights, the hunter drew a careful bead on the deer at the edge of the clearing.

"*This is it,*" he thought. "*The moment that counts. Everything in focus. Everything in balance. Life and death on the line.*"

Actually, he felt it more than thought it. That's what hunting with a muzzle loader was mostly about—feeling. He had felt the cool dampness as he left the car on the forest road and hiked into position in the early morning darkness. He had felt the cold burn of the steel barrel as he loaded the CVA Wolf hunting rifle from an earlier century—pouring the black powder down the long barrel, inserting the paper in the muzzle and then the ball, and then packing it all down with the long, thin ramming rod. He had felt the prickles of freezing air on his face as he waited for daylight downwind from the clearing, in a spot he had picked after months of walking the hills. He had felt the electric thrill of the hunt as an eight-point buck—unusual for this area and this time of year—stepped cautiously into view, sniffing the air, pausing for something edible that he spied on the ground, then sniffing the air again.

And now the hunter felt centered, as if everything in his life were on hold, hanging suspended between before and after. Looking carefully down the barrel, the front sight post exactly bisecting the *V* of the rear sight, aligned precisely with the motionless red-brown rib cage of the buck, just behind its right shoulder . . . the hunter raised his right thumb to the hammer of the rifle and pulled it back to the cocked position with an almost imperceptible click.

Almost imperceptible. But fifty yards across the clearing the deer froze and tensed his muscles for flight, then turned his head slightly to look in the hunter's direction. In turn, the hunter froze, feeling the long barrel of the rifle getting heavier by the second. With a slight pull he took up the slack on the trigger and then increased the pressure to the rear, waiting for the discharge. The deer shifted his gaze over the hunter, still on line with him but looking higher. The hunter's finger moved further to the rear. For an instant everything was fixed in time and space.

A deep throbbing hum sounded in the hunter's ears. A throb he felt more than heard.

In an instant the hum became a roar that exploded directly over his head. Just above the tree tops, a huge gray shape flashed past. The forest reverberated with the sound, tree limbs vibrating like tuning forks. What was left of the dry fall leaves shook from their branches and cartwheeled to the ground. The forest itself was instantly alive, moving to the pulsing roar. The buck snorted once, sprang to an amazing height, turned in midair, and touched the ground just long enough to bound off in a different direction. The huge white flag of a tail waved once and was gone, vanishing into the dry, brown thicket of the woods.

"Damn!" The hunter shook his head and exhaled at the same time. Whatever it was, it was big and low. And fast.

One of his personal means of getting in balance with nature was hunting as his forefathers had hunted, his primitive senses and primitive weapon pitted against the professional denizens of the forest. Another thrill was hunting after the legal season was over.

"*Damn game wardens!*" he thought. "*What the hell do they have now?*"

He had six seconds to recover and ponder how law enforcement might interfere with the Zen-like centering of the modern hunter, before a second huge shape thundered just over head. This time he got a better look—at the four great engines and the USAF painted under the wing—before the monstrous aircraft, which seemed just out of reach, roared past. He turned to follow its progress and saw the first plane farther away, sprinting down the ridge line with the second following a quarter mile behind. The noise was fading quickly, but still echoing from bare trees and rock outcroppings, when a third aircraft loomed overhead. Its throaty hum became a wave of noise as the engines passed by—a wave that followed the dark gray silhouette as it joined the conga line just above the outstretched tips of the wriggling branches. Another six seconds and a fourth monster shattered the silence and shook the trees with the hurricane from its propellers, then receded quickly in line with the others.

"*Good Lord*," the hunter reflected. Later he would be upset about the deer. But for the moment it was forgotten as he stood frozen in wonder at what he had just seen and felt. A low-level pass by a huge transport plane is an awe-inspiring sight. Four in a row, right over head, produces a memorable moment, as though you are seeing something special and private.

What the hunter felt was a strange mixture of emotions. Pride. Awe. And not a little bit of envy, as the lead aircraft, now nearly two miles away, lifted its right wing and the sun's reflection brightened the dull gray skin for just a moment. Then the plane slipped sideways, left, and down into the valley below.

Instinctively he raised his right hand as his left grasped the rifle midway down the barrel. It was a dumb gesture, he knew. They were miles away, focused to the front, skimming the tree tops at 250 miles an hour. It was futile and a bit immature. But he couldn't help himself. He waved.

The second aircraft in line raised its right wing as if to wave back. Then it slid with a rush a thousand feet down the mountain side, into the valley, and out of sight. The last two followed quickly behind.

★ ★ ★

The first aircraft in the line was a C-130 Hercules "E model" transport built in 1963. Although it had been well maintained and rebuilt once by the manufacturer, it was still eighteen years older than its pilot. Its four Allison turboprop engines were ripping through the morning air with 19,000 pounds of thrust apiece. But because of their age, planes of this model were subject to numerous problems that crews just had to live with. "Old things break in new ways," crew chiefs liked to say.

One perpetual problem was the engine and propeller system. Designed with a slide rule five decades earlier, it was a thing of power and beauty when it was running right. But over time, it became prone to unique and unanticipated malfunctions as modern replacement parts interacted with old and over-stressed metals, disrupting design tolerances in unforeseen ways. These malfunctions could be as simple as an electrical short. Or as complex and dangerous as a bleed air leak, a nightmare scenario where exhaust gases at 600 degrees Fahrenheit could escape through a pinhole in a worn tube, and turn like a cutting torch on wiring, hydraulics, and fuel.

The outcome could be catastrophic.

Old planes and new parts, under stress for years. For the crews, it was a constant game of striking the right balance—more art than science.

With most of the newer models gone to war, the E models were "hauling the water" and training the crews back in the United States. As the equipment wore out, the crews took up the slack.

The twenty-eight-year-old pilot, Captain Mike Middleton, sat rigidly in the left seat. He was strapped tightly to an aluminum frame encased by gray nylon, covering a wad of polyurethane foam that was collapsed in places and always slightly moist from the thousands of crews who had sweated out missions in the past. It was adjustable to the front and rear, and also up and down to allow each pilot to establish his own personal line of sight over the dash. Captain Middleton had it adjusted all the way forward and all the way up, with the back locked to incline slightly beyond the vertical. Most pilots would have thought the position uncomfortable, but this pilot didn't seem to mind. He thought it gave him a better view down and forward of the flight path, and a better feel for the aircraft in the air. It also made him look a bit stiff—distant and machine-like. He didn't mind that either.

As a man and a pilot, he wasn't rigid in an inflexible way, but more like a wing spar or a landing strut: overdesigned to flex and still bear more of a load than ever expected on a standard mission. But over time, even the best designed component tempered from the best of metals could become tired and brittle. The trick was knowing when the parts of the system—the men and the materials—were out of balance and when they were about to break. That was really hard.

The pilot had one hand on the half-circle control yoke that manipulated the movable surfaces on the wing and tail. His other was on the four throttle levers in the center console to his right. His feet rested lightly on the pedals that swung the tail to the left or right. His gaze shifted constantly between the vista through his front window, the trees and cliffs rushing by his left side window, the varied terrain he could see through the Plexiglas panels by his left knee, and the cluster of black dials and gauges directly before his face. He could not see the body of the aircraft he was forcing through the cold December air or the air itself as it rushed over the aluminum skin and control surfaces, pulling and tugging with the forces of lift and drag. He could not see it. But he could feel it.

The copilot was actually six years older and a major, with more staff experience but fewer flying hours. He was renewing his credentials on training flights, and so, in an arrangement unique to the Air Force, the junior person in rank was actually the pilot, in charge of the aircraft and the mission. Major David Barksdale was an experienced professional. He didn't mind taking instructions from a junior pilot with more experience. High professionalism, low ego. It was a great combination, if a bit rare for majors on the way up.

Riding in the right seat, his attention was focused primarily on the maps and trying to keep track of exactly where they were as the pilot constantly jinked up and down, and veered frequently off course using every valley and ridge they passed to mask the aircraft from view. Ever shifting his focus according to the mantra "clock, map, ground," the copilot kept careful track of their timing on each leg of flight, using the aircraft GPS and a stopwatch slung around his neck. Knowing the speed and the time after each checkpoint allowed him to know where they should be on the map, and what terrain features he should be seeing. Glancing out the window periodically, he would reconcile their real position with what he expected to see according to the map. Flying low and fast, and hugging the ground like a speeding snake could be disorienting without strict adherence to the process.

Behind and between them sat the flight engineer, Tech Sergeant Martin Jefferson. With nineteen years in the service, he was the oldest member of the crew. His understanding of how the aircraft operated rivaled that of the pilot, but was based more on doing, and less on reading and practicing in the simulator. He generally knew what the aircraft would and could do in a tight situation, even if he didn't know exactly why. But he was no slouch with a book. In preparation for upcoming retirement, he had completed a master's degree in aviation management online.

He was watching a different set of gauges, referring to a different checklist, and responsible for a different set of buttons and switches overhead. Some might have thought twice about the blur of rocks, cliffs, and trees rushing by almost close enough to touch. Some might have wondered about the people in the left and right seats ahead of him. Not Jefferson. He knew the aircraft. He knew these pilots. He knew the Air Force. He was part of something he trusted. And loved.

His only concerns at the moment were the left outboard Number 1 engine (whose rpm gauge refused to settle down), and the loadmaster in the back, nineteen-year-old newbie, Airman Ben Quinten, who was still getting used to the Air Force and his job.

Standing behind the engineer, hanging on to the pilot's seat with his left hand, an overhead handle with his right, and bracing his legs against the engineer's seat, was the navigator, Captain Bobby "Dale" Lee. Like all navigators, he really wanted to be a pilot. Unlike some, he had gotten over it.

His escape from South Vietnam on a helicopter at the age of three left him grateful to be in the American Air Force at all. He was just glad to be on the team. Although he had a checklist of his own hanging from a D-ring snapped to an anchor on the top instrument panel, he kept an eye on everything as a double check to the other professionals to his front. He was ready in an instant to pick up duties like radio calls for crew members focused on more immediate tasks. Although he was a little too informal in his approach for the taste of the tightly wound pilot, that demanding taskmaster genuinely liked working with this navigator—a preference that spoke highly of him.

As the plane bucked and rolled up and down, over the ridges and through the valleys, Lee rode the rises and falls with a studied indifference.

Not so in the cavernous back of the workhorse, where the young loadmaster rode out every mission by himself. With only a few weeks on the job, Airman Quinten was still prone to airsickness on these low-level missions.

Behind the pilots was a short passageway back to the cargo bay. On the right when headed toward the rear of the plane was the door by which crew and passengers usually entered. On the left was a small shelf used as a desk where the navigator sat when navigating. At the end of the passageway was a drop of several feet into the cargo bay. Descent was made easier by a ladder. At the base of the steps stood the loadmaster. Beyond him was a huge stack of lumber—several tons of it—lashed together to simulate a cargo load ready to be dropped on this practice mission.

Usually the loadmaster had one hand on a release lever and the other ready to control the switches on a black panel mounted on the bulkhead next to where he stood. But Quinten was using that second hand to hold a paper bag. As the right wing rose and the plane fell down and to the left, Quinten's stomach contents came up and to the right. And into the paper bag.

For a moment he looked at it. And for a moment he thought back to another bag— this one containing burgers and fries.

"Hello! Can I help you? Are you interested in our special today?" Twelve times an hour, four hours a day, four days a week, for two years in high

school he had handed meals in bags through the window of the fast food restaurant where he worked. Every day seemed the same. Every meal seemed the same. Every customer's face at the window seemed the same.

Compared to that, his current job was pretty cool, with or without the air sickness bag in his hand.

Carefully, he closed off the top of his barf bag, sealing the contents and quietly praying the bag wouldn't burst as he tucked it into a lower pocket on the leg of his flight suit, down near his boots.

"*Not bad,*" he thought. "*Only once so far this trip. Getting better.*"

With its wings at a steep angle, the sixty-ton airplane slipped gracefully 2,000 feet down the face of the mountain and into the valley below. The area was sparsely populated but not completely without inhabitants, and at 250 miles an hour and just above the tree tops, the aircraft flashed over many a surprised creature. Trailer houses and campers appeared through the Plexiglas windows and disappeared just as quickly. Two yellow canoes. A man fishing from the bank. A camper enjoying a cup of coffee outside a small red tent. All came and went in a blur.

The navigator touched the copilot's shoulder and pointed up the mountain, ahead and out the right window. Several hundred feet above them a black bear stood on its hind legs and gaped in wonder at what it saw. The crew members gaped back. The copilot thought of calling the pilot's attention to the sight, saw the intensity on his face below his sunglasses, and thought again.

The plane was loosely following SR 219, an approved FAA route through northwest Arkansas that at one point would pass close to an opening on the top of a small hill. Dropping their load of simulated supplies on a marker squarely in the center of that opening was the objective of this mission.

In combat, a determined foe would be populating the hills and valleys, seeking to kill the airplane and crew with rockets, missiles, and automatic weapons. And in combat, the troops receiving the supplies would be depending on this airdrop for ammunition, food, and medical supplies for their wounded. The stakes would be life and death.

This was not combat; it was a training mission. But it was just as complex. And the stakes for misjudging the clearance of a tree or mountain or narrow valley wall were just as high.

"Hold this route for 5 minutes present speed," the copilot said. "When the valley forks you'll see an intersection which is the IP, take heading 270 on the run-in. Three miles later we start the pop."

After five minutes of high speed contortions, the pilot stepped on the left rudder, banked the big bird sharply to the left, and focused on a spot where the valley narrowed to about four times the span of the wings. Forty-five seconds passed and the navigator said "Three miles to drop. Slow down, slow down . . . *now*!"

The pilot slid all four throttle levers back to idle and yanked back on the yoke. The aircraft nosed up and the crew simultaneously hunched down under a force two and a half times as strong as normal gravity, as the pilot traded speed for altitude to deplete their energy. Up front, the navigator pretended not to notice the heaving of the floor. In the rear, the loadmaster reached for another bag.

"Ninety seconds!" the navigator said.

"Before drop checklist," the engineer announced smartly across the intercom. "Defensive systems: TCAS?"

The navigator reached back to the station where he sat when he wasn't standing, and rotated a circular switch to the right. "Manual program one," he replied.

Meanwhile, the copilot reached down and flipped a switch on the Traffic Collision Avoidance System, which warns the crew when other aircraft are near. Because others would surely be near in this four-ship drop, the sensitivity of the system had to be reduced.

"TA," he advised.

Moving just his thumb on the control yoke to activate a radio button, the pilot spoke to all the planes in the formation.

"Wolf Flight go Green Seven," he commanded. This put all the planes on a common secure radio frequency just for the drop, so no outsiders might transmit confusing instructions at a critical moment. Each pilot confirmed the command with a brief response.

"Two."

"Three."

"Four."

Then the lead pilot dialed his own radio to the new frequency.

"Wolf Flight check," he called. Again the other aircraft responded cryptically as they checked in.

"Two."

"Three."

"Four."

The pilot called on the new frequency. "Blackjack DZ, Wolf 41 flight of four inbound with actuals."

The garbled and barely audible response was weak. "Wolf 41, this is Blackjack, no joy, continue."

An audible grunt from the navigator expressed what the entire crew thought. The soldiers on the ground did not have them in sight. Perhaps they were in a low spot on the drop zone. Perhaps the trees were taller than expected. Perhaps something was not quite right in the calculation of wind and flight times. But there was going to be some last second maneuvering required as they closed rapidly on a target they could not yet see. Just at the instant that they needed their entire focus on standard procedure, the drop sequence would be compressed. Without expert and methodical teamwork during the next few minutes, this entire airdrop would be aborted. "Game on," said the pilot.

Inside all four planes, crews were following the same intricate chorography.

"Aux hydraulic switch," the engineer read from his checklist.

The copilot reached forward. "On," he said. A dial sprang to life and a pressure of 3,000 pounds per square inch pushed hydraulic fluid through the lines to a cylinder in the rear that was about to lower the tailgate.

Ahead and to the left the pilot noted a distinctive yellow camp house along the stream. The valley widened at that point to a mile or more, and just right of center a clearing was visible on top of a small rise.

"Speed checks, door," the engineer said.

"Cleared open," responded the loadmaster.

The flight engineer reached forward and pressed a button on the center console.

Far to the rear, a horizontal seam appeared where the two sides of the aircraft curved together at the tail. The body split apart, like the swinging doors of an Old West saloon, except the doors divided up from down rather than side from side. The upper half-door began to swing in and up until it nearly touched the roof of the compartment. What had been a closed rear wall suddenly became an open tunnel, with a bright light at the end. The loadmaster could look straight down the length of the cargo hold and out into the air, 600 feet above the ground. Light poured in. The air turned December-cold. He saw blue sky and clouds and a brown smear of leafless trees extending back to the horizon like a carpet. Centered directly in the opening were the other three aircraft of the flight, staggered a half a mile apart, bouncing like his own, and thundering toward the target.

"Door open," the loadmaster announced over the intercom, the audible rush of air muffling his voice.

"Speed 165. Flaps" the engineer said without emotion.

With his left hand the copilot pulled back a lever in the center console. The numbers on a gauge in front of the pilot began to spool up. "Set 50 percent," the copilot said.

Outside, large rectangular extensions emerged from the back of each wing, increasing the curvature of the surface and the lift, but reducing the speed. Inside the crew area, the pilot focused on keeping the aircraft on the centerline of the valley. His feet shifted pressure rapidly between the pedals, and the aircraft rocked a bit from side to side as he compensated for the temporary change in the shape of the wing.

The engineer continued reading off a list dangling from the ceiling on a cord. "Speed checks, ramp," he said.

At his station by the stairs at the base of the flight deck, the loadmaster flipped a black switch.

"Coming open," he announced.

Far to the rear, the lower half of the huge rear door swung out and down, until it became an extension of the floor of the cargo bay. Soon it ran flat and level and stuck straight out into the air below the tail. On signal, the heavy load of simulated supplies was going to slide back on rollers, under the upper door, across the lower door that now stuck out like a ramp, and into thin air. To the left and right of the ramp were smaller oval doors that paratroopers would use if there were any on board. Today the doors were closed. Next to each, a red light glowed brightly.

"Ramp down and locked," the loadmaster said. Freezing air swirled around him. To the rear he was looking straight out into space while the ground disappeared behind him at the now slower rate of 150 miles per hour. "*Cool,*" he thought. "*I wish the girls in the burger place could see me now.*"

The right hand that used to pass burgers through the window had more responsibility now. It was grasping a lever about eighteen inches long, and recessed into the bulkhead. The lever disconnected the locking system on the rails that ran along the left side of the cargo bay—rails down which the cargo was going to slide when the drop began. The right locks were already released. As the aircraft bucked up and down in the turbulence from the uneven forest below, only the left locks held the five-ton load in place.

"One minute," the navigator said. "I'm starting to pick up the DZ."

Ahead, the clearing that was the drop zone began taking shape. "Right 20 meters," the navigator said. With his right foot, the pilot tapped the right pedal near the floor, and the aircraft slid just a bit to the right.

In the clearing on the hilltop an Army pathfinder team from the National Guard had placed an orange *X* fifteen feet across. "I have you in sight," one of them spoke into his radio. The voice was still not perfectly clear.

The navigator advised the crew of their status. "DZ confirmed. No red smoke. Positive comms with the ground. Press," he said into his intercom.

The formation roared on.

"Speed 130," the copilot said. "Forty-five seconds."

"Nuts," said the pilot, glancing at a clock. "We're about 15 seconds behind."

Smoothly he slid the throttle levers forward. The engines responded immediately, and the plane leapt ahead.

"Wolf Flight," he called to the other aircraft. "This is Lead. Going to speed 145 to shack this T-O-T."

No one responded, but behind him three gloved hands pushed three sets of throttles forward, and three aircraft bounded ahead to stay positioned on their leader. They were seeking to place their cargo out the door within thirty seconds of the Time-On-Target calculated three hours and 600 miles ago, and strike as closely as possible to the fifteen-foot cross. There was not much room for error.

Most military pilots are competitors by nature. They have to be. When they are not in a life or death struggle, they are preparing for one.

Fighter pilots think of themselves as lone wolves, seeking to best every other wolf they encounter. Special Operations pilots are pack hunters—alpha males (or alpha females) with the discipline to cooperate with other alpha males for the kill. Transport pilots are more like the warrior protectors of an agrarian society. They are more likely to play defense than offense, more focused on order, planning and rules than chasing prey. The whole existence of the system depends on the teamwork of the defenders. That teamwork depends on group cooperation and individual excellence in exactly the right balance. So the pilot of Wolf 41 engaged in an intense competition in every aspect of his job, every minute of every day: a competition against himself. His standard was perfection. It was very hard to win.

"Thirty seconds," the navigator announced. Suddenly it became quiet inside the plane. The checklists were done. The preparations complete. Nothing was left but the pilot's skill in hitting the mark.

In a final check, the navigator keyed his radio.

"Blackjack, Wolf Flight. Request surface winds."

Immediately a disembodied voice responded, "Wolf, Blackjack. Winds 230 degrees at 15 knots," he said.

The navigator figured rapidly, repeated the instructions to the pilot, and added, "Adjust CARP 40 meters west." The pilot responded for the first time with a hint of irritation in his voice.

"I thought the prebrief said winds 030 degrees at 5?" he asked pointedly.

"Hey, weather happens," responded the navigator, perhaps a bit too lightly.

Everybody knew weather changed in the hours between briefing and execution. But tension at the moment of drop was high and the pilot could not hide his irritation when the plan changed twenty seconds out. The navigator should have checked earlier.

"Forty meters west," the pilot responded flatly.

For all the complex modern avionics, navigation equipment, and communications the aircraft was carrying, the final adjustments depended on the pilot's eyes and a grease pencil mark that he made on the window to his front. He had been lining up his mark with a tall tree on the near side of the clearing and a rock on the far side. The invisible line ran just right of the orange X, because he expected winds to push the open parachute to the left. Now the actual winds were about to push the load more strongly and to the right. He had to adjust.

Quickly he picked an evergreen a bit west of the original near-side marker, and a dark hole between big trees on the far side of the clearing. After a quick adjustment of the aircraft's position, the imaginary line from the mark on his windscreen ran through these new reference points, and forty meters west of the orange X.

"Ten seconds," said the navigator. Pause. "Five seconds!"

"Green light!"

At this the copilot reached with his right hand to the panel on his right side and flipped a switch. The red lights in the rear flashed out and the green flashed on. Simultaneously, he used his left hand to press a button on the left side of his instrument panel. In the rear a weighted arm was supposed to swing down from the top of the cargo bay and drop a nylon extraction chute into the airstream at the rear. The chute was supposed to fill quickly with air, rocket out the back of the plane, and jerk the heavy load out behind it.

But despite the copilot's efforts, the drogue chute remained in place, and the load did not budge. Eager to make a good name for himself in a new unit, the loadmaster had been watching for just such an opportunity. When the arm did not fall within a split second of the green light, he grabbed a backup mechanical release affixed to the ceiling, and tugged with all his might. In the rear of the plane, the arm rotated down, the extraction chute dropped free, inflated to its ten-foot diameter, and shot backward into the wind stream the full length of its yellow nylon attachment cord. The cord jerked taught, and pulled savagely on the load with tons of force.

In less than two seconds, five tons of lumber lashed into a single stack had departed the aircraft. Two thirty-foot parachutes blossomed and slowed its fall. The package swung only twice under canopy, then touched the ground heavily, right on the edge of the orange marker. Six seconds behind that, a second load arrived. Descending beneath yards and yards of green nylon canopies, loads three and four pounded the ground shortly after that. The compensation for changing winds by those pilots had been a little slower and a little less precise. Their loads thumped to the ground a bit farther from the *X*.

Watching his own load depart the aircraft and the nylon canopies ripple to life behind them, the loadmaster cried, "Two good chutes." And after a pause, "Right on the *X*!"

"Completion drop checklist!" the pilot responded, advancing the throttles and rolling the nose of the plane toward the ground. They began to descend and accelerate. The crew turned to a reversed version of the previous checklists, closing the doors, raising the flaps, and "cleaning up" the outside of the aircraft to provide maximum control for the low-level ride home. Within minutes, a formation of four aircraft was making its getaway down the valley at high speed and low altitude.

The pilot glanced quickly at the clock. Drop within a thirty-second window was acceptable. "Within 8 seconds of calculated Time-On-Target," he announced. "Not bad guys, not bad." It was high praise from a taciturn professional. Everyone was pleased.

"Smoke in the aircraft!" the loadmaster announced. Then more urgently, "Pilot, we have a lot of smoke in the aircraft back here!"

For a moment, everyone paused to be sure they heard the message correctly.

Every member of a flight crew lives with the knowledge that even on the best of days, with great visibility, no other aircraft in the area, and everything running smooth, straight, and true, he might in fact be only moments from disaster. So many things can fail, from tiny electronic components to human judgment. The cost of even one minor failure at high speed and low altitude can be quick and disastrous. Every crew member lives with just a little voice of panic in the back of his head, like a scuba diver who is breathing fine under a hundred feet of water but knows this is not his natural habitat and he is just one breath away from disaster.

The panic is covered by training, professionalism, and courage. But every once in a while it shows its head. And now it was stirring in the primitive brain stem of every person on board.

"Are you sure?" the pilot asked. "Where is it coming from?"

"Can't tell," replied the loadmaster. "Near the rear door, I think. But yeah, there's a lot of smoke."

There was probably a simple explanation. The interior walls of the cargo bay were actually quilted insulation that just snapped into place. Between this quilt and the outside skin of the aircraft ran most of the wiring and hydraulic lines. The aircraft was old. Sometimes in old aircraft the stress of years of operations caused wires to chafe together, causing a short. If the short sparked against the insulation, boiling smoke could be the result. That would be a problem, but not a disaster.

On the other hand, the plane was full of plastic, electronics, and other combustible materials. A real fire would quickly generate toxic fumes that could overcome the crew before they realized they had a problem. Even a small flame could quickly become catastrophic. Smoke or fire on an aircraft was nothing to trifle with.

"Don't touch the fire extinguisher!" barked the engineer on the headset. He had trained a lot of new guys. He knew their instincts, despite their training. Civilians might smell smoke and think immediately of how to fight the fire. But a discharged fire extinguisher would not help against an electrical fire, and would make it hard to tell what caused the real problem. Changing a young civilian into an experienced pro takes time. Right now, they didn't have any time.

"Uh . . . okay," replied the loadmaster. Alone with the problem in the back, and not sure of what to do next, he had already taken the fire extinguisher from its bracket on the wall.

"Wolf Flight, this is lead." The radio crackled with the pilot's voice. "I am departing formation. I have an IFE. Wolf Two, take lead."

Everybody on every plane now knew that the first aircraft had some sort of In Flight Emergency, and the second aircraft was in charge of completing the training mission with the three remaining planes. "You fight like you train" is a famous military maxim. As a result of their training, the formation adapted immediately. Command passed to a new pilot and new aircraft in a matter of seconds. They continued the mission. Wolf 41 was on its own.

Without hesitation, the pilot pushed forward on the throttles with his right hand and pulled back on the yoke with his left. The plane nosed up and began to climb.

"Load, situation update!" he demanded.

"Still a lot of smoke back here—maybe more than before," the loadmaster responded. "I'm . . . I'm going to disconnect and move back to take a look."

"No, you're not! Don't move!" barked the pilot, who was already running the emergency checklist in his mind.

But it was too late. Although he had plenty of audio cable to reach the back, the inexperienced loadmaster pulled loose the connection to his communications box, and headed to the source of the smoke, expecting to plug back in closer to the problem. As the plane nosed up, the loadmaster found himself suddenly walking down a steep incline to get to the rear.

Still climbing, the pilot spoke to everyone. "Crew, this is pilot. We have a situation in the back. Check in on oxygen. SMOKE AND FUMES CHECKLIST." The voice showed no fear. It invited no discussion.

The difference between a crew and a group of individuals is the way they work together. This was an experienced crew. There was no panic, but no hesitation either. Each person reached to the place where his oxygen mask was stowed, extracted it, slipped it quickly on his face, snapped his communication cable into place, and checked in on the intercom. The calls were short and to the point.

"Pilot up."

"Co up."

"Eng up."

"Nav up."

But there was nothing but silence from the loadmaster in the rear. Having disconnected his intercom at a critical moment, the inexperienced airman headed back down the center of the cargo bay with his communications cable in one hand, and the fire extinguisher in the other. The acrid smoke burned his nostrils, and caused him to shake his head. He thought about retracing his steps to get his oxygen mask, but moved on to the source of smoke instead. Black puffs were emerging from behind a communications box next to the starboard door, and the airman started to plug in to report what he was seeing. But another puff of smoke popped out from behind the insulation, and he used the hand holding the cable to pull the pin on the fire extinguisher instead.

"Loadmaster report!" commanded the pilot. But the airman, unplugged from the intercom, heard nothing.

"Load report!" the pilot repeated.

Reaching for the source of the smoke, the airman was surprised by a short shower of sparks and another black puff right in his face. Starting backward, he tripped on the rollers that had sped the cargo out the ramp for the air drop, recovered, but lost his grip on the fire extinguisher. The bright red canister slipped from his gloved hand and made a quarter of a rotation before striking the floor precisely on its handle.

With the pin already removed, the extinguisher discharged just as the canister bounced back up. The internal chemical, escaping under pressure, spun the extinguisher in a rapidly climbing pinwheel. It struck the loadmaster squarely on the right ear of his headset, just at the point where the microphone joined the frame, then changed its trajectory, and clattered to the deck. The wiring connection on his headset was smashed and separated. Now he had no means of communication even if he remembered to plug into the comms box. The broken plastic connector slashed across his forehead opening a cut as long as his right eyebrow and an inch above it. It was not deep or dangerous, but like all facial cuts it bled profusely and in a matter of seconds blood was running down his face, past his ear, past his collar, and into his flight suit.

The loadmaster staggered backward and sat down hard on the floor. His intercom was useless now, and his oxygen mask nowhere to be seen. A steady stream of black smoke poured into the cargo bay.

"Load, nothing heard," the pilot snapped. "Navigator, please go back and check."

At this point, the pilot had two options: return to his home base, forty-five minutes away, or divert to a closer civilian airfield—perhaps one with medical assistance. He concentrated on leveling off at a safe altitude while the navigator plugged his mask into a small portable oxygen bottle, and moved back to the cargo bay to see why the loadmaster was silent.

Meanwhile, the flight engineer began switching off electrical systems, checking frequency and voltage, trying to isolate the source of a possible electrical short. The copilot worked a separate list. Together they turned off the generators, the connections to the battery, the air conditioning, and other systems.

Traveling the length of the bay, the navigator knelt quickly by the conscious but disoriented loadmaster, then snapped his communications wire into the comms box.

"Pilot, Nav," he intoned with a careful, steady voice. "Looks like the fire extinguisher discharged and smacked Load in the head. He's down on the deck and blood is running down his face. There was some black smoke in the air, but it is hard to separate it from the white stuff from the extinguisher. Suggest we open the doors back here."

The engineer cursed under this breath. These kids. They had seen too many movies. They were always too quick to act. Nothing in the cargo bay was going to explode right away. Think. Breathe. Focus. Then act. No matter how much you told them, they had to get it wrong before they could get it right.

It was decision time for the pilot. If he declared an IFE to the FAA and headed for the nearest hospital, only to find the loadmaster was all right, they would miss hours of training, and squander precious family time tonight because of a delayed return. If he took a training route home and the loadmaster was seriously hurt, the young airman could be much worse—even dead—before he got to medical attention.

"Nav, how does he look?" the pilot queried.

"Not good," came the reply. "Not good at all."

The navigator was thinking of how the loadmaster looked with his superficial cut and superficial bleeding. But the words conjured a different image in the pilot's head.

> Brilliant sunlight poured through the front windscreen and made the pilot squint behind the tinted face shield of his helmet. Yellow desert sand stretched away in every direction as the aircraft skipped over it at barely a hundred feet. The gear was still coming up, and the aircraft was still full of the dust stirred up by the landing and takeoff on a remote airstrip. Kneeling on the floor in the back, two Army medics worked furiously on three soldiers sprawled where they had been dropped. They were not moving. All three were bleeding profusely from wounds—head wounds, arm wounds, leg wounds, gaping wounds you could see, and worse wounds you couldn't see—exit wounds you couldn't always find until it was too late.
>
> One soldier moaned loudly, and tried to roll over and rise to his knees. But he couldn't. He only had one knee. The other leg ended in a mess of bleeding flesh and a tourniquet. There were more wounds than the medics had hands. They were losing the fight.
>
> "Load, how does it look?"
>
> The question came from pilot Mike Middleton, dressed in a brown desert jumpsuit and seated in the left front of the aircraft speeding across the Iraqi desert.
>
> "Not good," came the reply. "Not good at all."

★ ★ ★

Speeding across the hills of northwest Arkansas, Middleton blinked involuntarily, and made his decision. He pressed the transmit button on the yoke.

"Memphis Center, this is Wolf 41. I am declaring an In Flight Emergency. I am at radial 150 and 40 from Fayatteville at 5,000. Flash." He pressed a black button. On the radar screen in the FAA control center in Memphis, Tennessee, one of the green blips that identified the many aircraft they were tracking flashed to attract attention.

"Co, where do you think we'd find the nearest hospital?" the pilot asked.

The copilot's head snapped to the left. It was a good question the pilot was asking. It was a good decision to land. But it was all happening more quickly—and more smoothly—than the copilot had expected. The older pilot was less experienced. And he suddenly found himself struggling to keep up. He grabbed a map, rotated it and figured rapidly.

"Fayetteville most likely," said the copilot over the intercom. "About 6 minutes away." It was nearby, a college town, and had an excellent hospital.

"I have smoke in the aircraft and a crew member with an unknown injury," the pilot told Memphis. "Five souls on board. Three hours of gas. I am proceeding direct to Fayetteville. Request you contact crash fire rescue at that location and advise them we are inbound. Six minutes."

Very smooth. Very cool. Very in control.

"Roger, Wolf 41," Memphis answered almost immediately. "Stand by." Thirty seconds later he was back.

"Wolf 41 Emergency, this is Memphis. Talked to them by phone. They will clear you direct. Good luck."

"*Well, what do you know!*" thought the pilot. The guy was really on his game. Score one for the air traffic boys.

Quickly he rolled the knobs on the radio to a new frequency and called, "Fayetteville Tower, this is Wolf 41 Emergency. Inbound direct from the southeast."

The engineer stood, reached above his head, pulled a handle straight down, and pushed straight up. A 2 x 2 foot section of the ceiling popped up into the air stream. With the doors open in the back, the interior of the aircraft became a huge wind tunnel, as air tore through it at more than 100 miles an hour. Then he and the copilot pulled out their checklists.

"Roger Wolf 41 Emergency," said the tower. "You are cleared direct. Cessna 143, turn right 120 degrees. Clear the approach for Wolf 41 Emergency."

An instructor and student in a blue and white single engine Cessna turned right and away from the approaching C-130. In the fire station, a claxon sounded, the doors rolled up, and in less than sixty seconds, two bright green fire trucks and a white ambulance were out the door. Wolf 41 turned to line up with the runway.

"Five miles," the pilot reported. While he flew the aircraft, the copilot began speaking through the intercom. "Descent Checklist," he said. He was working through the yellow pages of a new booklet.

"Crew brief," called the pilot. "My plan is 100 percent flap landing, speed 135. Taxi to taxiway Delta and meet the trucks and shut down there."

"Before Landing Checklist," said the copilot. "Speed 163."

"Flaps 50 percent," answered the pilot.

"Speed 150."

"Gear down."

"Speed 140."

"Flaps 100 percent."

The headphones crackled with an outside transmission. "Wolf 41 Emergency, this is tower. I have you visual. Cleared to land."

Despite its size and speed, the great gray shape seemed to hang above the approach lights and inch its way to the ground. At sixty feet the ground pushed back, with the air exerting an upward force called "ground effect." Anticipating this, the pilot adjusted just a bit and set the wheels deftly on the numbers right at the beginning of the runway. There was a smooth sliding noise, and they were down.

As soon as the nose wheel touched the ground the pilot pulled the four throttles up and back to ground idle and the propeller blades turned completely flat. He pulled back once more and the pitch of the blades changed again, this time actually pushing air backward in a move civilians called "reversing the engines." The big plane shuttered and slowed to a fast roll. They were on the ground and under control in less than one-third the length of the runway. A combat landing could not have been shorter. A senior airline pilot could not have been smoother.

The copilot had only a moment to think how smooth the landing was, and how calm the young pilot had been throughout the event. He glanced at his watch. Just sixteen minutes since the loadmaster had first called out "Smoke!"

But there was no time for reflection. The crew still had work to do, slowing the aircraft, running through final checklists, turning off at the appropriate taxiway, and coming to a stop directly in front of the waiting emergency vehicles. The crew continued the checklists until the engines were shut down, the electrical systems turned off, and the rear ramp lowered.

"We're gonna have a bunch of disappointed fire guys," the navigator said from the rear. "Looks like just a couple of shorted wires behind the insulation."

The loadmaster was sitting up now, his back against the wall of the aircraft just forward of the rear door. He was holding his head, which sported a long cut over his right eyebrow. Blood covered his forehead, cheek, and chin. The navigator stood and walked down the ramp.

"Sorry guys," he called out. "No fire." The crew of the fire truck looked disappointed.

"But we do have a crew member hurt." The ambulance crew brightened. They put on their gloves and headed up the ramp.

The pilot turned to the copilot. "Sir, we probably ought to send Load to be checked out at the hospital. Do you want to go with him?"

The flight was over now, and rank mattered once again.

"Yeah, I think so," answered the major, who had moments before been a subordinate copilot. "I think I'll go with Load."

"Okay, sir," responded Captain Middleton. "Nav, you go too." He was walking a fine professional line now, deferring to the major as his senior in rank, but remaining conscious of his own responsibilities as senior pilot. "I will stay on comms with the tower. Eng, you want to call home and get maintenance started this way?"

"I'm on it," Tech Sergeant Jefferson answered, pulling his cell phone from his pocket.

"Hey boss," said the navigator over the intercom, oblivious to rank and protocol. "Our new boy here was trying to do the right thing. It was a new guy mistake. You might cut him a little slack."

"That's not good enough," the pilot snapped back. He was having none of it. "Trying is not good enough. This is all about doing the *right* thing, not just doing *something*. He needs to learn that *now*. Before he gets a lot of people hurt."

The navigator grimaced. Nobody else said anything over the intercom.

Now for the hard part. Waiting.

It would take thirty minutes to convince the maintenance crew that someone had to drive to the Fayetteville airport to find the source of the problem. It would take them two hours to make the drive. It would take more hours to find the two wires that shorted out, and more still to clear the plane to fly. Then they had to recover the rest of the crew from the hospital. They had been forty minutes from home and two hours from the end of the work day when the emergency started. Now they would be lucky to get home before dark.

The pilot pulled his phone from a pocket on his sleeve. He considered sending a text to tell his wife he would be late. Then he thought again. He wanted to stay focused on the mission. And he didn't want to start a flurry of messages and explanations.

Outside, three crew members and one headache boarded the ambulance for the ride to the hospital. As they pulled away the major thought again about how smooth the entire event had been. A multi-ship airdrop was a pretty complex operation. Response to an In Flight Emergency even more so. But the pilot had not lost his composure for a moment. He had been beyond cool. He had been mechanical. It was almost scary.

The navigator saw him lost in thought.

"Yeah, he's a pretty hot stick, isn't he?"

The major, his ego pricked, was a bit flustered by the question. But the navigator was right. Lots of pilots could have handled the situation. Few could have handled it so routinely.

Glancing once more at the aircraft, hulking and a bit bulbous on the ground, the major was struck by how precisely the nose wheel was parked on the taxiway. The dual wheels sat exactly astride the yellow line that marked the center of the pavement. However stressful the trip had been, cool professionalism had triumphed. After a difficult and emotional ride, they had found the point of balance.

The crew and the plane were safe . . . and back on the centerline.

CHAPTER 1

STORM WARNING

1930 hours 22 December: Little Rock Air Force Base (AFB), Arkansas

Giant snowflakes swarmed against the headlights like lacey moths. They skated over the hood in the airstream and bounced off the windshield without touching it. The wipers flailed after them—*thock, thock, thock*—without effect.

The driver, Captain-pilot-husband-father Mike Middleton, was late.

The pickup truck slowed on the wet streets and navigated a sharp *S* around the concrete barriers. Beyond lay a military housing area, neat as a monopoly board. But inside these identical plastic houses were real families, with real hopes, real dreams, and real fears. Many of them were incomplete, with an empty plate at the dinner table, an empty chair in the family room, and a cold, empty space in the marital bed. Eventually most of the missing would return. Most.

Middleton switched the headlights off and rolled to a stop beside the darkened guard post. Snow pirouetted erratically in the harsh glare of flood lights illuminating the checkpoint and the chain-link fence on both sides of the road. The guard emerged warily from the protection of bricks and special glass . . . and an electric heater.

"ID please."

The driver handed out his plastic card with his left hand, and with his right reached up to turn on the inside light. It wasn't required. It was more of a courtesy. It gave the guard a clear view of everything inside the cab, including the driver's face, and his hands, both resting atop the steering wheel.

Bundled against the cold, the guard relaxed his posture a bit. He examined the card with a flashlight, then switched the beam to the driver's face, then back to the card. He turned it over and ran his finger along the edge. Handing it back through the window, he snapped a salute. It wasn't required of the civilian contractor. It was more of a courtesy.

"Good evening, Captain. Merry Christmas."

Middleton slipped the card into his wallet, and the wallet into the zipper pocket on the left breast of his green flight suit. He answered the guard's salute with an easy salute of his own. It wasn't required. But it granted the other man status; it admitted him into the community of those who wore uniforms and stood on the wall in the dark and the snow so others could sleep warm in their beds.

"Evening buddy," he replied. "Appreciate your being out here."

"No bad guys getting past this gate, Captain. Not on my watch."

The captain nodded with a brief, tight smile, clicked off the cab light, and slipped the truck into gear. "*Attitude,*" he thought. "*Life is all about attitude. Knowing who you are. Staying centered. Good for him.*"

The truck proceeded straight for three blocks through the growing storm, turned left for two, then right again when the headlights glanced off a street sign that read "Florida Ave."

The streets in this housing area of Little Rock Air Force Base were named for states. But Alaska and Hawaii did not appear on any street signs, because the houses were built before Alaska and Hawaii were in the Union. In many areas of the military, repair and construction of base housing had kept up with civilian standards. In fact, on some bases, military families lived in housing that was better built and more attractive than in the local civilian community.

This was not one of those bases.

The light snow was beginning to stick. Cars lined the street on the left and right. The long row of silhouetted houses looked exactly alike. So did their yards and their carports.

Except for the lights.

Colored lights. All white lights. All red lights. Strings of lights in bare trees. Flashing lights that covered the occasional bush. Lights along the gutters and around the edge of the carports, revealing bikes and basketballs and skateboards, and piles of shoes around the door. You could tell which houses had kids. All of them.

The snow was clinging to the grass and the curbs, but the broken white centerline was still visible, and Middleton followed it between the cars to the only dark house on the street. He pulled slowly into the driveway, passed an empty trash can at the curb, and parked under the carport next to a bright red SUV.

After a deep, tired sigh, the captain/pilot closed his eyes and tried to make the transition to husband/father. Then he exited the truck with a green helmet bag in one hand and a full cardboard cup held gingerly in the other. He walked down the short driveway to recover the empty trash can. Wheeling it up to the house, he glanced at the bumper sticker on the SUV.

"God Bless Our Troops" it said. "Especially Our Snipers."

Pausing at the kitchen door, he looked down at the pile of children's flip-flops, cowboy boots size 12, and pink running shoes size 7. Setting down the helmet bag and balancing carefully, he unzipped each leg of his flight suit and slid off his boots—leaving them on top of the pile. "*The kids always like that*," he thought. When he dropped the second boot on the pile, one tiny pink shoe lit up with a circle of red LED lights chasing each other around the sole.

He pulled the cheap screen door out, and pushed the heavy wooden door in. "Joy," he said. "I'm home."

Inside the spare white kitchen the air was warm, but the atmosphere was chilly.

"It's late," Joy Middleton said flatly.

"Not so late," he responded in an upbeat voice.

"The kids are in bed," she answered. "Anything wrong?"

"Not really," he lied. "We had a little problem with a wire—spent a while on the ground while we taped it up—but it was okay. No big deal."

Actually an engine rpm gauge had fluctuated wildly on the trip home. After a maintenance crew had driven for two hours and spent two more hours repairing the wiring that caused the emergency landing, this different problem showed up on the final leg of the mission. The readings on the gauge suggested a surge in engine speed, but the engine itself seemed to behave normally. Old parts and new problems. That plus the emergency landing and repair of wires had made the return home late. Too late.

"I went off base and brought you mocha," he said, setting down his peace offering.

"I don't want to drink it this late. It will keep me up." She was not going to be mollified.

Seeking to change the subject, he scanned the room. Everything was neat, clean, and put away. There was no hint of food.

"What's that?" he asked, gesturing through the doorway and into the dining room. "In the box?"

A brown cardboard box about three feet long sagged against the wall. It looked limp and damp, and much the worse for wear.

"That's the tree," she replied. "It was in the storeroom. You said you'd put it up."

"Oh yeah." He tried to lighten his voice. "I didn't remember the box."

"You weren't here last year when I put it away," she observed coolly. "There's only one string of lights. The roof of the shed leaked and the other lights got wet and had some kind of mildew all over them."

"I'll get some more," he replied.

"Did you get the horses?"

Her brunette hair was pulled back in a short ponytail. She had an attractive, friendly face, when her mouth wasn't turned down in a frown.

As it was now. A long sleeved t-shirt and tight sweat pants suggested a trim figure underneath. It had been trimmer when she was able to get to the gym to work out regularly and could join friends for a run. But she couldn't do that when he was gone. And he was gone a lot.

"Damn," he said. "I was going to get it on the way home, but I was pretty focused on the . . . um . . . gauge."

She raised one eyebrow. "You said wires before. Now it's a gauge. What aren't you telling me?"

"We had a couple of small problems," he said. "Time consuming, but no big deal."

She paused. Other pilots on the street complained about parts and maintenance and problems with their planes. He always seemed to downplay any trouble. Perhaps it was supposed to make her worry less. It made her worry more.

"Okay," she said. "But I can't shop for Santa when I have the kids with me. If the Exchange runs out before you get it, we are going to have one very sad Christmas Day."

"I understand," he said tiredly. "I'll get it."

"It" was a plastic stable with five plastic horses in various poses, with manes and tails and combs and bows. A three-year-old-girl was going to be very disappointed if it was not under the tree three mornings from now.

"I'll get it. Is there supper?"

"There was. It was lasagna. Whatever it is now is in the microwave."

He crossed the yellowing linoleum floor—stylish in 1978—in his sock feet and opened the microwave. "Looks great," he said. "Sorry I'm late."

"There are bread sticks in the oven," she said. "Did you get the 'Power Pilot'?"

It was a needless question. If he didn't get to the Base Exchange to buy the designated Santa surprise for his daughter, then he didn't make it for his son's gift either. In fact, it wasn't a question at all. It was a dart, designed to wound. It worked.

He paused, his hand on the microwave timer. "I said I would get it. I'll get it," he replied with a little edge to his voice.

"It's okay," she said. Her point made, she relaxed her manner and her tone. "Tomorrow is a unit training holiday. I'll take the kids to see Santa in the mall while you finish up the shopping list."

Instead of heating his food, he turned around. He looked at her directly.

"I won't be here tomorrow," he said. "I have a mission. An Air Evac mission taking wounded guys home before Christmas. It just came up. It's important."

"It's always important," she replied heatedly. "We're important, too. Our children are important."

Her arms were crossed. Her weight was evenly distributed on the balls of her feet, and she leaned just a little forward. Her jaw was set and her dark eyes flashed. She was defending her home. This was going to be unpleasant.

"Look," he said. "These guys have all been wounded, some pretty bad. They all get down at Christmas. The docs want to get as many of them home for the holidays as they can. And most can't travel commercial. So we take care of our own. You know the score."

Yes, she knew the score. It was 272. That was how many nights he was away from home so far this year; 220 the year before; 236 the year before that. She knew the score.

"I thought Rusty was taking that mission."

"Rusty did take the mission," he replied patiently. "The ten-day mission. He's been gone a week. And some National Guard outfit picked up another mission. But they have more guys ready to go home than they have aircraft and crews to take them. So they need more lift. It's the Surge."

Yes, it was a Surge all right. A surge of troops into Iraq meant a surge of casualties out. And a surge of doctors and nurses attending to a surge of occupied hospital beds. And a surge of missing arms and legs. And a surge of crutches and wheelchairs. And a surge of broken bodies headed home to broken families. For Christmas.

And then she had a thought.

"This was a last minute mission. But you just finished a mission. You weren't next in line. You volunteered for this, didn't you? Didn't you!"

He leaned back against the kitchen counter, hands at his side.

"Yes," he said. "I won't lie to you. Yes, I said I would take it. But I will be home Christmas Eve. I'll be home for Christmas."

"Why?" she demanded, more perplexed than angry. "Why would you volunteer to leave us at this time of year? The gifts aren't bought. The tree's not up. You missed the preschool party and the kindergarten party. Your kids are the only ones on this block who don't have lights on their house. And you volunteered to leave again? Do you really love flying that much?"

She paused. Her voice thickened. "Mike," she said softly. "Don't you love *us*?"

His head snapped back as though he had been slapped. His eyes widened.

"Of course I love you, Jo-Jo," he replied with a pained voice and a pained expression. "Of course I love Brett and Bryn. Of course I want to be here with you to shop and decorate and bake. It's just . . ."

"Just what?"

He looked down, searching for words. "I feel . . ."

"What?"

"Guilty. I feel guilty." He looked up, searching for understanding. He didn't find it.

The pilot so cool under fire, so professional in an emergency, so solid in a crisis, was adrift in trying to explain his feelings to his wife.

"I feel guilty that they need me and I'm not there."

Now she was really exasperated. She rolled her eyes and raised her hands. "*We* need you!" she exclaimed. "And you're not *here*! You should feel guilty about *that*!"

"I do," he said. Now it was his voice that was flat.

"I do feel guilty about that. I feel guilty about not being *here* and guilty about not being *there*. I feel guilty about everything I do, and everything I don't do. And I don't know what to do about it. I . . . I don't know what to do."

The "hot stick" who was so good at avoiding ambush and evading attack could not get out of the emotional kill zone of his own kitchen. He looked away and retreated.

"But I do know this. I know there is a war on. I know we are short of pilots, and crew, and aircraft. I know that if I don't take this mission, they might not find somebody else. They certainly won't find anybody who is better at it than I am." It wasn't a boast. It was a fact.

"I know that if I don't do this some of these wounded guys might not get home to their families for Christmas. And you and I will have to live with that while we are opening presents on Christmas Day."

They were both quiet. The whole house was quiet. Down the hall a bunk bed creaked, and a tiny voice said, "Daddy?" just once, and was quiet.

"Look Mike, I can do all this stuff without you." Her voice was quiet, too. "I can get the kids ready and the house ready. But I don't want to. I want you to be engaged with your own family. I'm not angry Mike. I'm sad."

And she was. Her voice was sad. Her face was sad. Her whole body was sad.

"I'm sad for the kids that you are not here for the exciting parts of their lives. I'm sad for me because I miss you. Even when you are here you aren't really here. You talk *around* me, not *to* me. You talk *around* your life, not *about* your life.

"So I miss you when you are gone, and I miss you when you are here. And I am sad for you. You have no balance in your life, Mike. No center. We're supposed to do that for you. We are supposed to be the center. And you won't let us.

"I'm sad for all of us Mike. And it's getting worse. Really worse after your last tour."

She paused, then spoke gently, as if to a child.

"Did something happen, Mike? Is there something you need to talk about?"

The effect was electrifying. His head shot up and he showed his teeth. He snapped at her like a tethered dog.

"No! I don't need to visit mental health counseling, thank you! I don't need a psych eval! I'm fine."

The answer rocked her back. For a moment she did not recognize the man in her kitchen. It was as if she had poked an animal with a stick.

For his part, he was alarmed by the question and further alarmed by his own answer.

After a half decade of war, the mental health of those deploying over and over had become a touchy subject. In previous conflicts, it had been easier to separate soldiers in combat from those in support. And even those in combat had not faced the uncertainty of attack every day. Combat troops had been routinely rotated "off the line" for rest and recovery. But in Iraq and Afghanistan, security guards and truck drivers had to be as wary of attack as soldiers and Marines on patrol. The casualties were fewer in this war, but the tension was higher for a broader range of troops.

And with a volunteer military stretched thin, the stress of multiple deployments was taking its toll on military members and their families. The famous "Band of Brothers" that landed at Normandy on D-Day in World War II spent about eleven months in Europe before the end of the war in Germany—a good deal of that time in the relative safety of training or reserve assignments. This pilot had spent twice that time deployed to the tension and misery of "the sand box," and there was no end to this war in sight. Even the most rugged aircraft could only handle so many take offs and landings before it needed to go back to depot for repair. How long could fathers, mothers, husbands, and wives stand the stress and uncertainty of these missions before cracks appeared and the structure was compromised?

Senior military leaders recognized the danger and tried to convince their rank and file that there was no stigma to talking with professionals about the mental strain of the war. Not everyone believed them.

Mike Middleton was suddenly very still and very cautious. This was a dangerous situation. What did she mean by this question? "*Do you need to talk with someone?*" Did she doubt his sanity? Was she setting him up for something else? Would she raise this question with his commander? Was she out for revenge and looking to destroy his career? It had happened to others. And he had stepped into the trap. His answer was so harsh—so out of control. He had to protect himself. Now.

Joy Middleton had meant nothing of the kind. She loved her husband. She loved being his wife and the mother of his children. She loved being around him, riding in the car with him, shopping with him, having cocoa together at night. She missed him and she saw him miserable, and she felt like he was gone even when he was there. She just wanted him back. In the way of many wives, she thought maybe talking about it would help. And she was right. But what she had meant was not what he had heard.

His lips curved up in an artificial smile. His voice became light and upbeat. The openness between husband and wife was gone. He was back in his professional persona, talking to a loadmaster or a flight engineer.

"I'm sorry, Joy," he said formally. "I guess I'm more tired than I realized. I didn't mean to snap at you." His gaze was level. His tone was open and accommodating, without a hint of passion. He was the Pilot again.

"I'm sure things here at home are stressful, too." He was placing bricks in a defensive wall.

"I bet even you need someone to talk to." Another brick.

"And we will do that soon. We'll talk soon as I get back from this mission." He was calm. He was poised. He was protected. But the trust between husband and wife was completely missing. He was alone.

She knew something was wrong, but she didn't know what. She tried another tack.

"Something's got to change, Mike."

"I'm doing the best I can," he said levelly.

"That's not good enough," she replied. "Trying is not enough. You need to do it right."

He looked down again, struggling with how honest he could be. For a moment he almost spoke, then thought better of it. He decided he could not be honest at all.

"Well, I have to get to bed," he said in an upbeat tone. His half-smile was still fixed. "Early day tomorrow. Have to fly to Scott before the mission can begin."

"Don't you want to eat?" she asked. She was trying to reengage. He was having none of it. No reason to take another chance.

"No," he replied. "I'm not really hungry."

All she wanted to do was help him—help their family. But she had pulled the control rods from a nuclear reactor. In an instant the situation had flashed from manageable to critical mass. And she didn't even know it.

He brushed by her in a polite, professional way, like two crew members passing in a crowded aircraft. Then she made her second big mistake. She let him go.

He headed down the hallway past the small bathroom, with its small tooth brushes on the counter, a potty chair against the wall, and bath toys scattered on the floor.

He paused before the door to a darkened room with tiny noises, like mice moving in their sleep.

Then he moved on to the bedroom at the end of the hall, closed the door, and turned out the light.

Outside, snowflakes, large but light, danced on the icy wind. They stuck on the cars and the trees. They stuck on the curbs and the street. They covered the centerline. The storm might get better or it might get worse.

It was hard to tell.

CHAPTER 2

LUCKY FEW

0500 hours 23 December: Little Rock AFB to Scott AFB, Illinois

It was 5 AM, dark, and cold when the crew arrived on the flight line and began their pre-flight checks. It was 6 AM and still well before daylight when the C-130 lifted off from the runway of Little Rock Air Force Base, its tail beacon flashing a warning as it turned northeast and climbed into a threatening sky. It was 7:30 AM on a gray dawn when it touched down at Scott Air Force Base in Illinois. As the last engine wound down, and the tip of the last propeller coasted to a stop, Wolf 41 became Air Evac 1492, the call sign the pilots would use until this mission was complete.

At 9 AM, their mission planning finalized, the crew assembled in a small, bare meeting room in Building 505, the aging headquarters of the 375th Aeromedical Evacuation Squadron. The red plastic chairs were garish against the dingy beige walls. In the first row sat a team of five medical personnel: a doctor, two nurses, and two medical technicians, all in the same green jump suits that the crew was wearing. A sixth person, an enlisted man whose function was not entirely clear, sat alone on the row behind them. The copilot, navigator, flight engineer, and loadmaster took seats against the wall. In the back, separated by several rows of empty seats, sat the base public affairs officer wearing his Air Force blue uniform with tie. Next to him sat an attractive young woman with dark hair, a note pad, and a blue parka with a fur trimmed hood. She pulled a pen from her pocket and flipped the cover of the pad over the spiral wire on top to reveal a clean sheet of paper.

The pilot stepped forward, squared his shoulders to the group, and began to speak.

"I am Captain Mike Middleton, pilot of Air Evac 1492, your ride today to El Paso, Texas, and Garden City, Kansas," he said. The tone was not commanding or overbearing. It was practiced, easy, and professional. But it was very direct. It said that he was in charge, in case anyone had any questions. The senior nurse drew a long slow breath. Not a challenge exactly, but loudly enough that his eyes flickered in her direction for just a second.

"My crew sitting against the wall consists of the copilot, Lieutenant JT Williams; the navigator, Captain Bobby Lee; the flight engineer, Technical Sergeant Martin Jefferson; and the loadmaster, Airman Ben Quinten. Would you mind introducing yourselves?"

"Major Win Ames, Medical Crew Director for this team," responded the senior nurse in the first row. She had dark shoulder length hair that she would pull up under her hat as soon as they left the building. Her arms were crossed and she did not uncross them, gesturing instead with her head to the young male officer sitting next to her.

"This is Lieutenant Garrett Beauchamp, the other nurse on our team." Her tone was not commanding or overbearing. It was cool and professional. It said that she was in charge, in case anyone had any questions.

"*Great*," thought the pilot. "*I hope we aren't going to argue over who's flying the plane.*" But he said nothing, instead shifting his gaze to the doctor sitting on the other side of the nurse.

The doctor glanced sideways to the nurse with a bemused look, then back to the pilot. "I am Dr. Dan Woody," he said in an easy, friendly tone.

Like the flight engineer, he had enough experience and self-confidence that he did not have to worry about pride of place or challenges to his authority. No one in the room was better at what he did than he was, and he could demonstrate that without pointing it out. With some people ego swells with expertise. With some it shrinks. He was one of the latter.

"I'm not in the Air Force. I am a contract doctor—former Army—retired as head of emergency medicine at a public hospital. I'm helping to manage the load here at Scott."

"*Solid*," thought the pilot. "*Good to have him along.*"

"Staff Sergeant Zack Jones, Charge Med Tech," said the fourth member of the party. "Senior Airman Mary Wilson," said the second medical technician. "Sergeant Frank Gannon," said the last member of the group. "I'm not really on the medical team. I'm an admin guy, new to the unit. Just along for the ride."

"*Curious*," thought the pilot. But he said nothing.

The major in the blue dress uniform cleared his throat. Everyone turned to look. "I am Major Weston Howell," he said. "Public Affairs Officer for Scott Air Force Base." He smiled.

"And this is Ms. Taylor Webster, a reporter for *The St. Louis Post-Dispatch*. She is doing a story about getting our patients home for Christmas, and will be accompanying you on this mission," he informed brightly.

"*Oh crap*," thought the pilot.

"*Oh crap*," thought the nurse.

"*Oh crap*," thought everyone else.

The reporter nodded in a friendly manner, but did not speak.

"This is your mission brief," continued the pilot, as he regained control of the room.

"As you know, frequently we just pick up the medical team here and shuttle patients between hospitals. But today we are carrying 19 patients, 6 members of the medical team, and 1 reporter to 2 locations. We are batting cleanup for the flights that left earlier this week. Two of our patients are on litters and 17 are ambulatory. The 2 litters and 5 others get off in El Paso, along with Sergeant Gannon. The remaining 12, the reporter, and the med team are going to Garden City, Kansas. The 12 get off there, along with Major Ames. The rest of the med team and the reporter return to Scott with us. Because the stretcher cases are in the most immediate need of care we will take the longest leg to El Paso first."

Looking to Nurse Ames he asked, "Does that match your understanding of pax and missions?"

"Yeah. We've already done our team brief. Two corrections. Of the ambulatory pax, 16 are recovering wounded already released from the hospital, and 1 is a chaplain catching a ride home. And of the 16 medical cases, three are in wheelchairs, but I'm going to have them ride in litters. No sense running the safety risk of having them get up and down the ramp in their chairs." She was cool and professional. Not exactly hostile. Just distant. Using her professionalism as a shield.

"Roger," the pilot responded. "Thanks for the clarification."

The public affairs officer turned to the reporter. "Pax means passengers," he whispered. The reporter took a note.

"One of our litters is a TBI." She looked back to the reporter. "Traumatic Brain Injury." The reporter took another note.

The nurse looked back to the pilot. "He is still recovering from other injuries. The other one is going to . . . uh . . . keep pretty much to himself."

She paused.

Not all injuries are to the body. She decided there was no reason to mention that in front of the reporter.

"They are both moving to be closer to their families."

She paused again.

"I'm not sure it is a good idea to have a reporter invading their privacy," she said to the room as a whole. But the remark was obviously pointed at the public affairs officer.

He gulped and his Adam's apple moved rapidly above his tie. "Uh, we have an agreement that Ms. Webster will only write about people who give their permission. Her human interest story is about people going home, not their wounds."

"I'm their friend," the reporter offered with her most winning smile. "It's going to be a friendly story."

"No," replied the nurse. "*I'm* their friend. You only get to the litter patients through me. And you are not getting through me."

"They will be in separate parts of the aircraft," offered the pilot to keep things moving. "The litters will be in back. Ms. Webster and the other passengers will sit up forward until all the litters depart in El Paso."

No one said anything, which the pilot took for agreement. Or at least a temporary cease fire. He continued.

"Nurse Ames, as MCD, what would you like to brief?"

The senior nurse stood up, took out a laminated card, and glanced down the list.

"With only two in-patients and everybody else going home, I really don't have much left on my list, except for the things we want to say to everybody after they load the aircraft. Sometimes pressurization affects medications and wounds. Are you going to address that?"

"Yes ma'am," answered the pilot. "I will touch that in a minute."

"Ok," replied the nurse. "What else you got?"

The pilot stood up again. "Time is now 0905. Weather will be bumpy as we climb out, but should be okay at altitude. The little disturbance from last night is moving on through, so it should be clear today, before more snow for Christmas Eve. We should all be home by then.

"We will depart in about 50 minutes. Once all pax are loaded please strap yourself in. I would like to keep at least one person from the medical team on intercom at all times. I will ring a bell before engine start. Please be ready for intercom check at that time.

"Flight time is 3 hours. We don't expect any weather deviations today. If we get engine start at 0950 we will be on the ground in El Paso at 1300 in case you want to text anybody who is going to meet you. For official calls, we can set up a phone patch from your headset. The navigator will take care of that. If you really have to use a cell phone to support the mission, please check with me first.

"Flight level will be 220 (22,000 feet). We will keep the cabin pressurized at 6,000 feet. Will that work for all patients?"

The question was directed to the medical team in general. Nurse

Ames nodded yes. The doctor smiled again. This was a very experienced nurse. The nametag on her flight suit showed not just wings and nightingale lamp with physician's symbol, but a star and a wreath. She was a chief flight nurse with more than 500 hours in the air.

But sometimes experience took its toll. Sometimes the most hyperproficient—those always technically correct—were covering something else . . . a wound of a different sort. And like all scar tissue, that meant lack of flexibility. A scar would never tear again. But given enough stress, the flesh around it might.

The pilot continued. "Pressurized rate of climb and descent will be 500 feet per minute inside the cabin. Will that work for any intubated patients?"

Again the nurse nodded. "I don't expect anybody in that condition, but if that changes, that rate will be okay."

Now it was the nurse's turn to be impressed. A pilot who actually understood what she was up against. Good.

"We will have one more brief on the aircraft." The presentation had been short, crisp, and to the point. It was winding down. "The loadmaster will brief the other passengers when they arrive, and then go over safety issues and emergency procedures with everyone. I would ask the medical team to help us keep the patients focused during his brief. And of course, you can present your medical brief at that time."

Having the loadmaster give the safety brief was extremely important. Getting everybody to submit to the discipline of a brief by a junior crew member would establish the mindset required to maintain discipline during the flight. It was an important step, when some passengers might be in pain, or at the end of their emotional rope, or just tired of the military. It was a subtle little trick. And it worked. This was not the pilot's first rodeo.

The pilot finished, "Bottom line: if we do have an emergency, I will be the last one out so hurry up and get out of my way. Meet off the nose of the aircraft, at a 45 degree angle to the right and 100 yards out. If we have to egress, I will drop the ramp immediately so we can evac the walking passengers and litter cases. The crew will help with the litters. Watch for emergency vehicles trying to run you over as you leave."

It wasn't exactly humor, but it was delivered with a touch just light enough to make the pilot seem human.

"My team will stay with the patients," interjected Nurse Ames. "When we do the head count, raise your hand if everyone with you is okay. No hands up means you have a problem." There was no touch of humor in her voice. It was technically precise. Almost robotic.

The aircraft was parked a short ride by crew bus from the operations building. With most of the pre-flight done before the first briefing, the air crew zipped quickly through the remaining checklists.

The medical team had a greater challenge. In addition to themselves and their overnight bags, they had 800 pounds of equipment in a pre-packaged aeromedical evacuation "packet." They carried it from a truck on to the aircraft on litters, which they fitted into the stanchions the air crew had already rigged down the center of the aircraft. Some of it was opened and prepared for use, like the hand washing station, and the electrical converter that powered 60Hz medical systems from the 400Hz aircraft electrical system. Most—like the drugs and bandages—was left sealed until needed.

In civilian hospitals, doctors and nurses called a plumber or electrician or even an orderly to construct and repair facilities. On an air evacuation mission, the medical people did it all themselves unless the loadmaster lent a hand. This one did.

When the equipment was loaded and lashed, the team set up a spare litter in case someone became sick in flight. Then they prepared to receive patients.

The loadmaster had reconfigured the inside of the aircraft since the airdrop the previous day. Gone were the rollers that slid the cargo out the back door and the rails and locks he had tripped over during his accident. Instead the floor was flat and open, creating a smooth, cavernous tunnel broken only by the poles and clamps set into the ceiling and floor—clamps that would receive the litters, and hold them, one above the other, in flight.

Toward the front, along each wall, a metal pole had been folded down exposing seats created from wide orange-red nylon webbing. There was no padding and no pillows. The wounded going home sat in the same sling seats as troops going into combat or paratroopers going to a jump. It was very austere. But it worked. And it was cheap. The taxpayers should be pleased.

As the reporter tried to stay out of the way, she heard the sound of a bus approaching, then the squeal of brakes. She turned just as the doors opened. The story that she was assigned to cover, these lucky few who were going home for Christmas, stepped out of the bus carefully as if each movement of foot and leg was a major effort. Heads down, they trudged up the ramp into the plane. Some made the hike with difficulty. None asked for assistance.

In 1919, the French government staged a victory parade through the streets of Paris to celebrate the end of the Great War. It included veterans in wheelchairs. Amputees and paralytics by the squads. By the platoons. By the companies. By the battalions. The sound of wheelchairs clattered across the cobblestones, reverberating from the buildings, offices, apartments, and cafes. It was a mournful sound—the sound of a nation in pain. If drums and the rhythm of marching feet marked the beginning of the war, the cacophony of wheelchairs and the silence of missing feet marked the end.

There was no such parade for the wounded at the end of this war. In genuine gratitude for their sacrifice, in genuine admiration of their bravery, with a hint of guilt at staying home—and in some quarters, with the burn of hidden shame at how those returning from the Vietnam War had been treated—the American public embraced its military after 9/11. The outpouring of affection was real. The thanks from individuals to their fellow citizens in uniform in airports and on the street came from the heart. The urge to support the military overseas with cards, packages, food, and assistance welled up from deep in the American psyche. And the continuing efforts of individuals and groups to resettle veterans, help with job training, and even build houses for them was more than touching. It was inspiring. It was a wonderful display.

But the homecomings that Americans saw on their televisions were fathers and mothers surprising their children at school. They were all whole. The parade of crutches, canes, wheelchairs, missing limbs, and broken bodies that trickled home for years went largely unreported and unknown. Perhaps if the weekly discharge of Walter Reed's military orthopedic ward had traveled home through National Airport in Washington, DC, the nation's awareness might have been different. Perhaps if lobbyists and congressional staffers had stood in line behind thousands of wounded passing through security checks, perhaps if first class passengers had waited every day for wounded to make their halting way down the aisle first, perhaps if tourists to their nation's capital sat next to a soldier with a missing limb or a scarred face on the trip home, perhaps there would have been a different understanding of the cost of war.

The public did not see this human cost. Instead, in typical American fashion, a great logistical machine took over. Wounded were snatched from the battlefield and rushed to medical care frequently only minutes away. Trained teams with new skills and technologies cleaned and stabilized wounds that would have meant certain death in every previous war. Wounded from many locations were sorted by type and severity and grouped into packages to be loaded on the medical conveyer belt to home.

Like a giant international delivery service, wounded soldiers were routed to places where they could be best provided initial treatment, receiving better care in the aircraft than the best hospitals could have provided a generation before. Some went to Kuwait. Some to Germany. The worst cases went directly to the United States. Then on to specialists in different stateside hospitals with different capabilities to begin rehabilitation. Some went for a while to military hospitals near home to be encouraged by friends and family. Depending on the injuries, some went to long-term care where they were provided prostheses, then trained to live their lives within limitations where necessary and despite those limitations where possible. Some even stayed in the military, longing in a way they could never explain to get back into the fight.

And all along the way, this huge logistical train was pushed and pulled, lifted and carried by brothers and sisters in uniform. Although they could never put it into words, every pilot, every loadmaster, every nurse, every orderly understood that they were part of something special. They were not just helping people. These were *their* people. This was *their* family. And they took care of their own. Although they would never think about it this way, they were also the lucky few to be able to give to something that so clearly deserved their best.

Reporter Taylor Webster, her pen and notebook at the ready, watched a small piece of this worldwide drama play out. But like much of the public, she was interested and sympathetic, but without military experience. So she missed the enormity of the story she was watching.

Halfway through the short parade from bus to aircraft, attendants emerged with three litters. Each carried an amputee who was well enough to use a wheelchair, but for safety was being loaded flat on his back as if still a casualty. Their wheelchairs were being loaded separately. The last in line was an Army major. As he was lifted out of the ambulance, he began to yell.

"Down!" he yelled. "Put me down!" Confused, the attendants stopped and set him on the cement. The whole parade came to a halt. Nurse Ames flashed down the ramp like an angry bee.

"What's the problem?" she challenged. She was standing above the major, looking down at him. He lifted himself to a seated position and looked up. A short cloth tab sewn to the top left shoulder of his uniform said "RANGER." At the end of his trousers, the boots were laced tightly around two metal rods that extended down to artificial feet. She had read his record. He had been fitted with artificial legs, but was not yet skilled enough with them to get around on his own.

"You can't walk up this ramp yet! You know that! Lie down and let us get everybody on board!" She was severe with him. She needed to keep the parade on schedule.

"I can roll myself in the wheelchair," he said. "I know I can't walk up that ramp yet. But I can roll myself up. I've had enough of being carried around like a sandbag. I'm not going to ride all day lying down on a litter!"

She had no patience with this.

"Lie down! You know the drill. We can't afford the safety hazard of a wheelchair on the ramp. You can't guarantee your own safety. And I won't take the responsibility!"

He continued to look up at her steadily. "Yeah, I know the drill. I know you have a reporter on board to get our stories. Think she might want this story? Nazi nurse destroys dignity of war hero amputee?"

Her eyes narrowed. "I don't like to be threatened." she unloaded.

"I don't like to be bullied," he shot back.

She paused. "*Great!*" he thought. "*A weak spot!*" He pressed the attack.

"Look, let me try it. Put somebody behind me as a safety if you want. If I can't roll myself up that ramp, with no help, I'll lie back down here and you can load me like cordwood. Just stack me in the corner and I'll be quiet."

The nurse considered carefully, and glanced sideways up the ramp to where the reporter was watching.

"Okay," she said guardedly. "One try."

The attendants helped him stand, and he transferred shakily to the wheelchair. Once seated, he held tight to one wheel and pushed hard on the other, whirling quickly in a complete circle. Then he headed to the ramp, where he stopped, spun the chair in a half circle, and began backing up the incline.

Backing provided more leverage than trying to roll forward, but backing up a slope was still hard. Very hard. One of the medical technicians stepped forward to help, but the major shook his head no. He held the chair still with a hand on each wheel, then pulled back slowly toward his chest, rotating the wheels back a quarter turn in the process. The wheelchair moved a short distance up the ramp. Then he held a wheel in place on one side while reaching back out to grab a new spot on the opposite wheel. When that was secure, he let go with the close in hand, and reached forward to the wheel on that side, so that his grip with both hands was parallel. Then he pulled back again, inching further up the ramp. Steadying himself, he paused and repeated the process. It was an astonishing display of upper body strength. And determination. His forearms bulged.

Sweat broke out on his brow. His face reddened. His expression intensified. And slowly, he progressed. Near the top he paused.

All the other passengers were watching now. A medical technician reached for the chair again. Again the ranger dismissed the offer with a quick shake of his head. Another quarter turn of the wheel. And another. And another.

And then he was done. Hardly pausing, he whirled the chair around and started forward into the cargo bay. A patient with two crutches clapped them together. Another missing his left hand stamped his feet and raised his right with the thumb up. Another smiled and clapped him on the back. The junior flight nurse offered his assistance, and the occupant accepted it. Smiling broadly, he was wheeled to the front of the aircraft, where he again stood uncertainly, and plopped himself heavily into the mesh seats.

"Your boss is a pretty tough nut," the ranger commented.

"High standards," responded the junior flight nurse, Lieutenant Beauchamp, who seemed a little old for his rank. "And she's hardest on herself."

"Yeah, well . . . hard-ass and dumb-ass are not the same thing. What's her problem?"

The male Air Force nurse paused briefly to converse. He had been an Army medic on the *Thunder Run* into Baghdad in the opening days of the war four years earlier. Now he had a soft spot for Army wounded.

"I don't know," he said thoughtfully. "I'm a reservist on active duty. From New Orleans. I was an EMT in Hurricane Katrina, working my way through nursing school. I saw some responders who had a tough time after the flooding. Some of them just couldn't focus. Others did nothing but focus—got all hyperprofessional. It was like they lost their balance. I don't know. Weird."

Nurse Beauchamp collapsed the wheelchair and handed it to the loadmaster, who strapped it to other baggage and the floor.

"Tough nut." The voice was close and startled the reporter. It was Nurse Ames, who had been watching the small drama closely.

"Admirable," the reporter replied.

"Yeah. Unless he slips with that wheelchair, and rolls down the ramp and into somebody else, and we spend the next two months trying to recover the time and effort we put into the last two months of healing."

It was a solid professional assessment. But cold. The reporter was not sure how to respond.

Actually even the nurse herself had a glimmer of doubt about her answer. It was hard not to admire courage and determination, even when your professional judgment told you it was poorly applied.

"You made the right decision." It was the chaplain now, speaking to Nurse Ames. Everyone seemed to have an opinion about her job.

"These guys are fighters," he continued. "They need a fight. Give them something to fight for or fight against, even if it's gravity. Otherwise, they'll just fight you."

"*Interesting thought.*" The nurse pondered it briefly. But not for long.

The boarding continued. It was a diverse bunch.

A short lieutenant with a dark complexion moved up the ramp and through the aircraft with authority, although leaning heavily on a cane. A pale soldier who also carried a cane followed him, but seemed to walk without needing it. At one point he twirled the cane around his finger like a prop.

A strikingly beautiful female sergeant with coffee-colored skin walked unsteadily to her seat, holding herself stiffly as though she feared something inside might break.

A male sergeant with a ruddy complexion and shaved head followed her. He looked like he spent a lot of time in the weight room. He also walked with a pronounced limp, but carried his cane without using it. Inside one boot was an artificial foot. It was connected to an artificial leg.

Next, an overly gregarious infantry corporal made his way up the ramp. He wasn't just young – he was immature. Something about the way he carried himself said "surfer," or "skateboarder," or maybe "ski-bum." His hair was long, blond, and wavy—perhaps too long according to Army regulations. If he had a wound it wasn't obvious. He stopped several times to make jokes. The people around him were not laughing. A medal dangled from the left breast pocket of his uniform in violation of regulations.

A bookish-looking private first class entered carrying a backpack and a book grasped tightly between the two silver jaws of a steel hook that now substituted for his right hand. Two other soldiers with artificial arms followed him.

A tall soldier moved erectly through the crowd. He stopped to help several others settle into their seats, and did not appear wounded at all, until he turned around. His head and face were covered by a web of scar tissue from ear to ear. The tips of his nose and ears were missing. His hands below his sleeves showed the tell-tale scars of severe burns. Once his skin had been uniformly black, but now it showed splotches of pink and white as well.

This was not the end of the parade. There were others—sixteen in all. There was no special seating. Everyone had paid in full.

The whole process was well coordinated by the medical team. An attendant from the bus walked each passenger to the bottom of the ramp. A team member from inside attended each one to the top of the ramp, paying close attention to balance and footing. Then another team member walked each one to a seat.

As Medical Crew Director, Nurse Ames, stood at the top of the ramp, her head on a swivel, as she supervised the loading, stepping in immediately if the smallest action did not meet her standards for safety and care.

And weaving his way through it all, a chaplain—one of the passengers—moved from person to person, place to place, to help. Never taking the lead, always deferring to the medical personnel, he touched each passenger in some way. When everyone was loaded, he stood next to the stanchion designated to hold the bottom end of the yet-to-arrive litters. He was in the middle of everything, but without being in the way. The MCD did not miss anything on her aircraft. She did not miss this detail, either.

The two seriously injured litter patients arrived last. They were lifted out of the huge "ambus" that transported them and carried up the rear ramp by two attendants and the two technical specialists from the medical team. They passed through the big hole that would soon close to become the rear of the airplane again, and under the large rear door, held against the inside roof of the aircraft by hydraulic pressure. Soon it would swing down and lock them all into the metal tube that was the body of the plane.

The handles on the litters snapped into the special racks, one above the other, with the patients' feet toward the forward bulkhead, and their heads toward the tail of the plane. The procedure was quick and practiced. The nurses were attentive. The twenty-six-year-old reporter stood watching from the other end of the cargo bay.

The patient on top was tucked under a blanket pulled up to the top of his chest. His head was wrapped in bandages that crossed both eyes. His right arm was outside the blanket and his right hand gripped the rail of the litter. Both were wrapped in gauze. His left arm lay under the covers, and across his stomach. It was hard to tell from a distance, but a leg seemed to run under the covers for the entire length of the right side of the litter. There was no similar ridge under the covers on the left.

The patient on the lower litter showed no evidence of bandages outside the blanket and sheet that covered him to the chin. As the reporter watched, he rolled over and faced away.

Both patients were secured to their litters by two wide green nylon straps, one over the chest and one over the thighs. Each strap was locked in place by a large silver friction buckle.

Over the entire operation the lead nurse hovered like a worried mother hen. Nurse Ames supervised every detail. Was the latch on the stretcher too loose? Were the sheets too tight? Were the emergency tools where she could reach them easily? Were the medical technicians fully engaged?

"Where is the EPOX?" she barked.

"Got it," answered Beauchamp. Reaching into an equipment bin, he extracted two fat green nylon envelopes, closed on the edge with Velcro. In an emergency, there would be no oxygen masks dropping from the ceiling as on civilian aircraft. Instead, each passenger would open his own Emergency Passenger Oxygen kit. The folded material enclosed could be shaken into a hood with plastic vision port in the front and a small bottle of oxygen attached. The nurse placed one under the pillow of each patient.

The MCD was in her element. She was clearly very good at this.

"She is very good, isn't she?" It was the doctor, who had approached the reporter from behind. "I'll double check all the medical issues when she is done, but I bet I don't find a thing. Very professional.

"It's a hard profession, nursing," he continued. He was obviously making a point for the reporter's benefit, but she did not quite get it.

"It's very wearing on the body and on the emotions. After a while, all nurses change. They have to . . . to protect themselves. Some lose interest and get out of nursing. Some get tired and sloppy. Some become very exacting . . . very precise. Some lose themselves in the duty of it all. That's very dangerous. Duty is a bottomless pit."

He paused and looked at the reporter. "You're about what? Twenty-five? Twenty-eight? You don't know what I am talking about, do you?"

She decided to be honest. She shook her head no.

"Watch and learn," he said. "Watch and learn."

He moved up the aisle to the front of the aircraft and began looking over the patients. The nurse stood by stiffly until he was finished. Then he spoke to her and nodded. The reporter was too far away to hear what he said, but the nurse smiled and nodded in return, and relaxed her posture. The doctor turned and looked knowingly at the reporter, then sat in a nylon sling seat nearby.

Secretly, Webster was glad that the assignment specified she could not talk to the recently wounded. She would not have known what to do, or say, or ask in their presence. The nurse was right. Even watching them from a distance seemed . . . wrong. Invasive.

Once all the patients were aboard, Dr. Woody climbed to the crew deck, leaned past the navigator and over the engineer's shoulder. "Got just a minute?" he said to the pilot.

"Actually, I'm pretty busy," replied the pilot with a hint of irritation.

"Just want you to know that the quiet guy on the litter in the back—the one with no bandages—is a psych patient. I don't think there will be any trouble. We have him partially sedated. The admin sergeant is really a Raven—an airborne security officer. He's carrying a pistol with a special load that would wound but not penetrate an aircraft—like a sky marshal. I don't expect any trouble at all. But I did want you to have the info. And I was not sure who would be listening on the intercom."

Everyone paused. "Uh, thanks, Doc," the pilot finally responded. "How about fill in the loadmaster when he returns. Okay?"

"Sure," said the doctor. With a wave he was gone.

For a moment everyone on the flight deck was silent and motionless. "War is hell," said the pilot. "Everybody back to work."

The final settling in was a painfully deliberate process, but well organized, and in a matter of minutes everyone was seated and listing to the young loadmaster give his well-rehearsed safety briefing. It was Christmas and they were going home. The closer they came to take off, the more the passengers' spirits improved. They were in the grip of the system now, and it would move them inexorably toward their destination. They couldn't hurry it, and they couldn't slow it down. There was nothing to do but endure the trip, with good humor if possible. Most succeeded.

The wounded settled into the sling cargo seats and tried to get comfortable. It was not to be. Some were physically uncomfortable from the cramped surroundings and mesh seats. Some were still feeling the pull and tug of torn flesh not yet fully healed. All were wondering what they would find when the plane returned them home. They were changed. Would the world notice? Would it accept them? Would it disapprove?

They knew they were lucky. Lucky to have been wounded and not killed. Lucky to have good medical care. Lucky to be going home. But somehow, they didn't feel lucky.

Up in the crew compartment, the pilot briefly flipped a switch on the left wall of the aircraft up then down. A bell rang loudly in the rear. The medical technicians worked their way past every passenger making sure they had earplugs and were belted in. Nurse Ames picked up a headset and put it on.

The loadmaster grabbed a long communication cable, plugged one end into a communications box and the other into his headset and headed for the forward crew exit. He climbed up the steps to the pilots' level and then turned left and climbed down the stairs to the outside.

"Comm check," the pilot called. Every member of the crew responded, as did the MCD.

The phone in the pocket of his left shoulder buzzed. He snatched it out quickly and saw a text from his wife. "**How are you feeling this morning**?" it asked. "*Focus*," he thought. He turned the phone off and slipped it back in his pocket.

"Parking brake set?" the loadmaster queried.

"Set," the pilot responded.

Outside, the loadmaster ducked under the wings and recovered the "chocks"—wooden blocks that bracketed the tires to prevent the aircraft from rolling. He dropped them on the ramp in the back. Two members of the ground crew disconnected a large cable from the side of the aircraft and pushed the auxiliary ground power cart off to the side. The loadmaster moved to a position off the nose of the aircraft and announced, "Clear!" The pilot keyed his radio.

"Ground, this is Air Evac 1492. Parking location Bravo 6. Engine start. We have information LIMA. Clearance on request," he said.

The Ground Control responded, "Air Evac 1492, roger engine start."

"Clear Number 3," said the flight engineer. Out of the whole day of work, Tech Sergeant Jefferson liked this part most of all. It always seemed to have such promise. He turned the bleed air valve to "open."

"Number 3 clear," the loadmaster replied.

"Turning Number 3," said the pilot. With his right hand he advanced the Condition Lever, just to the right of the throttles. Above his head he pressed a red engine start button. He would hold it in for sixty seconds.

"Timing," said the copilot. The pilot checked his watch. And the dance was on.

What followed was a complex choreographed maneuver, with dozens of required steps, each due within seconds of the previous one. They checked for rpm movement within ten seconds, fuel flow within twelve—step after step after step in exactly the right sequence.

Outside the big turboprop engine growled to life. The propeller began to spin lazily, then faster and faster. Inside the compressor, a mixture of air and fuel was ignited with a throaty roar that grew steadily louder. Eventually the propeller was spinning so fast that the human eye could not distinguish individual blades, making it look like a gray disc spinning around the front of the engine. Then the inside engine on the left wing growled to life following the same sequence; then the right outboard, and then the left.

"Taxi checklist," the pilot directed. When those checks were complete, he keyed his radio.

"Ground Control, Air Evac 1492, on Bravo 6, request taxi for departure, Runway 32 Left, with information LIMA."

"Roger, Air Evac 1492," the Ground Control responded. "Clear to taxi."

The pilot slid the throttles forward. The plane began to roll. Outside a ground guide waved an orange guide stick to indicate they should turn. The pilot reached down with his left hand to a small steering wheel on the left side of his control yoke and turned it to the right. The plane obeyed. Like a ponderous elephant, it lumbered down the taxiway.

With permission from Ground Control, the pilot stopped the aircraft short of the last turn on to the runway.

"Crew brief," the pilot said. "We will do a rolling take off after the final turn on to the runway. I plan to rotate at 95 knots airspeed. That should put us at about 4,500 feet down the runway, with 5,500 feet left. We will pull the gear up as soon as I verify by eye and instruments that we are climbing.

"If we have any problem before rotation I will do a high speed reject on the runway. If we have a problem after 95 knots I will continue airborne and climb out north, then hold at 5,000 feet. Run all checklists. Take your time, cross your *t*s and dot your *i*s, and we will return to land.

"If I have a catastrophic emergency, weather is good so expect me to pull closed and land as soon as possible."

While they listened, the crew performed other duties. The flight engineer scanned all the gauges. The navigator updated and checked his GPS.

"We will climb out at calculated 4-engine speed all the way. That's 175 knots today. We will depart initially on the runway vector. We will get the departure vector from the tower for climb out. Then up to 22,000 feet for our en route segment. Any questions?

"Air Evac 1492, you are cleared for takeoff," called the tower. "Altimeter 2998. Winds are 270 at 10. Fly runway heading until 1,000 feet, then left turn heading 230, contact departure on 123.95."

"Roger," replied the pilot. He turned slightly so he could see the copilot out of the corner of his eye.

"Do you want to take it?" he asked.

It was a standard test for new flyers in the right hand seat. Take the pilot's duties right up to the critical moment, then quickly shift the burden to the copilot. It was not just hazing. It tested whether the new copilot had been following developments in her head or was just going through the motions. It tested her ability to adjust to changing situations rapidly. It tested her competency—was she ready to fly as an operational pilot, or did she have to go back to "the book" to think about the next step? And it tested her attitude. Was she going to be an aggressive pilot you could count on in an emergency, or a wall flower waiting to be invited to the ball?

"Do you want to take it?"

The whistle blew, followed by the horn, and the high school girls collected in a knot along the bench at mid-court.

"Time out, Lincoln," the referee said.

It was their last time out, but that didn't matter. There were only four seconds showing on the clock, and they were behind by one point. Time for one shot. They circled around the coach.

"Left post cutoff," he said. "Jamie, you pass in to Kim. Thomasina, fake around the forward to screen off your man, but stop short.

Kim, pass to her and Thomasina, take a long shot from the corner. They won't be expecting that."

The slight girl with the short blond hair, quick eyes, and quicker feet backed up just a little.

"Uh, I don't think so coach," she said. "They've been all over me all night. I'm not sure I can make the shot."

Everyone paused. They all knew she had the best shooting percentage on the team. They all knew she had a better chance from outside than any of them from inside the key. They all knew the game was on the line. And they all knew that at this critical moment their most competent teammate had turned timid.

The coach paused. The crowd was chanting and stomping so the bleachers rang, but he spoke slowly and just loudly enough to be heard. He looked directly into her eyes.

"Are you sure?" he asked. There was no missing his meaning. The game was on the line. It was her chance to be the hero. She had earned it. Did she really want to give it away?

"Yeah." She looked down. "They're all over me. Fake to me and feed Cathy."

"Okay," the coach said. "That's it."

He clapped his hands and the girls walked deliberately to their places on the court. The other team was already in place, each moving around slightly to make their intended defense a little less obvious. A girl in a green top and white shorts took the ball along the sidelines and held it above her head. The crowd roared to its feet and undulated in green and white, shirts and pompoms moving wildly as the noise level grew. The referee blew his whistle. The girl with the ball faked once along the sidelines, then threw it to a tall girl in the center of the court.

Jacquelyn Thomasina Williams broke down the left boundary line of the court in a hard run and angled toward the opposing forward in order to pass close behind. As she passed her opponent, she faked a shoulder shift as though she were cutting to the right, under the basket. The clock clicked to three seconds left.

A player in white jersey and purple shorts, matching her stride for stride, realized the move would cut her off from coverage, and force her out, away from the basket. So she broke to the right and headed instead to the point where Thomasina would emerge from behind the stationary defender.

But Thomasina stopped short and turned to the center as if to receive the ball and shoot from the outside corner. She was perfectly in position. Her opponent was perfectly out of position. If only Thomacina had the ball. The clock clicked to two seconds left.

But she did not have the ball. The play was a fake. The center turned instead to another girl in green on the other side of the court. She crossed from right to left and looked for the ball as she pounded toward a layup shot. The clock clicked to one second left.

The other defender was not fooled. Moving between the attacker and the ball, she was in exactly the right place to deflect the pass. There would be no layup. There would be no shot. The clock clicked to zero and the horn sounded. The opposing bleachers went wild with joy. The girls in green tuned dejectedly toward the bench. Their crowd applauded half-heartedly from the stands.

"Good try," someone yelled. "Good try."

He father met her at the bench.

"Thomasina," he said. "You choked in the clutch. You are a great player with great talent, but you lack confidence in your own ability. You know the standard. If you are not going to play to win, don't play at all. Winners always want the ball."

She hated the way he spoke in sports clichés. She hated the way he constantly referred to lines in sports movies. She hated his standard of perfection. And she hated how often he was right. With the game on the line, she had passed the shot to someone else. "Winners always want the ball." *She would not forget that again.*

"Do you want to take it?" the pilot repeated his question, wondering if she had heard.

She shook her head just slightly as if clearing it. "You bet," she said with a confidence that she didn't quite feel.

He took his hand off the throttles. She put hers on. She pushed all four forward as the pilot turned the taxi wheel to the left. The big plane lurched forward on the taxiway, turned left, then left again on to the runway.

"Rolling take off," she said.

The massive aircraft seemed ponderous at first. With the throttles advanced all the way forward and the propellers angled to take a maximum bite of the air, the engines roared and shook the whole frame and the passengers inside. The plane started forward only about as fast as a man could walk. Then as fast as he could run. Then as fast as a bicycle. It picked up speed quickly and those seated at the few small windows could see markers along the runway zoom by.

Four thousand five hundred feet later the airspeed read ninety-five knots, and the copilot pulled back gently on the yoke. The big metal bird responded without effort and the runway began to recede below. The machine was in its element. It had thrust. It had lift. It gained altitude. Suddenly it was a graceful thing of beauty.

Checking her artificial horizon, the copilot saw that she was climbing, and a glance out the window confirmed the same. "Gear up," she announced. Reaching to his right, the pilot pulled a lever up and the landing gear began to retract into the body of the airplane. In just a moment it locked into place and the doors closed with a thump.

"Flaps up," the engineer announced from a checklist.

"Flaps up," the pilot responded, reaching over from his position on the left, to advance a lever on the right of the center console. The copilot kept one hand on the yoke and one hand on the throttles, and her attention focused on the gauges

"Left turn, heading 230," the navigator said. The pilot shot him a look. "No hints," it seemed to say.

"Heading 230," the copilot responded. The aircraft veered left with its nose pointed slightly up toward the sky.

"Air speed 180," she announced. Then keying the radio she said,

"Departure, this is Air Evac 1492, heading 230, 1,000, changing to Kansas City Center."

"Roger, Air Evac 1492," responded the tower. "Merry Christmas."

The copilot smiled to herself. She felt lucky to be here. How many girls from the basketball team were piloting a sixty-ton aircraft across six states today? How many young women had earned their wings as she had? She was airborne and she was happy with her performance.

The pilot checked the airspeed again. He was not nearly so pleased.

CHAPTER 3

NOTHING TO REPORT

0955 hours 23 December: Scott AFB to El Paso
International Airport, Texas

They had barely cleared the end of the runway when Nurse Ames keyed the intercom. "I'd like to get up and check patients," she said.

"Roger," answered the pilot. "Use your own judgment. But please keep someone on the headset so I can warn you if we run into turbulence. I will keep it as stable for you as I can.

"Load, the med team will be moving around, but make sure the passengers stay seated until we level off at altitude."

"*Well*," thought the nurse. "*Surprised again.*" Some pilots were all about their own authority, but some understood that she had a mission, too. Very professional, this one.

She rose and moved down the length of the compartment to stand next to the chest of the litter-bound soldier with his head and face wrapped in gauze. His eyes were covered but his bandaged right hand, across the litter from her, gripped the canvas covered rail. He could not see but he was apparently conscious.

She placed her hand on his left arm to reassure him, and bent close to his ear to speak. "This is your nurse," she said. "Everything looks good here. Are you okay?"

She meant the words to be soothing, but he jumped as if he had been surprised in the dark. As indeed, he had. He relaxed his grip on the litter a little, and nodded in the affirmative.

"I'm going to check your drip," she said. "This won't hurt."

A bag of saline solution hung upside down on a hook two feet above the litter. A clear plastic tube ran down to the litter, then to a needle in his left arm under the covers . She pulled back the blanket to reach the needle. Frequently for long-term IVs, the needle was placed in the back of the hand. But this one was placed in his forearm. Because below the wrist, there was no hand.

The loading of the litters was complete, and the C-130 began to taxi toward the end of the remote runway. There it would turn and take off, carrying wounded from a field collection point to the hospital near Baghdad.

In the dirt, heat, and confusion of loading, the patient's IV bag had been disconnected and discarded. The nurse needed to rig another to replace the fluid being lost to bleeding and overheating. She hung the bag on a hook above the patient's head, selected a pair of scissors from a plastic cabinet between litters, and reached down to cut away his left sleeve in order to insert the tube into a vein on the top of his hand.

The fabric was dark and stiff with blood, and when she cut it open, the sleeve parted to show white bone and mangled muscle halfway between elbow and wrist. There was no place to put the IV—his left hand and lower arm were gone.

Quickly composing herself, she reached across the patient to his right arm, and began cutting away that sleeve so she could find a vein for the IV needle. The angle was more difficult and the cutting took more time and effort. But when the sleeve fell open, it also showed white bone and an empty spot where the hand should be.

The nurse was startled and her eyes grew wide. She was an experienced trauma nurse, but for a moment she was disoriented. The shock of twice expecting to see a hand and arm, only to find an empty sleeve stopped her cold. She tried to get her bearings. Involuntarily she grimaced and squeezed her eyes tight. "Ooof!" she exhaled, as though she had been struck.

Ten thousand feet above the state of Illinois, she reached forward with the IV needle and found no hand at the end of her patient's arm. She knew this from the charts, but seeing it brought memories flooding back. She grimaced involuntarily and squeezed her eyes tight. "Ooof!" she said, then looked around to see if anyone had heard. No one had. She turned back to her work.

After a slower than expected climb out, the pilot keyed the intercom again. "Load, pass the word that we are at cruising altitude. If anybody wants to get up and move around they are clear to do so."

A sergeant favoring one leg immediately tried to stand and move to the back of the aircraft. But he would have been unsteady on the ground, and he toppled over in the humming, vibrating bay of the aircraft. The male medical technician caught him, grabbed him by the belt, and whispered in his ear. The soldier nodded, and they began to move slowly toward the rear of the plane.

Reaching the rear ramp, the soldier tried in vain to negotiate entry into the small toilet area. No matter what angle he tried, he could not fit with his stiff new leg. After a few moments, the loadmaster approached the medical technician with a white plastic bottle. The technician held the soldier by the shoulders from behind, while the trooper balanced as best he could. He was facing away from the other seated passengers, but they all understood what was happening and looked down, or away, or closed their eyes as if resting. It was one of the many small indignities suffered by those recovering from wounds. Other passengers gave him as much privacy as they could, knowing that it could be their turn next.

All except for the reporter who seemed transfixed by the scene.

"Found something to write about?" It was the legless Army major, his artificial legs projecting awkwardly into the aisle.

"Uh, no," she stammered. "I'm sorry. I'm not used to all the . . . difficulties."

The major sighed. "It's okay," he said. "He would understand. I would understand. I'm sure you're a nice person. You mean well. It's just that you're an outsider and you live on another planet where there is such a thing as privacy, and people don't have to help each other pee."

She was quickly coming to realize that this was a truism she had not anticipated. She started to engage the major to see if he might expand on his statement for an interview. But his eyes were closed. He was not asleep. He had just withdrawn.

Up front the pilot had a question for the copilot.

"What climb speed did I brief?" he asked.

"Uh . . . the dash one says the standard is a staggered climb schedule—you climb at 180 knots to 10,000 feet, 170 knots to 15,000, and 160 knots to cruising altitude of 22,000."

"No," the pilot answered pointedly. "The dash one says a staggered climb schedule is recommended to prevent excessive nose-high deck angles, which is not my primary concern at the moment. With this load we want to get up to smooth air as soon as possible to let the medical people get up and do their job. And we want to get altitude quickly to conserve fuel in the thinner air. This is why the flight engineer calculates a steady 4-engine climb speed and posts it right over your head; ours is 175 indicated today, which is what I planned. And what I briefed."

"I was trying to go by the book to get it right." She knew it sounded weak the moment she said it.

"You don't get points for trying," the pilot lectured. "Don't try, do. Get it right. Look, every mission is different. When the dash one gives you flexibility, use it. I need a copilot, not an autopilot. Use your head."

As rebukes between senior pilots and junior pilots go, it was mild. But it was a rebuke. In public. Over the intercom. Her cheeks burned red, and she hoped no one would notice. She felt humiliated. It was a moment she would not forget.

That, of course, was the point.

In the back, the MCD reached under the litters into a blue plastic box lashed to the floor. From inside she pulled out the medical charts for each of the litter patients, as well as two bags of medicine. "Garrett," she called to the junior nurse while handing him a clipboard. "How about doing a med rec for this one, while I do the other. And be sure you use Zulu time."

Attached to the clipboard for each patient was a list of medications, doses, and the frequency with which they should be administered. Because the patients could be changing medical teams and time zones frequently—especially in flight—all times were recorded in Greenwich Mean Time (Zulu time), rather than in local time.

The two nurses began to reconcile the information available on the charts against the medicine remaining in the bags. In a moment they switched charts and continued. Then both looked up. As the doctor approached, the junior nurse spoke first. Indicating the soldier swathed in bandages, he said, "I get that this one can have morphine again in an hour. And the other one gets 2 tabs orally in 2 hours."

By this time the doctor was standing with them. "I get the same," Nurse Ames replied. Then she looked to the doctor for confirmation. He took the charts, read them quickly, and nodded. She made a notation on each chart.

"Okay," she said handing all the charts and bags to the junior nurse. "How about check all the vitals for me, and let me know if you see a problem. I'm especially concerned about respiration for the guy on morphine."

"Dr. Woody," she continued. "Shall we make the rounds?"

He smiled at her intensity. "Call me Dr. Dan," he said pleasantly. "Most of the patients do." He turned to walk stiffly toward the passengers at the front of the aircraft, stopping at one point to stretch his left arm.

Walking behind him, she noted that she was taking short, shallow breaths. She felt a little lightheaded and particularly energized. Perhaps it was the change in altitude. Or maybe just the personal confidence of knowing how to do a complex technical job well. The truth was she loved this part of every mission. She could forget everything else in her life and just focus on her duties and do them right. It was liberating. Because she had a lot she wanted to forget.

"Nicely done!" he said.

Doctors as a group were not famous for treating nurses well. In fact, quite the opposite—much of the difficult and essential job of nursing went unrecognized and unappreciated. The patient load of this hospital in the combat zone in Iraq made matters worse.

But this doctor was different. He was well known for the understanding he showed for the trials and tensions of nursing. He recognized and complimented technical competence, even in simple duties like medicine reconciliation. As a result, nurses liked working with him. And he had chosen to work with her.

Nurse Win Ames was not a blushing student nurse, enamored of the power and status of doctors on the staff. And she had seen the wreckage created by romances among members of the same medical unit. But this was different. This was not just a shallow physical attraction. He was a great surgeon, and she knew it. And she was an excellent nurse, and he knew it. It was only natural that they should enjoy each other's company.

He smiled and handed her the chart, then held it longer than necessary so her hand brushed his. Her hand was warm to the touch. So was his. And he held her eyes for an extra moment before turning to the next bed in line.

She felt a little lightheaded and particularly energized. She loved this part of her job. Especially when she was doing it with him. She wanted to remember every minute.

* * *

Reporter Taylor Webster glanced at her watch. Time to get to work. She really loved this part of her job. Research, writing, long hours, deadlines—all that she could handle, even though none of it gave her any particular reward. But this business of carefully selecting a few details of a person's life and spinning them into a narrative that engaged readers and sold papers . . . this was fascinating. The only problem was that the facts did not always fit the story she had decided to tell.

She had been a reporter for four years and during that time most of the friends who graduated from journalism school with her had moved on to other jobs. No two ways about it—newspapers were dying all over the country. People were less literate, less attracted to the written word. Most writing just could not compete with the power of images you could see, rather than just imagine.

But her writing was different. Her editor said so. She had been lucky to land her first job at a significant paper; not some little community rag but a paper with articles that were picked up by the national media. She started at the bottom, of course: obituaries. Of greater concern, she started at the bottom of a pyramid that seemed to get smaller every day, as reporters and staff members quit, changed careers, or retired, but were rarely replaced. Upward mobility was not just limited. It was disappearing.

Her solution was to weave an emotionally engaging tale from whatever facts she had at hand. It was a perfect approach to obituaries. The deceased were not just mothers, teachers, siblings, or elected officials. They were sacrificing mothers, inspiring teachers, beloved siblings, and dedicated officials or businessmen who put service above self. Her stories were inspiring, or ironic, or tragic or heroic. People loved them. Especially the families.

It wasn't hard. Most people had a positive side to them that others would prefer to remember. You just had to sift through the facts until you found a couple of tidbits that lined up in an interesting way. Take the right approach to interviewing those who knew the deceased, and a couple of carefully crafted leading questions, and the stories almost wrote themselves. Knowing the actual person turned out not to be important at all.

Her editor noticed. After a few months of talking to every funeral home director in a hundred mile radius, she moved up to what used to be called the society pages. Here the same formula worked, but sometimes in reverse. It did not take many carefully selected facts to create a titillating story that suggested something amiss among those who had the bad fortune to have both money and ego. It was such an interesting intellectual exercise to see how the exact same facts could make a wedding exciting or salacious. And she was clever. Yes, her editor definitely noticed.

In two more years of working regional news she had become the savior of some local figures and the bane of others. It wasn't so much a political bias that drove her writing as opportunity and challenge. Fitting facts together into creative narratives was fun. And she did have her standards. She let the occasional buffoon off from the consequences of his tomfoolery. She never willingly told an untruth or used a fact that could not be checked. Of course, the *way* you told the truth sometimes mattered. That was the interesting part.

And now she had a chance to break into the big leagues. Her editor needed an emotional story to draw in readers during the dead days between Christmas and New Year's. If it really pulled the right strings, it might go national. She needed to nail this one. The stories had to sing. So she set about writing the music.

"Lieutenant Buenavida—good morning! And a good life to you!" The reporter moved up the aisle and slid into the faded red nylon mesh seat next to the infantry lieutenant.

"Charlie. Please call me Charlie." The voice was wary, as if he sensed an ambush. "So you speak Spanish, Ms...."

"Webster," the reporter answered. "But please call me Taylor. I only speak a little Spanish. *Un poco*." She smiled pleasantly. "But enough to recognize your good fortune in having such a good name." Buenavida meant "good life." It was a start point for a story. She would see where it went.

She glanced at his West Point ring. She would try polite and formal with this one—every inch the professional.

He smiled weakly and extended his hand. It was a firm shake, but he grimaced just a bit as he shifted his left leg, which seemed stiff. He noticed that she noticed.

"It's the weather," he said. "Makes my arthritis act up."

They both smiled at the obvious joke. He was twenty-seven years old. His cane rested near his left hand.

"So do you have family in El Paso?" she asked.

"Yes ma'am," he said. "My mother and brother. My dad died when I was young. He owned a restaurant."

"And your brother—older or younger?"

"Older," he said.

He was in the fourth grade and small for his age. His shirt was clean and white, his trousers khaki, and his backpack new. It had been clean, too, until a moment before, when a bigger boy knocked him down and kicked it into the muddy gutter.

"You're new," he said. "You don't know the rules. Give me your lunch money if you want to go to school."

The lunch money was not much, but his mother had worked hard for it. His father was dead and the restaurant where he played as a toddler while his older brother cooked was gone. His mother cleaned rooms in a hotel to earn the price of his new shirt and trousers and backpack.

"No!" he said, trying to rise to his feet.

A second thug bent down behind him, and the bigger one gave the smaller boy a sudden push. He toppled over the kneeling delinquent and sprawled on the ground again. A third tormentor picked up the backpack, unzipped it, and began to throw school supplies on the ground.

"That's mine!" the smaller boy cried, and tried again to stand.

But the one who had tripped him from behind held him down, and the leader reached for the victim's pockets.

"Nothing is yours," he answered calmly. "It all belongs to . . . "

It happened so quickly that the small boy thought the larger had stumbled and fallen on him. But he had not stumbled. He was down and out—knocked cold by a blow from behind. The second thug tried to rise on his own, but a fist caught him under the chin and stood him up. Then a kick between the legs doubled him over and he crumpled to the ground.

The thug with the backpack stood watching for a moment, then dropped his booty and reached for his pocket. He was too slow. The blow caught him on the right ear and spun him around and to the ground. A new figure, larger than the others, stepped into the small boy's view. He raised the head of the third thug by his hair, then smashed it into the curb. Once, twice . . . the third time was accompanied by the sound of snapping teeth, and blood gushed into the gutter and ran toward the backpack now lying on the ground. The new figure picked it up.

"Hermano!" he said, reaching for the small boy's hand. "Three on one. They are cowards. You should wait for me to walk you to school. I will always take care of my brother."

"He's almost ten years older, my brother. But we always got along. He always took care of me."

"So why did you decide to go into the Army?" she asked.

"Free education," he said. She was startled by the honesty of the answer. He glanced down at his stiff left leg. "Well, almost free." He smiled self-consciously.

"After my father died, my mother worked very hard to get me into a good school, so I would be ready for college. A lot of kids where I lived were attracted to the street—drugs, crime. She really pushed me to want a better life and that meant getting a better education. But it cost so much to put me through high school that there was no money for college. So I took the tests, scored well, and went to West Point."

"Did your family support that decision?"

He was eighteen now. Still short, but stocky and well-muscled. He was standing alone in the alley. Three others were present, but not standing. They were lying where they had fallen. One bullet center of mass in each. Very neat. Very precise. Very methodical.

A less attentive, less focused person might not recognize these as the same three who had jumped a small boy on the same street ten years before. But he remembered. They remembered, too. But they did not understand that years of sports and the weight room and preparing for West Point had changed their odds.

His older brother was the first one to arrive.

"Hermano!" he said. "What have you done?"

"It was self-defense," he answered. "They jumped me. We fought. One guy had a gun in his belt. He pulled it out, but I kicked him and he dropped it. I picked it up. And I defended myself. It was self-defense."

The older brother took the gun out of his hand, then looked left and right. There was no one else in the alley. Yet.

"That was loud." He said. "Three shots. Somebody heard. Somebody called the cops. They will be here soon. You should have waited for me.

"Look, no one will believe you. There were three of them. Everybody knows they picked on you. Nobody will believe you took out three guys after they jumped you. The policia will think you were waiting for them."

He looked across the alley to a door with a padlock. In two quick steps he was hammering on the lock with the gun. When it gave way, he kicked the door again and again until the bolt tore through the frame. Several people were stopped on the street now, looking down the alley. In the distance a police siren wailed. The larger figure stood next to the door, shielding the smaller from view.

"Go!" he said, pushing the younger brother into the dark room. "Go to the other side of the building and go out the window. Then go to West Point and get rich. You are the smart one. That's why mamma pushed you. Go be a big man and save our family!"

The smaller figure backed two steps further into the darkness. Then he turned and ran deeper into the abandoned building.

The sirens were closer and more people were gathering around. The older brother quickly wiped the pistol with his shirt, then threw it down next to the bodies. He ran down the alley to the street, turned away from the abandoned building and kept running. The sirens followed.

"Oh yes," he said, in his best public affairs voice. "My family has always been very supportive."

"How long have you been gone from home?"

"Seven years," he said. "Four in West Point, and three in the Army. I've been back a couple of times to visit my mother."

"And your brother?" the reporter asked.

"He has been gone, too," he answered. "Seven years. He just got home last week. I called. He is coming to the airport to meet me."

"Was he in the Army, too?" the reporter queried, still trying to make her plot line work. She was trying to build a story in her head about family service.

"No," he answered carefully. "He has been working for the state." He looked away.

She tried another tack. "So what's next for you? Are you going to stay in the Army?"

"No," he replied, more relaxed this time. "I have a medical discharge. I will be getting some benefits from the government and from the state of Texas. I'm going to open a restaurant with my brother." The lieutenant smiled. "He used to be a pretty good cook."

Still looking for an angle for the story, she said, "Well tell me about your medal. You got the Silver Star. That's a pretty big deal. Do you think people will hear the story and want to come by to visit your restaurant? You're a war hero. Will that be good for business?"

They were stacked against the wall ready for the assault. Team A on the right, automatic weapon in the lead, and four riflemen behind. Team B on the left, in the same order. Team C, identical in organization, waited against the wall next door.

The lead through the door would look only at the far wall, scanning for additional rooms, doors, or threats, and shooting anything that looked hostile. Number 2 would take the same actions but focused only on the left wall. Number 3 would do the same with the right wall. Number 4 would enter and whirl, checking the back wall through which they entered. Number 5 would throw the initial flash-bang to disorient anyone inside, then enter last and look up, always up, for anything that posed a threat.

Every team member would be vulnerable in some way—to the front, the flanks, or the rear. But if he looked around to save himself, the whole team would be endangered. So every man focused on his job and depended on his teammate—his brother—to cover his back. Each little team was a tight little family.

Lieutenant Buenavida knelt along the wall behind Team A. He would follow Number 5 through the door. Usually the platoon leader stayed in the street to manage the other elements of the platoon. But once in a while he had to go with an assault team to maintain his reputation as a leader. You could manage from anywhere. You could only lead from the front.

The platoon sergeant and radio operator slid in next to him.

"Security up at both ends of the street," the sergeant said.

"Covering fire on the roof. Third squad in reserve two doors down. All ready to go."

The lieutenant looked at his teams—his boys, his brothers—spring loaded for battle. His gaze paused on the Number 3 man of the lead team—the smallest man in the platoon. His helmet always looked too big and the protective vest too large for the small frame. But the guy worked extra hard to make up for his size. He could be trusted.

The lieutenant nodded. "Demo!" he barked.

A soldier raced from across the street and slapped a web of charges to the door. He pulled down hard on a string attached to a short tube connected to a white ring of demolition cord. Small explosive charges dotted the cord like Christmas lights. "Fire in the hole!" he yelled.

The deafening explosion tore at the clothes of everyone along the wall. The door splintered, tore from its hinges in pieces, and flew inward. The explosion was still echoing when Number 5 stepped to the side of the door with a cylinder in each hand. With his right index finger he reached across and pulled the pin from the cylinder in his left, then he repeated the process the other way round. Then he tossed both cylinders into the room.

The "flash-bangs" were designed to stun an enemy with light, noise, and concussion, but not wound, in case non-combatants were in the room. In an enclosed space they worked magnificently. BA-BOOM!

The instant the second explosion went off, the Number 1 man was across the threshold. The others followed in a rush. The room was full of smoke and dust, but no people. Number 4 draped a three-foot long strip of bright orange nylon across the windowsill, so half hung outside. The room was clear. Across the street, security saw the orange banner and raised their sights to the second floor windows.

"Stairs!" announced Number 2. "Far left corner of the room"

"Locked door on the right wall!" called out Number 3.

"Team B!" called the lieutenant. "Upstairs!"

Team B rushed into the room and gathered at the base of the stairs. Number 1 stood up to advance.

Suddenly the door against the right wall swung inward, and arms reached out to snatch Number 3 of Team A from behind. "Hey!" he cried. But he had time to say no more before he was jerked violently through the door into an adjoining room. The door slammed shut, and the lock clicked in place, before anyone could move. Even the lieutenant was speechless. One of his team members had been kidnapped!

"Demo!" he cried. But not waiting for the demo man to cross the street and set charges, he rushed the door and threw his full weight against it. The ancient hinges gave way and the door collapsed inward.

Again everyone was momentarily stunned to inaction: the teams in the next room; the lieutenant on the floor; his soldier Number 3, about to be dragged semi-conscious out the window; and three men in Iraqi dress. One stood on the window sill, reaching back to pull the soldier through by his shoulders. The other two were fully inside the room, lifting the soldier out by his belt.

The lieutenant did not think. He reacted. Three against one. Endangering his brother.

He rolled off the door, took a quick bead on the assailant on the window sill through the bright round sight of his M-4, and shot him twice through the head before the man could let go and seek cover. Shifting his point of aim to the nearest target, he put two rounds through the man's chest and one in his head as he slid down the wall. He shifted aim again, but the rifle clicked without firing a round. Jam!

The third man was advancing on him now with some sort of an iron rod in his hand. The lieutenant rolled over again, ending up against the wall with his pistol out. He put two shots in the attacker's chest, but the man reached for a gun on the floor. Damn 9 millimeter. It didn't always take them down.

The kidnapper weakened and fell, but his gun went off with a flash, and the lieutenant felt a searing pain in his knee. Before Buenavida could follow up with a third shot to his opponent's head, someone kicked the pistol from his hand. There had been a fourth assailant trapped under the fallen door. Now he was up with a pistol of his own and drawing a bead on the lieutenant on the floor. The lieutenant surprised this attacker by rolling back the other way and taking him down at the knees. Pulling a knife from a sheath in his boot, the lieutenant fell upon the man in a murderous rage.

Suddenly, he was no longer a man in a fight. He was an animal released from a cage. Twenty years of outrage at being outnumbered and pushed around had escaped. Two decades of seeing the world divided into him and his brother against everyone else took over. He was no longer a soldier at war. He was a man possessed.

He did not stop because he was the victor. He stopped because he was exhausted.

He stood and looked around the room. Soldier Number 3 was backed against the wall, his head bleeding and his eyes wide. Three members of Team B stood open-mouthed in the doorway, their guns no longer at the ready, as they tried to take in the scene before them. Looking around the room he saw his handiwork.

Four bodies were in tatters. Blood was splattered on every surface. He looked down to find his clothes soaked and dripping red to the floor. A knife was clinched in his hand.

"Damn!" said a soldier standing in the doorway. "Damn!"

Suddenly the pain in his knee was intense. His leg would not hold him. He collapsed to the bloody floor. The last thing he remembered seeing was the wall. It was splattered with blood as high as a man could reach. Then he retreated into the dark.

He was sitting stock still. Perhaps he had not heard her.

"El Paso is a military town. Do you think people will come by the restaurant to see a war hero?" the reporter repeated.

He shook his head without speaking, and then looked away. "No war," he said. "No, no war hero. I just want to run a restaurant for my family."

He looked back at her. "I don't want any publicity about any of this. I don't want to talk about it. I would prefer that you not write about me please."

He looked away again. He was done talking. No permission here. She closed the notebook and looked for someone else to interview.

"Hi there," the reporter said brightly, sliding into a space next to Sergeant Connie Rodman. "How are you doing?"

"Fine," answered the sergeant shyly. "How are you?"

"Are you comfortable on the trip?"

"Yes," she answered quietly, "I'm just fine." But she wasn't.

"Are you healing up okay?" asked the reporter.

"Oh yes," replied the sergeant. "Everything is going to be great." But it wasn't.

"Do you have someone meeting you in El Paso?"

"You bet," replied the sergeant, warming. "My husband, and my dad, and a couple of my sisters." She smiled quietly. Her even white teeth were striking against her mocha skin. It was a warm, friendly smile. She looked down shyly. "*She could be a model*," the reporter thought.

"You could be a model," the reporter said. The woman's facial color darkened slightly. "*She's blushing!*" the reporter thought. She could not remember when she had last seen a woman blush. It was old fashioned. And endearing.

"Well, I'm not," the soldier replied. "I'm a mechanic."

"Really!" said the reporter, opening her notebook. OK, here was a story that might prove promising. "How did that come about?"

"My dad was a mechanic," came the reply. "In the Army. He worked on all kinds of stuff. Trucks, tanks, helicopters—he went to a bunch of schools, and now he's a manager for a big trucking company in El Paso.

"*Okay!*" thought the reporter. "*Here we go! Family story.*"

"So was he okay with you joining the Army?"

"Yeah, he was okay with it. I have three older sisters. They all went to college and got married and have kids. Good husbands. All settled down. I said I wanted to see something and do something before I did that. So I joined the Army. He made me promise that I would go to school eventually, and now I have the GI Bill, so that will make him happy."

She smiled again. Apparently making her father happy made her happy, too.

"So where have you been assigned?"

"Well, I work on trucks. So I can go pretty much anywhere. I had two years in Hawaii. That was great. Then two years in El Paso before I went to Iraq. That's where I met my husband—El Paso. He was in the Army, too."

"*Oh yes,*" thought the reporter. "*This is working.*" She leaned forward, "girl to girl."

"So did you know right away that he was the one?"

Nurse Ames was sitting nearby. It was the giggly sort of question that put her on guard. But not the sergeant. She actually seemed to enjoy talking to someone about her husband.

"Not right away, but pretty soon after I met him."

"What tipped you off?" the reporter asked in a conspiratorial whisper.

"You know," the sergeant replied. "He was just a really nice guy. He is very outgoing and I'm not. But he seemed to like me. He's funny and he's smart. And he wasn't pushy. Do you know what I mean? He said he just enjoyed my company and he could wait . . . " Her voice trailed off. She was blushing again. But she enjoyed telling the story.

Nurse Ames was listening intently.

"On about our third or fourth date he said he was not in a hurry to get married, but when he did, it would be for keeps. And he wanted a big family. That's when I knew he was the one. He says I set out to catch him, but I say he didn't run very fast." She was really enjoying this.

"And he has three brothers like I have three sisters. He said he wanted children and not many guys will say that." Suddenly she looked stricken. The reporter was looking down and did not notice. The nurse did.

"So what did he do in the Army?"

"He was a military policeman," the sergeant said. Her voice was guarded again.

"He was just back from Iraq when I met him, and we dated for about a year and a half. He got out and joined the Border Patrol. I was going to get out and maybe do the same thing, but then this deployment came up. I got caught in the extension. I was supposed to get out six months ago, but they extended me to do a tour because the whole Army was so shorthanded."

"So they sent your whole unit from El Paso?"

"No, just me. I was working on trucks in a missile unit in El Paso, but they sent me to a maintenance unit in Iraq because they had some people hurt. Then they had to have gate guards. That's where I was wounded."

"Wait a minute." The reporter sensed an interesting point. A narrative was taking shape. "So you were supposed to be out of the Army, and you were assigned to a unit that was supposed to stay home, but you were kept on active duty because they were short of mechanics, then sent to Iraq and instead of working on trucks you guarded the gate? And that's where you were hurt?"

"Yes," said the sergeant quietly. "Strange isn't it?"

The reporter wrote quickly. Lots of irony to work with here.

"And will you have a big crowd at the airport?"

"Oh yes," said the sergeant. "All three of my sisters have children, and my husband is the youngest of four brothers. All of them have children. We are going to have a big family Christmas in El Paso this year, as soon as I get home." Her face clouded and she withdrew. Again, the reporter did not catch the change. Again, Nurse Ames did.

"So," the reporter said, scribbling busily. "Lots of children at the airport!"

Now the sergeant was visibly pained. Nurse Ames turned to face her. The reporter did not look up.

"Well, I'm sure they are all glad to have you back and all healed up! Would you mind telling me about when you were wounded?"

"Nothing much to tell," the sergeant said. "I had only been in country two weeks. My second day on the gate. I was on with two guys who said something didn't look right about this car coming up, so they motioned it over. I never knew what they thought was wrong. It stopped and one of them walked up to the window and it blew up. That was the whole deal. Not much story."

"Were you hurt badly?"

"No," said the sergeant. "Not compared to them. One of the guys was killed. One lost his leg and an eye. It rang my bell pretty good—guess I was unconscious for a while. I lost my hearing and I was kind of in and out for about a week. But I just took some shrapnel in the abdomen. Came in under my vest somehow. It was no big deal."

After the tremendous blast of the car bomb, almost everything was a blur until she woke up in a hospital ward in Washington, DC. The arrival of the medics, being transported in the ambulance, the bright lights and doctors and nurses of the emergency room, being loaded on an aircraft, the flight to Germany and then to the U.S.—it was all just a mixture of faces and lights and noises. There was really only one thing she could remember clearly.

She was in a room with bright lights overhead. A lot of people were around. She could not talk. She could not move. She could barely hear. But they were talking about her. A woman was talking— a nurse. She was asking the doctor a question. She could make out one word— just one. "Children."

He bent over and looked at her stomach. Looked down where she could not see. And he shook his head no.

"Oh no!" said the reporter. "This is a great story! I want to get a bunch of pictures of you and your family and all the kids at the airport!"

The sergeant sat quietly.

"You know," she said. "I don't think so. I think I would rather that you didn't write anything about me at all."

She stood up gradually, grimacing and steadying herself by holding on to the aluminum rail of the seats. "I think I am going to take a little walk," she said. She walked down the aisle to the tail of the aircraft, turned and walked up the other aisle. She sat down in a seat on the other side of the plane and looked away from the reporter.

The reporter took a deep breath and shook her head in frustration.

The nurse took a deep breath and shook her head in anger.

"Nobody seems to want to talk," the reporter said.

"What?" The sergeant jumped, then turned to look her in the face. Lost in thought, he had not noticed when the reporter sat down.

"I didn't mean to startle you," she said.

"I'm not startled," he replied. "I'm embarrassed. I'm a scout. I'm supposed to sneak up on other people. Not the other way 'round." The name tape on his shirt said "Martel."

She smiled nicely at the small joke. And she meant it.

"It's frustrating," she went on. "Nobody wants to tell their story—about being wounded, about recovery, about coming home. You're all heroes. Every one of you has a great story, but nobody will let me tell it."

The sergeant smiled, too. They still had an hour to go. Might as well be pleasant. Might as well be polite. Took his mind off the arrival. He had a cane but set it down off to the side.

"Did you ever see the movie *Black Hawk Down*?" he asked.

"The one about the soldiers in Somalia? Oh yeah, of course."

"There's this one interesting part—actually, it's pretty realistic—where this convoy of gun trucks is lost, all screwed up in the streets. And they've been taking fire. And all the trucks are hit. And this colonel tells his driver to move out. The driver's just a young kid and he says, 'I can't drive. I've been shot!' And the colonel says, 'Hell son, everybody's been shot! Move out!'"

The sergeant smiled easily, remembering the scene in the movie.

"Well look around. Hell lady, everybody's been shot! Everybody in here is worse off than me in some way. Except maybe numb-nuts over there." He gestured toward the pale specialist with the cane. "I know a slacker when I see one. But everybody else is facing a hard spot in his life that he is trying to overcome. They're all worse off than me. And they are probably thinking the same thing when they look over here."

He paused. "We all know that the difference between being missed and being hit, or being hit and being killed is a random matter of a couple of inches. That's nothing to be proud of or ashamed of. We were lucky. Some other really good guys weren't. It's just not worth talking about."

Cautiously she unfolded her notebook. "Were others wounded with you?" she asked.

He was just stepping out of the truck when the IED went off. The door was open and his right leg was outside with his foot resting on the ground. His left leg was inside with the foot pressed against the floorboard of the Humvee as he began to lift himself out of the truck. The blast saved him the trouble. It threw him out of the truck, across the street and on to the sidewalk. His left leg stayed behind.

The driver was nineteen, from Pennsylvania, had played football in high school, and loved to talk about every game he had ever played. He was thirteen when the Twin Towers fell. He was seventeen when the Iranians began designing special armor penetrating weapons and smuggling them across the border into Iraq. He would never see twenty.

The metal tube that caused the damage was about two feet long and six inches across. At one end, it was capped and an explosive trigger was attached. The inside was filled with a special high-grade explosive. The other end was open and hollow to a depth of several inches. At the bottom of the opening a copper funnel held the explosives in place. When the charge was set off, the force of the explosive would be concentrated and focused by the shape of the funnel into a tight stream of super-hot gas and molten metal.

The Iranians had designed the weapon to penetrate the special armor of the American M-1 tank. So it cut through the driver's side of the Humvee in an instant. It also cut through the driver, throwing the top half of his body through the windshield. And it cut through the transmission. Then it cut through the sergeant's leg.

"Like I said, everyone here's been wounded. I got out. I recovered. I'm going home to see my kids. Life is good. I just don't have much to talk about.

"How about you?" he asked, trying to change the subject. "How long have you been a reporter?"

She didn't have a story and she was wasting time. She didn't parry the question. She ignored it.

"So who is going to meet you at the airport? Do you have a wife? Children?"

"Yes." He nodded. "But they might not be there. I'm not sure if my wife is bringing them."

"Did they visit you in the hospital, or is this the first time you have seen them since you were wounded?

The first grader was small and looked even smaller backed up against the wall of Ward 54 in Walter Reed Army Hospital. It was a wide hallway and many people were moving past. The boy's arms were crossed and his head was down. People passing by tried not to listen.

"Honey, your daddy is waiting for us," the woman said. "He is just right there in that room! Come on and let's go see him," she implored.

She had an attractive face, and dark hair curled for the occasion.

She was a little overweight, but she carried it in a vulnerable momish sort of way that made men feel protective. Those walking by wanted to help her, but they didn't know how.

"Come on," she directed, more strongly than before. "Let's not do this in front of your dad.

"Come on!" The voice remained quiet but the whisper became harsh. "Let's go!"

"Leave him alone!"

His ten-year-old sister was intervening now, trying to place her body between mother and son. "Can't you see he doesn't want to go? Can't you see he's crying? Leave him alone!"

The girl had adopted the role of protector, leaving the mother flustered.

"But honey, we came all this way. We need to see your daddy."

"I don't want to see him," said the small voice. "He's all broken. He lost his leg. You said so. I don't want to see him like that. I don't want to see him without his leg. I don't know what to say."

The daughter was crying now, too. And soon the mother joined her, dabbing at her eyes to keep her make-up from running.

Inside the room, Sergeant Roger Martel of the Third Armored Cavalry Regiment looked down at the sheet where his legs should be. But only one leg showed as a long white lump in the bed. On the other side the bed was flat below the level of the knee.

From just beyond the doorway, he could hear the conversations and the sound of his children sobbing. He lifted his hands and covered his eyes. And he wept, too.

"Sorry," he said. "I just don't have a story to share."

The reporter sighed deeply and closed her notebook. She could not afford to blow this opportunity. As she turned to move up the aisle, the sergeant turned the other way to look out the small round window. He glanced quickly to the side. No one was looking.

He raised his hands and covered his eyes. And he wept again.

"I think that rpm gauge is fluctuating again." The engineer reached forward to tap it.

"I know," said the pilot. I've been watching it for an hour. But I don't feel any vibration, and the reading is still within limits. Temperature is constant, no change in fuel flow. The engine's not surging. They wrote up that they changed the gauge, but maybe somebody made a mistake. That could happen."

"Not likely," said the engineer. "Not if they wrote it up."

"Roger," the pilot concluded. "Let's keep an eye on it. It doesn't look like there's any real trouble."

"We are 40 miles out," said the navigator.

"Load, tell the pax we are 15 minutes out from landing," said the pilot on the intercom. "MCD, recommend you make your final checks and get your team strapped in. Co, tell Albuquerque we want to start descent."

"Albuquerque Center, this is Air Evac 1492," said the copilot. "Request descent for landing in El Paso."

"Roger," answered the control center. "El Paso altimeter is 3002; descend and maintain 1–4 thousand leaving Flight level 220; contact El Paso approach leaving 1–4 thousand."

Quickly the team in back altered its actions and its tempo, as it went from constantly checking the patients in flight to preparation of patients for landing and hand off.

The medical technicians moved from person to person adjusting seat belts and checking for safety issues, while the junior nurse watched for facial expressions and non-verbal cues of pain or stress. The loadmaster wound his way between seats, passengers, litters, and mounds of baggage and equipment to ensure every strap and tie-down was tight. The MCD started toward the litters, then noted that the doctor was already standing on one side of the patients, and the chaplain was on the other. Together they provided two different kinds of comfort—both were needed to address two different kinds of pain.

And so she pulled out a medical off-load message form, about the size of a 5 x 7 card, and began to write. Briefly she described the patients on board, their condition, and confirmed the requirements for the transfer of the litter patients by ambulance to William Beaumont Army Medical Center at Ft. Bliss. Handing it to the loadmaster, she said, "Will you please ask the pilot to call this to the tower in El Paso? There should be someone there in operations waiting to receive it." The loadmaster nodded and headed up the ladder to the flight deck.

After making that radio call as directed, the pilot said nothing about taking control of the aircraft so the copilot started thinking about the landing. She was already behind the power curve. She just didn't know it.

"El Paso approach, this is Air Evac 1492. 20 miles Northeast of El Paso leaving 1-5 thousand for 1-4 thousand."

"Roger," responded the tower. "Cleared for approach. Report leaving 1-4 thousand. Stand by for LIMA 21 arrival."

There was a long pause. The copilot hesitated, but finally turned to the pilot and keyed the intercom. "What's LIMA 21?" she asked

"How were you planning to approach the runway?" he responded.

"I was just going to vector direct to Runway 22," she answered.

"LIMA 21 is the designation for a specific type of Standard Terminal Arrival. You need to look it up in a STAR booklet. It is different for every airport."

"Oh yeah, I knew that. It's for special approaches like noise abatement, or something like that."

"Thanks for the info," replied the pilot. "Didn't you check your STAR book before departure? Or during transit?"

She bit her lip. She just wanted the flight with this guy to be over.

"Call the tower and tell them you are a turboprop aircraft," instructed the pilot.

She frowned but complied. What was the point of this?

"El Paso approach, this is Air Evac 1492. We are a turbo prop C-130 aircraft."

"Oh sorry," answered the tower. "I was thinking you were a jet. LIMA 21 not required for a turboprop aircraft."

So the pilot was walking her through this just to rub her nose in it.

The checklist ballet was reaching a crescendo now, as every member of the crew reversed the procedures they had followed for takeoff.

"How about a crew brief?" asked the pilot.

Quickly the copilot organized one in her head, as she should have done ten minutes earlier. "My aim point is halfway down the runway," she began cautiously.

Together the crew worked through every step, checking each other, reminding each other, confirming each other, until the sixty-ton aircraft hung suspended over the runway and finally touched down just past the midpoint. The copilot efficiently brought the aircraft to a halt.

She looked blankly at the pilot. Now what? She had not thought about this.

"Nav pull out the diagram for this airport," the pilot snapped. "Ground Control, this is Air Evac 1492 on the ground. We are an Air Force C-130 carrying wounded to meet family and medical care. Want to park on the military ramp. Request progressive taxi."

"Roger," came the answer. "Turn left on Taxi Golf. Hold short of Runway 8 Right."

"*Request progressive taxi.*" Nuts. She had forgotten about that. You didn't need a chart. You could just ask Ground to guide you to where you wanted to go. There was just so much to remember. How did the pilot do it?

"Boss, that rpm gauge on Number 1 just died. Completely flatlined," said the engineer.

"Well nuts," said the pilot. "Let's get to parking and off load, then see what we can do. I hope we're not stuck here for three days."

By the time Air Evac 1492 made the final turn to its designated parking spot on the ramp, the two outboard engines had been shut down and the propeller blades were windmilling slowly to a halt. Following ground guides waving orange sticks, the plane made a final turn, then stopped, and the roar of the inboard engines was replaced by the changing pitch of the internal turbines winding down.

The loadmaster opened the back doors and jumped out carrying the chocks—then set them in place before and after the landing gear. The ground crew pushed up a yellow cart with a generator and attached it to the plane's electrical system by means of an umbilical cable plugged in near the crew door. The plane would have lights, radios, and some degree of heating and cooling as long as this generator was operational.

Meanwhile, the med team was organizing the passengers into three groups. The first included the two on litters, who would be loaded out to ambulances that should be waiting on the ground. The second would be deplaning under their own power to see friends and family who had come to meet them. The third group included everyone going on to Garden City. They would stay out of the way until the El Paso people had departed. Then they would receive instructions about the next leg of the trip.

Those hoping to meet friends and family gathered just behind the litter stack, and waited for the great ramp to descend and allow them to walk straight off the plane to the ground.

"Standby!" cried the loadmaster. Sergeant Martel was on his feet, trying to maintain his balance, when the ramp began to drop. The recon sergeant found himself breathing faster and faster. It was like the moments before a combat assault. Everything was beginning to move. Too late to stop it now. But no way to know ahead of time how it would turn out.

Two white ambulances were waiting on the tarmac behind the plane. As soon as the ramp was down, Nurse Ames was on the headset and in the middle of the action.

Two attendants for each litter helped the medical crew unlatch the handles and lift them out of the brackets where they rested. With one person on each handle, the litters and their human cargo made their way slowly down the ramp. At the bottom, each litter was placed on a wheeled gurney, and each gurney was pushed to the rear of an ambulance. The medical team lifted the litter and collapsed the wheels beneath, then rolled the entire package into the back of the vehicle. The soldier with his head bandaged spoke quietly to the medical attendants. The other soldier turned away from everyone and never spoke a word.

In a matter of moments the litters were loaded and the vehicles were ready to go. The "administrative sergeant" was the last into the last vehicle. He loaded his small silver suitcase into the ambulance, and the two vehicles pulled away, headed for the gate and the military base. They did not use their lights or siren. At this point, smoothness of ride was more important than speed.

As soon as they departed, those ending their travels in El Paso moved to the edge of the ramp. The medical team was abuzz with activity.

In a combat operation, the big mistakes are usually made at the end of a mission, when everyone lets down his guard. Medical operations are no different. In both cases, leaders counter the tendency and the danger by increasing their supervision and their intensity. This was difficult for Nurse Ames, who was already very intense.

Technically, the medical team's responsibility for those offloading on their own was over. These were discharged patients going home on leave or departing the military. But nobody wanted a final stumble or fall on their watch. So the team prepared to ease each person down the ramp as if they were fine crystal. Those departing were impatient, but they understood. Once they stepped off the ramp and on to the concrete, they were on their own. From a distance, the doctor checked one last time for anything out of the ordinary. The chaplain worked the edges of the small crowd. And Nurse Ames stood on the ramp to maximize her control over what she would soon be unable to control at all.

The plane was parked parallel to the fence line, so those onboard could not actually see who was waiting to greet them. The tension of how they would be greeted was compounded by the tension of whether they would be greeted at all.

As those departing lined up, Sergeant Martel stood at the top edge of the ramp. As MCD, Nurse Ames personally checked off the name of every person in the group. "Okay," she finally said. "You're clear to go."

The group moved gingerly down the ramp, one at a time, with a technician providing an arm and an assist to each. When they reached the bottom, the technicians returned to the top of the ramp for the next person. Meanwhile, those at the bottom turned to face the crowd.

The crowd was small—perhaps fifty people—but raucous. About forty seemed to belong to one family. There were nearly as many flags as people. As the wounded emerged from the shadow of the tail and walked toward the fence that marked the edge of the parking ramp, people began to applaud. "There she is," someone shouted. "Daddy!" said another voice. The people on canes and crutches and artificial limbs could not exactly run, but they could hurry. And they did.

The first through the gate and into the crowd was the female mechanic, Sergeant Connie Rodman. She was swarmed by a huge extended family. Her father. Her husband. His brothers. Her sisters. Her brothers-in-law and sisters-in-law. And children, children, children. It was a frantic scene with mothers chasing children, and her father beaming from ear to ear. Her husband hugged her warmly and held her hand as if afraid she might escape him again. In the midst of it all, Sergeant Rodman smiled wanly. At her feet, eight children, ages one to six, raced and shrieked. She looked at her husband, then looked down.

Watching from a distance, Nurse Ames drew a deep breath and looked away.

Her gaze fell on Lieutenant Buenavida, who was standing erect but favoring his stiff leg. His eyes scanned the crowd. He did not seem to recognize anyone. He moved past the platoon of well-wishers toward the parking lot and stood looking to the left and right. His face was impassive, but his shoulders slumped.

An older model car, clean but with faded paint, circled the parking lot and stopped by the fence. A rough looking man of indeterminate age exited the driver's side, circled the trunk, and opened the passenger side door in front. Tattoos covered both arms like sleeves. An older woman stepped out of the car with obvious effort. Her dark hair was braided in the back, and she favored one hip when she walked.

Together the two walked rapidly along the fence to where the lieutenant was standing. As they approached, Lieutenant Buenavida stepped haltingly toward them. Limping and leaning heavily on his cane, the lieutenant marched straight to the older woman and threw his arms around her. Even from a distance, Major Ames could see her shoulders shake. She was crying.

The lieutenant released her with one arm and turned to shake hands with his brother. It was a distant, tentative shake. The brother would have none of it, holding the shake with one hand and embracing the lieutenant with the other arm. It was a hard hug and a genuine one. The lieutenant rested his head on his older brother's shoulder for a long moment.

Then he stood erect, wiped his eyes, and took his mother's hand. The older brother hoisted the lieutenant's duffel bag on his back and turned toward the car with a broad grin. The group of three walked with two limps toward the car. But the stride was confident. The owners of the next successful restaurant in El Paso entered the car, backed from the parking space, and were gone.

"So what do you see?" The reporter had replaced the nurse at the top of the ramp, and was looking over the entire scene. The chaplain startled her with his question, but she was quick with a professional observation.

"They look uncomfortable—the wounded. Not hurt . . . just . . . ill-at ease. Maybe it's all the attention."

"Naw," replied the chaplain. "It's coming home. It's leaving the military. It's trying to remember who you are."

The reporter furrowed her brow and turned to look at him. He shrugged.

"I'm a chaplain in the Army Reserve. I have seen a lot of our guys come home. At the airport, I always see the same thing. Here they are, back from a very structured environment, hard living conditions, maybe a dangerous job. Maybe they're a squad leader or a company commander. Maybe somebody calls them 'pilot,' or 'Corporal,' or 'Top Sergeant,' or 'The Old Man.'

"And the family greets them and somebody calls them 'daddy,' and somebody calls them 'honey,' and somebody calls them 'son.'" Maybe their employer is there and says, 'So glad you're home, Frank. Can't wait to get you back to the garage.' And they look around and nobody is looking at them the same way people looked at them on patrol, or in the operation center, or even in the supply room.

"They don't know what name to answer to. They don't know who they are. How to get their balance. Especially if they've been wounded and can't do all the things they used to do. It's very disorienting."

It was a long speech. "*He's thought hard about this,*" thought the reporter.

"A lot of people talk about how hard it is to go to war. I think that for some, coming home is even harder."

Most of the arriving wounded had matched up with family members. The MCD's responsibilities were shrinking by the minute.

"Excuse me, ma'am, but do you have a cell phone I could borrow, just for a minute?" It was an Army private, addressing Nurse Ames politely.

"Sure," she said, pulling her phone from a zipper pocket on her flight suit and handing it over. "Miss your ride?"

"Not exactly," he replied non-committedly.

Quickly he pressed the number. He turned away and began to speak.

"Operator, can you please connect me with a cab company? . . . I don't care . . . the first one on the list. . . . Hello? I'm at the private side of the airport, where the military aircraft park. I need a cab please. . . . The nearest hotel. . . . No, I don't care, whatever is close. Yeah, I'll watch for him. Thanks."

He turned back to hand the phone to the nurse. "Thanks again, ma'am." He offered a quick salute with his right hand, which she returned.

"Where are you going," she asked. "Don't you have any friends or family here?"

"No," he answered. "My unit's still deployed. And I don't have any civilian friends that I want to see again. That was sort of before the Army, if you know what I mean."

She nodded. He was so young. Eighteen. Maybe nineteen. She wondered for a moment if he shaved.

"I'll find a place. I'm processing out. This is my Home of Record—where I was when I joined up. I'll try to get a room at transient billeting on post tomorrow, and get an appointment at personnel for the day after Christmas. Then start clearing the hospital. And I'll catch a cab over to the chow hall for Christmas dinner. I'll be okay." His words were confident. His voice was not.

Hoisting the duffle bag on his left shoulder, he turned, and began to walk away with a slight limp. At the end of each step, his right foot fell unnaturally on the pavement.

Christmas dinner in the mess hall. A room at transient billeting. Someone to care about his wound at the hospital. The Army was the only family he had. And soon it would cast him out because he couldn't keep up.

Suddenly she remembered why she hated this part of the job so much. So many of them left her protection just as the healing process was really beginning. They returned . . . to what?

While she pondered her limited healing power as a nurse, Sergeant Martel passed her taking long if somewhat uncertain strides toward the fence. His cane was nowhere to be seen. "Dad!" yelled a girl's voice. "Daddy!" cried a younger boy. Martel bent down, opened his arms, and braced for impact as the two children flung themselves the last few feet to greet him. He stood unsteadily, but managed to swing them in a circle. He set them, laughing, on the cement, then turned to his wife.

She did not speak—just embraced him tightly. She stayed disciplined before the children. But on his shoulder, her face collapsed and she sobbed once before regaining control. "I'm just so glad you're home," she said wiping tears.

"Me, too," the sergeant said. "Me, too.

"Who's up for pizza?" he asked loudly. "Me! Me! Me!" two small voices cried at once.

Together the four turned toward the parking lot and set off, only to be brought up short by the youngest member of the squad after a few steps.

"Daddy?" he said tentatively. "Can I see it?"

The mother caught her breath and put her hand to her mouth. The daughter frowned and balled her fists.

Slowly the sergeant bent over and pulled at the trouser of his left leg, tucked neatly into his boot. After a moment the cloth slid out, and he pulled it up and up, until it was halfway up his lower leg.

Except there was no lower leg. There was only a shiny titanium rod connecting the human leg above with an artificial foot in the boot. He stood for a moment without saying anything.

The boy's eyes were fixed on the rod. His face was expressionless. "Can I touch it?" he asked.

"Of course," said his father.

The boy reached out gingerly with a single finger—touched the rod—then tapped it with a finger nail. He looked up with a smile.

"Cool!" he said. "Like Transformers!"

The sergeant tucked his cuff back into the boot, and his happy squad resumed its trek to the car, a pizza, and something like a normal life.

Not every soldier who was wounded returned home. Not every soldier who returned home found it as he had left it. But for some, the story did have a happy ending.

Reporter Taylor Webster stood watching the little dramas play out. There was so much human emotion out there—she should get several bylines out of this! Too bad she had to get people's permission to tap that well. Because waiting for them to tell their stories left her with nothing to report.

CHAPTER 4

BROKEN

1305 hours 23 December: El Paso, Texas

As the personal drama played out in the back of the aircraft, a professional one was playing out up front.

"Eng, did you catch the tail on that parked C-130 we passed during taxi?" the pilot asked.

"I think it was Texas National Guard," said the engineer. "Looked like the ramp and doors were open. You thinking what I'm thinking?"

"Yeah," responded the pilot. "Most Air Evac missions are Guard or Reserve. I bet those guys picked up a 10-day mission like ours out of Scott. They got here late last night on a regular run. They're not going anywhere until after lunch. And they usually travel with maintenance. If they have some wrenches and a gauge, they could save us a day on the ground here. We could get out today instead of everybody spending Christmas by the coffee pot in Base Ops."

"I'm on it," said the engineer.

"Take the lubricant," reminded the pilot. "We really need this. Take the Blue Label."

Johnny Walker Blue Label Scotch was less than $140 a bottle in the Base Class Six store. The Guard crew was probably paying $200 a bottle back home in their day jobs. A bottle was a powerful motivator. The engineer opened a small cabinet, reached far in the back, and extracted his prize.

"Not the first time this has gotten me home," he said. Then he was gone, two steps down the alley toward the back, right turn out the door, and into the glaring Texas sunlight.

The pilot turned his phone on. He had a new text. "**I really wish we had talked more last night,**" it said.

He typed a response. "**Bkn in El Paso.**" His finger hovered over the send button. Then he deleted the message and snapped the phone shut.

"So why did you miss the STAR chart?" he asked the copilot, as if continuing a conversation.

Her stomach roiled. She began to sweat. "I knew I needed to check," she said. "I just thought I would do it in route. And when I tried to get to it, other things came up during the flight."

"Right," the pilot said coldly—almost mechanically. "That's why we do all our planning before we take off. Before. We don't wait until later, because sometimes later gets real busy. And we forget. And people get hurt."

"*Or killed,*" she thought. He was right. How could she have forgotten? She was too focused on the takeoff.

"I tried, but I was too focused on the takeoff," she said, trying to join in her own critique.

"Which you also blew," he answered.

This was not an ass chewing. She could have taken that. You could always charge part of a screaming session off to dramatic effect or to personalities. But this pilot was like a scientist examining a bug under a microscope. No secrets. No place to hide. No passion in the dissection. Just a pin holding her in her seat, arms and legs flailing.

"And the landing was unsat," he added.

This was too much. "I thought the landing was fine," she said defensively and a little defiantly. "It was very smooth."

"It was too far down the runway," he said.

He had been sorting through books in a bag. Now he stopped and looked at her directly.

"You said your aim point was 'in the first half of the runway.' The runway is 9,000 feet long. At 120 knots ground speed you're moving about 2 miles a minute, or 200 feet per second across the ground. Best case, you gave up 2,500 feet before you began the flare. Then you floated for 5 seconds while you tried to get through ground effect. That cost 1,000 feet. That's 3,500 feet. And it takes 4,000 feet for a standard stop, which is all you can handle. So you are up to 7,500 feet. You have 1,500 feet to spare—about 7 seconds. So you would have had 5 or 6 seconds to recognize and respond to a crisis—a blown tire, a prop that wouldn't adjust, an engine surge, a hung throttle . . . .

"I was one second from taking the aircraft away from you and making a go-around. One second. If I had done that, the whole base would be calling you 'Go-around Sue' for the next three years. A good pilot aims for the numbers. A fair pilot aims for 1,000 feet down the runway. A poor pilot aims for the middle."

He paused. His tone was still flat—all precision, no passion. "You blew it. You blew the take-off. You blew the in-flight. You blew the landing. I don't want to hear that you tried. It wasn't good enough."

"You blew the shot," he said.

She was ten, with her hair in pigtails. She was wearing white shorts, soccer shoes, shin guards, and a Kelly green shirt with the number 12 and the name "Thomasina" on the back.

The other girls were smiling at their parents who were smiling back. Her dad was not smiling.

"Do you want me to make you feel good because you are a little girl, or do you want me to tell you the truth so you can get better?" he asked. "You blew the shot."

This was the part of an ass chewing where they stopped yelling and started talking softly so you would remember it. But the pilot's voice had not changed. It was flat, precise, and he was absolutely correct on every point. Damn.

"Look," he said. "You are flying inside the cockpit. You are dealing with each moment as it comes up. At 300 knots you are moving 5 miles a minute. You have got to be 5 minutes ahead of the aircraft to give yourself some decision time. That's 25 miles. You've got to be flying the aircraft from *in here*, but you have to be thinking from 25 miles *out there*—ahead of the aircraft."

Her cheeks were burning red again and sweat was staining her flight suit under the arms. The navigator was listening to every word, and seemed to be enjoying it. She just wanted to crawl into a hole and pull it shut behind her. She wondered if he talked to junior male pilots this way.

"And don't give me any of that 'I bet you don't treat men this way' crap," he said, still in a soft flat voice. "I don't care whether I am flying with a man or a woman. I *do* care whether I'm flying with a competent pilot. Catch up. Stay up. Pull your own weight."

She felt like she had been stripped naked in public and everybody was watching. It was horrible. She was humiliated.

"Hey guys!"

All three crew members turned to see a large white-haired man in a Christmas aloha shirt, standing at the top of the stairs behind them. He had a full white beard and sunglasses. He looked for all the world like one of those postcards of Santa Claus at the beach. Except he was wearing a blue American Legion hat covered with buttons and pins.

"I'm 'J' Nicholas. Kind of a fixture around here. I volunteer at the USO in the commercial terminal, and I meet all the planes bringing the wounded guys home. Guys and girls," he said, nodding to the copilot. "No offense intended.

"You're shut down with people in the back. Looks like you are going to be here for a while. Anything I can do to help?"

The navigator found his voice first. "Not unless you own a restaurant," he said. "Looks like box lunches again."

"Actually, I do own a restaurant," answered Santa merrily. "That's why I'm here! And I have a friend who owns a bus. When I saw all the people stay on board and the engines shut down, I gave him a call. He'll be in the parking lot in five minutes!"

"We have to clear it with the medical team," interjected the pilot. This wasn't a flight issue, so it took him a moment to focus on the question. "If they say okay, then it's okay with me."

"Oh yes," said Santa. "Got to clear it with the doctor." He smiled broadly, laying a finger aside of his nose. "And the nurses. Thanks!"

He turned and moved rapidly to the rear, then down the ladder into the crew compartment, and directly to the lead nurse. He was a bit rotund, but his movements were . . . well . . . lively and quick.

The navigator followed to the end of the crew deck next to the ladder and reported on activities in the cargo bay.

For a moment the nurse squared her shoulders and crossed her arms. But Santa smiled broadly and gestured energetically. In a moment the nurse smiled, then looked back at the passengers, already tired from many days of hurry up and wait. She nodded her head yes.

"Well, Donner and Blitzen!" the navigator exclaimed. "I think the old guy pulled it off! Everybody's getting up and moving down the ramp!"

"You better go, JT."

Apparently the lesson was over. Suddenly the pilot was a friend again. They were coworkers. The copilot found it very disorienting.

"You too, Dale," Captain Middleton directed his remarks to the navigator, senior to the co-pilot now that they were back on the ground. "Be visible. We're responsible for this mission. Don't let them forget that. Leave Ben with me. Jeff will need him if we get the gauge fixed and do some engine starts."

No more "Nav," "Eng," and "Load" now. The aircraft was on the ground. The hierarchy defined by crew position had morphed into one just as structured but more personal. Yet responsibilities remained clear and defined by rank.

"Time hack—1305 now. I want everybody back here and seated at 1430. If we get it fixed, we'll be off before 1445. Both of you keep your cells on. See what Ben wants to eat and bring something back for him and Jeff."

Captain Lee, the navigator, sighed. Mike Middleton was a good guy and a great pilot, but professional to a fault. How did people get that way? The military could turn a picnic into an unpleasant, by-the-numbers ordeal. But he smiled good naturedly and nodded his head. "Yes, sir, 1430 hours," he said.

Middleton paused to pull his phone from its shoulder pocket. He read another text message from his wife, then snapped the phone shut without replying, and turned back to his paperwork. The copilot climbed awkwardly from her seat and walked without a word back to the ladder. For her, changing rolls was not so easy as just changing names. She took it all much more personally.

Down she went with the navigator and out through the cargo bay. They stopped to converse briefly with the loadmaster who looked disappointed, but nodded, placed his order, and returned to his work.

Across the parking apron, Lieutenant Williams and Captain Lee followed the crowd, through a gate in the fence and past a guard, then up to a huge tour bus emblazed on the side with an American flag and the words, "See America the Beautiful."

As they started to follow the group up the stairs and through the open door, Lee paused at the bottom step. "An elf!" he whispered to the lieutenant behind him.

And sure enough, the driver looked like the polar opposite of Santa-the-restaurant-owner who had issued the invitation. A short, dark man in a matching Christmas Aloha shirt smiled broadly and welcomed them aboard.

"I'm Gus Gutierrez!" he announced loudly. "All aboard! Plenty of room!" His feet barely reached the gas and brake. His black VFW cap moved vigorously with his head. His enthusiasm was infectious.

"So glad to have you!" he said into a microphone. His voice boomed through the bus. "Thanks so much for serving our country! You're gonna have a great time! Come on in and let's get started."

Without instruction the passengers had moved to the back of the bus. They limped. They leaned on crutches and canes. They leaned on each other. They were tired and a bit dispirited, but took care of themselves. The medical technicians took the ranger from his wheelchair, lifted him under the arms, and helped him up the stairs into the bus. Then they returned to collapse the wheelchair and place it in the cargo space underneath the passenger compartment. They repeated this with two other patients in wheelchairs. The med techs were perspiring heavily by the time they were done.

Each passenger took a seat by himself. Nurse Win Ames moved down the aisle and spoke to each patient, asking how they felt and paying close attention to how they responded. Wounded never told the nurse it hurt, not until it was very bad. So she had learned to be sensitive to how they spoke in addition to what they said.

The chaplain followed two rows behind her, pausing to pass out candy from a cargo pocket, and exchange a word with each person he passed. His manner was easier and less formal. He was performing a check of his own—more psychological than medical—but just as important as the regime the nurse was following.

After talking with each wounded soldier, Ames moved all the way to the back, where she could watch everyone and everything. The doctor joined her on the same seat. One medical technician sat in the middle among the passengers. The chaplain shared a seat with him. The other technician and Lieutenant Beauchamp, the second nurse, sat at the front of the group. The navigator and copilot sat all the way up front, with the reporter a few rows behind. No one invited her to sit with them.

While they were waiting for the medical team to approve how everyone was settled in, the navigator tapped his copilot on the arm and said, "Hope we get to the cafeteria before the senior's early bird supper. Could be a crowd."

There was no response to his attempt at humor.

"So how do you like flying with Yoda?" he asked

"What?" the copilot replied. In her mind, she was still on the plane and still in a funk.

"You know, Yoda." Lee crooked one finger and spoke in the high squeaky voice of the *Star Wars* character. "Do . . . or do not! There is no try!" he said.

The copilot was roused from her self-pity. "Does he do that to other people?" she asked.

"He does that with every junior pilot he is assigned to teach and mentor. Everyone he thinks is worth the effort," he replied.

Lieutenant Williams was silent. "Seems pretty arrogant to me," she said. "Is he really all that good?"

"Oh yes," nodded Lee vigorously. "Very good. Very instinctive. But really knows the book too. I'll fly with him any time, any mission, any weather. And with the pilots he trained."

He paused for a moment to let that last point sink in. Then he leaned back in his seat.

The driver peered over the steering wheel and out through the door. "Is that everybody?" he asked. "That's everybody!" Nurse Ames replied from the back. Standing at the top of the stairs, Santa nodded.

"Okay!" said the elf. The engine roared. The gears clashed into place. He was, after all, the owner of the bus company, not a regular driver. The door whooshed shut. And like the down of a thistle, they were off, headed for the main gate.

All the responses from the wounded to the nurse had been positive but subdued. It was a somber group. Watching others arrive home, limping down the ramp and across the tarmac—meeting awkward families, some bravely protective but clearly avoiding the missing limb or site of the wound—it had been a troubling experience. They were all thinking about how they would be received at home.

The question had been in the back of each mind for months, bubbling up now and then as a fear, then stuffed back down inside again. Visits by family to the hospital had not helped on this point because the hospital setting made it clear that they were hurt and needed special treatment until they were well.

But now they *were* well. As well as they were going to get. Now they had to fit into real life in a new way—incapable of doing some things they had done before. Were they less of a man or a woman for their loss?

Would people think differently of them? Treat them differently? Ignore them? Leave them out?

The younger ones thought about the way they had treated disabled kids in school. Mostly they hadn't treated the kid with the broken body meanly. They just ignored him. They just moved on by in their own world. Now they *were* that kid. Who would ignore them? Wives and husbands? Other young men and women? Dates? Everybody?

The bus passed through the gate and the guard threw a salute. The elf at the wheel—an officer during the Vietnam War—saluted back. Just half a mile after they turned on to a busy street, traffic slowed to a crawl. Ahead, flashing lights marked the site of an accident and black smoke boiled into the air.

Off to the side, on a cross street, a car had hit a utility pole and burst into flames. It was far enough away that the police kept traffic moving on the main thoroughfare. But it was close enough that everyone on both sides of the bus could clearly see the car on fire, the flames licking the sky as a fire crew began to pump a mist of water on to the wreck. The mist knocked the fire down but not out. A second truck began to supply foam. Looking through bus windows that all reflected the same scene, each wounded passenger saw something different.

For one it was a burning Humvee, for another a burning truck, for others a burning tank or helicopter. Inside were people they knew or people they did not, friends or strangers, or a voice they had known well but only on the radio. In every case, what they saw in the street was something they had seen in the war. The aftermath of an explosion, wheels or treads blown off or windows blown out. And somebody inside. Always somebody inside.

"Get out!" their minds screamed. But nobody got out. Nobody ever got out.

The bus crawled past the site of the crash in silence, with its own load of crash victims in the back. The black smoke turned to white steam. Traffic picked up speed. The bus left the scene behind. The passengers did not. Everyone was quiet.

At the next red light, the reporter moved quickly up the aisle and squeezed in next to Captain Lee, who was sitting against the window. In the row ahead, Lieutenant Williams still sat in a seat by herself.

"So!" began the reporter, her voice just a little breathless, her shoulder slightly raised, her chin tucked and head canted forward coyly, and her blink lasting just a moment longer than necessary. "Tell me about being a pilot!"

"Navigator," replied Lee brightly. He recognized the game but was perfectly willing to play along with a pretty girl. "There's a pilot there" he said, nodding to the seat ahead. "They just drive. I'm the one who gets us to the right place at the right time."

Turned in the seat so her back was to the bus window, the copilot rolled her eyes, then looked at the reporter. "*Boys,*" the look said, with one eyebrow raised in disapproval.

The reporter remained cheery. She was willing to play along, too. It was a game she had played before. In fact, she thought she had invented it.

"What's your name?" she asked, flipping open her pad.

"Lee," he replied. "Bobby Lee."

Her pen hesitated on the paper.

"Lee—you're Korean?"

"No, I'm from Texas," he said cheerfully. "My momma wanted to name me 'Robert Edward' after Robert E. Lee, but my daddy said "Bobby' was good enough."

The reporter's pen started, but stopped again abruptly. His voice did have a Texas twang, but he was clearly of Asian descent. Was he putting her on?

"Ooo-kay," she said, betraying a hint of suspicion. "Okay, Captain Robert E. Lee. Do you have one of those pilot nicknames?"

"Well, that's mostly for fighter pilots," he said helpfully. "Transport guys don't usually get call signs unless they have an especially strong

". . . personality." He raised his eyebrows and flexed his pectoral muscles beneath his shirt in an exaggerated motion.

Lieutenant Williams in the seat ahead rolled her eyes again.

He leaned toward the reporter intimately. "My call sign is 'Dale.' After Dale Earnhardt. I'm a big NASCAR fan."

The reporter started to write again, then put down her pad. "Okay," she said. "Sorry I bothered you. I can tell when somebody is pulling my leg."

"No really," said the navigator, this time with a serious look on his face and a serious tone in his voice. He backed off, then re-engaged politely.

"I'm Vietnamese, but I was an orphan. I ended up with a farm family in Texas—Willie and Bessie Lee. I went to Texas A&M, and was in the Corps of Cadets there. Now here I am. When I was in college I drove at the Texas Speedway on weekends, and I really am a NASCAR fan. And my friends do call me 'Dale.'"

Lieutenant Williams was listening with interest now. So was the reporter.

"A Vietnamese orphan." She counted rapidly in her head. "You're a little old to be a captain."

"Senior," he said. "Not old. I'm thirty-five. I was in the Air Force for a while, then got out to be a cartographer. I made maps for the government. After 9/11 I knew I had to be back in the game—not just a civilian here at home while my country was at war."

The reporter paused. "Were you evacuated from Saigon?"

He was very young and his mother was holding him tight against her chest. She was running. Beside them other people were running. "Don't worry," she was saying in Vietnamese. "It will be all right. Don't worry."

There was a lot of noise and suddenly a crowd formed and everyone was pushing. "Mother!" he cried. He was afraid she would drop him and he would be lost. "Mother!"

She pushed and the crowd pushed and she pushed back. A man fell and she stepped over him. Suddenly they were at the edge of the crowd and he could see out. The surface was flat and hard and stretched far away. There was a big machine in front of them. A helicopter. It was beating the air with its arms. The noise was overwhelming. The wind stung his face. Behind the helicopter was another and another. The people were pushing toward the noise and the machines. A line of men with guns was pushing them back. The helicopter was full of people. The noise got louder and the machine lifted a bit off the ground.

A man next to them swung a stick at a soldier, who turned to strike him to the ground with his rifle. A woman screamed. But when the soldier turned, it opened up a slight hole in the line and his mother darted through carrying him across her chest.

As she ran to the helicopter, the people inside waved their hands and shook their heads. "No! No!" they cried. Behind her, soldiers chased and shouted in Vietnamese, "Come back! Come back!" She ran harder.

The wind was swirling and the noise was deafening. The helicopter just barely lifted off the ground. There was no room inside. Every inch was jammed with people.

His mother took him under the arms with both hands. Holding him away from her body, she spun in a circle, then released him, flinging him toward the open helicopter door.

"Fly!" she cried. "Fly!"

Hands inside the helicopter caught him. Some tried to push him out, but stronger hands pulled him in. Something whistled loudly, then there was a tremendous bang, and smoke. The helicopter rose unsteadily, skidded sideways as the pilot struggled with the load, then tipped forward, caught air, and began to run, nose down, along the ground. After a few moments it lifted up with a rush. He felt as if he were falling. But a man held him tight. A white man in a green uniform. He pulled the boy close, and put the boy's head on his broad shoulder, covering it with his huge hand.

The helicopter struggled to climb. Slowly the ground looked smaller and smaller. Then there was no more land underneath. It was all blue sea. The boy closed his eyes and buried his head against the big shoulder. The nametag near the big shoulder read "Lee."

"Were you evacuated from Saigon Captain Lee?" she repeated gently. She wasn't acting now.

"I guess so," the navigator replied. "I was pretty young."

They were both quiet. JT Williams stared intently.

After a while the reporter asked, "So why did you join the Air Force?" He smiled slightly. He was a whole different person now. Very vulnerable.

"When I was about ten years old—living on the farm with my folks in Texas—I heard this guy on television telling this story. It was President Reagan. And he was telling about how this Navy ship had found this group of Vietnamese floating at sea and had rescued them. It wasn't me. I flew out. But this big U.S. Navy ship stopped to pick up this little boat and these people floating in the middle of the ocean. And a Vietnamese guy in the boat looked up to a sailor standing at the rail and yelled out 'Hello, freedom man!'

"When I heard him tell that story, I felt like he was talking to me. And I realized what I wanted to be. I wanted to be the 'freedom man.'"

He was blinking rapidly. It was all very unexpected.

"And now here I am. I've been to Bosnia, the Philippines, Bangladesh, Turkey, Afghanistan, Iraq. Every time there is a storm or an earthquake or a war, they need us. Everywhere I go, somebody there needs me. Now I am carrying these guys home for Christmas. I'm the 'freedom man.'"

He had said more than he had intended—it just spilled out. He looked out the window, then down at his boots, then up sharply.

"But you can't write about that," he said. "I wasn't wounded." He gestured to the back of the bus. "Those are the wounded guys. Talk to them. Tell their story. I don't want you to write about me." He glanced up.

"Looks like we're here," he said.

The bus slowed, turned carefully to the right, out of traffic and into a parking lot, then coasted to a stop. While it was still rolling, the navigator stood, pushed past the reporter, and into the aisle.

The reporter followed him with her eyes, then turned back to Lieutenant Williams who was looking at her levelly with a protective expression that brooked no compromise.

"*My guy,*" it said. "*My team. Back off.*"

With a sigh, the reporter folded the top of her spiral notebook closed, and shook her head. No story here either. She was failing. Her editor was going to be unhappy. She was going to miss her shot at a national byline.

In the back of the bus, the passengers slowly stirred from the monotony of the ride. One glanced out the window.

"Holy crap!" he exclaimed.

Others turned to look at him, then followed his gaze out the window. Those who did stopped as if turned to stone.

"Here we are," said Santa happily.

"Everybody out," said the elf.

The white beard and blue American Legion cap bounded out the door. "Hope you like the food," he said over his shoulder.

The reporter craned to follow everyone else's gaze. "Good Lord," said the copilot.

Outside, a huge orange neon sign loomed over the bus. "Hooters" it said.

The solemn individuals unloading from the bus were not a pretty sight. One soldier hopped down the stairs with crutches in one hand and nearly fell. Three who could not climb down the stairs by themselves were carried by the medical technicians, then were seated in wheelchairs that had been stored in the luggage compartment. Even Dr. Dan walked with two stiff legs. "It's my knees," he said.

Major Ames was clearly distressed by the scene and nearly intervened to put everyone back on the bus and return to the airport. But Santa spoke up.

"It's going to be okay," he said. "I've been doing this a long time. So have you. You know they need this regardless of what the regulations say."

The nurse did not reply. She stood still and erect with her arms crossed, watching the passengers unload. The patient safety people would have a cow.

The Air Force was a strange place. You could be well respected among your colleagues for twenty years and never get the attention of your senior leadership. Then you could take one chance—make one decision that was the right thing to do for the right reason—and lose everything from one instant of bad luck. She was taking a big risk. But the troops *did* need this, and it *was* the right thing to do. She stood at the door of the bus and supervised every person who departed. But she did not stop their progress.

The group that crossed the short space from the bus to the door created a sad little parade. Just about any group of young men in America would have approached the door to Hooters with barely concealed anticipation. But most of this group was strangely apprehensive. Maybe this was not such a good idea after all.

"It's a good idea," said Santa. "You are doing the right thing. You'll see."

Major Pike, the Army ranger, rolled up beside the nurse and threw her an appreciative glance.

"I'm impressed, Nurse Ratched!" The words were ironic, but the tone was not. It almost seemed genuine. He gave the wheels a strong spin and propelled himself forward. Then another spin.

"Really," he said. "I know you could kill this. I know you probably should. I'm glad you didn't. Shows leadership. I like that."

After the unexpected compliment, he spun the wheel even harder and the chair leapt ahead of the walkers. In front of him was the pale surly soldier leaning on a cane.

"Hey numb-nuts!" the major called. "You're limping on the wrong leg!"

The soldier did not acknowledge the remark. But after a moment, he switched the cane to the other hand, and began to limp on his other leg.

The major in the wheelchair shook his head.

The group dragged in slowly—almost apologetically—and stopped just inside the door. Some were left outside.

"Clear the choke point!" cried the major. "Don't bunch up!"

The remarks were ludicrously out of place: tactical instructions to an assault team, not warm and encouraging words to patients under care. But the effect was immediate. Suddenly they were soldiers again, and each man moved to clear the door as quickly as his wounds would allow.

The sidewalk provided a slight incline up to the door. The major didn't seem to notice. "Make a hole!" he barked. Someone held the door and he rolled rapidly past the crutches, canes, wheelchairs, and artificial limbs to the stand where a hostess was waiting to assign tables.

"Lafayette," he announced with an exaggerated salute, "we are here!"

Not one soldier in ten knew his reference to the arrival of doughboys in France in World War I. But they understood his attitude. And they loved it.

To her credit, the manager was equal to the task.

She stepped forward past a very uncertain hostess and said, "Welcome to HOOTERS, heroes. Follow me, please."

The manager was wearing a tight fitting black top, like the torso of a leotard, but without sleeves and cut low in a swooping curve that crossed the middle of her breasts. This exposed ample curves but in a matter of fact way that seemed both striking and normal at the same time.

Below the waist she wore khaki shorts and a broad black belt. The shorts were very short and very tight, but at the same time, professional in a curious sort of way. It looked like the uniform of a whale trainer at Sea World, not a bar room stripper. The lead members of the group fell in behind her without a moment's hesitation. It looked like she was leading a hunting party. And in a sense, she was.

The building held more than thirty tables divided into four serving areas. Each had four or more large flat screen TVs, and each TV was showing a recording of a different sporting event—twelve football games, three baseball contests, and three basketball matchups. There was a bar with dozens of types of beer on display, but the stools there were mostly empty. It was lunchtime.

As the group crossed the main dining area, the reporter noticed that almost every table was full. Only two tables held men alone—one with four beefy bikers quietly enjoying a meal, and one with five businessmen in ties, talking animatedly about a week old football game playing out on the closest screen. All other tables held a mixture of men and women. Four tables included children. And at one table three boys and one girl, all under the age of eight, were busily coloring paper table mats. At two tables, four women sat alone, dressed casually for shopping.

The reporter had heard about HOOTERS, but had never been inside. "*Good grief,*" she thought in surprise. "*Nobody is looking at the girls!*"

The group followed the manager/safari guide to a dining area apparently reserved for them—all the tables were empty. Those in the middle of the room were set up for four people each in standard chairs. Tables along the wall were higher and accommodated six or more guests on tall stools. Dark orange plastic table cloths clashed a bit with the yellow pine walls, stained and shellacked to emphasize the grain and knotholes. The ceiling looked unfinished; it was black with various lights, wires and air conditioning conduits hanging down—all painted orange.

The reporter moved directly to a table with three young soldiers—all amputees—she had identified previously as potential stories. They sat quietly, with their hands in their laps.

"Hello," she offered eagerly. Two nodded a bit, but remained withdrawn. The third, sitting to her right, extended his left hand. She shook it naturally with her left. He smiled slightly. She had passed the first test.

"Well, welcome to our club!" he said brightly. Even for a journalist, it was intimidating to approach three strangers at a table and ask to sit down. He was making it easy.

"I'm Lefty. This is Lucky. And this is Squeeze." He pointed to each in turn, again with his left hand.

They all smiled pleasantly, but Lefty was eying her closely. He was a good looking guy with close cropped black hair, strong features and gray eyes. She tried to size up her interviews early so she knew what role to play, but his mannerisms were hard to place. A little older than the others, he wore the mantel of informal leadership easily. His left elbow rested on the table and his left hand supported his chin. She could see him in a college book store or in a coffee shop. But not in the Army.

Still smiling, he was watching her closely, almost studiously. He casually lifted his right hand from his lap and set it on the table. Except it wasn't a hand. The arm apparently ended somewhere below the elbow. A silver metal hook protruded from the cuff of his sleeve.

She glanced down, and then back up to look him in the eyes. "Well, I see why they call you Lefty." She turned to the soldier seated on her left. "And why do they call you Squeeze?"

All three of them appeared quietly pleased. They were playing a little game. She had refused to be shocked. She was playing, too. She had passed the second test.

The soldier she was addressing was actually little more than a boy. And something about him said "farm kid." He raised his right arm from his lap and set his hand on the table. It was pink plastic—close to his flesh tone but not quite right. There was a false thumb and four false fingers fused together. All together they formed a stiff U, as if the false hand were holding a phantom glass. As she watched, the hand closed—the fingers squeezing toward the thumb in a motion more like a crab's pincher than grasping hand. Then it opened. Then squeezed shut again. Then opened.

She almost jumped at the motion, but controlled herself, and was glad she did. "Clever," she said. Turning to the occupant across the table. "And you're Lucky."

He was a bit withdrawn, too—but not because he was shy. He was smiling but wary. His features were a bit irregular, and his eyebrows wild. He wasn't hostile, but he seemed to be looking for a weakness—an opening. This was a kid with street smarts, no question about it.

Without speaking, he raised his right hand to the table. Again somewhere in the sleeve the arm ended, but what protruded from his cuff was a plastic hand with individual fingers. As she watched, each finger lifted by itself, then lowered with a slight thump to the table. The motion started with his pinkie and continued, one finger at a time, until it reached the index finger, then it began again, starting with the pinkie. The speed increased and the fingers became a wave rising and falling over and over, from first finger to last. The fingers made a rolling thump on the tablecloth.

He was drumming his artificial fingers on the table.

She stared for a moment, then lifted her gaze. "Good to meet you, Lucky."

All three chuckled at their own joke. "We were just hazing the new kid," Lefty confided. "You did fine. I'm Tom Milton. This is Mark Wilson. And this is Anthony Santini. And you're—"

"Taylor Webster," she answered. She eased her pad from her purse and extracted a pen.

"Sorry, you need a nickname to sit at our table." It was Lefty speaking. "I'll call you Bartleby. Bartleby the Scrivener."

Her pen stopped in mid-air, and she sat back, a surprised look on her face.

"Don't mind him," said Squeeze. "He talks like that. We're all use to it. Sometimes I don't have any idea what he's talking about."

"No, I don't mind it," she said, recovering quickly. "I just don't hear many references to an obscure Herman Melville short story in day to day conversation."

It was Lefty's turn to be surprised. "Oh! A journalist *and* a literature major!"

"Minor," she said. "Literature minor. Not many jobs out there for lit majors."

"Plenty in the Army," Lefty responded. "You could have been a mechanic and a wrecker driver. That's what I was, but the other way round from you. Lit major and journalism minor."

"I bet that's an interesting story," she said, her pen moving again toward her notebook.

"Nice try, Bartleby." Lefty was still smiling, but firm. "No write ups at this table. All the heroes are over there at the nurses' table."

The reporter pursed her lips and set down her pen.

Meanwhile, Major Pike had paused at the door when the others followed the manager to their seats. He backed his wheelchair against the wall behind the stand where the greeter waited. This obscured him from a group of waitresses gathering near the entrance to the area that held the special customers. They were looking in at the customers from a distance. They were nervous.

"I just don't know what to say," said one. "I want to help. But I don't know what to do. I don't know where to look."

"I know," said another. "There's a guy in there with a hook for a hand. There are a couple of guys with no legs. There's one with his face all burned. I don't know how to act." Two other girls nodded.

"Did you ever have a date with a really good looking guy?"

The major had rolled up behind them silently. Now he was speaking in a friendly voice but with authority.

"Did you ever date a guy you really wanted to know *you*? To listen to *you*? To get past your looks and focus on the real *you*?"

He had their attention. They were listening closely. Nobody moved.

"What did you want when you were on that date?" the major continued. "When you were hoping he would get past your hair and your make up and see the real you, what did you want him to do?"

They were still quiet. Then a tall blond girl spoke up.

"I wanted him to quit looking at my chest and look at my eyes!"

Everybody giggled. Several girls looked down and smiled.

"Well that's what *they* want," said the major. "They don't mind if you notice their wounds. But they want you to look past that and see the person inside. They want you to look in their eyes."

Several of the girls were looking at his wheelchair. They shifted their gaze to his eyes.

"They want to know that a pretty girl like you can look past what isn't there, and see what is there. Just treat each one like a really good customer."

The major paused.

"A customer who did you a very big favor not long ago."

He looked around the group. All their eyes were locked on his. No one broke his gaze.

In the parking lot of the Commissary on Little Rock Air Force Base, Joy Middleton pushed a basket loaded down with Christmas dinner and a recalcitrant three-year-old toward her SUV, while keeping an energetic six-year-old under control. With a practiced motion, she swept him from one side of her body to the other and away from traffic. The wind was gusty and cold, and the three-year-old managed to drop both shoes and a sock before they got to the car. Getting coats off, children into car seats, and groceries loaded in the back was a tough task—she felt outnumbered

Finally settled behind the wheel, the frazzled mother took just a few seconds to send a text on her phone. "**Picked up Xmas Eve dinner. Hope you are home on time**," she wrote. She hoped that sounded positive and encouraging.

"Mommy, I have to pee-pee bad!" said a little girl's voice from the back seat.

"I think she already did!" added her brother helpfully. "It stinks back here!"

"Okay, honey. We'll hurry," answered the mom.

She turned the key in the ignition. Under the hood, something groaned once and clicked three times. Then everything was quiet.

She was momentarily stunned by disbelief. An icy blast of wind shook the car.

"*This can't be happening*," she thought. She turned the key again. This time it clicked only once. Then nothing.

"*Of course*," she thought. "*Every time he leaves. It's something every time he leaves.*"

Her shoulders slumped forward and she rested her head on the steering wheel. The wind shook the car again. She got exactly three seconds to feel sorry for herself before she was interrupted again.

"I mean it really stinks!" said the boy. The girl began to cry.

She drew a deep breath and reached to open the door.

"It's okay," she said to the back seat in general. "I'll fix it. I can fix everything."

In the cockpit of Air Evac 1492, pilot Mike Middleton watched over the shoulder of a visiting National Guard mechanic trying to change the faulty gauge, just as a wrench dropped from the airman's hands and clattered its way into the linkages below the rudder pedals. They both sighed. This was going to take a while.

The phone in his shoulder pocket buzzed with a message and he took it out and opened it.

" . . . **Hope you are home on time**," he read.

"*Damn*," he thought. "*Like I'm not trying? Like I'm going to forget?*"

He closed the phone without answering the message and turned back to his duties. The gauge was not the only thing broken in his life.

CHAPTER 5

FIXED

1320 hours 23 December: El Paso, Texas

"May I have your attention?" It was Santa. Standing just inside the room, he turned to face the guests, then the waitresses, then the guests again.

"I want to welcome our guests, all members of the United States Military who have sacrificed for their country."

An employee turned down the background music. The other serving areas were separated only by a low wall, and all the other customers in the restaurant turned to look.

"Everybody in this room has been wounded, or is taking care of our wounded, or is working to get our wounded home for Christmas.

"We can't repay you, but we can show you how much we appreciate what you have done. To make sure you get the service you deserve, a number of our girls have come in on their day off and on short notice to serve you lunch. And to let you know your country remembers and cares, Gus and I"—he gestured toward the elf—"are going to buy your meal."

He paused.

"We didn't do so well taking care of our guys after Vietnam. We won't make that mistake again."

He paused again and looked down, lost in thought. After a while, he looked up and smiled.

"No alcohol," he said. "Sorry guys, but I don't want the medics to have to worry about who is on what medication." He waved toward Nurse Ames, who half saluted him back.

"And I don't want to have to card any soldiers who are old enough to fight but not to buy a beer." A small laugh swept the room.

"So thanks for your service. Have a good time."

The bikers in the next room stood and applauded. So did the businessmen. And slowly, so did the rest of the room. The soldiers looked around at each other, and then down. Several blushed.

Suddenly, the HOOTERS girls burst into the room like a squadron of honey bees.

The servers moved quickly and with a purpose. One went directly to each table. Their sudden presence, and the movement of so many dressed alike, was electrifying. The way they were dressed was electrifying, too.

Taylor Webster tried to take in every detail with her reporter's eye. The servers were absolutely uniform. Each wore a white, form fitting top with no sleeves, low cut with the same swooping curve, skin tight, and shaped somehow to emphasize the breast, but without any seams. Without any bra lines. And without any nipples. All curves, no lines. "*How did they do that?*" she wondered.

Every girl wore an orange name tag with white letters, pinned high on her chest. Everyone had long hair that fell over her shoulders and just kissed the top of the breast. From time to time each girl reached up and used a single finger to sweep the hair back behind her ear in a practiced motion.

They wore no jewelry. Their necks were absolutely bare. And so were their hands and arms. They wore no watches or rings. No makeup—or at least very little. If it was there, it was in natural colors—no colored eye shadow, no bright lipstick—all fresh and clean as if each girl had just washed her face with soap. There were no tattoos. And no tan lines.

The lack of adornment had a striking effect. It made the girls look . . . naked. But in reality, their clothing was more suggestive than revealing.

They all wore orange short shorts—very short shorts—with legs cut high in the back to show the lower curve of the buttocks. Each girl was wearing stockings that glistened just a bit as she walked. Especially where the light reflected from that curve.

The reporter had fished a lot with her grandfather as a child, and as the girls walked across the room, she thought immediately of a favorite lure that wiggled and flashed as it hurried through the water.

In the front, each girl wore a flat black bag, secured by a cloth belt looped through rings on the side, and holding the tools of her office—straws, an order pad, and a row of brightly colored pens. These flashed as the waitresses walked, and drew the eye to the crotch. But at the same time, the bag hung low and covered the crotch from view. "*Very clever,*" she thought. Like a cheerleader's pom-poms, they enticed and covered at the same time.

The girls wore identical socks—heavy, tall, white athletic socks—over the shiny stockings. Each was scrunched down to a full, blousy effect. Each wore white athletic shoes and white laces without a hint of color. This highlighted the curve of the lower leg, and left the impression of a fit, athletic body. But these were not hard-bodied female athletes. They looked more like sorority girls in a college gym class.

On their backs, each girl sported the same motto in bold orange letters: "Delightfully Tacky, Yet Unrefined."

As they bubbled around the tables, their attitudes were uniformly friendly, outgoing, and just a bit flirtatious. A few leaned forward on the tables they were serving—never toward the women, she noticed. Each was quick with a smile that flashed dazzling white teeth. "*Is tooth whitening a company dental benefit?*" the reporter wondered.

And they were busy. They walked quickly, with a purpose. They carried drinks and plates of food, but no big trays. So they made more trips. Which meant more lean, attractive bodies moving constantly between the tables. It brought them back to the table more often than waitresses in other restaurants. But it also made them obviously too busy for small talk. It's hard to hit on a girl who pauses only long enough to smile and pull her hair back from her face, before hurrying on to the next table.

The reporter had never visited HOOTERS, and this was not what she had expected at all. This was not a bar or a strip club—this was the commercialization of the American Girl Next Door. It was Judy Garland in the twenty-first century. It was Andy Hardy's girlfriend in short shorts. It was Sally Field in white Reeboks. It was the Beach Boys' "Little Surfer Girl" without sun damage. This wasn't *Pretty Woman*. This was Princess Leia.

"Worried about the competition?" It was Lefty. He had been watching her watch the girls.

"Professional curiosity," she answered lightly.

"Okay," he said. "Watch this."

Their server had already delivered water on her first pass by the table. Now she was approaching again. Just as she arrived, each soldier put his artificial arm to use.

Lefty used the hook to extract a pair of reading glasses from his pocket. He held them still with his hook while wiping them clean with a handkerchief in his left hand. Then he used the hook to set them deftly in place on his head and concentrated on the menu—although he seemed to be looking over the glasses instead of through them.

Squeeze reached for his water glass, closed his prosthetic hand around it, and lifted it for a drink.

Lucky drummed his artificial fingers loudly on the table.

The server's nametag said Joyce. She positioned herself between Lefty and the reporter, leaned forward on the table, then canted her body slightly toward the soldier. She ignored the movements of the various artificial limbs, instead looking each male occupant of the table directly in the eyes with a long and meaningful glance. She ended with Lefty and flashed a hypnotic smile. "Do you guys want to order drinks first, or are you ready to eat?" she asked.

Squeeze glanced once at her breasts, then down at his menu, and turned bright red.

Lefty drew back slightly, but kept his gaze locked on hers. He was short of breath and surprised at his own response.

"Oh, we're ready," he said, then paused dramatically. "Pepsi and a Western BBQ Burger," he said. "Medium rare."

"That's what I would have guessed," she responded coyly. Then shifting her attention across the table, she asked "And how about you?" Again she leaned forward and smiled brightly.

Lucky was drumming his fingers furiously. "Chicken fingers and a Pepsi," he said fiercely. He tried to offer a seductive smile but couldn't quite pull it off.

"Great," she said, returning the smile, and letting it linger for just a moment. She brushed her blond hair back behind her ear with a finger, then shifted her weight against the table and leaned to the left. Looking Squeeze full in the face, she lowered her forehead in an intimate gesture. "And what about you," she asked.

The soldier reddened again, and used his good left hand to steady the drink in his right. He just could not break the lock on her hazel eyes, and for a moment he forgot the question she had asked.

"Um . . . um . . . what he's having." He motioned to Lucky without looking, then lost himself again in her eyes.

"Super!" she said brightly. Again she held the gaze for just a moment longer than necessary, then turned to the reporter.

"House salad with vinaigrette dressing," she said flatly, without being asked. "And just ice water to drink."

"You bet!" responded the waitress. "We girls have to watch our figures!" she added with a conspiratorial wink.

"Anything else?" Her eyes swept the faces around the table. "Okay. I'll be right back." She took one deep breath. Her breasts rose and fell. The three soldiers took a deep breath, too. They held it. And then she was gone.

The reporter slumped forward and gasped in mock surprise. "Do you guys really go for that stuff?" she asked.

The soldiers ignored her. Suddenly they were lost in their own discussion.

"I think she liked me!" said Squeeze.

"It was the fingers," said Lucky. "The fingers always get 'em."

"No way," countered Lefty. "It was the hook. They always go for the hook. It makes me seem mysterious and exciting. Like a pirate."

He paused.

"I'm gettin' a frickin' eye patch," he said.

The reporter's jaw dropped. "You guys are too much," she finally said. "Send my salad over there when it arrives, would you?" She pointed toward the table with the doctor and the nurse.

Lefty was suddenly alarmed. "Hey, I'm sorry. We didn't offend you did we? I mean—this is just our way of dealing with . . . all this."

"No, no." She smiled reassuringly. "I just have to deliver some stories for my editor, and you guys said you didn't want to be on the record."

"I'd like you to stay," said Lefty. It was a genuine invitation.

She paused.

"No, really," she said. "I have to look for a story. But I'll be back."

She paused again. Then leaned forward like the waitress and crinkled her nose in a smile.

"I'm hooked."

Dr. Dan and Nurse Ames were sitting on stools at one of the higher tables along the wall. They were accompanied by Santa and the chaplain, leaving two empty stools. The reporter arrived at one empty place, just as the ranger rolled up to the other.

"Mind if we join you at the grown-ups table?" he asked.

Before anyone could answer, he pivoted his chair in a short arc, locked the wheels, and stood up—holding the side of the table while he balanced precariously on his new legs. He turned sideways and sat back on the stool next to the nurse. The reporter took the stool across from him.

"Guess you haven't seen my new trick yet," he said to the nurse. "Not bad for a dumb-ass, huh?"

She turned to face him. "Hey congratulations," she responded. "Really, I mean it. I know how big a deal that is. It's the big hurdle. When you get back from the holidays and you can practice your balance in therapy, you'll be walking in no time." Clearly, she really did mean it.

"Thanks," he said. He looked down, then up. "Sorry about giving you a hard time before. I know it's your tail in a sling if a patient gets hurt. I understand you were just trying to keep us safe. It's just . . . the whole helpless thing gets old."

She smiled and nodded.

"And thanks for this. I know you're taking a chance. But the guys really needed this. Thanks."

Nurse Ames smiled and looked him as levelly as he had looked at her. "Yeah," she said. "Not bad for a hard-ass, huh?"

"Needed what?" asked the reporter.

A waitress interrupted to deliver the reporter's ice water from the other table, and a soda the major had previously ordered. She paused to flash him a smile, then moved on.

"Needed that. That smile."

The reporter looked puzzled.

"Look," said the major. "Every wounded soldier here left something behind in Iraq or Afghanistan. An arm, a leg, a hand, maybe most of his face. Maybe just a sense of invulnerability. 'It can't happen to me.' They'll never feel that way again.

"And now they want to know that they can fit in—can be accepted—can be appreciated and loved, even though they're not like everybody else anymore. That's what these girls are doing, even if they don't know it. They are telling these guys, 'It's okay. Somebody is still going to want you when you get home.'"

The reporter looked unconvinced.

"Tell her, doc," said the major.

But before the doctor could speak, Santa weighed in. "He's absolutely right. When I came back from Vietnam, I thought no woman would ever want anything to do with me because of the things I had seen and done. Took me a long time to get my head straight. Maybe that's why I bought this place. Because the girls are nice to everyone here.

"Not like bar girls," he continued. "It's not like they are trying to sell you drinks or anything. There's no touching here. No bad stuff. Anybody gets the wrong idea, we help him out the door. It's just nice to be around good looking girls who are friendly to you. Everybody goes home happy.

"Some people think this is a nasty place for nasty old men. Some think it cheapens women. I think it's therapy."

The reporter was still not satisfied. "Dr. Dan," she queried. "Is there something to this?" She was trying to spin this as a story in her head, but it didn't quite compute. It was too hard—too subtle for casual readers.

"Speaking not as a medical professional, but from personal experience," he replied, " . . . You bet." He was moving his left wrist in a circle to stretch the arm. He grimaced briefly, then continued.

"I was wounded pretty badly in Vietnam. I would have died except some kid pulled me out of a firefight, threw me over his shoulder, and ran me back to safety. Afterwards, I was bitter—thought I was a failure. I made a lot of money in the stock market, but that didn't help. Until I met this girl. I still don't know why she liked me, but she did. Made me want to be around her, just because she wanted to be around me. One day she sat me down and said 'You are wasting your life. I have always wanted to be married to a doctor. Get busy.'

"And I did. And here I am. Pretty clever girl, my Susan. Made me understand you never get over it. But you can get past it."

"I'm not sure I would have picked this cure," contributed the chaplain. "But I do think you've identified the disease. The biggest thing they want to know is that it's all going to be all right. That there is someone out there who will accept them for who they are."

"Really?" asked the reporter. She was looking at the nurse now. "Are there really a lot of wounded guys who think this way? Who need this kind of reassurance?"

"In my experience . . . yes," Nurse Ames responded. "Men and women."

She swished her iced tea around in the glass, and poked at the lemon with a straw.

"Almost every single one. It's just amazing. . . . It's actually a bit disorienting. With some of these guys, I'm old enough to be their . . . uh . . . older sister." Everybody at the table smiled.

"And yet every one eventually says the same thing. 'Would you date me? Would you pay any attention to me? Would you ever marry a guy like me?' Even the women ask if I think they will ever find a guy who will overlook their scars or their artificial leg or missing finger."

The major was watching the nurse closely—taking in every word. This was getting pretty close to home.

"I'm lucky," he finally said. He spoke first to Nurse Ames, then turned to the reporter. "I have a fiancée who is okay with the new me. I've never had a moment of doubt that she would stand by me—accept me the way I am. Help me with the things I know I have to do now. That got me through everything I had to face. I don't know how the guys do it who have no one to lean on. I'm really lucky to have a committed fiancée I can depend on."

"It's the best I can do until we get back to the States," the doctor said. "I'll get you a proper ring then."

He was very handsome. And persuasive. And gentle. Some doctors abused nurses constantly. Some just discounted them, dismissing their ideas and experience out of hand. And some of them worked as colleagues with the nurses on their staff, even soliciting their ideas. He was one of those. Every nurse wanted to work on his shift. And he had picked her.

"I think this one is beautiful," she said

She held out her left hand. Around the ring finger was a rubber O-ring from an oxygen bottle. This made it official. No matter what ring they got in the future, she would always love this one.

"Just one thing," he said. "I think we ought to keep this our secret until we get home. It just creates too many problems out here. There are too many rules—we would never get to see each other. We need to keep this our secret."

"Ok," she said reluctantly. She slipped the rubber ring from her finger and into the pocket of her Desert Combat Uniform.

"We don't need a real ring," she told herself. "This is our pledge to each other—our commitment—and that's good enough."

★ ★ ★

"Well, let me ask this." The reporter was not letting go. "You don't have to answer if you don't want to. Do you see a lot of romantic relationships between patients and medical staff?"

The question took the nurse aback.

"*How can you be so ignorant of what we do?*" she wanted to say. The life of a deployed military nurse was hard, hot, and dirty. They helped put up the tents and move equipment. They wiped up pus and changed adult diapers. They handled people in pain and hurt them more as they cleaned wounds. They breathed in fumes from jet exhaust and dust from helicopter landings. They washed sand and blood and hydraulic fluid from their clothes and God-knows-what from their hair. They used outdoor latrines and sometimes just squatted down behind a truck while the guys looked the other way. They were always making decisions—big decisions, little decisions, decisions that relieved pain or ended life. "*When I got a few minutes to myself,*" she thought, "*I felt sleepy, not sexy.*"

And yet . . .

"No," said the flight nurse. "To be honest, sometimes we see a relationship or two within the medical staff. But the relationship with patients is just not like that."

"It's much more intimate than sex," interjected the ranger. "Much more complex."

Everyone turned to face him.

"It's like when you have a girlfriend, and you get hurt, but you don't want to look weak in front of her. And at the same time, it's like when your mom cleans your skinned knee and holds you and lets you cry. And it's like with your wife when she touches you in places and ways that you would never admit to anyone else, but it's okay because of who she is. It's all of that at one time.

"You know, you might be married twenty years and not remember any specific thirty minutes in bed with your wife. You spend thirty minutes with a nurse in the emergency room having your leg sawed off, you remember her pretty well. It's very intimate."

It was a startling little speech. The nurse was looking at him in an entirely new way.

The glare of the emergency room lights was always so bright. They projected straight down on a patient stripped naked and writhing in pain. His chest was clean—it had been protected by body armor. But both arms and one side of his face were burned and freckled with black shrapnel, scattered like grains of pepper across his body. Below the waist he was miraculously unscathed—no damage to his stomach or genitals. But his upper thighs were flecked with black. And below his left knee his leg just ended. She could see six inches of jagged white bone, then a gap where you could look through the leg right to the bloody white padding underneath. Below that, the leg began again . . . sort of. The upper and lower parts of the leg were held together by strips of flesh and muscle. The foot was just a ball of hamburger.

"That's it, doc," someone was saying. "More on the way by air. Be here in about an hour."

"Too long," said the doctor. "This has to come off now. We have to clean it and stop the bleeding. And we need the table. We can't wait an hour."

The doctor leaned over the patient's face. The soldier was young—they usually were. He was groggy. But he knew what was going on.

"Son," said the doctor. "You are going to be okay. You are going to live and you are going to keep everything that's important. But the left leg has to come off. We can't stop the bleeding and clean up the rest of the leg with this mess hanging on. So I'm going to take it off. You will keep your knee. But we are out of morphine. I've given you the strongest stuff we've got, but it's still going to hurt until I can get the morphine to you in about an hour. Do you understand?"

"Yes, sir," answered the corporal through a fog. "If I could just have something to hang on to . . . "

The nurse leaned across his body and laid her chest on his. She put one arm under his head, and one arm over his right shoulder. She buried her head in his neck and pulled him close to her. The soldier reached around her with both arms and held on.

"Thank you ma'am," he said politely. "Makes it almost worthwhile."

His courage, his politeness, his attempt at humor at this moment of pain and crisis—it all struck her very deeply. Suddenly he stiffened.

"Oh my God!" he said. He cried out again, but stifled it with a wrenching groan. He squeezed her so tightly that she could barely breathe. Then he whimpered. Then he fainted.

"What you don't understand is that everybody who went to war was shot." It was the ranger, Major Pike, still trying to explain himself to the reporter.

"Some were shot in the body. Some were shot in the head, like that kid on the litter today. And some were shot in the heart. Everybody got shot. And everybody needs to recover."

Dr. Dan nodded thoughtfully.

"*Wow*," thought the nurse. "*Wow.*"

Quickly she snapped her head to the side, as if looking across the room. And quickly she wiped her cheek as if brushing off a fly. But what she brushed off was salty and wet.

"Ouch!" said the waitress at the next table over. She straightened up and backed away from the pale soldier with the cane. He was returning his right hand to the table. She looked at him severely. Santa slid his stool back to get up.

"Hey numb-nuts!" It was Major Pike calling out to the offending party. The soldier did not look up.

"Yeah, I'm talking to you." The major was using his parade ground voice. Soldiers at other tables turned to look.

"Keep your hands to yourself, or you're gonna go down in history as the first person to ever get his ass kicked by a guy with no legs!"

Nurse Ames covered her mouth and smiled.

It wasn't much of a standoff. The waitress turned and left. The two other soldiers at the table stood up and moved. The offending party slumped down in his seat and studied his food. The major held his position and his posture, then took a deep breath and flexed his chest and arm muscles before turning back to the table. The nurse thought she should have been put off by the primal display of an alpha male. But she wasn't.

The food arrived, and several waitresses slid their youthful bodies between the customers to set the plates down with a smile.

"Thanks," said Santa across the table to the major.

"No problem," the major replied. "The guy's a jerk. I saw him in orthopedics at Walter Reed. Twisted his knee jumping off a truck. Been hanging around first one hospital and then another for months complaining about the pain. Docs can't find anything wrong. Guess he finally found a sympathetic doctor or maybe they just got tired of him. He's going home on a medical discharge and planning to collect benefits for the rest of his life."

"Oh really!" said Santa. He pursed his lips, then winked. "We'll talk later."

Across the room, the dining resumed. The girls buzzed between tables, pollinating their guests with smiles and French fries. The mood was improving by the minute.

As the meal was winding down, the doctor stood stiffly and slid around the table to whisper into Santa's ear. He smiled and nodded and left for the back of the restaurant. When he reappeared in a couple of minutes, the doctor slid around the other side of the table and approached Nurse Ames.

"Would you like to dance?" he asked.

The nurse looked around, confused. "There's no music," she said.

"There will be in a minute," he replied. "Do you like Bill Haley?"

She stiffened and widened her eyes, then looked around. Everyone else at the table was looking back. Quietly she said, "I was in a dance club in high school." She took his hand and slid off the stool.

Together they walked to an open spot near the entrance to the room and asked the occupants of several tables to slide back. Then they stood looking at each other for a moment. Some of the others in the room had noticed the commotion and paused to watch. Others went on eating. She seemed to be steeling herself for a difficult task and took a deep breath.

Suddenly, the speakers overhead blared a familiar voice.

"One, two, three o'clock, four o'clock, rock!"

Everyone in the room stopped eating and looked up.

"Five, six, seven o'clock, eight o'clock, rock!"

The servers stopped and looked toward the dancers.

"Nine, ten, eleven o'clock, twelve o'clock, rock!"

People in the other rooms stopped eating and some stood up to see better.

"We're gonna rock around the clock tonight!" Wearing green flight suits and boots, the doctor and nurse faced each other and stepped off.

"I was in a dance club in high school," she said. He took her hand and led her to an open spot on the floor.

It was one of the rare days in Baghdad when the weather was neither scorching hot nor miserably cold and wet. The sides of the tent were rolled up, and the floor of wooden pallets had been overlaid by sheets of plywood, making something like a smooth surface for dancing. The smoke from the barbecue barrels outside had shifted and was wafting through the tent, but that was actually a pleasant change from the pungent odor of whatever hazardous waste they were incinerating in the burn pit today.

She had been watching with friends from a seat at a folding table, as he took turns with nearly a dozen women on the dance floor. He was very accomplished, very smooth at fast dances, slow dances, classic rock, country and western, and even a bit of rap, as the DJ tried to meet the diverse tastes of his diverse crowd. And the doctor was clearly enjoying himself with a diverse set of partners—nurses, clerks, orderlies, motor pool guards. He seemed to be working his way around the room before he approached her table and extended his hand.

"You know I'd like to dance every dance with you," he whispered in the brief seconds before the music began again. "But we mustn't let anyone know." He smiled and winked. "We can get together later in my room when Frank takes his shift in the ER."

Then the first bars of the classic song by Bill Haley and His Comets filled the tent, and the crowd began to applaud.

"Put your glad rags on and join me, hon,
"We'll have some fun when the clock strikes one . . ."

Across more than fifty years, the familiar voice and the well-known twelve-bar blues-based melody for guitar and saxophone reached out and touched three generations at once: the doctor, the nurse, and their patients scattered around the room. Their first few steps were hardly award winning. They were dancing in flight suits and rubber soled boots. They could barely slide across the floor. But the audience appreciated the effort and broke into smiles.

"We're gonna rock around the clock tonight, "We're gonna rock, rock, rock, 'til broad daylight . . ."

It was a basic dance step in eight counts: Right toe to right side, right toe to left instep; right toe to right side, hold right there; step right behind left, step left to left side; step right across the front, hold right there; and reverse. Then repeat. Nothing fancy. That was it.

But the tempo was so upbeat that the simple footwork felt dazzling. The doctor's steps were actually a bit too small. So when the second verse began, Nurse Ames began to circle him without letting go of his hand. The audience whistled and clapped in response.

During the second verse a soldier stood up from a table against the wall across the room. It was the tall soldier with the scars on face and hands. Normally the eye would have been drawn to his missing nose and ears, to the unnatural curl of his lips, and to the overbroad forehead that extended down to where eyebrows should have been. But his eyes were so bright and enthusiastic that they seemed to dominate all his other features.

He turned to the statuesque blond server who had spoken up to the major earlier, and extended his hand. She looked quickly to Santa—this was against policy and she needed permission—but a wink of his eye and a nod of his head soon gave her to know she had nothing to dread, and they made their way quickly to the open spot between tables. When the guitar solo began after the second verse, the couple entered with a rush.

She was good. He was fantastic. His feet were so quick that it was hard to tell what they were doing, but he seemed to be moving twice as fast at the eight beats per measure. His partner broke into a broad grin, and accompanied his quick steps with exaggerated movements of her feet and hips. The effect was to swing the female partner in a much wider arc than the nurse and doctor had occupied, and with a smile they slid off to the side to give the new pair more room. The move was just in time, as the soldier picked up his partner during the break between measures and set her down four feet away to start the new stanza. The audience loved it, and began to clap to the music.

As the new couple entered the dance, the slouching soldier with the cane stood and moved slyly over beside one of the servers watching from the side. Reaching around her, he placed his right hand on her hip, and began to slide it down as he drew her to him. When she reacted with surprise, he invited her to dance. When she spun away he turned to the girl next to her and reached out to take her hand. She jerked it away and turned to leave as well. Frowning in frustration, he shifted his cane to his other hand and limped toward the restrooms with an exaggerated motion.

The major slid off his stool and balanced precariously on his legs for a moment, then turned and seated himself in the wheelchair. He deftly removed the brake, and wheeled rapidly toward the men's room.

When the fifth stanza gave way to the dueling saxophones instrumental, the dancing soldier seemed to break free from the laws of gravity. His body went up and down. His legs went in and out. He head went back and forth. And the HOOTERS girl used her long hair to exaggerate her own movements in a circle around him. At the end of the section, the audience exploded with laughter and applause.

"When the clock strikes twelve, we'll cool off then, "Start a rockin' 'round the clock again . . . "

On the last stanza the two cooled their intensity a bit and shortened their movements, making room for the doctor and nurse to move back to the center of the floor. In the final measure, each couple added a flourish that left them with arms outstretched to the audience at the end. And again the audience responded with appreciation.

As the music ended and the hard breathing dancers turned to each other to exchange high fives and handshakes, the room broke into applause. The soldier with the burns gestured broadly, bowed to his partner, and returned to his table. The server returned the smile, then returned to her duties. The nurse tightened her smile and gestured to her medical crew to prepare for departure.

But the doctor stopped in the middle of the space cleared for dancing and looked squarely at the occupants of two wheelchairs sitting on the perimeter of the dancing area. They had been smiling, but were more reserved than the rest of the audience.

Still standing in the middle of the floor, the doctor held their eyes as he squatted and grabbed his trouser legs below the knees. Then he stood and jerked the flight suit up, so the bottom twelve inches of each leg showed to the crowd.

But what showed were two shinny titanium rods.

Dr. Dan had been dancing on artificial legs and feet. Still looking at the soldiers in the wheelchairs, he dropped his flight suit legs and nodded in their direction. The meaning was clear. *"If I can do it, so can you."*

Both wheelchair occupants dropped their jaws in surprise, then quickly recovered and began to applaud again. The wave this time was even louder. Every guest stood to applaud. And every soldier in the room stood a little straighter.

"I see. You were proving something," Nurse Ames said to the doctor.

"You bet," he answered.

"Me, too," she said grimly. "Me, too."

"We gotta go," the navigator said to them both. "I got a call from the pilot. Gauge is changed out and they've run up the engines. We are good to go!"

"Roger, I'll pass the word," Nurse Ames replied. In the blink of an eye, she was again the Medical Crew Director—again the soul of professionalism. She seemed happy about the change.

"*Curious*," thought the doctor to himself. Most people did what they had to do at work, then relaxed when the job was over. She seemed at ease only when she was working. It was relaxation and time to herself that made her nervous.

Nurse Ames whispered a message to the med techs and they spread it quickly from table to table. The elf rose to start the bus. Santa passed some final words to the manager.

Suddenly, a cry arose from the restroom. Everyone stopped and turned in that direction. "Ouch!" said a man's voice. "Damn! Stop it! Ow! Stop! Hey, stop! Ooof!"

Without warning the troublesome soldier who had pinched the girl came tumbling out of the restroom area. He hit the ground in a ball, clutching his crotch and gasping for air. He grimaced and groaned and pulled tighter into a ball.

His cane flew through the air behind him and struck the ground with a clatter.

Moments later, the major rolled out of the men's room in his wheelchair. As he sped past the soldier still lying on the ground in a knot, he turned his head to speak.

"Be careful there buddy!" he said in a booming voice. "That floor is slick!"

As he rolled back to his table, the nurse barred his way, her arms crossed.

"Where have you been?" she asked.

"Making history, Nurse Ratched" Ranger Pike replied. "Making history."

It was a joyful parade that returned to the bus. Santa stood at the door to shake every hand as they departed. The businessmen stopped by to give him twenty dollars toward the lunch. The bikers contributed twenty dollars apiece. Several other couples contributed as they left, and a five-year-old-girl skipped up to Santa with a five dollar bill from her mother "for the soldiers."

The soldiers returned the compliment with generous tips on the tables.

As the crowd stacked up at the door, two waitresses approached the ranger from behind. One was the girl who had been pinched by the sullen soldier. The other was the girl he tried to pull to the dance floor. Looking around to make sure Santa was not about, they bent down and kissed Major Pike quickly—one on each cheek. He smiled broadly and looked up at the nurse.

"Jealous?" he asked.

She tried to muster a disapproving frown, but it wasn't very disapproving and it wasn't much of a frown.

He turned serious. "You know," he said, "this is what I want to do with the rest of my life. Take guys like this and show them what they can do instead of what they can't."

He wheeled along beside her until they were outside. They didn't talk. He was thinking about his future. So was she.

Moving quickly, they soon overtook the other two soldiers in wheelchairs. They were on their own this time—nobody pushing from behind. As the major wheeled past, he cried out.

"Pick up the pace! Pick up the pace!"

And he was off. A moment later they were off behind him. The nurse closed her eyes, put her hand to her forehead, and shook her head. But not for long. Soon she was watching him from afar with a new appreciation. In his own way, he was as much of a healer as she was.

The trail of wounded soldiers, medical team members, and aircraft crew was animated and happy. Those on crutches fairly winged their way across the parking lot. Having made their way to the bus, those in wheel-chairs were engaged in a race around it. The major was letting the other two win.

Only the sullen soldier with the cane still had a poor attitude, and he seemed even worse as he made up the rear. He was not really limping on either leg, but was walking gingerly on both. As he started to board the bus, Santa caught up with him.

"Hey, just something for you to think about," said Santa. "I have a friend who works Veterans Fraud out of the Kansas City office. They follow people around with digital cameras and approach them on the street, looking for fakers who pretend to have a problem to get money from the government. See, it's easy to fool a doc for a couple of weeks, but it's hard to do without a job for a lifetime if you really aren't hurt. And once they have your name, you never know where or when they'll be watching you.

"And thanks to a phone call I made a few minutes ago, they definitely have your name."

The soldier stood still for a moment, then turned and handed Santa his cane. "The leg is much better," he said.

As everyone took a seat, Nurse Ames slid in next to the chaplain.

"What's the deal with Ricky Ranger?" she asked.

"Who?" the chaplain asked. "Major Pike?" He chuckled. "Pulled your chain, did he?"

She frowned impatiently. "No, I guess he's a nice enough guy. But he seems to be trying too hard. Maybe he's overcompensating for the legs."

The chaplain struggled to stifle a smile. The idea of princess-over-control thinking that someone else was over-compensating was humorously ironic.

Then he gave the question a second thought, and rubbed his chin.

"Actually, you might be right," he said. "I was in the hospital downrange the day he came through. I had just arrived in country. He kept asking about this medic who was with him when he got hit. The other guy didn't make it, and the major took it real hard. Maybe there was more to the story. I don't know."

The group that joshed each other and jostled for seats was completely different from the group that had dragged off the bus just an hour before. The travelers bubbled like high school students on a field trip. Loaded with the old passengers but a new attitude, the bus pulled away from the therapy session and headed back to the airport—where it appeared that, at least for now, everything had been fixed.

CHAPTER 6

QUICK TURN

1440 hours 23 December: El Paso, Texas, to Garden City, Kansas

It was a happy platoon of warriors that made its way on to the Air Evac plane at the El Paso airport. The nurse worried a bit on the return drive about losing control over her patients after the emotional high of the lunch. But every passenger on the bus responded quickly to instructions and cooperated in moving to the aircraft and settling in. The single exception was the "team" of three wheelchair patients. They refused as a group to be carried into the plane on litters, but Nurse Ames defused the situation by allowing them to be pushed up the ramp in their chairs, then transferred directly to the seats inside. Two medical technicians pushed each chair in turn, with the male nurse behind as a safety in case they started to roll back.

Nurse Ames resumed her position at the top of the ramp where she could see and control everything. "Nice call," said the chaplain standing nearby.

"What?" she asked.

"The compromise," he answered. "I understand your point about safety, but their pride is pretty important, too."

As they watched, the Army major took his place in line and allowed himself to be pushed up the ramp. As he passed by, he grinned and winked. "How do you like my gun crew?" he asked.

"That's all he wanted," offered the chaplain. "A little control over his life."

"*Don't we all?*" thought the nurse. "*Don't we all.*"

The loadmaster repeated his safety briefing. The medical team went seat to seat checking health and safety. The chaplain went seat to seat checking attitude. The lead nurse went seat to seat checking everything. And the doctor stood by to intervene if required. The team in back finished their duties, the team in the front ran quickly through theirs, and soon the big propellers began to turn. Number 3, Number 2, Number 4, Number 1 . . . the engines roared to life. The gauges behaved correctly. The cargo compartment hummed and vibrated. Major Pike put in his ear plugs. Nurse Ames put on her headset. The doctor noted the location of each member of the medical team, nodded approvingly to Nurse Ames, then stretched his left arm over his head before buckling his seatbelt and settling in. The plane eased forward and began to roll.

At the end of the taxiway it made a neat U-turn on to the active runway, and began a rolling take off. At the prescribed airspeed the nose rotated up, the flaps and gear retracted, and the plane turned on to the proper heading for Garden City, Kansas. With her left hand on the throttles and her right hand on the control yoke, the copilot checked the climb rates calculated by the engineer and posted on a paper above her head. Staying tightly within those parameters she raised the nose of the big gray bird and headed up into the dazzling blue sky.

After the hectic activity of the takeoff had settled into the routine of flight, the navigator reached over the engineer's shoulder and deposited a white plastic bag in his lap. Tech Sergeant Jefferson opened it to find a flat Styrofoam box emblazoned with the word "HOOTERS." The *O*s were in bright orange, and an owl peered through them as if they were large spectacles on his face. The engineer opened the top to find two round hamburgers staring up at him, with an olive on a toothpick in the center of each.

"Aw-w-w-w-w," he said in mock appreciation. "You went to HOOTERS and thought of me."

"Not exactly," said the navigator. "I thought of your wife."

"Then you should have ordered the jumbos," replied the engineer.

The pilot chuckled and went back to his work. The copilot glanced back over her shoulder, sighed deeply, and shook her head.

"Nothing for you, sir?" asked the engineer of the pilot.

"Just gum," the pilot replied. "Saving my traveling money."

"Your wife's a beautiful woman," the navigator observed to the pilot as the engineer picked up a full round burger in both hands. "You should think of her more often."

But the pilot was thinking of her. And of the phone in his shoulder pocket with its list of unanswered messages. And of their argument last night. He turned back to his checklist.

"Is she still mad at you?" the navigator asked. Middleton glanced back disapprovingly, then focused again to the front.

"Cause if she's still mad, that's good! Means she still loves you and thinks she can change you."

The engineer looked up from his burger. "He probably knows what he's talking about," he said to no one in particular. "He has enough ex-wives to start a basketball team."

"Not true," answered Lee. "The number is only four, not five. And that last one doesn't even count. It was in the Philippines."

"What?" he said defiantly to the copilot's glare. "Can I help it if women throw themselves at me?"

He faced back toward the pilot. "I'm just telling you that as long as they are mad, you're still ok. It's when they get all lovey-dovey that you have a problem. That means she has already been to see the lawyer. And the bank."

"When they have daughters," the chaplain said to the nurse. He was wearing a headset along with the lead nurse and the doctor, and had listened in on the crew exchange. Now he was talking to her around the earphones and without benefit of the intercom.

"If you are wondering when men stop acting like boys around women, it's when they have daughters. Gives them a whole different perspective. Changes everything."

The nurse slipped the headphones down around her neck. "You have daughters?" she asked.

"Hundreds of them," he replied. "A congregation full. Counseling women is an eye opening experience. Especially women soldiers. They have a whole set of problems I hadn't ever thought about. Things that apply to civilian women, too, but that I never thought about before I went to Iraq. Yeah, I see my whole job differently now."

The reporter, sitting on the other side of the nurse, leaned forward. "So how long were you in Iraq?" she asked.

"Six months," the chaplain answered. "I told you—I'm in the Army Reserve. Was called up for deployment. Now I'm heading back to my congregation in Kansas."

"What faith?" she asked.

"Methodist," he answered. "But more on the Baptist side of Methodism than the Episcopal side. More like a traditional John Wesley Methodist."

Clearly she had no idea what he was talking about.

"I have a rural congregation. I stick pretty close to the fundamentals of the scripture," he said in explanation. She nodded her head.

"So what did you do in Iraq?" she asked.

He looked away. "*I held people's hands while they died,*" he thought.

The soldier's clothes were still smoking when the chaplain got to him.

He was not a staff chaplain. He was on patrol with an infantry platoon. The first two soldiers made their way warily down the side street and had passed the dead dog without event. But when the squad leader signaled them to stop, the third soldier dropped to one knee right beside it. It exploded with a roar. The chaplain was knocked to the ground by the blast, but sprang up and raced to the soldier's side. The medic began to run in their direction from far down the street.

"It's going to be okay," the chaplain said to the soldier lying in

the street. He picked up the limp hand and held it as he bent close to the soldiers face.

But the soldier was already pale. His face turned blue-white while the chaplain watched. He glanced down. Everything below the waist was gone. Not just legs but groin and hips, too. Some of the soldier's intestines lay in a pile next to him in the dirty street.

"It's going to be okay," the chaplain lied again.

Now the soldier's skin was alabaster in color. There was no strength in his grip. He turned his head to look at the chaplain, stared deep into his eyes, and shook his head slightly from side to side. Then he was gone.

"Counseling," he replied. "I did a lot of counseling."

"I missed it," said the medic. "I thought I checked everything. But I missed it."

The medic was sitting on the ground, rocking back and forth. Next to him lay a soldier on a litter. He was turned on his side. His arm was neatly bandaged. But with his protective jacket half off, a huge exit wound was evident in his back. By some terrible miracle, the bullet had entered from below and under the jacket. It passed through the liver, the intestines, and the lung before exiting the back.

The medic had treated him for an obvious arm injury while he bled to death from the massive wounds inside.

As the medic rocked, the chaplain knelt next to him and cradled him like a child.

"Nobody could have saved him," he said quietly. "Nobody could have seen the wounds inside. Nobody could have fixed it."

The soldiers who had carried the litter to the evacuation site stood awkwardly nearby. A helicopter with a white square and a red cross *on the side landed only yards away, covering them with dust and noise.*

"I missed it," said the medic. He was weeping uncontrollably. "I missed it." *The chaplain held on and prayed.*

"So," said the reporter, reaching for her notebook, "Did you feel like you made a big difference by being there?"

"What story line do you create for a chaplain?" she wondered.

"No," replied the chaplain. "I didn't feel like I made any difference at all."

The reporter stopped writing before she began, and the nurse and doctor turned to look at him.

"Look," he said. "You asked a good question and I'm ready to answer it. But put away your notepad. I don't a want a story on this. It's just the truth as I see it."

Reluctantly, the reporter set down her pad.

"I'm not whining or crying about life being unfair. I'm just telling you the conclusion I reached after six very bad months with a group of brave guys given a damn near hopeless task.

"And my conclusion is that I am not very good at being a chaplain. I gave it my very best. It just wasn't enough.

"I worked hard. I tried to be where the action was. I tried to be a good servant. And it just didn't matter. They got shot, or burned up, or died anyway."

He paused to look at the faces around him. They were all frozen in uncertainty, wondering how to react.

"Hey, don't worry," he said. "I'm not giving up on life or going postal or anything. I'm just going back to my wife and family and get a new job. Maybe I can be a teacher, or a manager, or a salesman or something. It's a big world. I'll find something to do. It just won't be pretending to help people when I can't. I'll explain that to my congregation next Sunday morning, and then I'll leave."

He leaned toward the reporter. "I can see you are in a spot—nobody wants to talk about their experiences. But there is one guy over there who is willing to talk to anybody about anything. Bit of a blowhard, but he does have a combat story you might use. He's that corporal right over there." He pointed across the aircraft. The reporter gathered her things in a flash.

"Thanks for the tip," she said. "I hope things work out for you."

After she climbed past the doctor, he turned to the chaplain.

"Seems to me you gave up pretty easily," the doctor said.

"Nothing easy about it," answered the chaplain. "Not so hard on me. Hard on the guys I let down. But I've thought about this for a long time. I just wasn't ready. In the hospital, in the field, in the headquarters. I just didn't have anything useful to tell them. I'm not used to failure, and I felt like I failed at everything I did."

"Maybe that's the problem," countered the doctor. "If you've never failed before, maybe you don't know that's the price of success."

The chaplain smiled. "That's very good as a platitude, doc. You would be a good counselor. But it doesn't work so well in practice. Shot is still shot. Burned is still burned. Dead is still dead."

Nurse Ames leaned forward to join the conversation. "All I can tell you," she said, "is that I have seen chaplains make a big difference to the people I work with and the people I work on. Even doctors and nurses have to have somebody to talk to once in a while."

Even me. She finished the thought in her head, but did not say it out loud.

The chaplain smiled again. "Thanks for your concern. You're right—some chaplains do a great job. I'm just not one of them. I'm not giving up on myself. I'm not giving up on God. I'm just giving up on being His spokesman."

He leaned back in the sling seat and crossed his arms. The conversation was over.

The nurse sat back with a troubled frown.

"So what's your name really?" asked the Army ranger. He had changed seats since the last flight and now sat next to her. His legs projected oddly into the aisle, but otherwise he looked like a normal passenger.

"No more Nurse Ratched?" she asked.

"No more Nurse Ratched," Major Pike confirmed. "That was a good call you made back there. I admire leaders. Sometimes you gotta push the troops in front of you, like pushing a rock. Sometimes you gotta pull 'em behind you, like pulling spaghetti. And sometimes you gotta know when to let go and let somebody else drive. Good call."

She smiled and looked down for a moment. Then turned to face him and placed a finger on the nametag on her flight suit.

"Ames? Nurse Ames? Nurse Cherry Ames?" He grinned broadly. She sat back tightlipped.

"Hey," he said. "No offense meant. I wasn't making fun. But really, what are the odds?" He was being pleasant. She decided to give him the benefit of the doubt.

"That's a very old series of books," she said. "How do you happen to know about *Cherry Ames, Student Nurse?*"

"I come from a small town outside Cheyenne, Wyoming," he explained. "Long winters. I read just about everything in the local library. Which included the whole series about Cherry Ames. My favorite was the one where she was a nurse on Bataan."

"*Mine, too,*" she thought. "*What are the odds?*"

"So what's your first name?" he asked.

"Win," she answered.

"Win?" He wrinkled his face in puzzlement. "Who names their daughter 'Win'?"

"Wait a minute." He leaned forward and pointed to her directly. "It's not 'Win' is it? It's Wendy! Wendy Ames. Ha-ha! Perfect!"

Again she started to take offense, but he was so excited about his discovery that she decided to tell the truth.

"I grew up on a farm in Kansas," she said. "Not far from Garden City. I'm getting off there to visit family. My mom's favorite book was *Peter Pan*. Her favorite character was Wendy. And so . . . "

"I always loved Wendy." He sat back and smiled again. "She was the real leader in the book. Part girlfriend. Part mother. The closest thing to an adult in Neverland."

He sat quietly for a moment. "Do you ever feel that way? Like you're the only adult and all your patients are just Lost Boys and Girls?"

"Only all day every day," she answered. Then stopped. That was more honest than she had intended. She leaned forward to take it back.

"No need to take it back," he said. "I understand. Being in charge is really hard. Lonely. It's the only job worth having in the world. But lonely."

They were both quiet.

"You know," he said in a distant voice. "Being a Lost Boy is no piece of cake either." He was somewhere far away. She was a good nurse. She didn't interrupt.

"But that Tiger Lilly was pretty hot, too," he said finally. She laughed. It had been a while since she had found anything humorous. Wherever he had gone for a moment, he was back, and she was glad for him. And for herself. She pointed at his name tag.

"Pike? Like the fish?"

"What?" he looked puzzled. "No. No! Not like the fish!" he replied in mock exasperation. "Like a spear. Like a pikeman. You know—like a soldier who carries a pike."

She shook her head.

"Really?" he asked. "You really don't know?"

"Back before gunpowder, when war was between real men, pikes were these extra long spears. The pikemen stood together in ranks—like this huge porcupine."

"So how did they fight?" It was a serious question. She was interested.

"They supported each other, defended each other, covered each other. They faced down everything the enemy could throw at their ranks. Maintained discipline. Then they advanced. Together."

"And that's you? Major Pike-man?"

"No," he said patiently. "That's what a pikeman does. Did. I'm George Pike. Not the same thing."

"Actually, I'm kind of thinking it is the same thing," she answered thoughtfully. "Stay disciplined when life attacks. Take care of your friends. And keep moving forward."

He frowned and looked away. "Well . . . " he said. "I hadn't thought of it like that."

They were both quiet again.

"Are you married?" he asked.

She didn't usually talk shop with patients. And she never talked about personal issues with them. At least her own personal issues. But it had already been a long day, and the mission would be over soon, and there didn't seem to be any harm in it.

"No," she answered. "Never married. Sort of engaged once."

"Me neither," he responded. "But I have a fiancée. Want to see a picture?"

"He pulled out his wallet before she could answer, jerked back the Velcro on the black nylon cover, and flipped open the top to show a gorgeous blond beauty with striking eyes.

"They're not really blue," he said. "They're violet. 'Violet eyes to die for.' That's what they used to say about Elizabeth Taylor."

He took the wallet back and studied it for a moment. "I've been in love with her since the fourth grade," he said quietly. Then the story rushed out.

"She never paid any attention to me until I joined the Army. Even when we were students together in Laramie. She moved to Kansas for a job. I visited her on leave and she said she realized how much she missed me when I was gone to school and training, and she was ready to marry me and move anywhere in the world where I was assigned. She said she liked the idea of traveling around with the Army."

He folded the wallet and put it back in his hip pocket. "She wrote me every week until I was wounded. I called her once I got to the states, and told her not to come to Walter Reed. I didn't want her to see me until I could take care of myself."

He pursed his lips and then looked at her. "Look—I can't let this be the end of my life. I'm here because of somebody else who isn't. Now I have to do something—be something. Accomplish something. And I can't do it alone. I need her. She's not going to see me carried off the airplane. Understand? I don't want her to think I'm going be a burden.

I'm going to make her proud. We're going to be a team. We have a commitment. A commitment. I'd do anything for her. Understand?"

"Yes," answered the nurse. "I do. I really do."

"That was wonderful," the doctor said casually.

They were in a small steel shipping container, barely ten feet on a side, which had been converted into a bedroom for two. Metal bed frames with thin mattresses lined two walls. Two wooden footlockers occupied the third, with a horizontal pipe mounted into the wall overhead to hold uniforms on wire hangers. A single small desk and chair and one table lamp filled the fourth wall, along with the door. It was a tight fit for the two people who lived there—in this case, two male doctors. But unlike the tents where most of the medical team lived, it did offer some privacy. And when the other roommate was on shift, the little cell was about as close to a private room as could be found in Baghdad.

The doctor was already standing, putting on a sweat suit. Win Ames sat up on the cot and pulled her t-shirt down from around her neck. Her bra was still in place. Then she recovered her underwear from the end of the mattress and swung her legs over the edge of the bed. She was still wearing her tan polypropylene socks, and she felt the sand from the gritty floor underneath her feet when she stood to pull up her uniform trousers with their desert tan pattern. She sat down again and crossed her left leg over her right knee, dusted the bottom of the sock, and inserted her foot into her boot. Then she did the same with the other foot. In the process, she kicked the gold foil from a condom wrapper across the floor.

Lacing the boots took a while, and the doctor did not speak while she dressed. By the time she was finished, he was sitting at the table with his back turned. He was pouring a red-brown liquid out of a mouthwash bottle into a glass and drinking it. When she stood up he turned around to face her.

"Sorry," he said. "You know how this paperwork piles up."

She stood awkwardly for a moment, until he stood and said, "Come here." It took only two steps to cross the tiny room. He embraced her tightly. She didn't resist, but she wasn't passionate either. He smelled strongly of whiskey.

This was not what she had imagined. This was not what she had expected with him.

"I would do anything for you," he said. "And I know you would do anything for me."

She didn't respond. But as he bent his head to nestle against her neck, she could see her left hand high up on his shoulder. On the third finger of the hand was a black rubber ring.

"Committed," she thought. "We are committed to each other."

But something just didn't feel right.

On the other side of the aircraft, the reporter was taking notes as an Army corporal spoke rapidly and with enthusiasm. He had signed a release. She was smiling. His tassel of blond hair was a breach of Army regulations. So was the medal that dangled from his left breast pocket.

"Oh, it's all official," he said. "I have lots of copies of the write up for the medal in my luggage. I'll give you one when we land in Garden City. Nine enemy dead. Two rocket-propelled grenade positions. A machine gun team. Some sort of unit commander. I shot them all. Just moved from position to position taking care of business. I got the bronze star for it. With *V* device. The battalion commander showed up just after the fighting was over, and I walked him through where everything happened. And he said 'Great job—we're going to put you in for a medal.' And I got it."

"Where are you from?"

"Denver. My folks are from Wisconsin, but I haven't seen them in a long time. I have some friends driving over from Denver and we're gonna take a road trip—going skiing."

"Is your wound recovered enough for you to ski?"

"Oh yeah," continued the specialist. "It was just a flesh wound in the arm. They would have just treated it in theater, except I was ready to rotate home anyway, and my enlistment is up. So they routed me through the medical system, I got a final checkup at Scott, and now I'm headed home and out." He emphasized the last three words.

"So you weren't wounded in the fight?"

"Oh no, I was wounded recently. Actually, it was sort of an accident—I thought the pistol was unloaded."

"Okay. Tell me about the fight."

"Well, the area was supposed to be safe, and we were just scouting a road where our colonel was supposed to go meet some local guy. So we only took two gun trucks."

"Gun trucks?" the reporter asked.

"Humvees with machine guns mounted on top," he answered. "We took two, but the lead triggered an IED planted in a guard rail, I guess. I think it killed everybody in that truck right away. Spun it completely around on the road.

"I was the vehicle commander in the second truck. We started taking heavy fire from one side of the road. Maybe three or four positions. The .50 caliber on the top was chugging away, but the gunner didn't have any cover. Every time he fired in one direction, he got pinged by fire from another direction.

"Then my gunner got hit, and while my driver was trying to take his place, he got hit too. Then an RPG hit the lead truck. Big explosion, rolled the truck into the ditch and set it on fire.

"I was gonna go help but it all happened so fast, and I guess I must have hit my head or something, because I woke up in this ditch. But the new position gave me a shot at the guys who ambushed us. So I started working my way through the positions I could see, one at a time. I got some grenades off the wounded guys and threw them and then charged the enemy positions and shot the guys who stayed behind."

"All by yourself?" the reporter asked.

"Well, yeah," answered the corporal. "Everybody else was dead or wounded. After I hit the last position this wrecker drove up, but he was too late to do anything, so he drove off. Then my battalion commander showed up with a couple of gun trucks and a rescue team. I was the only one left standing so I showed him around."

"Amazing," the reporter said. She was delighted to finally have a story.

"Let me get some more details," she said. "Where did you go to high school?"

Two seats down, Lefty was listening intently. His hook opened and closed reflexively as he tried to clench his fist. His mouth turned down at the corners and his jaw was tight.

"So," asked the navigator. "How can you tell if you have a fighter pilot at your party?"

The flight was routine now, everyone was relaxed, and the navigator felt free to tell his joke over the intercom.

"I don't know," answered the pilot, joining the game and implying his permission for others to do the same. "How *can* you tell when there is a fighter pilot at your party?"

"You don't have to," answered the navigator. "He'll tell you."

It was an old joke, but new to the copilot and loadmaster, and everybody laughed along.

The engineer entered the fray. "What do you call a guy with the personality of an accountant, the social graces of a computer nerd, and no sense of direction at all?" He paused.

"A navigator."

"Zing!" said the pilot.

Before anyone else could step in, the engineer played another card.

"What are the only two types of music a loadmaster listens to?"

Everyone waited.

"Country and Western," said the engineer.

"Hey!" said the loadmaster to another round of chuckles.

Taking a chance, the copilot stepped in. "How can you tell you are halfway through a date with a command pilot?" she asked. Everyone paused. This was risky.

"He says, 'But enough about flying. Let's talk about me.'"

"Ow-w-w-w," said a chorus of voices.

"Real nice," said the command pilot in a good humored way. The copilot smiled. It was going to be okay.

"So this doctor finishes his examination and stops at the end of the patient's bed to write on his chart."

It was Dr. Dan, listening in the back, and now joining in. This was going to be interesting.

"So he tries to write on the chart but he can't make a mark. He tries again, still no mark. He tries again—same result. And the nurse says, 'Doctor, that's a rectal thermometer.' And the doctor says, 'Oh my God—where's my pen?'"

The unexpected entrance of the doctor into the game, and the unexpected turn of his story resulted in a belly laugh at every station on the intercom. The pilot laughed so hard that he wiped tears. The navigator laughed and filed that one away for future use. The copilot laughed robustly, delighted to be one of the team. The chaplain laughed with the abandon of a man who appreciated a joke he knew he would never be allowed to tell. The nurse had heard the joke many times before, but never told by a doctor. It took a special confidence and humility to make yourself the butt of a joke like that before a crowd. *"Butt of a joke."* Even she was getting into the mood.

The doctor smiled at the joy he had brought others. He continued smiling broadly as he leaned back in the seat, stretched both arms out to the side and arched his back. He brought his right arm in to his chest and yawned, still smiling at the joke. Then he frowned slightly, and pulled the left arm into his chest. Then he grimaced and reached across with his right arm to grasp the inside of his left arm at the elbow. Then he bent over sharply at the waist as if in pain.

"Heart attack!" exclaimed the chaplain. He unsnapped his seatbelt with a single motion, and fumbled in his pocket as he made three quick steps to where the doctor was curled up, struggling for breath. He extracted a bottle from his cargo pocket, removed the cover with a press and a turn, and threw two white tablets into his palm. He jerked the headset from the doctor's head, lifted him up from his fetal position and shouted into his ear, "You are having a heart attack. Are you allergic to aspirin?!"

The doctor raised his head to reveal a face contorted in pain. But he understood the question and shook his head no.

"Okay!" said chaplain. He forced the two white tablets between clinched teeth and commanded "Chew!"

The doctor was struggling with pain and breathing rapidly, but he understood the importance of the action. He crunched the tablets as best he could, attempted to swallow, and crunched again.

"Get him to the down litter!" The nurse had been just a moment behind the chaplain in recognizing the problem, but she recovered quickly. The two medical technicians wrestled the doctor on to the litter set up in the middle of the aircraft for just such an emergency. Nurse Ames was in her element now. Organizing a lifesaving response in a moment of crisis was her specialty. And it showed.

"You, get the airway open—tilt that chin and lift it. Then check the breathing. If it is clear and unobstructed start an IV drip.

"You," she indicated the other nurse. "Focus on circulation—check the vitals. Check the carotid pulse and the brachial pulse. I need a BP and pulse ASAP."

"You, start the patient oxygen and get a tube on him.

"I need an EKG, O2, and IV *now*!"

The 800 pounds of medical equipment had been hauled on and off, strapped and unstrapped, wrapped and unwrapped, charged, checked and stored, set up and taken down time after time after time. Suddenly it was critical that it all be working and accessible. Every tube, tie, box, valve, bottle, extension cord, scalpel, bandage, tweezers, and cardiac defibrillator had to be in exactly the right place—and the team had to know where to find it all without looking. That came from uncompromising training and discipline on the hot, cold, dry, wet, busy, boring days and nights between emergencies.

"Muscle memory" some trainers call it—doing the right thing in a crisis entirely out of habit. Such training is the direct result of the personality and personal habits of the leadership "where the rubber meets the road."

Generals and medical commanders may issue commands, directives, and policies. But readiness at the moment of crisis grows from the leaders on the line. The Medical Crew Director—Nurse Ames—had worked hard to keep her skills sharp, when every pressure of every day sought to dull and compromise them. In the next fifteen minutes her efforts would pay off. Or not.

While her crew began a well-rehearsed drill, the MCD began the critical flow of information.

"Pilot, I have an emergency"

"Crew," he replied immediately. "Stay off the intercom unless you have something critical. MCD, go."

"The doctor has suffered some sort of medical emergency—maybe a heart attack. This is beyond our capability to handle. We need to get him to a hospital ASAP. And I need a phone patch to medical operations at Scott. They will have a flight surgeon on duty."

"Roger," responded the pilot. "Co, you fly. Eng, stay on it with her. Nav, set up the phone patch—then break out the charts. I'll talk to Albuquerque soon as we have a plan."

In less than a minute the phone patch was complete, and the nurse was talking to a doctor about treatment for a sixty-three-year-old-man with chest pains, a thready pulse, irregular blood pressure, and artificial legs. The navigator looked quickly at a map, then, taking care not to tie up the intercom between front and back of the aircraft, he leaned over the engineer and shouted to the pilot: "We are about 25 miles from Lubbock. I used to date a girl there. College town. Pretty good hospital—they're used to dealing with sports injuries and emergencies on football weekend. Probably has a cardiac unit."

"Okay," said the pilot. "Check it with the MCD."

"Good plan," answered the nurse after the navigator briefed her over the intercom. "I talked to AMC—they have an accepting provider there. They are calling the hospital by phone. Let's do it."

The navigator was working feverishly at his desk. "It's actually only about 18 minutes out," he said. "Anything else likely to have the hospital we need is at least 45 minutes away."

The pilot moved his thumb to the radio transmission button. He paused and took two deep breaths. Then he pressed the button.

"Albuquerque center, this is Air Evac 1492. Emergency." His voice was calm—direct—informative—very in control.

The center responded immediately. "All other traffic stand by. Air Evac 1492 go."

"Albuquerque, Air Evac has a crew member with a life threatening emergency. I have 23 souls on board and gas for 4.5 hours. We wish to divert to Lubbock—we have ground contact with a hospital there."

"Roger Air Evac. I will clear other traffic out of your way. Stand by for details."

"Thank you Albuquerque—departing flight level 220 for 5,000—direct for Lubbock, beginning my descent. I will get the weather. Please advise Lubbock to roll crash rescue. Will change to tower frequency and advise them of details on my emergency shortly."

Two expert teams were working the problem now, one in front and one in back. And professionals at Scott and in Albuquerque were also in high gear. Teams in the tower in Lubbock, in the fire station there, and in the hospital would soon be engaged. Connected by radio, training, and professionalism, fifty people across several states were moving rapidly to save one. It would have been a wonderful story. But the reporter—like most people not part of these professional teams—knew nothing about the complex operation unfolding around her.

With the opening moments of the crisis behind her, Nurse Ames opened a fat binder from her battered briefcase, and pulled out a checklist. She began to read:

- "Oxygen therapy." The green box on the next litter over was repositioned and activated to convert liquid oxygen to a gas, which was routed by clear plastic tube into the doctor's nose.
- "Fluids." The IV drip was up and running.
- "Relieve pain." The doctor had twice mouthed the words "No nitro!" Apparently he was worried about some drug interaction. She talked by radio-telephone patch to the flight surgeon at Scott Air Force Base and reported consistent systolic blood pressure under 180. He approved morphine through the saline

drip. That would open the blood vessels and aid circulation to the heart.

- "Check and control arrhythmias." A portable EKG hookup showed no abnormal heart rhythms, but the ZOOL cardiac machine, also lashed to the next litter, was charged and ready to defibrillate if necessary.
- "Stop further clotting." The chaplain had already administered aspirin, so she held off on the Plavix, and was waiting for permission from Scott to administer Heparin.
- "Beta blockers." That would have to wait for the hospital. She hoped they would be quick about it.

The doctor was resting easier now, but he was not out of the woods.
"Pilot, MCD."
"Pilot, go."
"Please tell them on the ground that we suspect acute myocardial infarction. We need an ACLS ambulance with cardiac monitor, IV pump, and oxygen. Their destination is Lubbock Heart Hospital."

Up front, the pilot quickly relayed that information to the tower in Lubbock. In the back, Nurse Beauchamp was asking the now resting doctor a series of questions, then relaying the information to Scott for relay to Lubbock.

"Do you have a history of heart problems? Do you have peptic ulcers? Are you using anticoagulants? Have you had any major recent bleeding? Have you ever had a stroke?"

Nursed Ames keyed the intercom again. "And pilot, one more thing." She was on her game now.

"Pilot, go."

"It's absolutely critical that they get him some thrombolytic drugs immediately to dissolve any clots that have formed. Every second counts." She paused. "Do you think we might do an engine running offload with the civilian ambulance that meets us?"

"I doubt it. But I will do my best to convey that to the tower," the pilot answered. "Any further intercom traffic, please send to the copilot."

The copilot looked at him quizzically while he passed the request to the Lubbock tower. They were now less than ten minutes out.

"Co—I've got the plane."

"*What the hell?*" she thought. She was doing fine. Why take the aircraft away?

The pilot continued: "Crew—my plan is direct into Lubbock.

"Co, get out the FLIP charts and get me the airfield dimensions.

"Nav, double check weather and check the NOTAMs.

"Eng, my approach speed will be 150 knots—we will keep that up as long as possible. Need to figure a rapid slow down to touch down speed in the last 2 miles. I want to set it down just past the numbers."

Two minutes later the navigator interrupted: "Pilot, I have information ROMEO—winds 300 at 12 knots. That checks with tower—they directed Runway 35 Left. There is construction on taxiway Bravo."

"Pilot, this is Co." She was checking a chart. Runway is 11,500 feet long. I'm guessing that will mean a turn off to the military ramp on taxiway Victor."

The navigator continued: "Runway altitude is 3,282 feet MSL. Surface concrete. Clouds broken at 5,000 feet. Ten miles visibility. No LIMA approach required."

As they neared touchdown, the loadmaster prepared all the passengers for landing. Everyone was strapped in except for the medical crew. They were standing around the doctor's litter. And closest to his head, whispering constantly in his ear, was the chaplain.

"We were able to use the phone patch to contact your wife. I talked to her personally. It's a long drive but she will start early tomorrow and be here in time to spend Christmas Eve with you."

The chaplain paused. "Dan—do you want me to stay with you until your wife gets here tomorrow? This can be pretty spooky. Even for a doctor."

With the morphine in his system, the doctor was feeling much better. Much better.

"You know, chaplain, I bet you would. I bet you would do just that. With your family waiting for you after six months at war, I bet you would get off this plane and spend Christmas here with me just to make me feel better." The doctor paused.

"You're a good guy, chaplain. A good guy." He paused again. The morphine was great.

"But you are making a mistake about leaving your job. I've watched you. You are good with people. They like you. They like being around you. They listen to you. Because you don't just preach at them. You live with them. You really do put others first. And you have patience with people." The words were slowing. The doctor was woozy.

"That's a rare gift, padre. I don't have it. I'm a good doctor, but I have no patience. I know it. I try to compensate for it."

The chaplain was smiling and shaking his head no. The doctor seemed ready to nod off. Then he roused and grabbed the chaplain's uniform by the front and pulled him closer. It was a surprisingly strong grip.

"I'm telling you, buddy," he said quietly but with passion. His head was weaving. "From one guy who has been there to another. You have a gift. Don't waste it."

The doctor lay back, suddenly tired. His eyes closed. He slept.

Up front, the copilot was trying to focus on her job and sulk at the same time. "*What did I do wrong,*" she thought, "*that he would take the airplane away right in front of everybody?*"

Just as they crossed the numbers at the end of the runway, she noticed a different noise from the back of the plane. It took a moment to register. It was the wheels on the runway. The landing had been so smooth that she couldn't tell the moment of touchdown. Standing in the back, the medical team never felt it. "*Impressive,*" she had to admit to herself. "*Very impressive.*" And infuriating. If the pilot would make one human mistake, it would be a lot easier to work with him.

A moment later, as they turned off the runway to taxi, the pilot said,

"Don't be upset that I took the aircraft. I think you could probably give them a smooth landing, too. But I am not positive. And with the doc feeling every jolt on that litter, and with the whole medical team standing up, I had to be positive. I was pretty sure you could do it. I was positive I could do it. Pretty soon I will be positive about you, too. Just be patient."

Well, that helped—since everyone was listening on the intercom. Maybe he was right and things would soon take a turn for the better.

"Also." He was in the instructor mode again. "Watch your voice. It tends to get high when you stress. Drop it down. When the guy on the other end is dealing with a problem, the last thing you want to do is amp him up. Take two deep breaths. Drop your voice an octave. Then key the mike."

The lesson was over. His voice changed. It was more collegial. "This will put us even further behind," the pilot said to everyone. "Let's make this a quick turn."

As they taxied up to a parking spot on the ramp, the pilot received another radio call from the tower, and passed it on to the MCD and loadmaster.

"Tower says the ambulance is ready to do an engine running offload soon as we drop the ramp."

After communicating with the pilot again, the loadmaster began to lower the ramp. The engines were reduced to their lowest idle speed, but the noise and fumes and heat entered the cargo compartment immediately. The nurse would not have allowed this if the patients were in bad shape physically. But the only one in bad shape was the one who needed to get to a hospital immediately. So she held her criticism as the ramp touched the cement, and a ground guide backed the boxy ambulance deftly into position.

Two civilian medical technicians from the ambulance, the male nurse and the chaplain lifted the litter out of its brackets and carried it down the ramp to the flat cement. There the ambulance driver met them with a wheeled gurney. He locked the wheels in place, and together they lifted the patient off the litter and on to the gurney, which the driver pushed up to the back of the ambulance. As he continued to push, the wheels collapsed and the entire mechanism slid into the back of the ambulance where another attendant and a nurse were waiting.

As the litter bearers headed back into the aircraft with the litter, the attendant closed the rear door, and started for the driver's side. Nurse Ames grabbed him by the arm. "Thanks for the quick turn!" she said.

"No problem!" he shouted over the roar and the heat and the flying dust of the running engines. "I was a Navy corpsman with the Marines in the Gulf War. I've done this before. Glad I could help!"

Lights on, the boxy blue truck sped through a gate, turned south on Highway 27, and was gone.

With a start, the nurse realized that she had not even had a chance to say good bye to Dr. Dan. It had been quick.

"That was a quick turn. I didn't even get a chance to say goodbye to him." It was Major Pike. "There's a guy who really did something with his life. Really made a difference."

He had been thinking hard about that subject—again—since they left El Paso. "*How am I going to do it?*" he thought to himself. "*How am I going to stay in the Army? How am I going to command? How am I going to make my life worthy of the life it cost to get me here?*"

He was relieved to think that he would have a wife to listen and help.

It had been so quick.

It wasn't even a runway really—just a flat spot on a desert road that the Air Combat Control Team had surveyed and marked. But it was close to the objective, and the C-130s could drop them in under the cover of darkness, let them off with engines running, and spin around for a quick take off. If things went as planned. But sometimes things turned around quickly.

The plane landed with the ramp already part way down, and by the time it stopped, the Rangers were pouring out the back in an air assault, going to ground on either side of the makeshift dirt runway, and waiting for the aircraft to depart in a hurricane of dust before regrouping and moving on the target. He hit the ground running, and took only four or five steps into the soft sand off the side of the road before it happened.

He actually felt it more than heard it. "Click!" The anti-personnel mine was designed to blow its force up and out. And that is exactly where his boots and feet and lower legs went—up and out.

It was so quick that he didn't actually feel anything right away. But he knew right away what had happened. "Mines!" he yelled. "Stay back."

"Medic!" someone else yelled. "It's the major!"

And sure enough a medic came hustling through the night, through the sand and through the mines, to slide to a stop on his knees next to the prone figure in the dust.

"Mines!" cried the major again. "Everybody back! Get back!"

The medic was already searching his belt and cargo pockets for tourniquets. "Like you got back last week when I fell through the floor and into that basement? And you jumped in after me and covered my ass 'til we got out? Don't worry, sir. We'll have you out of here in a flash."

Not finding everything he needed immediately available, the medic shucked his aid bag off one shoulder and threw it to the ground so he could open it rapidly.

"Carlos!—no!" the major cried.

"Click!"

The medic had just enough time to throw himself between the prone figure and the blast. It saved the major's life. It did not save his own.

Everything else was a blur. Somehow he was back on the floor of the C-130. And someone was leaning over his legs. Or where his legs used to be. It was so quick. In a single moment he had lost his legs and a friend. And gained the responsibility for living a life that deserved the sacrifice someone else had made for it.

"Things can turn so quickly," he said thoughtfully.

"Yeah," agreed Nurse Ames. "They sure can."

She was walking back from the doctor's small living quarters when she first noticed the noise. Although it was a warm afternoon, she felt chilled—like she needed more clothes. And a hot shower. There was no one else walking this street between container/rooms. She crossed her arms across her chest, and hunched her shoulders as if to keep out the cold.

The noise was noticeable but not alarming at first. It did not have the rushing-freight-train sound of artillery overhead. Or the whistling-shriek of an incoming shell. Or the fluttering-birds sound of a mortar. It sounded like a truck rattling or something loose banging in the back of a trailer. Except there were no trucks or trailers around. And it was moving. Overhead.

Too late she realized—rocket!

The living area was a sea of tents, metal container/rooms, and cement blast walls dividing and protecting them. The first rocket rattled past and landed with a loud "CRASH!" on a road between tents about two blocks away. It did not sound like an explosion exactly—more like a high speed collision between two large trucks. And the impact was not marked by a flash of fire, but a cloud of rocks and dust and dirt.

She had barely turned to follow the sound of the first rocket to its impact, when a second exploded two blocks ahead—right where she had been headed. Because it did not reach her, she never heard its approach. This one fell among tents, and the crash was followed by screams. Someone was hurt.

She was still trying to decide whether to run toward the injured party or a bomb shelter, when a third rocket rattled overhead. This time it was low and it landed very nearby—close enough that the force of the explosion sucked at her clothes and knocked her to the ground. KA-BAMM!

It landed right behind her—just a few rooms back—near the room she had just left—near—Andre!

"Andre!" she yelled. She got up a bit wobbly, grabbed the side of a container/room to steady herself, and yelled again.

Then she ran the thirty yards to where smoke was rising from between two rooms. The walls of both were smashed inward. Both roofs were collapsed and the contents riddled by large holes where big pieces of something jagged—shrapnel—had ripped through.

She stopped before the container that Andre shared with the other doctor—the one on shift in the OR. It was not just collapsed. It was destroyed. It was scrap. The metal sides were lying flat on the ground. Of the things inside—beds, chair, table—almost nothing identifiable remained. And it was leaking a trail of blood out of the scrap and into the street.

Two more rockets rattled overhead and landed some distance away, but she was only dimly aware of their passage.

The trickle of blood became a stream, then a torrent. So much blood. But it didn't go far—it was swallowed by the dust and gravel.

"Andre!" she cried again. There was no answer.

"Yeah, *'quick turn,'*" she thought. It doesn't take long for your whole life to turn around.

CHAPTER 7

EVASIVE MANEUVERS

1620 hours 23 December: Lubbock, Texas, to Garden City, Kansas

The incident with Dr. Dan had a sobering effect on everyone. The medical crew was shaken by the unexpected loss of a popular leader whose quiet competence had infused confidence into the whole team. The passengers were reminded of their vulnerability and retreated into the shells created when their bandages were first applied. Major Pike tried to raise spirits with some light banter, but it fell flat. The chaplain moved from seat to seat offering a smile and an encouraging word, but it had no effect. Nurse Ames hardened her voice and increased her direct control over the team. The passengers did what they were told, and otherwise shut her out.

"It's pretty grim back there, boss," said the navigator to the pilot as he returned from a trip to the cargo compartment. "Looks like everybody's dog died at the same time."

The pilot did not acknowledge the comment, but continued to examine the maps and charts he was using to plot a revised flight plan to Garden City. The phone in his shoulder pocket buzzed again with a text message from his wife. But he needed to focus on the mission. And he didn't want to focus on the problem at home. And so he ignored the text. After a moment he looked up.

"Crew brief in two minutes," he said. Then he looked over his shoulder to his navigator and continued, "Pull out the local charts and check for towers, buildings and obstacles over 100 feet AGL north and east, then in a circle west and south of this airport for a radius of 5 miles. I want to do a low level exit and circle around the field with a pass over the runway on departure."

The copilot pursed her lips, raised an eyebrow and looked over at the pilot. The engineer smiled and looked down at his calculations.

"MCD, this is pilot" said the pilot over the intercom. "I would like to do a tactical departure for training purposes. Do you have any pax who would be negatively impacted?"

"No," replied Nurse Ames. She did not know exactly what the pilot had in mind, but she was a flight nurse with an emphasis on flight. She was not afraid of aggressive flying, as long as patient safety was not endangered.

Under different circumstances, she might have challenged anything except straight and level flight with a minimum impact on patient comfort. But these patients were all far enough along in healing that they were going home—some for good. Nobody was going to be hurt by a couple of tight turns, and it might give them something to think about besides the sight of the doctor leaving the ramp on a litter with oxygen and an IV.

"Everybody back here is in good shape," she continued. "Maybe that would break the mood a little."

With engines still running, the crew moved quickly through the remaining checklists. Garden City was still sixty minutes away, the pilot realized, and it would be dusk when they arrived. It would be a close call to get on the ground, discharge the passengers, and get out in time to return to Scott Air Force Base before their crew day expired. The pax would make it home for Christmas. But if the crew was slow, and the regulations for crew rest kicked in, they would be trapped on the ground at Garden City, and perhaps miss the chance to be home for Christmas. Joy would never understand. Never forgive him.

On the other hand, as a leader, and a pilot, and a trainer of other pilots, he had certain responsibilities.

The big plane eased away from the parking space, and trundled down the taxiway. Near the end of the runway, it stopped.

The pilot turned to the copilot and said, "Pay attention. This is not a game. We are not joyriding. You're going to take off like this ten times a day when you get in the box. I wish somebody had practiced this with me before my first trip.

"There is a fence about three quarters of a mile off the end of the runway," he continued. Everyone on the intercom could hear.

"We are going to assume that beyond that fence is Indian Country. We are going to take off at max power. As soon as I'm satisfied I have lift I will get the nose up and rotate. Gear up and flaps up immediately. When we cross that safety line, I want to be clean at 400 feet AGL and 220 knots—and climbing like a bat out of hell. I will turn sharply on to our heading to Garden City which is about 010—maintain 220 knots at full power, and we will take whatever climb rate we can get.

"But that's the best time for the bad guys to take a shot with a heat seeking missile because it's as low and slow as we are going to get. So we are going to pretend that Load sees a missile out the back at four o'clock.

"Load," the pilot raised his voice a bit, "soon as you hear the gear thump into place you start counting—one–one thousand, two–one thousand, three–one thousand—and when you hit thirty, you sing out 'Flares! Flares! Flares! SAM—four o'clock!' Got it?"

"Yes, sir," answered the loadmaster. In the back, the nurse raised her eyebrows and looked at the chaplain who was listening on the doctor's headset.

"Co," the pilot continued his lesson. "We will be at about 600 feet doing more than 200 knots in a hard left turn. We have a missile to the right rear at four o'clock. What do we do?"

"Chop the throttles to reduce the heat signature and turn right into the missile," answered the copilot.

"Great!" replied the pilot. "I'll do that and drop the nose to gain back the speed we lose when we chop the throttles. Nav, hit the flares. Not really, of course. We're just simulating. Then we'll descend to Minimum Altitude Capable. For me MAC is about 80 feet, but that would scare the hell out of any civilians in the area, so we will hold it at 200 feet AGL.

"*But!* We are going to assume the bad guys are as smart as we are. Or at least as smart as the navigator."

"Hey!" the navigator responded.

"And they have created an ambush off the nose. So when we turn right and slow to counter the heat seeker, they shoot two rockets from the left across the nose where they think we are going to be. What do we do?"

"Even though they are not heat seekers, turn into them, so hard back to the left. We can't afford to lose any more altitude, so we will lose some speed." She felt strangely good about this—not at all like a school girl reciting her lessons. This was the real deal.

"Affirmative," said the pilot. "Turn into rockets and missiles, away from ground fire. So we turn toward the rockets back to the west. That will cost us speed and I want at least a 50 knot buffer. So, Eng, help me watch the airspeed and we will call 'knock it off' at 180 knots. Power up, hold the turn at low level around the west side of the airport and come back into the approach, then begin max climb directly over the runway. At the far end turn back to our departure heading, and continue max climb. At 10,000 feet, we will back off the speed and climb rate to match what Eng computed to save fuel.

"Meanwhile, Nav—you help me watch to the front during all this and make damn sure nobody put up a new tower and forgot to tell the charts.

"Everybody ready? Okay—Load—tell everybody in the rear to tighten their straps and why. I don't want anybody surprised."

"Roger, sir." In the back the loadmaster rapidly passed the word down the line of passengers. "Tactical take off. Evasive maneuvers. Strap tight. Hold on." He glanced around the compartment to make sure everything was lashed down. Then he keyed his intercom. "Load to pilot—all set back here."

"Tower, this is Air Evac 1492," the pilot said evenly. "Request clearance to depart. I would like to pause on the end of the runway to run up the engines, and then execute a high speed tactical military take off for training purposes."

The engineer looked at the pilot with a question on his face and mouthed "high speed tactical military take off?"

The pilot glanced at the engineer and shrugged his shoulders. "I just made it up," he mouthed back.

Continuing on the radio, he informed the tower, "That would include several low-level turns north of the airport, and a low-level circle of the field to the west, with climbing pass over the runway before departure on heading 010 for Garden City."

The tower was a little slow to respond. Finally a somewhat skeptical voice said, "Ooo-kay Air Evac. You are cleared to turn on to the runway and depart. We have no one in the pattern, no one in contact, no commercial flights scheduled for arrival for another 30 minutes, and I don't see anything moving on the FedEx ramp."

"Roger, sir," answered the pilot.

"Okay," he said on the intercom. "Let's rock 'n' roll."

Lifting his right hand from the throttles, he jerked down one more time on the straps holding his body against the seat. First the left, then the right. He was no longer attached to the aircraft. He was part of it. Lifting his foot off the brakes, the pilot wheeled the ungainly gray elephant-with-wings in a 180 degree circle, ending up stationary on the white lines that marked the end of the runway, with the nose wheel directly on the centerline. Then he stopped.

With his hand spanning all four throttle levers, he advanced them forward until they reached the end of their range. The engines responded rapidly—more quickly than a jet—until the propellers disappeared in an invisible whirl. The hot exhaust whipped the grass behind them. The whole plane trembled and groaned for release. In the back the passengers looked at each other. The more experienced ones pulled their seat belts even tighter.

"Hot damn," said the ranger, Major Pike.

"Hot damn," replied the male flight nurse, Lieutenant Beauchamp. The chaplain smiled at them both.

And then—when it seemed the brakes could not resist the pull of the frantic engines any longer . . . the pilot lifted his feet from the brake pedals and the plane lunged forward.

It was not like being slung from a catapult in a fighter jet. It was more like accelerating up a highway ramp in a sixty-ton truck to join traffic at highway speed. But that acceleration was quite different from the take off in most passenger and cargo flights, and several passengers leaned forward in response. Sitting as they were in sling seats against the wall of the aircraft, and thus without a way to brace themselves, those who did not lean sideways and forward found themselves tilting sideways and backward as the plane picked up speed. Anyone looking through the few small windows on the side wall noted runway markers whizzing past.

A standard passenger jet take off requires a runway roll of about thirty-five seconds. An Air Force cargo plane is a little quicker. But barely ten seconds after releasing the brake—just over one thousand feet down the runway—the pilot noted ninety knots of airspeed and pulled back on the yoke. The nose rose off the ground, followed by the four huge wheels under the center of the plane. First looking at his artificial horizon, then glancing out his side window, the pilot pulled back harder on the yoke and said, "Two positive indicators of climb—gear up! Flaps up!"

"Gear up!" responded the copilot, making the appropriate adjustments.

"Flaps up!"

A high pitched whining sound marked the action of servo motors, followed by a thump as the wheels nestled into the belly and the outside doors locked shut. With wheels and flaps retracted, the air flow around the aircraft was no longer disrupted. Shed of that drag, the plane surged forward and continued to climb. The navigator was standing now, behind the engineer, holding tight to his handles, scanning intently through the forward windscreen. In the back, the loadmaster began counting slowly to himself. "One–one thousand, two–one thousand. . . . "

Five thousand feet later, Air Evac 1492 crossed the far end of the runway at 100 feet and 130 knots. Three thousand feet after that, it crossed the fence at 500 feet and 190 knots. In the cold heavy air it was climbing even faster than the pilot had expected. The seconds ticked slowly. Nose up, the plane clawed for the sky. In the back, the passengers, sitting in sling seats along the sides of the aircraft and facing inward, struggled to right themselves and lean forward. They were smiling. It was an exertion no one seemed to mind.

Everyone up front was expecting the call, but it still came as a jarring surprise.

"Flares! Flares! Flares!" cried the loadmaster from the back. "SAM, four o'clock!"

"Flares!" simulated the navigator. "Armed! Fire!"

Riding with his hand on the throttles, the pilot pulled them rapidly to the rear. He pushed the right rudder pedal with his foot, and turned the yoke hard to the right. The engine noise quieted to a hush. The right wing dipped and the left went up. The nose dropped hard to the right and rushed toward the ground.

"Flares! Flares! Flares!" cried the loadmaster from the back. "SAM! Two SAMs! Four o'clock!"

It was cold and dark, and the lights of Balad Air Base shone brightly out the open rear cargo door as the C-130 clawed for altitude in the Iraqi sky. Combat lighting painted everything inside the cargo compartment in red light or black shadow. The loadmaster stood at the end of the cargo bay, tethered to a ring in the floor by a harness and strap. He held tightly to the edge of the opening where the door would fit when closed, and watched two balls of fire leave the ground and begin to curve up toward his position. They left a dull gray trail of smoke reflected by the moon.

"Flares!" responded the navigator. Picking up a gray, rectangular box linked by a spiral cable to a connector overhead, he manipulated a switch at the top.

"Armed!" he declared. He pressed the switch below.

"Fire!"

More than a dozen brilliant balls of fire were ejected from under the nose. They curved apart, seemed to hang in the air for just a moment, then plummeted straight down.

Others leapt rapidly to the left and right from under the wings, spreading apart and many yards away from the aircraft before curving downward and racing rapidly toward the earth. Behind them, parabolic trails of smoke marked their plunge.

Although all the flares looked the same to the human eye, they were made from different chemical mixes, so they burned at different temperatures and gave off different frequencies of light. This in turn had differing effects on different sensors that might be carried in the nose of the missiles streaking toward the hot engine exhaust.

The exact composition and combination of these chemical compounds was a closely guarded secret. But the technique was a very public success. And once again tonight, the combination of distracting flares and maneuvering aircraft defeated the deadly seekers streaking toward the crew. One missile chased a flare straight down and right; the other chased a different fireball in a long curve to the left. Neither followed the aircraft as it began a tight turn that minimized its heat signature.

Riding with his right hand on the throttles, the pilot pulled them rapidly to the rear. He pushed the right rudder pedal with his foot, and turned the yoke hard to the right. The engine noise quieted to a hush. The right wing dipped sharply and the left wing went up. The nose pointed hard to the right and toward the ground. The whole aircraft dropped sideways with a sickening rush.

Turning in a tight arc, the pilot felt his lift decrease and saw the speed rise on the indicator to his front. The aircraft was in a hard bank. In response to the drop, forces pulled the pilot slightly upward in his seat. He wished he had pulled the straps tighter before takeoff. Ten seconds and 200 vertical feet later, the navigator, standing over the engineer's shoulder, sang out in an excited voice: "Rockets off the nose, ten o'clock!"

Damn! Ambush! Most of the ground fire the pilot had received in Iraq was uncoordinated and from a single source. But sometimes a couple of clever boys coordinated their fires. If they missed with their first shot, then they would anticipate where the pilot would be when he took evasive maneuvers, and position additional attackers there, to get a second or third shot. The maneuvers were tricky business—high speed, low altitude, and in the dark. The pilot wished he had more practice at this—it was all about judgment and timing.

Transferring pressure to his left foot on the left rudder pedal, he also turned the yoke hard to the left. The maneuver would cost precious speed and altitude. An experienced pilot could recover both by adding power. But this pilot was a little slow. Too late, he advanced the throttles all the way forward with his right hand, and the engines responded with a roar. The blades changed angle automatically to bite more air. But it took time. And the rockets were in a hurry.

"Holy crap!" cried the navigator. The rockets had no engines and did not show a fireball or leave a trail of smoke like a missile. But the tails were hot, and they glowed bright green in the night vision goggles the crew was wearing. If the pilot had been quicker on the throttles, they could have climbed higher and traveled faster. In a game where every bit of speed and altitude mattered, the pilot had been late. He won, but just barely. The rockets passed close underneath, and fell away below.

The pilot stayed in a tight turn to the left.

The whole aircraft dropped sideways with a sickening rush and picked up speed. Turning in a tight arc to the right, the pilot felt his lift decrease and saw the speed increase on the indicator to his front. The plane was in a sixty degree bank. Straps were pulling bodies down, forward, and to the right with the aircraft while inertia pulled them hard in the other direction. Ten seconds and 200 vertical feet later the pilot said matter-of-factly, "Rockets off the nose, ten o'clock!"

Transferring pressure to his left foot on the left rudder pedal, he also turned the yoke back hard to the left, and simultaneously advanced the throttles all the way forward with his right hand. Unlike jet engines, the massive turbo props required no time to spool up. The reliable old Allison engines responded with a roar, and the blades changed angle automatically to bite more air. The plane jumped forward. The engineer grunted in appreciation.

In the back, each passenger dealt with the quickly changing g-forces of the rollercoaster ride in his own way. Those with a missing arm held on more tightly with their legs. Those with a missing leg held on more tightly with their arms. Those with all appendages reached over and grabbed a brother or sister by the sleeve. The nurse watched warily, ready to call a halt on the intercom at the slightest indication of a problem. But with everybody belted in tightly, there was no hint of an issue. Some faces were smiling. Some were more focused and intense. But no one showed any sign of distress.

Except for the reporter. Her eyes were wide.

Pressed against his seat by the straps and the speed and force of the turn, the pilot looked down and left through the side windows of the cockpit just in time to see a blacked out Apache helicopter flash by under his nose.

"Tower, Hatchet 36 declaring self-defense ROE in effect. Engaging just off the northwest corner of the runway." The voice was cool and professional—not a hint of excitement.

A pencil-thin line of fire reached out from the Apache's nose. It was actually tracer rounds from the cannon, flying so fast that they looked like a solid stream of red-orange vengeance. The line broke once, then emerged as another stream seconds later.

But what was a single stream to the eye above arrived at the target as scores of explosive warheads. A dark figure had dropped his rocket tube the instant his explosive took flight, and dashed to a pickup truck waiting by the edge of the road. He jumped in and pulled the door closed as the truck roared away. But it had traveled only a few feet before explosions smacked the dust and pavement like ferocious hail all around. Then the shells found the truck, penetrating and exploding in the engine, passenger compartment, and fuel tank at almost the same instant. Pieces flew off the engine block, and the rocketeer's head flew off his body. The dashboard disappeared along with everything above the driver's waist. The truck veered momentarily to the side, then overturned and exploded in a single motion. A huge fireball blossomed. What was left behind burned fiercely.

Just behind that, a second truck never even got into motion before it was enveloped by the hail of fire.

Still turning left but now looking up and through his upper windows, the pilot saw a second helicopter further back from the first. It was stationary and oriented back toward the origin of the initial surface-to-air missiles. At the very instant he looked, a Hellfire missile ignited with a flash, dropped from its rail, and accelerated so rapidly that it pulled ten times the force of gravity. Weighing 107 pounds, it scrambled across the ground like a wasp on fire, homing in on the reflection of a laser beam fired by the same gunner who had released it. Passing under the plane, the missile chased the reflection to a stack of concrete blocks that marked the remains of a house. Behind the wall crouched two men. They remained still and quiet in their hiding place in the dark. But it didn't matter.

The missile was traveling 950 miles an hour when its eighteen-pound high-explosive warhead penetrated the pile of blocks and exploded with a roar. Four sandals flew in different directions. Not much identifiable was left besides the shoes.

"Good God!" said the loadmaster from his perch at the tailgate of the retreating C-130. Then more quietly and with reverence: "Good God."

With the throttles all the way forward, the pilot leveled out his wings and held his heading, then dropped closer to the dark earth. At barely a hundred feet off the ground he skimmed over buildings, huts, cars and trash until he was well outside the flight path of any approaching aircraft. Then he spoke briefly with the tower before easing back on the power, turning back to his original heading, and climbing at a reduced rate into the night sky.

Five friendlies endangered, six enemy killed, smoldering bodies and implements of war left behind. "Just another night at the office," thought the pilot. He felt he had done well, but not well enough. "There must be a better way to learn this stuff," he said to himself.

Still turning left but now looking up and through his top windows, the pilot saw cattle flash by, then a pickup truck on a dirt road, then a farmhouse.

"One hundred eighty knots," the engineer said. "Knock it off."

The co-pilot was impressed. They didn't teach this sort of thing in flight school.

With the wings at an angle and in a turn they were losing lift. The plane wanted to drop toward the earth. To keep it from doing so the pilot was pulling back slightly on the yoke. Physics demanded that something had to give, and it was speed. Even with the throttles forward, the plane was losing speed as it tried to turn sharply without losing altitude.

"Knock it off," echoed the pilot. He dropped the right wing sharply, flattening out at about 250 feet above the ground. He dropped the nose slightly, then pulled back a bit at 200 feet and dipped the wings cautiously to the left again. The effect was to increase the speed a bit immediately, then continue the increase slowly and steadily as the plane began a sweeping left turn around the airfield, with throttles wide open. At barely 200 feet off the ground, the gray monster skimmed over farmland, fences, cars, and outbuildings.

Strapped tightly to a seat inclined slightly forward, the pilot was acutely—almost supernaturally—aware of every vibration in the aircraft, of the engines humming furiously on the wings, and of the wind sliding smoothly over its skin. Even in cool weather, low-level flight entails a surprising number of bumps, thumps, and "disturbances in the Force." Every change in the surface of the earth—every road, forest, plowed field, and tree-lined creek—creates an updraft or a downdraft, either strong or weak. In hot weather they are violent, in cool weather more gentle. But even with a promise of winter in the air, they jostled the aircraft up and down in its low-level progress. That jostled the crew as well. And any cargo they were carrying. And any passengers in the back.

"*Cool*," said the loadmaster to himself, as the aircraft completed its wild gyrations, flattened out briefly, then began a series of ups and downs. The right wing was slightly inclined now and the aircraft obviously was picking up speed. He looked around the cabin, where a smiling group had broken into applause. All except for one rumpled soldier. It was the sullen troublemaker who had lost the confrontation with the ranger. He was sitting by himself and retching into an air sickness bag. The loadmaster looked at the bag in his own hand, empty and unneeded. He smiled. "Cool," he said, this time out loud. "That was great!"

"Why is everybody smiling?" asked the reporter. While she had seen everyone else getting ready, and had heard the warning about "evasive maneuvers," the violence of the roller coaster ride had taken her by surprise. Trying not to show her discomfort, she was bothered by the fact that everyone else seemed to be enjoying events immensely.

"Really," she asked of the soldier with the hook sitting beside her. "What's so funny?"

"It's not really funny," answered Tom Milton—the soldier also known as Lefty. "It just feels good to be a soldier again."

She was puzzled for a moment, but, sensing a story, replied "What do you mean?"

Lefty smiled broadly, then spoke slowly and distinctly over the roar of engines at full power. "People come into the military for lots of reasons. Most end up hating all the stupid rules and regulations—what to wear and what to eat and when to sleep. But most end up loving it when they get to be a soldier. They like doing something hard and dangerous with a good group of guys. They like cutting it close to the edge and getting away with it. Then they like talking about it later.

"They like the responsibility—the fact that other people are depending on them to do their job right—to man up when there's a problem." He paused, then pointed with his good left hand to the seats on the other wall of the cargo bay.

"You met Squeeze, right? Country boy. Shy. He was a tank gunner. Took over when his tank commander was killed. Ran the tank into a house to get the guys who shot his sergeant. Killed 'em both. Then parked the tank sideways across the street to protect a bunch of infantry guys who were pinned down. Bullet smashed his right elbow. Big piece of cement broke his left hand. Before he fainted from blood loss he broke a tooth trying to open a can of machine gun ammo with his teeth. How old is he? Twenty maybe?"

The reporter thought briefly about her twenty-four-year-old cousin, who spent four years at three different junior colleges, and now played video games all day while living with his folks. She looked around the plane at the faces of the wounded going home, struck for the first time by how young most of them were. And how in control they were, even when their bodies were not whole. Mature beyond their years. How had she missed that before?

Tom Milton was still talking. "Being wounded takes all that responsibility away from you. You go from being a soldier to being a kid again, doing what you're told while the adults run your life."

He was straining to be heard over the roar. He paused.

"Everybody wants to get back to doing something that was hard and exciting and made sense—something rewarding. And everybody here knows that they might never get another chance. Some just kind of sense it. Others know it for sure. For the rest of their lives, they will never again do anything this important or exciting. Some will spend the next forty years trying to regain the feeling—talking about how it was back when their lives mattered. And now here we are again, acting like soldiers. It's like another turn at bat."

His voice was hoarse and he was done. He sat back. The plane jerked straight up ten feet, then dropped straight down again. Then it banked hard to the left.

Taylor Webster widened her eyes and grabbed a strap. Tom Milton leaned back, closed his eyes and smiled.

The plane was in a hard left bank now, still holding at 200 feet and lining up on the runway. But it was not going to land. With wings level and engines running full out, it accelerated quickly, and when it crossed the south end of the runway it was doing nearly 250 miles an hour across the ground.

As they crossed the white stripes at the end of the runway, the pilot pulled back quickly on the yoke and the nose pointed sharply up. With a clean airframe and no maneuvers to bleed off lift and speed, the plane began to climb hard and fast. By the time it crossed midfield it was at nearly 1,500 feet and headed up. By the end of the runway it was at 2,500. Inside the cargo compartment, the passengers had their hands raised like they were going up a roller coaster in an amusement park.

The nurse looked around. The mood was different. Nobody was thinking about the doctor being carried off the plane.

"Pretty cool, Air Evac," said the tower. "Haven't seen anything like that around here before. Please change to Ft. Worth Center at 1–0 thousand and request higher altitude."

"Roger, sir," responded the pilot. "Thanks for your help during our emergency. Good day."

The pilot switched to intercom. "Could you do that?" he asked the copilot. "Could you jink on take-off like that?"

"I'll give it a try," she said.

His head snapped to the right, and he looked at her hard without speaking.

She turned her head just slightly and looked at him out of the corner of her eye. "Yes, of course," she corrected. "I'm sure I could."

"Good," he responded, turning to look forward and left through the windscreen. "Because next week you will."

At 10,000 feet the plane reduced its speed and rate of climb and turned on to heading zero-one-zero toward Garden City. In the forward compartment, the crew busied themselves with their duties. In the back, a dozen recovering veterans dropped their arms and became mortal once again. Unseen on the instrument panel, the pointer on the rpm gauge for the Number 1 engine flicked twice into the red range, then returned to normal. The plane and its cargo of former superheroes grew smaller and smaller as it retreated toward Kansas and home.

"So Lefty, if you have a college degree in literature, what are you doing in the Army as an enlisted man?" It was the reporter speaking to the soldier with the hook. The engines were quieter now, and it was easier to converse.

"I already told you 'no story,'" He replied. "There are lots of guys here hurt worse than me. Talk to them."

He was quiet for a minute.

"Traffic accident," he said. He turned slightly to watch her expression. "I lost my arm in a traffic accident in Iraq. We were in a cloud of heavy dust and my convoy got crossed with a convoy of armored vehicles. A Stryker t-boned me at an intersection. I never saw him. He never saw me. I don't even know exactly what happened. Somebody pulled me out, and I woke up in a hospital missing my right arm. That's the whole story. Not very romantic."

"I didn't ask," she said quietly. She didn't avoid his eyes.

"Yes you did," he responded. "Everybody asks. Sometimes with their lips. Sometimes with their eyes. It's okay. It's the first thing everybody wants to know. 'How'd you get the hook?'"

He paused again. Then he smiled. "So now you know. No mystery about me."

"Okay," she said, and put away her notebook. She also put away her professional "talk to me" smile, and leaned back as if talking to a friend.

"I really didn't think it would be this hard to find a story in a plane full of people with stories."

"Sometimes life plays tricks," he said. "You might find a story here yet. Just don't quit."

"So is that your big 'lesson learned?' Just don't quit?"

He thought for minute. "Well . . . actually, yes . . . I guess so. But it's not any big personal revelation. Look around you. That's what everybody here learned. Bad things happen. Don't quit."

She was quiet again, then crossed her arms. "So really," she asked. "How did a guy with a name like Milton and a degree in literature end up as a truck driver in the Army?"

"Mechanic," he said. "I drove a wrecker, but I was a mechanic." He smiled as if enjoying a private joke. "Money from the Army Reserve helped put me through college. And I was looking for something to write about. I thought I would find it in the Army."

"Like Marion, the Marine in that World War II movie."

"Yes!" he said. "Marion Hodgkiss! The character was Marion Hodgkiss. Actually it was a book first. *Battle Cry* by Leon Uris. How did you know that?"

"I minored in literature, remember? Plus, I've spent a lot of time alone. I'm a big fan of old movies. TCM—Turner Classic Movies." But she was focused on asking questions, not answering them. "Have you done much writing before?"

"Yeah, some," he answered. "But nothing anybody would ever read—except my mother."

He was in the eighth grade and sitting at the supper table. The conversation had been excited and one-sided for ten minutes, as his

father discussed the big news of the day: his older brother had been named to the first string of the high school football team.

He served himself a second helping of corn, then put down the bowl and waited for a lull in the conversation. When his father paused to take a bite of chicken, he spoke quickly.

"I got an award at school today," he said. "At the assembly. In front of everyone."

His father was a big man, arms and shoulders broad and tanned from years of farming. He stopped chewing and looked in the boy's direction. "Really!" his father said. "For what?"

"Writing," the boy said. "For the best story in the eighth grade. I got some money, too. Fifty dollars."

"Well that's great," said the father. "Put it in the bank. You're going to need it, unless you learn to play ball and get some kind of scholarship." It wasn't a mean comment. It was just the hard truth. His father continued chewing.

"Tommy, we are so proud of you," beamed his mother. She was a small woman, direct and energetic, but with a soft smile. Some farm women became dry and bitter after years of hard work. Some became kind and generous. She was the second kind, directive toward her children but in an encouraging sort of way. She valued reading and writing almost as much as she valued religion. And she valued that a lot.

"You bet," said his father quickly. "Very important."

Turning back to the older brother, he asked, "So, is coach moving you to a new position?"

The younger boy looked down at his plate and set down his fork. He wasn't hungry anymore.

"So did you find it?" the reporter asked.

"Find what?"

"Find something to write about?" It was a friendly question, not an interview.

He considered for a moment, then said, "Well . . . yes I did. Balance. Balance and resilience. How do people come back from something bad in their lives? How do they get back on center, back to normal?"

The reporter looked startled for a moment, then smiled and shook her head. "Glad to hear you are going to start small!" she said.

"You think that's funny?" he asked defensively

"No!" Now she was the one on the defensive. "Not at all. I just don't meet many truck drivers who want to write about balance and personal resilience."

"Wrecker."

"What?"

"Wrecker driver. I was a wrecker driver. Hemingway drove an ambulance. Why couldn't I drive a wrecker? It's actually better preparation for a writer."

"Really?" she asked skeptically.

"He just dealt with pain and loss. I was a mechanic. I found hidden problems. And I didn't just look at them or analyze them. I fixed them. Good writing can do that. It can highlight problems so you can fix them and make the world a better place."

She was impressed. He seemed unusually self-aware. Self-confident. For a . . . mechanic.

"So how will what you write help people redeem themselves?"

"Oh, I can't redeem people. I want to be Johnson, not Jesus."

"Why not Joyce?" she retorted. She was up for the game.

"Oh please!" he sighed. "Joyce is too tired, clichéd, worn-out. And I don't have 17 years to read his books."

"*Finnegans Wake*," she said. "It took 17 years to write, not read. But clichéd and worn-out is the way he described the world, so I think he would take that as a compliment. And I can see where Samuel Johnson might have said the same thing."

"Everybody's a critic," he said, then paused. "Get it? Samuel Johnson? Literary critic? That's like a triple word score. But you guessed 150 years too late. I was admiring Ben Johnson, not Samuel Johnson. One of the real classics. The father of the Cavalier poets. Understood people and the fact that life goes on."

He grew expansive. "Drink to me only with thine eyes, And I will pledge with mine."

"Or leave a kiss but in the cup," she smiled, "And I'll not look for wine.'"

Suddenly, he was looking deep in her eyes. Not challenging. Not hostile. Not mocking. Searching. Looking for something. . . .

She broke off the gaze. "So you think he wrote Shakespeare's stuff?" she asked.

"Anarchist!" he cried. "Enemy of civilization! Take it back!"

She laughed. He didn't. She furrowed her brow. "Really?" she asked.

"People like you are always trying to create some emotional tale for their own benefit. I think the truth is usually simpler than that. Shakespeare worked hard, that's all. "

"People like me?"

"Romantics. Wordsworth. Coleridge. Shelley. Keats. And when the world lets them down, Romantics become cynics. Eliot. Beckett. Woolf. Thomas."

"Dylan Thomas was a cynic?" she asked.

"I take it back. Dylan Thomas wasn't a cynic. He was just a drunk."

"So you dismiss the last 200 years of English literature."

"I like the Victorians. They had discipline. Structure. Tennyson. Browning. Rossetti."

"Gabriel?" she asked.

"Christina," he answered. "'Goblin Market.'"

"My God, it's obscene!" she said.

He smiled and lifted his eyebrows twice. "You think?" he replied.

"What about American authors?" she queried.

"Edward Arlington Robinson was the last American poet I really like. Died 1935."

"Really?" This was not a conversation she had anticipated. "You like 'Richard Cory'?"

"Piff," he responded. "High school. 'Mr. Flood's Party'—now there's rhyme, reason, structure, narrative, and pathos all together. The newer poets are all emotion. No structure. Free verse. Playing tennis without a net," he replied.

"Robert Frost," she observed. "Frost said that. So you drive wreckers by day and read poetry by night?"

"I've had the last couple of months to brush up," he replied. "'Stone walls do not a prison make, nor iron arms a cage.'"

"Richard Lovelace." She was on this one. "Cavalier poet—English Civil War. And it was 'iron bars.' 'Iron bars do not a prison make.' Not 'iron arms.'"

"Well," he replied. "Lovelace had his war, and I had mine." He lifted his metal arm and snapped his hook twice.

They were both quiet for a while, and she took stock. She was actually having a good time. It was completely unexpected.

But something was troubling her. "So," she said. "You've already decided I'm an out of touch romantic tale teller?"

"I don't mean to be offensive," he said. "But I hear your questions. I see what you are trying to do. You're trying to make up a story, and then fit people into it.

"You need to listen to the people first—understand them—have some sympathy with them—then you can figure out the story. Or maybe you'll figure out there isn't really any story at all. It's just people trying to get through. Isn't that interesting enough? Isn't that inspiring enough? Just people getting back up when they've been knocked down. Just people regaining their balance. Isn't that a good enough story? Does everything you write have to have a crescendo? Some phony cosmic point?"

He was on a roll now. Not hot. Not angry. Just philosophical and a little sad.

"That's what the great authors do—the really great journalists. They tell us about the people and let the people tell us the story. You want to be a great journalist? Let *them* talk. Build some trust. Then don't abuse it, and your readers will trust you, too. It's all about trust."

She was taken aback. He had worked all this out in his head, while lying in a hospital bed for three months. It took a moment to gather her thoughts.

"So this is what you do as a mechanic? Gain their trust and they bring their problems to you?" She meant it as a push back against his assessment. He didn't take it that way.

"Exactly!" he said. "Do you go to a mechanic who starts by writing up the bill and then listens to the problem? Every engine has a story. Listen to it before you try to take it apart. Work first. Learn something. Then you can write."

"Work before you write. Sounds like you heard that from somebody."

"Yeah," he sighed. "More than once. From my dad. He's an expert in work. Not so much in writing."

He paused.

"Did you ever read *Don Quixote*?" he asked. "Did you know that Cervantes—the author—lost his hand in battle? Gives you a whole different perspective on the idealistic old knight. He wasn't crazy. He understood loss. And nobility in the face of loss.

"Do you know what Cervantes said about his hand?" Milton lifted his hook again. "He said 'My wounds may not be beautiful, but they are honorable.' Now *there's* a story to tell. No embellishment. Just the truth."

With the hook on the end of his right arm, he lifted the flap on his breast pocket and extracted a pair of glasses. With his left hand he unfolded them, then reached back and extracted a handkerchief. Using the hook, he raised the lenses to his mouth and fogged each with his breath. He held the glasses with the hook and with his good left hand wiped each moist lens with the handkerchief, then lifted the spectacles to his eyes and returned the handkerchief to his pocket.

"Actually, I only need them for distance," he said.

Two seats down, the overeager corporal with the award clipped to his chest sat straight up in his seat, mouth agape.

Turning in the sling seat, Tom Milton looked out the small, porthole-shaped window to his left and was quiet. Then he lifted both the hook and his good hand to the glasses, and replaced them in the pocket.

"Looks like we are almost back in Kansas, Dorothy," he said quietly.

"Frank Baum," the reporter said. "*Wizard of Oz*. So have we established enough trust for you to tell me your story?" she asked.

"You don't want a story that you can tell. You want a tale that you can spin. And I don't have one of those.

"Ah! What avails the classic bent
And what the cultured word,
Against the undoctored incident
That actually occurred?"

Leaning back he crossed his arms and closed his eyes.

"*Undoctored incident that actually occurred,*" she said to herself. "I bet that's Rudyard Kipling. And I bet I get your story yet."

CHAPTER 8

COMFORT AND JOY

1700 hours 23 December: En Route Garden City, Kansas

She sat for a moment wondering how to respond. Then she took a deep breath and looked around. The loud corporal, the one so eager to talk, caught her eye. He motioned her over with his finger. As she slid in next to him with her interview smile, he leaned over and whispered, "Did that guy tell you what he does in the Army?"

"He's a mechanic," she answered. "He drives a wrecker."

The blood drained from the soldier's face and he leaned back in his seat. The was no sign of his boisterous behavior now. He sat still for a long moment, then turned to face her.

"I didn't recognize him until he put those glasses on," he said.

"Can I trust you? Can I tell you a story?" He went on. "No notes. Nothing in writing. I just have to share this with someone I can trust." His look was urgent. There was no bluster in his voice now.

"I'm going to be honest with you. The story I told you before was a lie. But you can't write this up. I could get in trouble. You gotta promise. You gotta promise!"

"Ok," she said warily. "I promise I won't write it up."

The wrecker slid to a stop on the shoulder of the hard top road, spewing gravel and a cloud of dust. Rifle shots immediately panged against the door, the fender, and the steel boom in back. With his right hand, the driver grabbed the rifle wedged upright in the seat next to him. With his left he rotated the door handle, opened it, then crashed through the opening. His left foot touched the high step only for a moment, before he collapsed to the ground. Two bullets cracked overhead and one broke a headlight. The driver rolled underneath the truck, and more bullets struck the pavement before and behind.

The highway was a divided four lane. To his left front a section of the guard rail was blown out, where the IED had been hidden. To his right front, off the road and partly in a ditch, lay what was left of a Humvee, rolled on its side and burning with a hot orange flame. The huge explosion had killed the driver instantly, and cut the gunner, riding exposed in the top turret, in half. The patrol leader had been mortally wounded by the explosion, then crushed when the vehicle was hit by a rocket and rolled on to him in the ditch. The bodies were trapped in the burning wreckage.

Behind the wrecker sat a second Humvee crosswise on the main route. All four tires were flat, and the doors, fenders, and hood were thoroughly ventilated by multiple holes from rifle and machine gun fire. There appeared to be someone lying still at the bottom of the gun turret in the back seat. The passenger side door was open. The driver lay sprawled in the road, sheltered behind the vehicle and moving one arm feebly.

The passenger was huddled in the ditch below, unharmed but curled tightly in a ball. His M-4 assault rifle lay some distance away, while he used both hands to pull his knees tightly to his chest.

Even from under the wrecker, the newly arrived driver could size up the situation immediately. Usually IEDs were left unattended.

But in this case, a team had stayed to ensure perfect timing for the detonation. And additional attackers—he counted fire from at least three positions—were waiting around to ambush a light relief force if one arrived. If heavier vehicles responded, they would fade away into nearby buildings and mix with the populace.

The one unwounded member of the patrol could have called for a heavy relief force, but only if he left the safety of the ditch and returned to use the radio in the Humvee on the road. Head down and curled up in the ditch, he did not seem inclined to do so. Meanwhile, the radio in the wrecker had lost its "fill" earlier in the day—gone was the daily electronic code that allowed secure frequency hopping radios to stay linked with each other for communication. It was a routine electrical problem—usually an inconvenience; now perhaps a fatal malfunction. So the only way to call for help was to run smack into the kill zone around the remaining Humvee. That would be suicide. They would have to fight it out.

Firing at the wrecker had ceased while the enemy evaluated the situation. The driver realized that they were probably not sure exactly where he was located. Carefully, he crawled forward in the dust under the truck until his body was completely obscured by the right front tire. Removing his helmet, he peeked around the tire and saw three heads sticking over a pile of rubble barely thirty yards away. They were looking for him and the missing passenger from the second Humvee. He looked down in the ditch, caught the eye of the other soldier, and gave a quick nod. The soldier in the ditch made no motion in reply.

As a mechanic, the driver was armed with a standard M-16A3 rifle—much improved since the Vietnam War edition, but still a descendant of that ancestor with a solid plastic stock and a long twenty-one-inch barrel. That length would make it difficult to maneuver while under the wrecker. He worried about exposing himself when he fired, but fortunately a cloud of thick smoke from the burning Humvee drifted between him and the nearest enemy position. He rested the bottom of the thirty-round magazine on the ground, and lifted his head higher to compensate for the uncomfortable height of the rifle. The bottom of the magazine provided a stable platform as he tried to get off three aimed shots at the three residents of the close-in position.

With his right thumb he rotated the safety lever down until it clicked. Then he pointed the weapon through the smoke, centered his eye on the peephole of the rear sight, aligned it with the front sight post, and waited. The smoke thinned, then cleared. He aligned the sights with a body in the enemy position. A man in jeans and a faded blue shirt rose in a crouch to see over the wreckage. The driver pulled the trigger.

TAT! ... TAT!

The M-16 always sounded so light and unrewarding compared to the heavy bark of an AK-47. But when the larger 7.62 millimeter bullet from the enemy weapon entered a body, it passed right through. In contrast, the M-16 bullet was specifically designed to "fishtail" and tumble once it penetrated a target. As a result, the small .223 caliber round made an unimpressive sound when it was fired, but had a devastating effect on the target.

And the first two rounds did indeed reach their targets. The first struck one attacker squarely on the chest bone just below the thorax, exploding the ribs and the lungs. The second caught another attacker in the throat, severing the carotids that ran there. Both men fell back dying.

But instead of the sharp report the driver expected to hear when he pulled the trigger a third time, he heard nothing. The trigger was stuck—jammed by the ever-present dust, the round refused to seat properly in the chamber. Again, fortune, or God, smiled on him. The smoke from the wreck and the muffling effect of his position under the truck confused the enemy about his location.

From deep in the ditch, the surviving patrol member saw the driver pull the charging handle to clear the weapon, attempt to force the bolt forward, and then try to fire again. Still no luck. Then, to the astonishment of the terrified combat soldier, the wrecker driver began to dissemble his weapon to clean it.

There under the wrecker, the driver depressed a lock on the side of the rifle with his right thumb and extracted the thirty-round magazine. Pulling the charging handle to the rear, he ejected a round from the chamber, then used the tip of the bullet to depress a pin holding the rifle together. The pin slid to the right, and the rifle split apart top from bottom. Inverting the rifle, he pulled the charging handle to the rear, and turned the rifle over so the bolt package would fall into his hand. He fumbled for a moment with the small folded metal clip that held the firing pin in place, and then shook the pin into his hand.

Wild shots were splattering the area now, as the enemy sought to make him reveal his location. Holding the firing pin firmly, he used it to reach inside the bolt and scratched with a circular motion. Inverting the bolt, he shook a pile of black carbon into his hand. Reaching down to the cargo pocket on his right trouser leg, he extracted a broken toothbrush wrapped in a rag, and a green plastic bottle of lubricant.

Firing was picking up now. Bullets were coming with greater frequency—and striking closer to the driver's hidden position. It was a recon by fire.

After thoroughly cleaning the bolt and the chamber that holds each bullet before it is fired, and lubricating everything, the driver deftly reassembled the rifle, inserted the magazine, and slapped the rifle on the side. The bolt snicked forward and locked a round in place. The driver slid off to the side of the tire once again, and once again drew a bead on the third member of the close-in ambush team. A single shot dispatched him, striking the target just above the left eye.

The enemy fell backward, and in that instant, the driver rolled out from under the wrecker and down into the ditch next to the cowering member of the patrol team.

"Did you get a radio call off before you slid down here?" the driver asked. The patrol member shook his head no.

"Okay—we'll do this ourselves," the driver responded. "Can you cover me while I get the grenades off that guy on the road up there?"

The patrol member waited a long time, but finally nodded his head yes, and picked up his rifle.

"I'm going on three," said the wrecker driver. "One, two . . . "

On three he was up and running toward the soldier lying in the road. And to his surprise, the corporal in the ditch raised his rifle above his head and actually discharged twenty shots on a flat enough trajectory to keep all the enemy heads down. The driver was back before the twentieth shot, carrying four fragmentation grenades and two white smoke grenades.

"Jackpot," he said. "Can you throw grenades?"

The patrol member, a corporal according to the rank on his shirt, shook his head yes.

"Okay," the wrecker driver said. "I'm going to throw these two smoke grenades out there. Try to block the view between where we are and where they are. Did you see them? Behind that little rise of dirt off at one o'clock, about thirty yards from here. We'll let the smoke build up, get the frag grenades ready, and when you see me throw, you throw. We'll wait for four explosions, then run through the smoke and try to come out the other side and shoot whoever is left before they can recover. Can you do that?"

"I don't know," the corporal replied.

"Do your best," the wrecker driver said.

Turning to sit with his back against the berm with grenades in his lap, he picked up one gray-green cylindrical smoke grenade in each hand. Holding the spoon of each grenade down with the respective thumb, he reached across and pulled the circular safety pin with the opposite index finger. One . . . two . . . then still down in the depression and with his back as square as possible to the enemy position, he heaved both grenades backward in a high arc. It was an unorthodox throw, but it worked. The grenades sputtered to life, and rolling smoke soon obscured their position from enemy observation.

Turning to face forward toward the enemy, the driver handed the *patrol member two round fragmentation grenades, and they began snapping off the wire thumb safeties and preparing them for use.*

"*Ready?*" *the driver asked.* "*One, two. . . .* "

On three, both men pulled the pins and hurled their grenades as far as they could through the wall of smoke. Immediately, each picked up a second grenade, pulled, and heaved again. Then they dropped prone in the bottom of the ditch.

Two separate explosions rocked them almost immediately, followed by two more seconds later. The driver sprang to his feet. He snapped the selector lever of his rifle through two clicks to the "auto" position so it would fire three rounds each time the trigger was pulled. Then he dashed over the top of the berm and through the smoke. An eternity later the patrol member in the ditch heard four loud reports from one or more AK-47s, at almost the same time as three three-round bursts from an M-16.

TAT, TAT, TAT!

TAT, TAT, TAT!

TAT, TAT, TAT!

It seemed to take forever for the smoke to clear, but when it did, the driver was lying on the ground on the friendly side of the enemy position. Two enemy dead were visible, and the driver's demeanor clearly indicated that any other threats in the position had been eliminated.

He waived to get the corporal's attention, then pointed back to a third pile of rubble a long seventy-five yards or more away.

With his right hand he lifted the flap on an ammo pouch on his belt, and extracted his glasses. With his left hand he unfolded them, then reached back to the pouch and pulled out a handkerchief. He raised the lenses to his mouth and fogged each with his breath. He held the glasses with his right hand while wiping each moist lens with the handkerchief, then lifted the spectacles to his eyes and returned the handkerchief to his pouch.

He flipped the rear sight to provide a smaller circle for a finer sight picture and a distance shot. Now that he was in the second enemy position, he had a flanking perspective on the third. The driver squeezed off a very careful single shot, and a hundred yards away an attacker threw his hands in the air and tumbled backward. A second man broke from the position and began to run. He was clearly carrying a weapon. The driver clicked the selector back to three-round burst, drew a careful bead, and pulled the trigger. The man stumbled and fell. He did not get up.

The wrecker driver looked back toward the patrol member. He was looking back up the road at nearly a dozen Humvees moving in their direction. The cavalry had arrived.

"There was a lot of confusion," the corporal said to the reporter. "Some gun trucks took the wrecker up the road to the next town to recover another Humvee. I never saw the driver again. And when this officer showed up later in the day asking how it all went down . . . well . . . I just explained it as if I were the guy that did it.

"But I wasn't. I recognized him for sure when he put his glasses on. He was *the man* that day. Can you get word to him without getting me in trouble? Can you give him this from me?"

In his outstretched hand was the bronze star he had been awarded by mistake. Or more precisely, by falsehood.

The pitch of the engines changed and the plane slowed perceptibly. Ever so slightly, it began to descend. Inside the cargo compartment, conversations ceased and everyone became quiet.

"Everybody doing okay?" It was Nurse Ames making the rounds. No one on this flight was still undergoing inpatient treatment, so the medical team remained seated. A professional eye would recognize that they were not randomly distributed, but carefully paired with the most difficult recoveries. A professional eye had in fact put them there. Wounds might be healing, but the patients still required personal care and personal attention.

This was the part of the job that she hated the most. Blood and gore, terror and pain, burns and bleeding—these she could do something about. In the heat of a crisis or the groove of a routine she could turn off the personal part of her brain, and rely on the well-trained professional. Lately she was doing this more and more. She convinced herself that this meant she was becoming better and better at her job. The concern that she was becoming less and less human in the process she pushed deep inside and tried to forget.

But once she began the descent toward landing with a load of wounded going home, the concerns crept back. She looked around the aircraft at the broken bodies. Missing hands and arms. Missing legs. Burned faces. Scared souls. She had done all she could do. She and her team, and the other teams, and the whole compassionate machine that was health care for the wounded had scrubbed and cut and mended and sewn and covered and treated and prescribed and rehabilitated until they had run out of time and techniques. They had done their very best. And now the long trip from the bewildering moment of the injury to the moment of return was almost over. Some of the wounded, she knew, would find home bewildering all over again.

Like the medical team, the wounded had made this whole trip with a goal in mind. Survive. Heal. Restore. Get up, get moving, get on with it. Don't stop, don't think, soldier. Clear the choke point. Gain ground every minute, every hour, every day. Move, move, move!

And now they had arrived at the objective. Home.

Now what?

They had been soldiers. They had carried weapons and worn body armor. They had a place, a role, a rank, a position. People took orders from them. People depended on them. What they did had significance. Their duties mattered, and so their lives mattered.

Now all that was gone.

Who were they now?

Some of them would return, regain their balance, and do well. Some would take longer. Some would never regain their balance at all. And she couldn't help. She couldn't stop it. She couldn't even slow it down.

"This is what I want to do with the rest of my life. Take guys like this and show them what they can do instead of what they can't." That's what the Army

ranger had said. Now there was a goal in life. It made her feel empty. Cheated. Incomplete.

Somewhere servos whined and the flaps extended as the plane turned on final approach. Then a rushing sound filled the compartment as doors opened in the belly, followed by a thump when the landing gear locked in place. The plane was going slower and slower. The trip was going faster and faster. Almost there. Almost home. Almost out of control.

"Everybody doing okay?" It was the chaplain finishing his own rounds and plopping down in the sling seat next to Major Pike.

"Oh yeah," said the ranger. "I'm good to go."

"Anybody meeting you?" asked the chaplain. It was a friendly, casual question. Also professional in its own way.

"My girlfriend," answered the major. "Fiancé. Ruby. Don't worry padre, I'm okay."

"What do you mean?"

"Come on," replied the major. "I do this for a living, too, you know. I recognize the old leadership turn around the foxholes when I see it. But keep it up! You're doing fine."

The chaplain's mouth turned down. "Am I that obvious?"

"Hey, you're fine!" replied the major. "You're supposed to be obvious. You're supposed to be predictable. That's part of what you do.

"Every sergeant is different. Every officer is different. And the good ones change all the time—they change with the troops to keep things balanced. When the troops are down, the leaders amp them up; when the troops are up, the leaders tone them down. But you guys . . . you gotta be the same all the time. You're like McDonalds. Anywhere a soldier goes in the world, the chaplain has to have the same menu, and it's gotta come out the same. Hot, fast, and good. Always the same.

"That's not easy," Pike concluded. "Really, my hat's off to you."

The chaplain raised an eyebrow and half-smiled. "Well, some of us do it better than others."

The major was quiet, but not for long. The ground was rushing up to meet the plane now. Not much time left to talk.

"Anybody meeting you?" he asked.

"My wife," the chaplain said. "I'm sure she will be there."

"Nobody from your church?"

"I doubt it. It's the end of a long day and just before Christmas. People are busy."

"But you were their—whatever—reverend, for a long time."

"Yeah. We have a lot of good people in our congregation. A lot of friends. But it's a small town, and we've had a substitute pastor for eight months while I trained up and deployed. Young guy. Very good, I hear. I'm sure people are looking to keep him now."

The major looked at him squarely. "I think the doc was right," he said.

"About what?" asked the chaplain.

"About giving up too easily. You told him you felt like you didn't make a difference over there. Now you tell me you think you didn't make a difference over here. You give up pretty easily."

"Don't make it so dramatic," responded the chaplain. "It's no big deal. I can still contribute. It's just that I thought I was prepared for what I would see and do over there. And I wasn't. I wasn't as much help as I thought I would be. So I'm moving on to something else that I might do better."

The plane was just off the end of the runway now. Then over the white stripes. Then the numbers.

"I'm telling you," said the ranger—the leader of men. "You're pretty good at this. Maybe you need to give it more time."

"Um . . . can you give me some time, sir?"

The chaplain paused and looked up from his work. He was pushing a squeegee across the floor. Ahead of it rolled a small tide of bloody water. He was cleaning the floor of the receiving room at the aid station—pushing the bloody residue of a medevac delivery toward the drain.

"Uh—okay son," he said tiredly. "If it's really important, sure."

"It's kind of important. But if you want, I can come back." The

soldier was a specialist, and he was holding his patrol cap in front of him, like a supplicant.

"No," said the chaplain. "We can talk now. I'm about done here." He paused. "Or we can get together after chow. I made two patrols today, and haven't eaten breakfast or lunch. Would after chow be okay?"

The specialist seemed to shrink a bit. His voice dropped. "Actually, sir, tomorrow would be fine. Maybe after breakfast."

"Ok," said the chaplain a bit too hastily. "Right after chow tomorrow morning." He smiled and the soldier retreated through the door to the street.

The chaplain wiped the blade off the squeegee with a paper towel and dropped it in the trash. Then he stacked the squeegee in a cleaning closet with two brooms and a mop.

As he was turning around, two orderlies ran past him pushing a gurney toward the door. A medic pushed past him carrying a bag. A fourth aid man started by in a run, but the chaplain snagged him by the arm. "What's up?" he asked. "What's going on?"

"Some specialist shot himself out in the street," the medic replied breathlessly. "Just walked right out the door here and shot himself in the head."

The chaplain released his grip, and the aid man dashed through the door. God's representative was left standing, paralyzed by shock and guilt. The chaplain closed his eyes. The doors to the emergency room slid shut with a thump.

The chaplain closed his eyes momentarily. The wheels thumped down solidly on the runway. Two soldiers clapped halfheartedly.

"Thanks," said the chaplain to the major, "but I think I know myself better than you do."

As the plane taxied toward its parking spot near the tower, Nurse Ames and her team busied themselves with a host of final duties, some medical and some administrative. Every patient was getting off here—some to rest for a few days before returning to a rehabilitation unit, some for leave before returning to a regular army unit, and some for discharge from the military. All needed their vital signs checked. All needed one last look before she released them from her care and into the care of whoever was meeting them at the airport.

Assuming that someone *was* meeting them at the airport. That was not always the case.

As usual, Nurse Ames stood at a key spot where she could see and control everything. Without the litter patients, the back of the aircraft was open and largely free of equipment. But that did not make it safe for patients from her perspective, so her head continued to swivel constantly as she tracked every person and process under her supervision. She bit her tongue as technicians transferred wheel-chair patients from seats to chairs to roll down the ramp. This was a big exception in her book. But the chaplain's words rang in her head: *"These guys are fighters. They need a fight. Give them something to fight for or against, even if it's gravity. Otherwise, they'll just fight against you."*

The engines were stopped now. The passengers were crowding by the back of the compartment, waiting for the ramp to start down.

"You know," said Major Pike. "Maybe you got it backward."

His chair was positioned next to the chaplain, who turned and looked down. The major continued to look forward—he was not going to look up.

"You were disappointed that what you did *here* didn't prepare you for what you did *there*. But maybe what you did *there* is supposed to prepare you for what you are going to do *here* from now on out."

He spoke the words and rolled away, seeking the best avenue out once the ramp was lowered. The chaplain was left standing by himself ... thinking.

Lefty was left sitting alone in the sling seats. Taylor stepped over and sat down next to him. The reporter and the mechanic watched the others crowd toward the ramp. Neither seemed in a hurry to leave.

"Did he give you another story?" he asked.

"Uh-huh," she replied. "Do you know what it was?"

"I can guess," he said without looking at her. "Are you going to use it?"

"Great story!" she said. She was looking at his face. "He signed a release earlier."

He was still looking away. "Who's it gonna help? That story. If you tell it. Will it help him? These other wounded guys here? The nation, who thinks they are all heroes because most of them are? Besides you, who's it going to help?"

"How about you?" she asked.

"I don't need the help," he said. He still wasn't looking at her. "I know who I am. I don't need an award. Or a promotion." Now he turned to look her full in the face.

"How about you?"

The question hung in the air.

"Will telling that story help you?"

"Yeah, how about me?" she asked sharply. "You never asked where I'm from or how I got here. You never asked how you could help. For all your talk about listening to people and letting them tell you the truth, you never asked me anything about myself. You just gave me a lecture on literature and refused to help me get the story I need.

"Well, I'm not from anywhere," she continued. "Because we moved a lot." She was looking him squarely in the eye.

"I never knew my father. I ran away when I was 15 because all the "uncles" my mother was bringing home started taking an interest in me. And she let 'em, so they would still be interested in her.

"I lived with a friend and her family until I graduated from high school. And I worked hard and got into college. But I didn't have a scholarship from the Army Reserve. I worked my way through—four years—as a dancer. And I don't mean the ballet."

She was on a roll now, and she was hot and passionate—not a bit philosophical.

"And no I didn't sleep with any of the customers. Any."

"I didn't ask," he said quietly. He didn't avoid her eyes.

"Yes you did," she responded. "Everybody asks. Sometimes with their lips. Sometimes with their eyes. As soon as they find out I was a dancer, it's the first thing everybody wants to know. 'Did you sleep with the customers?' Same thing at the paper. 'You got promoted. Did you sleep with the boss?'

"So don't give me any crap. You just assumed I'm some romantic twit. I worked hard to get here, just like you. And I need that story, ok?"

She was immediately sorry for telling the truth. What was she thinking to tell this story that she had swallowed down and hidden from everyone? She steeled herself for a counter punch. She didn't get it.

"You're right," he said, softening. "I should have been asking about you, not talking about me. I just haven't had anybody to really talk to in a long time. But I won't ever make that mistake again." His manner had changed. The solder was gone. He was quiet and gentle, as if approaching a wounded bird.

She was off balance now, uncertain of what to say next.

"Just tell me one thing," he said. "Did you get back up?"

"What?"

"All those times you were knocked down. Did you get back up? Did you regain your balance? Did you get on with life? Because that's a great story if you did. It's not just romantic. It's heroic."

He didn't recoil from her. He didn't mock her. He didn't press her for details. He just looked her in the eyes and talked to her. He showed an interest in her. And in doing so, he touched her in a place she did not want to be touched.

Taylor Webster jumped to her feet, grabbed her belongings, and joined the crowd at the ramp.

The servos turned, the ramp descended, and the sound of voices filled the air.

"*Joy to the world!*" they sang. "*The Lord is come!*"

It wasn't a few voices. It wasn't a choir. It was a crowd—a big crowd.

"*Let Earth receive her King!*"

It was dark outside. There was a short space of tarmac between the aircraft and a fence that kept people away from the flight line. And beyond the fence was a sea of flashlights. And of people.

"*Let ev-rey heart, pre-pare Him room,*

"*And heaven and na-ture sing!*

"And heaven and na-ture sing!
"And heaven! and heaven and na-ture sing."

The medical technicians were everywhere. Nurse Ames' continued to move her head constantly, looking both ahead and behind. Most patients made it safely down the ramp and started across the short space of tarmac as a group. A uniformed guard appeared and opened the gate. A dozen people passed through—family members all—while the rest of the crowd stayed respectfully outside.

"Mark!" called a mother, and hurried toward "Squeeze," the soldier with the pink artificial arm making his way carefully toward the gate. A man in overalls strode quickly along behind her.

"Tony!" barked a man with a New York accent. "Lucky" looked up. His father's accent seemed strangely out of place in Kansas.

"Carl!" a woman's voice cried out. A young woman with dark hair, slim and attractive even under a winter coat, broke out of the crowd and hurried to the soldier with the burns on his face and hands. "*A dancer,*" thought Nurse Ames. "*She's a dancer.*" The girl embraced the soldier tightly.

Three sketchy characters in matching hoodies and low-hanging pants stood against the fence and waited. A sullen Private Sylvester Fox separated himself from the crowd and sauntered toward the gate with a duffle bag over his shoulder.

"Hey, dude! Where's your cane?" one of the characters called out.

Private Fox turned to look at Major Pike in his wheelchair. Pike raised a hand to his face, two fingers outstretched like a *V*. He pointed them toward his eyes, then toward Fox, then repeated it. The gesture was clear. "*I'm watching you,*" it said.

Fox turned away and passed through the gate. He joined the group and slipped off his uniform top. A friend handed him a hoodie. He put it on, and the group disappeared into the crowd, headed for the parking lot.

Taylor Webster stood waiting at the top of the ramp just inside the body of the aircraft. It was cold outside, and she had her parka on with the hood up. There was snow on the ground. Treeless Kansas prairie stretched away in every direction, except along the fence line. There several tall bushes of some sort helped to mark the boundary. Each was covered with colored Christmas lights. The reflection on the new fallen snow, and the crowd of flickering flashlights made the scene festive. And the mood of the carolers completed the effect. Almost everyone was smiling.

Across the open tarmac she saw two young women and a young man converse momentarily with the guard at the gate. They pointed to the previously boisterous corporal walking toward the fence by himself. He waved back weakly and the guard let them through. They approached him in the manner of friends: smiling, walking expansively and with arms outstretched, but without the joy of family members. He greeted them like friends, with a smile but without enthusiasm. They were all wearing ear buds, white chords extending down to their pockets. The young women danced to their own music, bobbing and weaving back toward the gate. The soldier and his male friend were more reserved. The soldier looked back toward the C-130 once. He saw the reporter standing at the top of the ramp and locked eyes briefly. Then he turned, ducked his head, and disappeared into the crowd.

Inside the aircraft, Lefty picked up his bag with his one good hand and headed out. The reporter was walking down the ramp toward the crowd. He fell in walking beside her.

"Who's coming to meet you?" she asked. They did not mention their recent exchange.

"Should be several people," he answered. "My mom and dad, two sisters, older brother, all married, all live near here. So there'll be a big crowd at Christmas."

"Cool," she said. "I always thought having a big family would be neat."

They did not have much farther to walk.

"Are you going to stay on at the farm?"

"Going to have a hard time farming with one arm," he said. "I would really like to find a job writing. Or maybe as a photo journalist."

She looked at him quizzically. He held up his hook.

"Just put a screw on this thing, and I'll have a built in mount for the camera," he said.

She smiled easily.

"You don't know any journalists who need a partner do you?" he asked. It sounded like a joke. But he looked at her steadily. She started to laugh again, then stopped—open mouthed—as she realized he might be serious.

They were near the gate and before she could answer, a dozen relatives of all shapes, sizes, and ages rushed out to meet him. After a few moments of happy confusion, his mother turned to the reporter. "And who is this beautiful young lady," she asked. She had an open, direct way about her that was immediately endearing. She was gentle, but in charge.

"Mom," answered PFC Milton, "this is Taylor Webster. She's a reporter for *The St. Louis Post Dispatch* in Missouri. She is doing a story about the flights bringing wounded soldiers home at Christmas time. Taylor, this is my mom, Abigail Milton."

"*Trying* to do a story," the reporter said, shaking hands. "Nobody wanted to talk much. Looks like I have to go home and face my editor without a story. I'm afraid it is going to be very unpleasant." She looked at Lefty without saying anything.

"Gracious, you wouldn't have that problem at our house. You can't get people to hush," the mother beamed. "A writer! I always wanted to be a writer. Tried to push Tommy in that direction."

"Yes," the reporter responded. "Tom told me that."

"He did? Well you must be somebody special if you could get him to talk! He's *The Quiet Man* around our house."

"Short story. Written by Maurice Walsh" Lefty muttered under his breath.

"Made into a movie starring John Wayne," added Taylor.

"So why don't you stay at our house for Christmas?" Mom was beaming again. "You could do a story about a wounded soldier coming home to a family Christmas."

Taylor felt a wave of relief wash over her. Maybe she could pull this off after all. Maybe she could get a national level story yet.

Maybe the old lady was not as innocent as she looked.

"That would be a wonderful idea!" the reporter responded carefully, scanning the mother's face for a clue.

Abigail Milton winked.

Taylor was taken aback—and unaccountably pleased. She felt like she was colluding with a girlfriend in high school. Her face seemed warm. She wondered if she was blushing.

"I'll call my editor and tell him I will be a couple of days late getting home. He wanted the story for the slow days between Christmas and New Year's, so that should be okay."

"You see!" exclaimed the mother. "The Lord always works things out for the best. Tommy, you go get her bags. Everybody else back to the parking lot! See you at the house."

Lefty looked patiently at his mother, then to the reporter, then down to his hook. "Sure," he said. 'I'll just grab a handful of bags." He turned to do as he was told.

"You're injured, dear—not an invalid!" his mother called out helpfully. She leaned close to the reporter. "We mustn't let him feel sorry for himself," she whispered confidentially. She paused, then continued. "I knew the instant I saw the two of you walking together."

Straightening up, she regained her commanding stage voice. "And this is my husband," said the mother, gesturing formally.

He had been watching from a distance with a bemused look on his face. "Great to have you," he said. "Mother here is a force of nature. And she likes you already. I can tell."

"Daddy doesn't think very much of writing," the mother continued. "He thinks it interferes with farming."

"So did Nathaniel Hawthorne," Lefty contributed. He was back with one bag and set it down before returning for another. "Or maybe the other way round. That's why he left Brook Farm."

"It's not polite to show off dear!" his mother called as he departed.

"That's ok," commented the reporter. "I knew that actually."

"Really! How wonderful!" The mother seemed genuinely pleased. The father pursed his lips and blew a long breath. Both women looked at him.

"Sorry," he said. "Only big name I can drop is John Deere."

"That's why I love you, dear. You keep us grounded in reality. And you provide for us very well." She patted his hand.

"Which reminds me—I have food in the oven. Daddy, you get Tommy and Taylor and their bags. Bring them along in the truck. I'll herd the rest of these cats into the cars and back to the house."

The father stood awkwardly with the reporter. They were suddenly alone.

"Sorry about your son's arm," she said.

"Yeah," he answered. "I don't see how he is going to do any work around the farm."

They were both quiet.

"From what I've seen, Tom can do pretty much anything he sets his mind to," offered the reporter.

"Well, maybe," said the father politely. "He's a really good kid. Not much interested in farming anyway. Doesn't have quite the grit of his older brother."

"Really!" said the reporter. Reaching into her pocket, she pulled out the bronze star and handed it to him. "Well," she continued. "Have I got a story for you."

As a non-patient, the chaplain brought up the rear of the group "There he is!" someone shouted. "Reverend Wordman!" Two hundred pairs of gloves clapped in appreciation. A slim, forty-ish woman holding a spray of greenery and poinsettias emerged through the gate. Everyone else stayed outside.

"Kelli!" the chaplain exclaimed.

His wife crossed the tarmac toward him and ran the last three steps. She flung her arms around him, buried her head in his shoulder, and cried.

The chaplain was overwhelmed by his own emotions. He hugged her back hard, then was quiet for a moment. "Who are all these people?" he asked. "Our congregation isn't this big."

"Oh honey, these are people from lots of congregations. When they heard you were coming back, they took off from work and their own churches and families and came to see you. People in this county know you, John. They trust you. They believe in you. You make a difference in their lives. They're glad you're back.

"Honestly—sometimes I think we know you better than you know yourself."

The chaplain had no answer for that.

He walked arm and arm with his wife through the gate and into the crowd. Well-wishers surrounded him.

The crew was helping off load luggage now. They were in a hurry—trying to get back to Scott before their crew day ran out. Little knots of families were gathered around talking excitedly. Nurse Ames picked up her own bag and turned to the second nurse.

"Garrett, looks like everyone is matched up," she said. "I'm going to break station and head to my sister's house. You got it chief."

There would be no passengers for the return trip—no responsibilities except accounting for medical people and equipment on the other end.

"I got it," answered Lieutenant Beauchamp. He feigned a salute, and Nurse Ames smiled and feigned one in return.

As she turned to leave she noticed that among all the pairs and groups on the tarmac, one figure was still alone. Major Pike sat erect in his wheelchair, his bag at his side, looking back toward the tower and parking lot. Far away a blond woman in a long winter coat stood under the tower with her hands in her pockets.

As the nurse watched, a man emerged from the crowd, passed through the gate, and headed directly for Major Pike. He approached from behind, and extended his hand when the startled major turned back in response to his greeting. The nurse was too far away to hear the conversation. But she did not have to be a psychic to understand what was going on. As the man talked, Pike leaned forward sharply in his chair, continuing to look down the fence line to the woman standing under the tower. Then he slumped a bit, but nodded his head slowly.

Finished with his message, the man straightened, and extended his hand again. Pike did not look at him, but waved him away without shaking. Then he continued to look down the fence line toward the woman.

The man withdrew back through the gate, and walked briskly along the fence all the way to the tower. The woman turned. He put his arm around her. They began to walk away. She glanced back once. Then they disappeared into the distant parking lot. A moment later a pair of headlights circled the inside of the lot, turned toward the exit, and were gone.

"*Bad surprise*," the nurse said to herself.

"*I really appreciate your help,*" *the lieutenant colonel was saying. Anytime we lose someone it's important to go through his things before we send them home. Prevents any bad surprises for the family. And I always want a second person to sign the inventory.*"

Nurse Win Ames was seated in a folding chair in the tent that served as a supply room for the medical unit. Before her was a footlocker marked with the name "LTC Andre Fontaine."

It was scratched and dented from the effects of the rocket. A single piece of shrapnel had punched a hole through one end and into the contents. But the wooden box was otherwise miraculously undamaged.

The lieutenant colonel opened the lid and began to lift things out. Nurse Ames began to write.

"Watch," he said. "Timex. Huh. I've known Andre since med school. He was a watch collector—has some really nice pieces. Expensive.

"Six Bic pens, gel. Same with pens. He had a collection of Montblancs. Guess he just used the cheap stuff out here.

"Six pairs of green wool socks.

"One box of condoms. Yeah, see what I mean?"

The nurse blushed and hoped the doctor doing the inventory didn't notice.

He open the box and found it about one-third full of gold foil discs.

"See—what if we sent that back to his wife. Think that's going to be helpful? I think not."

Nurse Ames stopped writing. She noted how much of the box was empty as the doctor tossed it into a round green metal trash can. "His wife?" she said in surprise. "I didn't think Dr. Fontaine was married?"

"He didn't act like it," the doctor continued. "But trust me, I've known him since before they were married. He has a wife and two kids. Married a rich girl—a real class act."

"Are you sure?" she managed to get out without gasping. "Maybe he got a divorce recently." She looked down. "I thought one of the nurses told me he was single."

"That nurse probably thought he was *single. I wouldn't be surprised if he told her that, himself. He's been two-timing his wife that way for years. But I had supper with the two of them two weeks before we deployed. Nope, he was married."*

He continued to inventory the contents of the footlocker.

"One wedding band, gold."

He paused. "Hell of a surgeon," he said. "Terrible husband. One of the most selfish people I've ever known.

"Now what do you suppose this was for?"

He picked up a small cardboard box containing rubber O-rings, turned it over in his hand, then tossed it in the trash.

"Guess he just used the cheap stuff out here," she thought.

Behind her the big propellers began to turn.

Nurse Ames set her bag down and shifted her purse on her shoulder. She picked the bag up again. Then set it down again. She paused. Then she picked it up and walked to the figure in the wheelchair.

"Bad news?" she asked.

Pike did not look up. "Good news," he said. "Would have been bad news if I had gotten it several years from now. Guess she found somebody else to show her the world. The guy's a software salesman."

She took a breath. "Some people can't handle it," she said. "The separation. The time and distance. The wounds."

"Some people don't have a choice," he said. He was quiet.

"But I don't blame her. Truth is I knew it was coming. Something like this—you know when it doesn't feel right. You may kid yourself, but you really know."

She winced. He was right.

"So where are you going?"

"Hotel," he said. "Until I can get a flight out of here to San Antonio. I've got a report date at the Wounded Warrior Center right after New Year's. Maybe I can check in early."

Now they were both quiet.

"Look," she finally said. "My sister has a big farmhouse outside of town. Plenty of room. Guest room on the ground floor. No stairs. Do you want to stay there for the holidays? Or at least until you can get a flight?"

He squared his shoulders and looked up at her. "You know," he said. "That's a really decent thing to do. I really appreciate it. Very tempting. But I can't walk in on your sister at Christmas without warning or permission."

With its engines running, the plane began to taxi to the far end of the runway. Nurse Ames waited a moment for the noise to die down.

"Don't take this the wrong way," she said. "But my sister and her family have gone skiing for the week. They offered me the place just to be alone and get my head together. I would be in a different room on a different floor. But I wouldn't mind the company. No—actually I'd enjoy the company."

He paused to consider. "That would be great," he said. "Really."

Then he smiled. "But I gotta warn you—I'm not easy."

"That's fine," she responded. "Been there, done that. I'm not in any hurry."

"Well," he said. "That explains a lot."

She was embarrassed. "No, that's not what I meant," she said.

"Yes it is," he said levelly. "That's exactly what you meant. But it's okay.

I've been there and done that, too. And let me tell you—whoever he was, he was an idiot. You're a very attractive woman. You care about your work and you care about people. He didn't deserve you."

"Enough," she said, sliding behind the chair and grabbing the handles. "You had me at 'He was an idiot.' Can you pick up my bag?"

"Geez," he said, lifting the bag easily on to his lap. "Could we have a little respect for the cripple?"

"*Something to fight*," she thought. "Can you get your bag too?" she asked.

With a remarkable display of upper body strength, he lifted the heavy duffle bag from the tarmac and set it in his lap.

The group with the flashlights began another carol.

"*God rest ye merry gentlemen*," they sang.

At the far end of the runway, Air Evac 1492 turned on to the runway and began a rolling takeoff. The sound of the engines echoed across the small airfield.

"*O ti-dings of Com-fort and Joy*," the voices continued. "*Comfort and Joy!*"

As Nurse Ames began to push, Major George Pike turned in his chair and took one long last look back across the ramp toward the tower where no one was standing. Then he looked up at his nurse. His teammate. His friend.

"Wendy," he said. "You better drive."

"I plan to, George" she replied.

"For now," he added.

"*O-oh ti-dings of Com-fort and Joy.*"

The song ended. The crowd dispersed. The wounded soldiers began the rest of their lives.

Up in the cockpit of Air Evac 1492, the pilot's phone buzzed again with a text message. "**Got time to talk?**" it asked. The message went unread.

The big gray shape rose rapidly from the runway, pointed its nose toward Scott Air Force Base, and climbed through the clouds, into the starry night.

CHAPTER 9

"I'LL BE HOME FOR CHRISTMAS"

1120 hours 24 December: Scott AFB to Randolph AFB, San Antonio, Texas

Both hands were full and the phone in his pocket was buzzing as he tried to let himself into his room at Scott Air Force Base. Transferring a plastic shopping bag to his teeth, Captain Mike Middleton tried slipping the plastic card into the door slot three times before the lock glowed green and allowed the handle to turn. As soon as the door opened, he dropped the bags across the threshold, unzipped his pocket, and pulled out the phone. He pressed "talk" without looking at the return number.

"Oh hi, Joy. No, no. I'm glad it's you. I was afraid it was Operations," he said. He found himself eager to talk to her. Then he stopped short. Better stay neutral.

"Uh . . . Where are you? There's a lot of noise. Oh—okay—just today at the Base Exchange? Well great, I'm glad you went. Hope you got a picture. No, I don't care how much it cost. Brett is six—he's not gonna want a picture with Santa for many more years.

"Yeah, me too. I really wanted to be there to see it.

"Yes, this afternoon I hope. We got in from Garden City really late last night. Slept late today to get our crew rest. They told us that unless they had a mission for us by noon, we would be released. That's forty minutes from now. So I'm packing, and I hope to be headed your way soon."

"Can I talk to the kids?

"Yeah, that's probably true. That's exactly what they will ask."

"No, I agree. I don't want to tell them I will be there until we actually land."

"Yeah, I know—too many promises in the past. I know trying doesn't count."

"I'll do my best, Joy."

"Well, that's all I can do."

"Yeah, I got your texts. Just been really busy."

"Okay, I'll try to call you when I know something for sure."

"Okay. I love you Jo-Jo."

"Hello? Hello?"

He set the phone on the desk that held the large screen TV, and finished packing his bag. It did not take long. One spare flight suit, two civilian shirts, one pair of trousers, a shaving kit, running gear, some socks and underwear. Life was pretty simple on temporary duty. Simple and Spartan.

He unfolded a second bag—one with straps so you could carry it over your shoulder. He filled it with the contents of his shopping bags from the Base Exchange. He was just picking up both bags to leave the room when his phone began to buzz again.

"Middleton," he said. "Yeah Ops—go.

"Roger—got it. Will be there in fifteen minutes to file the reports and get the rest of the information. Roger. Fifteen minutes."

Hanging up, he touched the speed dial. The copilot answered her phone.

"We have a mission," he said. "Please contact everybody. Tell them to check out and meet me in the lobby in five minutes. They should be about ready to go anyway."

Five minutes later a dour group met in a semicircle around the pilot, just in front of the coffee bar in the lobby.

"Okay, guys. Here's the deal," he said. "About thirty-six hours ago two suicide cars hit a fuel convoy south of Baghdad. Five guys burned over most of their bodies. Very bad shape.

"They tried to evac them direct to San Antonio by C-17, but one of them had some sort of a seizure, so they landed here. They all spent last night in critical care. The guy with the seizure died. The other four are stabilized and they want to send them on to the burn center at Brooke Army Medical Center ASAP. We're here and ready to go. We got the mission.

"I know everybody wants to get home for Christmas. But these guys are really in bad shape. Some have their faces burned off. You should know that there's a storm shaping up out West. If we go to San Antonio, it might close in behind us. We might not be able to get home tonight. But we need to do this. It's worth your Christmas, okay?"

He looked around the group. Four solemn faces looked back. He could have ordered, but he didn't. He asked. Everyone agreed.

"I'll get the van," said the engineer.

"I'll get a cart for the bags," said the loadmaster.

Ten minutes later, the pilot, copilot, and navigator were at Operations planning the mission. The engineer and loadmaster were configuring the aircraft. The three joined the two in time for a quick crew brief, before a regular medical care team—a doctor, a nurse/Medical Care Director, a second nurse, and two technicians—arrived with their equipment. Then two special burn care teams arrived—each consisting of a doctor, a nurse, and a respiratory technician. Each would focus on just two patients. The pilot and MCD conducted a joint brief with everyone in the back of the aircraft. They would need no seats. No one would be sitting down for this flight.

The four litters would be mounted in a single row straight down the center of the aircraft, so the medical crews could reach both sides of a patient at once. Equipment would be stacked toward the front of the aircraft, litter patients to the rear, extra litters holding equipment in the middle.

In addition to the standard package for medical evacuation missions, each burn team carried one specialized medical equipment package per two patients. That made a total of about twelve litters carrying equipment—nearly 2,500 pounds. The plane was going to be jammed.

The burn care teams looked exhausted, and they were. But they were bonded with their patients now, even if those patients existed in a state of morphine induced-unconsciousness. The teams were not giving up. They would get off the plane with the patients in San Antonio, then stay several days to ensure a smooth transition in care, before returning by air to the forward hospital, ten time zones away. It was an exceptionally tiring routine. And they did it all the time.

The teams pulled their gear off the shuttle trucks and set to work setting up their stations. Two large busses arrived, each carrying two patients on litters. They were off loaded by hand, carried carefully up the ramp, and secured into the stanchions now rigged down the center of the cargo bay. After a flurry of work, all four patients were settled, secured, and sedated. The new Medical Crew Director told the pilot over the intercom that they were set, and the engines began to turn. In a matter of minutes they were launched down the runway and climbing toward San Antonio.

They reached cruising altitude at 24,000 feet with the copilot at the controls and a flight plan for maximum speed and minimum fuel savings in route.

"I know weather is closing in on us from the west, and there may be a lot of last minute traffic this afternoon. I don't want to do a bunch of zigzagging around up here to avoid people and clouds. Let me see if I can get us some help," said the pilot over the intercom. He switched to the radio.

"Memphis Center, this is Air Evac 1492."

"Air Evac go," came the crisp response.

"Memphis, I am carrying wounded Marines from Iraq to the burn hospital in San Antonio. Every minute counts for us, and I wonder if you could route us INS direct to Randolph Air Force Base?"

There was a slight pause before the voice responded. "Roger, Air Evac. I can clear you direct to the edge of my area, but you will have to clear with Ft. Worth when you enter their area."

"Thank you, sir," answered the pilot. "These guys were burned up in a fuel truck ambush thirty-six hours ago and we really need to get them to San Antonio ASAP. I wonder if you might call Ft. Worth for us and see if you can clear us straight through?"

"Good call," said the navigator. "If they agree, they'll be moving aircraft out of our way for the whole trip."

Two long minutes later the voice was back. "Air Evac 1492, this is Memphis. I talked to Ft. Worth. You may hold your current heading all the way to San Antonio. We will make a hole for you. Godspeed, sir."

"Thank you, sir," said the pilot on the radio.

Then on the intercom, "This will save us a lot of time. But it will jack around a lot of commercial flights. Hope they don't give us grief about it . . . Uh-oh. Here it comes."

The radio was crackling.

"Continental 955, this is Memphis. I need you to turn right on heading 060 for 60 seconds, then resume initial heading.

"American 3991, I need you to descend 2,000 feet to flight level 200, and hold that altitude until I contact you."

The calls went on for several seconds as four aircraft were rerouted at a cost in time and fuel to give Air Evac 1492 a direct route. More would be redirected all along the way.

"Roger, Memphis," came the first response. "This is Continental 955. Turning now. Air Evac 1492, Godspeed to you, sir."

"Roger, Memphis. Air Evac 1492, this is American 3991. Godspeed."

"Air Evac, this is Delta 1555. Godspeed."

Other aircraft that had not been contacted by Memphis began to call as well.

"Air Evac 1492, this is United 704. Godspeed."

"This is US Air 7329, Godspeed."

"Southwest 454, Godspeed, sir."

CHAPTER 9: "I'LL BE HOME FOR CHRISTMAS"

In a room full of computers and telephones and radar displays in Memphis, Tennessee, a controller called for his supervisor. As it happened, the supervisor—a short rotund man—was already standing over his shoulder, listening.

"This is pretty irregular, sir," said the younger man. "Do you want me to tell them to knock it off?"

The supervisor looked down at his coffee.

The short thin soldier looked down at his paper cup of coffee just in time to see it slapped from his hand and fly across the floor.

He was not quite twenty. He had been in the Army for nineteen months. For twelve of those months he had been in Vietnam—eleven of them in an infantry platoon chasing an elusive enemy across the Central Highlands. He had been back in the United States for sixty minutes. Traveling alone, he had a six-hour layover in San Francisco, where he knew no one, so he visited the USO.

He had just emerged from the small facility, wearing the uniform of his country, carrying a bag in one hand and a cup of coffee in the other, when a boy his own age but with long hair and a mustache slapped his coffee to the ground.

"Killed any babies lately?" he asked in a mocking tone.

Actually he had killed someone recently, but it wasn't a baby. Two weeks before, in the dark confines of a dirt tunnel, he had been quicker with his pistol than an enemy he could not really see. After he shot the North Vietnamese sergeant, the hole collapsed behind him, and he had to crawl over the body of his dead adversary to get out. He still remembered how the dead man smelled. Now he thought about it every day.

As he stood looking at his spilled coffee, two girls with long blond hair, tie died shirts, and jeans, walked by him and laughed. Across the passage way at an opposing gate a businessman in a suit and tie observed the scene. He turned his back and took out his paper.

★ ★ ★

The supervisor looked up from his coffee. "No," he said. "If it gets to be a problem, call me. But otherwise, let it go."

"Air Evac, this is Northwest 808. Godspeed."

Then a formal voice with a heavy British accent took the air. "Air Evac 1492, this is Speedbird 404. You Yanks are not there alone you know. Godspeed to you and your Marines."

And a less formal voice followed. "Air Evac, this is Qantas 1111. My brother is in Baghdad with your soldiers. Godspeed, mate."

As the crew did everything they could to maintain a straight and level flight for the medical team working in the back, the calls continued from planes across Missouri and Arkansas.

"Godspeed."

"Godspeed, sir."

"Godspeed, Air Evac 1492. Godspeed."

Two hours and thirty minutes later, the flight had been uneventful. The fact that all traffic was vectored out of their way actually made things a bit boring. It was as if they were alone in the sky.

"Pilot, this is Navigator." The call on the intercom roused everyone. "You asked to know when we were about 45 minutes out."

"Thanks," answered the pilot. "Co, I'll take the airplane. I want you to go back and check on the medical teams."

"Uh, roger," answered the copilot. It seemed a needless task that someone else could handle. She keyed the intercom. "Load, this is Co—can you tell me who is on headset from the medical team?"

"Cancel that, Load." It was the pilot. "Co, I didn't ask you to use the intercom. I can do that. I asked you to get out of your seat and go to the rear compartment and check on the medical teams. I want you to go personally and get me a personal report. Is that clear?"

He wasn't yelling. It was worse. It was like he was talking to a child. Over the intercom again. Where everyone could hear. What did she have to do to get on this guy's team?

The copilot turned to look at the others on the flight deck. The navigator and engineer were busily avoiding her eyes.

"You have the aircraft," she said to the pilot. Then she began the arduous task of freeing herself from everything that held her in place, and climbing out of the tight seat without touching any of the dozens of knobs, wires, switches, buttons, and other protuberances trying to impede her movement. Finally she was free. She disconnected her headset. She would plug it in again when she reached the cargo compartment.

Carefully she navigated the passageway to the rear, then paused at the top of the stairs leading down to the cargo bay floor. The scene below stopped her cold. It was like something from a horror movie—except it was real.

The bright white lights illuminated eleven people vying for room around four litters in a line. Every patient had a tube carrying saline fluid into each arm, an oxygen tube in his nose, and a tube coming out from under the covers and connecting to a bag full of liquid hanging below the litter. The liquid in some bags was bright yellow. In one it was dark orange.

Working in their own small world, the medical teams were focused on three issues for every patient.

The first was temperature management. When second and third degree burns destroy the outer layers of skin, they also destroy the body's means of regulating its own temperature. So the environment in the back of the plane would have to be kept warmer than usual, and the patients needed individual blankets and coverings.

The second was fluid management. The swollen burns were leaking enormous quantities of fluid. The medical response was to mount two one-liter bags above each patient, rig a fluid line and large bore IV to each arm, and run them through a triple lumen pump that would force the fluid into the body.

The third issue was pain management: All of the patients were sedated before they began their trip, but everything about flight—movement, pressurization, and so forth—made pain management harder. And so as necessary, a nurse would confirm prescriptions from the chart, load the additional pain killer into a small orange "ambIT" infusion pump, and push the anesthetic directly into the fluid lines running to the patient.

Beyond that, each patient had his own individual problems, ranging from sensitivity to antibiotics to organ stress and potential failure. So each was individually watched, tested, monitored, and treated.

Of course, the copilot did not know any of this. She only knew what she saw—which was four litters holding four human figures wrapped in white gauze, submerged under various coverings, and connected to a variety of wires and tubes. It was the best in-transit medical care in the world, as the patients were rushed to the best burn center available. But it looked horrible—as if the Air Force were experimenting on aliens in a movie.

Climbing down the ladder into the cargo space, she moved carefully past the stacks of luggage and equipment lashed to the floor and gingerly approached the first litter. The medical team was focused on some problem with the next figure in line, so she found herself alone facing a prone white mummy, his green litter suspended about waist high above the floor.

The head was wrapped in gauze with holes for breathing and an opening for the mouth. Two dark red and hugely swollen lips protruded through the hole. A clear oxygen tube rested on the face and directed its flow into the nose.

Below the head, the neck was covered with a thick white paste that extended down to where a green hospital gown peeked from under the covers. The bottom cover was a foil blanket that reflected body heat inward. This was covered on top by a civilian quilt—one of thousands produced by loving fingers in church groups, community centers, and service organizations, then donated to soldiers in the combat zone. Although she knew nothing about quilts, she recognized the pattern as one she had seen many times—something early American in red, white, and blue. An expert would have called it a "Log Cabin:" repeating squares made of carefully arranged rectangles of cloth. She marveled at the thousands of individual stitches, put in place by patient fingers, and sent 10,000 miles to warm a stranger coming back from war.

Over the figure's chest and the quilt stood a black steel tent about two feet wide, forming a shelf for stacking equipment. On top rested a pump busily pushing saline and drugs into the patient, a suction device to pull liquid out of the body, and a ventilator to push air into the lungs. None were in use in this patient—but similar devices were in use on others further down the line.

Glancing back at the head, she saw the lips move and realized the figure inside was saying something.

The medical teams were busy with infusions and outputs and talking to each other. None of them heard the burned Marine whispering quietly to himself. It was hard to tell whether he was conscious or unconscious—did he know what he was saying or was he just repeating a phrase that his mind had locked on to before it was overwhelmed with pain and a reality from which it could not escape?

The copilot moved closer, being careful not to interfere with the medical team in action. She could hear the breath rushing past the swollen lips, but the words were not clear—not distinct. So she leaned closer.

The sound was whispering out of the mouth from between the teeth. It was a message from the other side of some terrible threshold of pain. The lips could not form the words properly, but the message was becoming clearer. She leaned still closer. She could hear it. She could get some of it. She could get all of it.

"I'll be home for Christmas," it said.

"I'll be home for Christmas, I'll be home for Christmas . . . "

Over and over and over . . .

She stumbled back in horror until her back was against the padded wall of the aircraft. She breathed hard for a moment, regaining her composure. The loadmaster was on the opposite side of the litters. And nobody on the teams was paying attention to her. Nobody had seen. She gathered her wits and made her way along the aircraft wall toward the rear, taking care to stay out of everyone's way.

As she passed the next litter, she encountered a doctor—a lieutenant colonel—who was reading a chart. Remembering her instructions from the pilot, she asked: "Is everything OK? Do you need any help?"

He did not answer at first, then shook his head and looked up in exasperation. He had deep circles under his eyes. He looked tired.

"What?" he asked. "Lost my train of thought. What do you need?"

"I was just asking if you needed any help. If everything was okay," she responded. It sounded lame.

"No. No!" he replied in irritation. He shook his head and went back to the chart. "We'll call if we need anything. I know how to use the intercom."

Once more feeling like an idiot, the copilot slid behind the team, inching along the side wall, giving them as wide a berth as possible.

The third figure in the line of litters had an additional tube extending from a box on the steel tray across his chest, to his mouth and down his throat. It was taped in place across the mouth, and rhythmically pumping air into the lungs.

Whir-pause-phisss-pause-whir-pause-phisss-pause . . .

As the air came out the hole where the mouth should be it whistled slightly through a space where there should have been lips. But there were only teeth. It was like one of those haunted houses with a dummy whose face was gone leaving just the bone structure underneath. Except this was no dummy. There was a person inside.

For some strange reason, this patient's arm rested on his chest instead of under the covers. The only skin she could see that was not blistered red or burned completely off was a bicep. By some accident of fate, it was completely free of injury. And it was marked by a tattoo of an eagle holding a flag. Below the eagle a short scroll said "USMC." Over the tattoo, a longer scroll read *Semper Fi*.

She crossed the ramp and passed by the head of the fourth patient. One of the nurses was taking pulse and reading monitors. She was obviously not satisfied, as she called over another nurse to join her. They both became agitated and called a doctor. He listened for a moment through his stethoscope, then checked a mobile read out on an EKG. He called a second doctor to confirm, and two technicians carried up a metal box labeled ZOOL on the outside. They set it on the shelf over the patient.

Opening it and extracting the famous "chest paddles," the nurses cleared the patient's chest and stepped back.

The copilot turned away and continued back toward the front of the aircraft.

Having reversed her course, she passed on the other side of each litter. As she passed the next to last patient, a nurse stepped in front of her and lifted the plastic fluid collection bag attached to a tube running out from under the covers. There was not much fluid inside, and she shook her head disapprovingly. Peeling back the covers and pulling up the gown, she uncovered a body wrapped mostly in gauze. But the genitals were free of burns. With a shock, the copilot realized it was a woman.

The nurse reached for the catheter extending into the body. She pulled it out several inches, then pushed it back in. A dark orange-red fluid gushed through the tube, swirled down to the bag, and collected until it was nearly half full. The nurse lifted her eyes and looked at the copilot levelly for a long time without speaking a word. Then she turned back to her work.

Completing her circuit around the floor of the cargo compartment, the copilot returned to the first Marine. He was still whispering his mantra: "I'll be home for Christmas; I'll be home for Christmas; I'll be home for Christmas. . . . "

He too had pulled an arm from beneath the covers, and the bandage looked heavy and stained. A nurse swept in to cut it off and replace it. As she pulled back the bandage, the copilot saw what she guessed were fingers—except they were red and black, and swollen until unrecognizable. At this moment the moving air in the cabin delivered a whiff of something she recognized. It was burned hotdogs—like when you leave them on the grill too long, and they swell and split.

Instantly she was nauseous. She felt the vomit rise up her throat—felt the acid rush on the back of her tongue.

Then from nowhere the loadmaster was by her elbow, handing her an air sickness bag. Twice her stomach convulsed and she vomited into the bag. When she was done she was weak and shaking. Cautiously—awkwardly—he patted her twice on the shoulder.

"I got it, LT," the loadmaster said gently. He closed the mouth of the bag with a deft twist. "You didn't plug in your headset, Lieutenant. The pilot needs you."

For a moment she was too overcome to speak. Then she shook her head without looking him in the eye, or turning to look at the scene she left behind. Instead she focused on making it to the ladder, then climbing to the crew deck. Without a word she reoccupied her seat, happy that her job took her way from the pain and suffering they were carrying in the rear.

Shortly after she returned to her seat, the aircraft was down on the runway at Randolph Air Force Base in San Antonio, and taxiing toward an isolated spot on the west side of the field. Once again there was a crowd to meet the plane, but it was not made up of smiling family and friends. Instead it was a crowd of nurses, drivers, technicians, and baggage handlers set to complete the massive logistical movement that began less than two days before, when another young man, possessed by a murderous idea, swerved a car full of explosives into a fuel convoy half a world away. There was no time to appreciate the medical accomplishment, or express pride in the professionalism of the team involved. There was only time to complete this mission, and get the whole team ready for the next.

Because that was the only certainty of this entire exercise in war, politics, brutality, and humanity. There would be a next time.

Finally, the litters and medical teams were gone. Their equipment had been transferred by a labor gang that made quick work of the ton (literally) of equipment lashed to the ramp. The pilot had dispatched the navigator on some task. The engineer was in the rear assisting the loadmaster in reconfiguring the cargo space. The pilot and copilot were alone on the crew deck.

The pilot was fully engaged in his logbook, and it took him a while to notice that the copilot was not talking or moving or writing. She was sitting stock still, facing to the right with her face hidden from view. She was not wearing her headset, so he spoke to her directly.

"What's up?" he asked. "Is there a problem?"

At first she didn't speak or move. Then slowly she turned to face him. She was crying. Hard. Tears had streaked her face, dropped off her chin and wet her flight suit.

"I didn't know," she said, haltingly at first. "I didn't know it would be like that.

"I can fly," she said. "I can handle the airplane. I can handle the work. I can handle the physical labor. But I don't know if I can handle that. It was horrible."

She looked away. She could not bear to look him in the face while they discussed her failure.

"Yes," he said. His voice was different again. Softer. Warmer. More private.

"The blood and gore of war are terrible. Absolutely terrible. If you haven't seen it, you can't imagine it, or describe it, or understand it. It's horrible.

"And *you* have to be able to function right in the middle of it. You have to be able to fly your aircraft when they carry a guy on board with his eye hanging out of the socket. You have to be able to fly—*and lead*—when a guy is bleeding out on your ramp and you can't get the engine to start. You have to focus on the mission when they drop a guy on a litter in the back and his intestines spill out on the floor.

"Do you think you can do that?"

She paused for a long time. "I'm not sure," she answered. She was still not looking at him.

"Don't be stupid!" he snapped. "Grow up! Of course you can! We've all learned to do it. You can, too. That's why I sent you back there—to see it up close. To learn what it looks like and smells like and tastes like. To look at a guy with his lips burned away and nothing left but teeth, and realize there is a human being in there—and know it could have been you. And then do your job anyway. Because that is how we save them.

"See it now," he said. "Learn it now. Get over it now. So when the time comes and the chips are down, you can do your job."

It was curious. He was not yelling. He was not lecturing. He was not demeaning. He was . . . teaching. And he did not appear angry. Instead, he was . . . sad.

She turned back to look at him. "Okay," she said. "I got it. I can do it. I'm sorry I cried. I just didn't think it would be like that."

"It's ok," he said. His tone was completely different. He was almost friendly.

"And here's a secret, JT." He leaned closer. "Sometimes it bothers me, too. When I'm alone and I think back over what I've seen and done. Sometimes it gets to me, too."

He glanced over his shoulder and back down the passageway to the rear. Then he winked at her. "But don't tell the guys, okay?"

She looked away again. He was so easy with her. So natural. This is what she thought the Air Force would be like—conversations with comrades. Not a steady stream of ass chewings and humiliations.

She smiled and looked back at him. But he was focused on the logbook again. Once again every inch the detached professional.

"Did you get the clock time when we shut down the engines?" he asked. It was as if nothing had happened. But something *had* happened. She had had a glimpse—two glimpses—into the best and the worse the Air Force had to offer. Casualties and camaraderie.

It was going to be all right now. She was going to make it. The pilot and other experts like him—they were eventually going to be her friends. She felt strangely at home. This was where she belonged.

Inside she smiled at her private joke.

She was home for Christmas.

CHAPTER 10

INTO THE DARKNESS

1745 hours 24 December: Randolph AFB to Home

The patients were gone. The attendants were gone. The equipment was gone. The medical team was gone. No one was left in the cargo space of the aircraft except the crew. They were breaking down and securing to the walls and floor the pieces of their standard equipment that had been set up for the special needs of the last mission.

Technically this was the duty of the loadmaster. But the crew as a whole did what the pilot asked. And this pilot was a leader who shared the burden of manual labor with his team. So when he said "Let's help Load break it down," there were no groans or complaints. They just moved as one to help finish the task as quickly as possible.

The loadmaster's mentor, the technical sergeant who flew as engineer, had told him that flying with this pilot was a different experience. He had now been in the service long enough to realize that some pilots (and thus some crews) always had something else to do when the loadmaster needed help with physical labor. Not Captain Middleton. When there was work to be done, he was there. Nobody said anything, but the crew knew what he expected and so they made their way to the back and set to work. They set about the task with determination, if not exactly with enthusiasm.

Many hands made light work and they were almost done when the navigator hustled in.

"Boss!" he called out from the flight deck overlooking the cargo bay. "I took a look at weather and routes like you asked. I think we can still get home tonight!"

Everyone paused and looked up. "The direct flight in got us here way ahead of schedule," he said breathlessly. "I've been talking to weather and operations. If we can get out of here in the next half hour or so, we can get ahead of the storm and into Little Rock before things get bad. We can get home for Christmas."

He stopped and looked around. The other members of the crew straightened and looked at each other. The engineer spoke for them all. "Hot damn!" he said. "Let's get out of here."

The pilot took charge immediately.

"Eng, get us gassed. I will tell you how much soon as I finish here."

"Co, get started on the flight plan. You work it, I'll check it, and then you can file it.

"Nav, get back to your desk, get everything weather can give you, and check every current Notice to Airmen for any special instructions or warnings. Then feed everything you've got to the Co so she can make a plan we can file ASAP.

"Load, you finish locking everything down. Then start your pre-flight checks. I've gotta make a call."

The copilot started back a step. She had filed many flight plans. But given the situation, with bad weather inbound, this was a heavy responsibility. A heavy investment of trust.

"Everybody back here and on a headset in 20 minutes," the pilot continued. "I wanna be out of here in half an hour."

He clapped his hands twice. "Let's go."

Like a football team breaking from a huddle, the crew turned quickly to their individual tasks.

CHAPTER 18: INTO THE DARKNESS

For a moment the pilot stood still, wondering if he should call his wife. She was a good wife and a good mother. He loved her. And he respected her. She deserved to know where he was and what he was doing. After they were first married, he loved to call and hear her voice. He loved to share what he had seen and done. But then the pressures got heavier and heavier, and the things he was seeing and doing were less and less pleasant. As he found it harder to talk, she became more demanding. And the discussion two nights ago (only two nights!) had driven a deep wedge between them. "*Do you need to talk with someone?*" Damn. What was she thinking?

Before he could decide about the call, the engineer approached. "Gas guy is here. How much you want to load?" he asked.

"Well, I want 32,000 pounds," the pilot replied. "That's 15,000 for a 3-hour trip, plus 7,000 for margin, plus 10,000 to give me 2 hours for a divert with this weather coming up. But when we left this morning TACC only authorized us 24,000."

"Twenty-four thousand?" the engineer frowned. "What's up with that? Is this that new cost saving deal? Carry less fuel to save money?"

"Yep," replied the pilot. "Save a quarter on this end, and cut us close on the back end. But traffic will be light tonight. We should get a straight vector out. If the weather doesn't get ahead of us, we'll be ok. Twenty-four thousand."

Now he was late. He hustled to operations to get an update and make a different call.

In fifteen minutes on the dot, the pilot returned to the crew deck and climbed carefully into his seat.

"Who'd you call?" asked the copilot.

"The Weather Guy," the pilot replied.

"Dale already called weather," she said perplexed.

"I didn't call the weather section. I called 'The Weather Guy.'" His voice changed. He was teaching again. "Look, the weather section is full of people like you and me. They know their business, but they come and go. But every base has some civilian squirreled away who has been doing his job at the same place for twenty-eight years. Pick a subject—fuel, weather, maintenance. There's always a guy at the bottom who really knows the score. You need to find those guys—get to know them. Use them when you have a question.

"This is a close call—long way to go—big storm. I don't want us to get a case of the 'hurry homes.' I don't want to get this sled to Little Rock and find out I've got no roof top to land on. So I called The Weather Guy. At home. On Christmas Eve. He never batted an eye. Said that if we can get out right away, and stay up at cruising altitude and cruising speed, we should be okay—should have about an hour slack.

"Then I called the Ops Officer. Never surprise the boss. He said okay, so we're headed home."

He paused. "Teaching point—if you show superior judgment, you won't have to show superior flying."

Five minutes later the crew was running the drill. Each member ran his individual checklist, then checked his neighbor. Avionics checks. Electronics checks. Numbers calculated, checked, and rechecked.

At engine start the big propellers began to turn—slowly at first, then faster and faster. The loadmaster bounded up the stairs with his long cable looped in his hand. He slammed the door shut and rotated the handle to lock. After contacting Ground Control, the pilot began to taxi out, delivering a compressed crew brief as they rolled down the taxiway.

"Straight home," he said. "Nav, stay on the radar and Co, help me stay in touch with Houston Center on the climb out. With a little luck we will pass just ahead of the weather front as we're south and east of Dallas. If not, I will need some help diverting around any big cells.

"Rolling take off."

The ungainly gray machine with its blunt nose and rounded belly lumbered straight down the runway, picking up speed. At ninety-two knots the beast so awkward on the ground broke free of the earth's clutches, and rose majestically into its element. The nose was up. The engines were throbbing. Ten thousand pumps, pipes, tubes, and wires did their job. Electrical messages flashed down the copper nerves from sensor to sender to solenoid.

With its medical mission complete, the aircraft reverted to its normal call sign. Wolf 41 pointed its nose to the northeast and climbed in a hurry. The crew was headed into the dark. And into the storm. And home for Christmas.

At 21,000 feet the pilot leveled off and set the throttles for his calculated "max cruise"—the optimum balance of speed and fuel consumption to get him home as quickly as possible while saving gas. He was in a hurry. But he was not taking any chances.

Below him a broken cloud deck reflected silver light from the first sliver of a rising moon. To his left front, far against the horizon, a dark wall indicated the edge of the weather front racing him for home. Below, through the side windows on the left, the ink black earth was smeared with lines and dots and patches of light. Barns and shopping centers, individual houses and massive apartment complexes, narrow country roads and broad urban highways—each contributed its own glow, glimmer and twinkle to the mix. The combination looked like some sort of living creature—like he was looking at the neural network for the earth.

And in a way he was. Because what he was seeing was evidence of man's collective neural activity—of his imagination and creativity, of his drive and determination, of his initiative and hard work. Covered by a cloak of darkness was all evidence of mankind's darker side. From this distance in space and time, there was no sign of war or man-made famine, of man's cruelty and brutality, of the daily barbarism that made people wonder if there was a God, and God wonder why He ever made people. It was enough to make some soldiers returning from a war forgive and forget. Some even forgave themselves. But not this pilot.

And above! Overhead was a galactic cathedral created from the light of a billion stars. The starlight flooded into the cockpit, and spilled across the instruments, and the pilot's lap. Like dimly glowing quicksilver, it lit the copilot's face, as she studied the instrument panel, and the back of the engineer's head, as he used a small flashlight to recheck his calculations. The starlight highlighted the oblong wing against the dark of the earth. It kissed the edges of the spinning propellers, creating four silver arcs that pulled them through the sky.

With individual dots that gleamed and shimmered and burned with distant fire that looked like ice, the sky overhead cried out for humility and worship. The pilot tuned the setting on one of his radios, and the sound of Christmas carols filled the headset. The members of the crew continued their duties, but each reflected on the starlight in his own way. The feeling of awe and humility was overwhelming. The humanity of what they had seen and heard and experienced in the last forty-eight hours—suppressed in the name of duty and professionalism—began to peek through. They would not need to attend church tomorrow for Christmas Day. They had attended tonight in God's majestic chapel.

"*I wish Joy could see this,*" the pilot thought to himself. "*I wish I could share this with her. She does so much for me and the kids. I wish I could do more for her.*"

Seventy minutes later, as they passed over highway I-20, a bit southeast of Dallas, Ft. Worth Center interrupted their reverie.

"Wolf 41, we are seeing some pretty bad storm cells ahead of you. Can you see them?"

The pilot whipped his head around to look at the navigator. Sitting at his navigator's desk behind the flight engineer, Captain Lee was staring intently at a forty-year-old radar screen while trying to determine where storms were emerging along their route. Unlike more current digital radar in newer planes that gave a complete and constant picture, this vintage analogue system made a circular sweep every five seconds. So the navigator's job was like picking his way through a dark room littered with landmines by using a flashbulb that illuminated every few seconds. Technically it was a reliable system. But it told a confusing story.

"Oh yeah," said the navigator on intercom. "I see it, all right. And not just west of us. Some of it is already northeast, right across our flight path."

Together the pilot and navigator searched for every advantage in the rapidly changing situation. Then the pilot took a deep breath and keyed the radio.

"Ft. Worth Center, this is Wolf 41. Request permission to vector twenty miles northwest or southeast of the established course.

"Is that enough extra space to help you work us around the worst cells?" the pilot asked internally.

But before the navigator could answer, Ft. Worth was back. "Wolf 41," the voice in the headset responded. "We have a pilot report of severe icing ten miles northeast of your course. Do you need approval for more maneuver room?"

"Roger Ft. Worth, request fifty miles deviation north or south." That was a pretty big variance. If they had to go that far to get around the big storm cells more than a couple of times, they would be cutting it short on fuel to get home.

"Approved," answered the center. "Not much traffic tonight."

"So Nav, what do you think?" called pilot.

"I just got off the radio with weather in Little Rock. This whole storm is moving a lot faster than they expected. We're okay as long as we keep our speed up. But we're gonna have to stay high and pick our way through it."

A good navigator—and this was a good one—could "see" turbulence and bad weather by interpreting the changing radar reflections on his scope. As weather intensified, he could recognize concentrations of rain and snow and ice, and predict the worst buffeting by winds. But although the radar on this older model plane could see heavy weather, it could not see through it. In a big storm, the effect was like outdriving your headlights on a dangerous road. As major concentrations of snow or rain or ice loomed ahead, Captain Lee began suggesting route changes to the pilot—hoping that the next sweep of the radar would not reveal an even bigger problem smack in the path he had just suggested.

"Boy," he said to no one in particular. "I wish we had a J model." Loaded with state-of-the-art technology, the new C-130s were entering service first where they could have the greatest impact on the war effort. That was not Texas and Arkansas.

So this crew was stuck with an exhausting and repetitive routine that took the full attention of pilot and navigator.

The engineer broke their focus. "Um—Pilot, the engine rpm fluctuation is back again. This is the third gauge in two days, but I am still seeing a problem with the readings."

The pilot was annoyed. The heavy weather was going to take his full attention. The aircraft felt fine, and there were no other indications of a problem. He was tired of this problem that did not act like a problem. But he answered coolly. "Roger, Eng. Keep an eye on it. Let me know if it looks like trouble."

A sudden shudder rocked the aircraft briefly from nose to tail. Then it was gone. This was a big storm. Its effects were reaching out hundreds of miles.

Below, the network of roads and towns and lights was now obscured by a silver-gray haze. On the ground they would call the sky overcast. From four miles up, what the crew saw was a lumpy gray carpet, angling up ahead as the carpet grew thicker. In the distance the dark wall now extended from horizon to horizon. This was going to be a footrace to home.

It was after midnight and full dark. The sliver of a moon gave the desert a silvery glow, almost as if the sand were dirty snow. Over the horizon to the front was the glow of lights from Baghdad. Somewhere in that glow was the safety of Balad airport and home. But off to the left loomed the wall of a massive dust storm, brownish-black even in the dark. It was headed for Balad, too. This was going to be a footrace to home.

"Wow," said the copilot. "That was lightening in those clouds out ahead. Lightening in that snowstorm. Anybody else see that?"

No one else spoke. No one else was looking out of the cockpit.

"Wolf 41, Memphis Center," crackled the radio. "We are looking at some very intense cells out in front of you. Recommend you vector left 45 degrees for 35 miles, then right again to recover your original course."

With his left hand on the control yoke and his feet on the rudder pedals, the pilot brought the nose of the aircraft to the left. With his right hand he eased the throttles back slightly. He was starting to worry about fuel.

"Co, take the aircraft, please, while I run the numbers with Eng.

"Eng," the pilot continued. "Please check the numbers again for me on speed, altitude, and fuel consumption. What is the absolutely best setting to get us home? And I mean all the way home."

Soon the pilot, engineer, and navigator were consumed by charts and calculations.

"Fire!" said the copilot. "Fire Indicator Light on Number 1!"

The pilot's head jerked straight up as his eyes swept the bottom of the overhead panel. There five T-handles were lined up side by side—electrical shut offs for fuel and other essential engine functions. No lights were lit. There was no indication of fire.

"Are you sure?" asked the pilot.

The copilot hesitated. "Pretty sure," she said. "I just saw it from the corner of my eye."

The pilot took a deep breath. "OK," he said. "If you say you saw it, I trust that you did. Everybody keep an eye out for fire lights."

He could not solve this problem. And maybe it wasn't a problem anyway. So he put it aside and focused on more immediate issues.

"Pilot?" the engineer interrupted. "This is really goofy. I now have several gauges showing anomalies on Number 1—rpm looks like it is surging, fuel flow shows 200 pounds higher than the other engines, but it's not putting out more power. The engine temp is low, but the engine oil pressure is high. Meanwhile, I have no physical indication of a problem. I really don't understand what's happening here."

"Very intense cell coming up," called the navigator, apparently oblivious to the other discussion going on. "Recommend vector right 45 degrees for 20 miles.

The copilot tapped the rudder pedals with her feet, and the aircraft nosed to the right.

"There it goes again," chimed in the engineer. "Several gauges moved at the same time, then it stopped."

"Crew brief," said the pilot. "Okay guys, I am starting to get task saturated. I am going to break out specific duties so I can think through this.

"Nav, I want you to pull out the charts and figure out where we can divert if we have to.

"Eng, get me some numbers on fuel, speed, and distance. Work it against what Nav is coming up with. We are doing a lot of zigzagging. It's costing us gas. Work out the possibilities."

"Co—fly the plane—keep an eye on everything while I think through this.

"Load . . . it's gonna get rough back there. Come on up and sit in the jump seat if you want."

A moment later the loadmaster made his way up the ladder to the crew deck. He had been all alone in the back, listening to the rest of the crew discuss the problems. He folded down a seat from against the wall to the rear of the navigator's position and sat down, snapping the seat belt around his waist. He left it loose so he could move more easily. It was a new-guy mistake.

The pilot paused. He was thinking rapidly, but the pieces just did not add up.

Air turbulence shook the plane again. Their bodies were suddenly snatched upward against the straps holding them to their seats, as the plane dropped quickly. Then they were all squashed down into their seats by gravity as the plane rose rapidly back to the original altitude.

"Ooof!" said the loadmaster.

"Tighten your straps," said the engineer.

The loadmaster did as he was told.

"I have an rpm fluctuation on Number 2!" said the engineer.

The plane shook from another violent spasm. A three-ring binder leapt from the navigator's desk, slapped the floor loudly and scattered its pages down the short passage to the rear.

"Engine fire light on Number 1!" announced the copilot. Then, "Nope—blinked out again."

"Eng," said the pilot. "I can only think of one thing this could be. A bleed air leak."

"Not likely," replied the engineer's voice in the headset. "That's pretty much assuming the very worst case."

CHAPTER 18: INTO THE DARKNESS

"What else can it be?" asked the pilot. "We've eliminated everything else. I have lots of independent instrumentation problems, but no indicators of a real physical problem. Something is causing all these gauges to read wrong. What else could impact them all at once—from more than one engine?"

"What's a bleed air leak?" said the loadmaster to the navigator over the roar of engines and storm. He leaned up close to the navigator's ear. He was off the intercom, so no one else could hear.

"Bleed air is air drawn directly off the jet exhaust," said the navigator. "Maybe 600 degrees Fahrenheit at 125 pounds of pressure per square inch. It is routed through a bunch of tubes to do a lot of different things. For example, it runs hot air along the edges of the wing to prevent ice buildup. It helps to heat and pressurize the cabin. But if you get a crack in one of those lines, then you have super-hot air squirting out on to whatever is close—wires, gauges, solenoids. Anything it touches might give a false reading. Eventually it could burn through anything—even a fuel cell. It's like having a live welding torch rattling around inside the wing."

"It could burn a hole in the wing?" the loadmaster asked, alarmed.

"It could set fire to something and burn the whole wing off," answered the navigator.

"Fire light on Number 1!" announced the copilot. This time the light stayed lit.

The pilot and engineer looked at each other. "Bleed air leak," they said in unison.

Of course, it might not be a fire in the engine at all. It might just be wiring or sensors cooking in the extreme heat of a super-hot leak. But they could not afford to take a chance.

"Commence emergency shutdown, engine Number 1," the pilot commanded sharply. "Bold Face immediately. I've got the plane!"

He turned to look out the left window to engine Number 1.

As he looked out the left window to engine Number 1, it coughed

fire out of the exhaust—red and orange and evil black—out into the airstream. In the dark of night it illuminated the wing and both engines with an eerie yellow flash of light. All the features of the wing were blurred by the sand in the air sweeping by—sand that was really more like dirty dust—gray and tan even in the harsh light of exploding fuel. The flash lit the whole of the window, and the pilot's face staring out in shock. "Fire!" someone shouted. "Fire in Number 1!"

The crew jumped immediately into action, following steps printed in bold type in the manual—steps that had to be memorized and not simply read from a checklist.

"Co, use the condition lever to shut down Number 1!" the pilot barked.

The copilot reached for a worn yellow lever directly to the right of the throttle levers. Of the four identical levers, she picked the one on the left.

"Confirm Condition Lever 1!" she said.

"You have Condition Lever 1!" the engineer replied. Pulling the lever back would starve the engine of fuel and shut it down immediately. But they could not afford for the copilot to pull the wrong lever by accident. Every step that anyone took in this emergency would be confirmed by someone else. The copilot announced her action. The engineer confirmed it.

"Shutting down engine Number 1." The copilot lifted the lever up until it snapped, pulled it rapidly to the rear until it clicked gain, and held it in place until she knew it was locked. There had been cases in the past where the lever had jumped back out of lock. When that happened, the angle of the propellers on the dead engine changed in an instant, and so did the drag on one side. Controlling the plane would become ... difficult.

Even in the midst of the emergency, the pilot noticed the copilot's attention to detail. "*Good job,*" he thought.

With the lever in its new position, fuel stopped flowing to the combustion chamber. The noise level dropped immediately as the thrust in the engine on the far left end of the wing dropped to zero. The sustained explosion that spun the internal parts of the jet engine and transferred power to the propeller suddenly stopped. The engine was off.

The aircraft slewed to the left as the two operational engines on the right wing pulled harder through the air than the single remaining engine on the left. The pilot compensated immediately with his controls. He added rudder trim to the right. He pulled back on the power to Number 4 engine—the far engine on the opposite wing. Wolf 41 was no longer flying straight and true like a fat arrow through the air, but skewed and twisted slightly to the side.

The pilot kept both hands on the controls. "Fire Handle Number 1!" announced the copilot.

The engineer looked up to see if the copilot was about to pull the handle on the correct engine.

"Confirm Fire Handle Number 1!" he answered.

The copilot tugged. Now electrical power was cut off to Number 1 as well. And the fire bottle was armed, in case fire suppressant had to be dumped into a flaming engine. For such an emergency the aircraft carried enough agent for two attempts to douse the flames. After that . . . well . . . there was no after that.

"Agent discharge not required," she continued. "Confirm no discharge."

"Confirm," replied the engineer.

After a moment's delay the copilot said, "Pilot, the solenoid doesn't indicate that the engine feathered. Do you want to take a look outside?"

Pulling the condition lever should have activated a series of pulleys and cables that would cause the propeller blades to rotate until they were edge-on to the wind. This was called "feathering" the propeller. It ensured the big blades would create the least resistance and the least drag, as they hung fixed and motionless in the wind stream. But the process should have created a vacuum that changed a button on the instrument panel. The button remained unaffected.

The pilot glanced out the left window again. The propeller was flat into the wind, and not moving.

"Damn," he said. "It's not going to feather. This is gonna cost us speed and gas.

"When Bold Face is complete, everybody go back and complete their standard checklists."

The crew became a blur of motion as they checked and rechecked steps.

"Eng, we've got to shut off all the bleed air to all the engines." It was the pilot on the intercom again. "Even if that's the problem, we don't know for sure where it's located. I think that means we've got to get down."

"This storm is ugly even up here boss," interjected the navigator. "It's gonna be really bad down below."

"But when we shut off the bleed air, we won't have any anti-icing on the wings—it's going to start to build up pretty quick," responded the engineer. "The lower we get the better."

The ice would change the shape of the wing, making it harder to fly the aircraft, and throw off all their calculations about weight, thrust, and speed. What no one said was that it would be impossible to calculate the speed at which you would lose control of the aircraft. The pilot could take no chances—he would have to land at a much faster speed than usual.

"We won't be able to pressurize correctly—so we need to go on oxygen or get down below 10,000 feet." said the pilot. "And we'll have no heater—it's gonna get 20 below here on the flight deck if we stay up high."

"Ok," said the engineer. "Let's go down. Just throw away the charts and fly at 165 knots. We can't figure it any better than that."

"And come right to course 070," added the navigator. We've gotten pretty far north. Hell, we're only a little more than an hour out. Almost time to start the descent anyway."

The pilot took two deep breaths. "Memphis Center, this is Wolf 41," he announced on the radio. "I'm declaring an In Flight Emergency. Number 1 engine shutdown. Five souls on board and two hours fuel. I'm

CHAPTER 18: INTO THE DARKNESS

direct Little Rock Air Force Base, altitude my discretion. No assistance required—standby further calls."

The response was immediate. "Roger, Wolf 41 Emergency," spoke the disembodied voice. "You are cleared for immediate descent. You are cleared to Little Rock direct. Do you want me to make any calls for you?"

"No thanks, Memphis—we will call direct."

"Roger, Wolf 41 Emergency. Be advised that you have a very bad line of weather between you and Little Rock. A number of airports left and right of your vector have shut down operations because of heavy ice and snow. Good luck."

"He's right, Mike" added the navigator. The stress of the moment had caused a break in protocol. "We're moving slower than we expected, and the weather is moving faster. I've been on other frequencies checking diversion sites. There is nothing open between here and Little Rock. Both the air base and the civilian airport are still open there. If they close, we may have to go to Memphis to find some place to land."

"Not good," said the engineer. "All this working around storms, dropping down in altitude, and now dragging a dead engine that won't feather—this has really sucked the gas. We need to get into Little Rock."

The pilot turned to the copilot. "Sometimes superior judgment doesn't work out, and superior flying is required."

He turned to look forward through the windscreen. "We are going to Little Rock," he said.

The huge gray shape began to let down into the darkness. It was much harder to fly now. It rocked and shook, and rattled violently as it descended into the bowels of the storm. The stars were gone, along with the black of the sky, and the gray of the ground. The pilot's eyes flicked out through the windscreen to look ahead, and he had just a moment to wonder at the sight of snow so heavy that it was white and dark at the same time. Groups of flakes flung themselves at the windscreen, then spun right or left or over or under just before impact, as the buffer of air around the aircraft pushed them away.

The pilot was struggling to control a plane that rocked and shook in the unstable air just ahead of the wall of dust. As the dust grew heavier, a brownish-black enveloped the plane. It was as if someone had placed a blanket over the windscreen. He could not tell whether it was two feet away or two miles away. There was just nothing to see. Inches outside the cockpit, dust swirled at the windows, clutching at them, desperate to get in, before the rush of the plane through the air swept it away.

Suddenly, something loud whacked the skin of the aircraft directly overhead. Then another report, like a marble hitting metal at high speed. Then a blow fell directly on the wind screen to their front. It sounded for all the world like the window had cracked, but it wasn't the wind screen after all. Instead it was the projectile that shattered, leaving crystal shards adhering to the window for just a moment before they, too, were swept away. Then the blows came more rapidly until there were too many to count.

"Hail," said the pilot.

"Hail Mary," said the engineer.

As they passed through 10,000 feet the pilot contacted the tower at Little Rock Air Base and requested permission for a straight in approach.

"Roger, Wolf 41 Emergency," came the reply. "We are trying to stay open for business, but get here soon. We may have to close down any time now."

"Nav, take the charts and get on the radio and check everything an hour past Little Rock in case we can't get in." The pilot was on the intercom again. "And look at the line up for the long runway at Little Rock International, in case we have to divert there."

"I've already been checking," answered the navigator. "The storm has hooked around and is approaching Little Rock from the north. Everything is closed north and west and south. And given our gas situation, there's not much close in out to the east."

CHAPTER 18: INTO THE DARKNESS

"Wolf 41 Emergency," called the tower. "Be advised Little Rock civilian had a DC-9 slide off the side of the long runway. They are shutting down operations. Do not plan to divert there. I say again, do not plan to divert there. Looks like you are coming here."

"This is Wolf 41 Emergency. Looks like we are coming there," answered the pilot. In the blink of an eye, his options had disappeared. "Game on," he said.

It had to be pretty important for the MCD to leave the patients and medical team in the back and climb the ladder to the flight deck. But there she was, standing behind the navigator and leaning over the engineer's shoulder. She held on tight as the plane rattled and bucked in the sandstorm. They were descending and the crew was busy. Her team in the back was busy, too. But here she was. Something was up.

She was wearing white latex gloves, covered with blood. Blood was on the front of her uniform and on her forehead. Her eyes were ablaze.

"Listen to me," she shouted to the pilot over the roar of the engines and the storm. Apparently she had something to say that she did not want broadcast to everyone on the intercom. "I'm out of blood. I have two guys bleeding out on their litters. Maybe more. I heard you talking about diverting to get out of the dust storm. If you divert, they die. Get us in. Get us on the ground."

The pilot looked her squarely in the eye. Then he looked at the navigator, then the engineer, then the copilot. "Game on," he said. He turned back to the instruments. "Game on."

The pilot advanced the power settings for the three remaining engines. Speed was the key now, even more than fuel. They had to get to the runway and get down before the storm made that impossible.

He really wanted the luxury of a few minutes to think about what he had done—the calls he had made. Had he done the right thing when they first guessed it was a bleed air problem? When they shut down the engine? Should he have landed hours ago? But that was before he knew how quickly the storm would build. Still . . .

Then it occurred to him that everything they had said had been recorded on the "black box" (which was actually orange) in the aircraft. If this went bad, future pilots in training would listen to his voice and his decisions and try to guess what they would have done in his place. What he should have done. It was not a comforting thought. But what the hell. Let them listen.

"Load," he said. "Where are you going tomorrow for Christmas dinner?"

The question hung in the air while everyone tried to digest it.

From his seat at the rear, out of the action, the loadmaster looked around.

"Uh . . . yes sir. I'm going to Tech Sergeant Jefferson's house."

"Of course," the pilot said. "Good man. He takes care of his people."

"So Eng," he continued. "You gonna show him how to use a knife and fork?"

Everyone smiled a bit at the weak joke. "Gonna try, sir," said the engineer.

"*Nice play*," thought the navigator. He glanced at the copilot. Two minutes before she had been a ball of nerves. Now she seemed relaxed—in the groove. The pilot thought there was going to be a tomorrow. He thought they would be back in the world tomorrow, sitting at dinner with family and friends. His one question—off the checklist—conversational at a moment of maximum tension—had steadied everyone.

It was a tough call. They needed to be on their game—no distractions. But at some point, too sharp becomes brittle. The pilot was walking a fine line, a line that technicians never understand but leaders get by instinct. And it worked. The navigator saw the trick, and yet even he felt better. The crew was centered and focused. Balanced. They were not just flying now. They were going home.

"Twenty miles," the navigator reported. While the pilot wrestled the balky aircraft, the copilot began speaking through the intercom. "Descent Checklist," she said. She turned through the yellow pages of a booklet.

"Crew brief," called the pilot. "My plan is 50 percent flap landing, speed 150. We have to have more speed and less flaps than usual because we don't know how much icing we have or the minimum control speed. We have to be hot when we touch down.

"We will approach on instruments—Runway 25. Frequency 109.9. Dial in 250."

In addition to a GPS that indicated where they were, the pilot had two instruments to help him find the runway and land.

The first was an Attitude Directional Indicator. A mechanical arrow on the side of a dial would show when he was descending at exactly the right rate—neither too fast nor too slow.

The second was the Horizontal Situational Indicator, which told him when to turn left or right, and how hard, in order to align the aircraft with the runway.

If this combined Instrument Landing System was functioning correctly, he would be able to tune in to its frequency (109.9) and follow its guidance on a properly aligned, three degree descent, all the way to Runway 25 with its heading of 250 degrees. But even with this assistance, once he got close to touchdown, unless he could see the runway, he was forbidden to land. Once he had the runway in sight, he would stop flying the instrument approach and land visually.

"If we break out in time, I will land visually and touch down on the first 100 feet of the runway," he continued the briefing. "If we can't see until the very last minute, we'll land by Instrument Flight Rules a thousand feet down the runway.

"We will reverse engines symmetrically, Numbers 2 and 3 only. Cut Number 4 to ground idle when we touch down, and keep it there."

The pilot was taking no chances that reversing two engines on one side and only one working engine on the other might slew them off the icy runway.

"We can't make any mistakes here—we have no margin for error. Stay off the brakes—there will be ice on the runway so let it coast to a stop.

"Assuming the runway surface is good, I will turn off at the far end of the runway and taxi to park. Any questions?"

Everyone had the same question. "*Would it work?*" No one asked it.

"What about a go around?" It was the copilot. "When will you decide on a go around?"

"No go around," answered the pilot. "We have gas and weather for one shot at this. We are going to stick this landing. No go around."

"No go around," said the pilot. Despite the darkness, the dust was visible inside the cockpit, hanging in the air. "There is no go around for the guys in back. We are going to stick this landing. No go around."

The copilot broke the silence. "Before Landing Checklist," she said. "Speed 180."

"Flaps 50 percent," answered the pilot.

"Speed 165."

"Gear down. No night vision. The reflection from the snow will just make it blank out."

The copilot reached up and left to pull the landing gear selector down. Then just to the right of that, she used two fingers to flip up two switches that extended the landing lights. On either side of the fuselage, sealed beam flood lamps unfolded from under the wing and rotated down, then past the vertical to shine straight ahead. Shifting her hand straight up, the copilot used two fingers to flip up two more switches. The landing lights flashed on. At the same time, the engineer reached to a panel above his head and flipped two switches illuminating the taxi lights affixed to the main landing gear doors.

These four lights were joined by two others, with one positioned on the underside of each wing, far out toward the tips. All together, six bright white beams reached forward, hit the snow, and illuminated a wall of brilliant white, constantly in motion. It surged toward the plane as though it would impact any instant, but dashed away just before it struck. Always racing toward the snow but never striking it, the plane hung suspended in a cloud. It rocked, and banged, and flexed and skidded through the air. Somewhere metal squealed in distress. But despite the constant movement, the plane never seemed to move. It hung suspended in a cloud of white.

The pilot glanced out the window. The dead engine hung silent near the far end of the wing. The blades were flat, immobile like a vertical cross.

The bright beams of the landing lights hit the dust and illuminated a wall of dirt—dirty brown sand, constantly in motion. It surged toward the plane as though it would impact any instant, but always skipped away just before it struck. Always racing toward the wall of dust but never striking it, the plane hung suspended in a cloud. It rocked and banged and flexed and skidded through the air. Somewhere metal squealed in distress. But despite the constant movement, the aircraft never seemed to move. It hung suspended in a cloud of dirty brown.

The pilot glanced out the window. The dead engine trailed smoke, a darker black than the cloud of dust that surrounded it. The side of the engine was black and scorched and threatening. The propeller hung motionless like a flat X, resisting the wind and pulling the aircraft hard to the left.

"Speed 160."

"Weather says ceiling is a thousand feet," interjected the navigator. "We should break out anytime now."

"Wolf 41," called the tower. "Looks like weather has taken the rabbit lights out. We have somebody working it. Hope to have it back up shortly."

So the flashing white sequential lights that marked the center of the runway were dark. Now even finding the airport in the storm might be tricky.

Pilot Mike Middleton continued to descend along the imaginary line described by his Attitude Directional Indicator and into the brilliant white nothingness. He watched the arrow on the right side of the scale align with the indicator line, then continue to descend until it was too low. He pulled back on the yoke and raised the nose of the aircraft just a bit, and the arrow and indicator became perfectly aligned. Simultaneously he adjusted the track of the aircraft across the ground until the HSI indicator showed him perfectly aligned with the runway. Now if he could just see where he was going to land. . . .

At a thousand feet above the ground, the thick white haze thinned and turned to streaks. Through the streaks, the pilots could see snow covered earth and bright lights intermittently. As they dropped down, the landing lights went from illuminating a white wall to illuminating individual snowflakes. Just over their heads, thick white clouds reflected the lights like a white ceiling stretching away into the distance. The snow was still heavy, but now it existed as squads of flakes, and not as a protoplasmic mass. The copilot realized with a start that they had been flying in both snow and clouds. Now they were below the clouds and flying in heavy snow alone.

"Anybody see anything?" the pilot asked. "We should be about three miles out." All was quiet in response.

"Beacon!" announced the navigator. "Green, green, white—that's it!" he called out excitedly.

It is amazing how difficult it can be in the dark of night to see something as big and well lit as an airport, even when instruments tell you exactly where to look. But tucked in among the light displays of streets, buildings, and shopping malls—and especially at Christmas—and especially in heavy snow—it can be hard to see where you are supposed to land.

Once the beacon told them where to look, it was clear that the runway stretched out in front of them on the ground. Three horizontal rows of red lights and a row of white crossed their front. Then two vertical rows of white lights, marking the edges of the runway, ran in parallel directly away from them, disappearing into the snow and darkness off the nose. As they watched a long row of white lights begin to flash in sequence describing a path right down the center of the runway. Somewhere in the dark and falling snow, a work crew had restored power to the lights. Just in time.

The great gray shape was moving fast—faster than normal for a landing. It flashed over the approach lights and headed for the numbers painted on the end of the runway—numbers completely obscured by a coat of white. It did not hang in the snow. It fell rapidly from the sky.

"As we cross the end of the runway, the white lights shining directly up in the air and bouncing off the heavy snow are going to blind us for a moment." The pilot was speaking to the copilot in his teaching voice; as though it were a simulator and they were preparing to break for a cup of coffee. "Don't worry. We'll pass through it quickly. Be ready for it—squint hard—and just ride it out. Don't change anything. We'll do fine."

"What?" asked the copilot. "How do you know that?"

"Don't worry—we're almost home," the pilot said.

"But how do you know?" asked the copilot again.

"I've done this before," the pilot answered.

The great gray shape was moving fast—faster than normal for a landing. It flashed over the approach lights and headed for the numbers painted on the end of the runway. It did not hang in the dust. It fell rapidly from the sky. At sixty feet the ground pushed back. The air exerted an upward "ground effect" causing the aircraft to float a little.

Just at that moment, the aircraft crossed the bank of white lights marking the end of the runway. Most nights they would have had no effect on the landing. But tonight with thick dust hanging so heavy in the air, they created a vertical wall of light, blinding the pilots at exactly the moment they should be adjusting for the ground effect. They were surprised by the sudden glare, and when it passed, their unprotected eyes could not adjust rapidly to the dark. The pilot wearing night vision goggles was hit especially hard as the green light amplification screen flashed white and turned itself off. Both plots strained in vain to see forward. Instead they saw only pools of black while their eyes recovered.

Meanwhile, the aircraft floated down the runway. Five hundred feet went by. A thousand. Two thousand. Three.

Flying blind and realizing he had waited too long, the pilot forced the nose down to the ground—just as the ground effect was exhausted and the aircraft began to settle to the runway by itself.

The result was a terrible jolt and a smashing noise as the landing gear slammed into the runway. The plane bounced once, skipped up, and returned to the ground with renewed force.

It was an acceptable landing under the circumstances. No metal was bent. No parts of the aircraft were damaged.

But the human cargo in the back was not so lucky.

At sixty feet the ground pushed back. The air exerted an upward "ground effect," causing the aircraft to float just a little.

Just at that moment, the aircraft crossed the bank of white lights marking the end of the runway. With snow hanging so heavy in the air, it created a vertical wall of light that the great ship had to penetrate.

At the critical moment, just as the reflection flashed to blinding brilliance, the pilot squinted his eyes. In an instant they were through, and with the flash of light behind them, the pilot concentrated on settling through the ground effect. Just past the numbers on the runway, the massive bird set its wheels carefully on the snow. There was no impact. There was no bounce. They were down.

Instantly the pilot reached for the throttle levers of the three working engines and pulled them up and back to the idle position. He was lifting all three to pull further back when the copilot said, "Confirm—just reversing Engines 2 and 3."

"Uh . . . confirm," answered the pilot. He adjusted his hand to grasp only the center two levers, picked them up, and pulled rearward. The angle of the propeller on the two engines on either side of the fuselage reversed to push air forward, slowing the plane rapidly but in a balanced way. The dead engine on the far left provided no thrust at all. Neither did the Number 4 engine on the far right position, which continued to turn its perfectly flat propellers furiously, but without providing either push or pull.

Still, the huge plane was splashing through an accumulating layer of slush. The pilot struggled to use his foot pedals to keep the aircraft centered on the runway.

"Stay off the brakes!" he commanded the copilot.

The copilot tucked her feet in close, and kept them away from the rudder pedals and brakes.

As the aircraft slowed, the pilot made a brief attempt to guide it with the steering wheel. Beneath the massive plane, the nose gear merely moved sideways in the slush. Nearly empty of fuel, they were riding a fifty-ton sled now, and the pilot immediately abandoned the effort to steer it. Instead he reached to the throttle levers and adjusted them deftly one at a time, applying a bit more power on one side, a bit less on the other, then correcting again, as the big plane, again a creature of the earth, fishtailed down the runway.

At approximately the 7,000 foot mark, the plane eased smoothly to a stop.

"Tower this is Wolf 41. The runway is very slick with ice. Request we stop here and wait for a tow to parking."

"Roger," answered the tower. "Nobody else in the air tonight. Request approved. We will send a tow out to you. And we will be shutting down operations. We are below minimums now. You guys got in just in time."

"Thanks tower," answered the pilot, realizing that the tower crew had been sweating the shutdown call for some time. "And a Merry Christmas to you."

After a few minutes, a glow appeared followed by headlights feeling their way through the blinding snow. The engines were all stopped now, and a figure heavily bundled against the cold dismounted from a yellow tractor. Trudging through the rapidly accumulating snow, he stopped below the left window and gestured with a flashlight. The pilot waved an okay, and the driver returned to the tractor, circling in an arc to a spot directly in front of the nose.

Behind the tractor trailed two long yellow metal bars on wheels. The driver backed them deftly to the nose wheel and dismounted carrying a shovel. He scooped snow away from the wheel, and shifted the bars until he could align them with holes on the gear. Then he then snapped two locking pins in place. As he turned back to the tractor, his glance fell to the spot he had shoveled. White paint showed against the dark runway before snowflakes could cover it up.

Curious, he hoisted the shovel off his shoulder and cleared a space a little longer. Then a little longer. Then a little longer than that.

With each shovel of snow removed, a bit more paint was revealed. Then a break in the paint. Then another stripe of paint. After a few minutes of shoveling he looked back over his handiwork. Behind him was a cleared strip stretching a hundred feet back to the plane. Snow and ice were accumulating to the side of the bare swath he had cut. Within the cleared space, the black of the runway showed through, straight between the lines of white lights and into the darkness. And running through the center of the cleared space was a dashed white line. It was the centerline of the runway.

Through yesterday's ghosts and today's storms, the pilot had guided his plane and his crew to safety. The trip was over. They were right on the centerline.

CHAPTER 18: INTO THE DARKNESS

Ninety minutes later, as the crew was just completing a blizzard of reports, safety forms, and logbook entries, the Flying Safety Officer pushed the door open and entered with the gusty wind at his back.

"Hey, Mike," began a lanky captain. "Glad you guys are back safe."

The pilot turned in his seat, and the rest of the crew focused on the new arrival.

"Jimbo!" said the pilot in surprise. "So they got you out of bed on Christmas Eve for this?" he asked. His decisions had been good. His flying had been superb. Now he had to worry about being second guessed by administrative weenies.

"Oh yeah!" the new arrival exclaimed loudly. He rubbed his cold hands together. "A dead engine and a bleed air leak, then landing in a storm at a base that should have been closed an hour earlier? I'd say you're famous. Your little flight bounced from the tower to the squadron commander to the wing commander, to the base commander, back to the squadron commander, to me. Everybody is going to want a report."

Then his manner softened. "But don't worry—looks to me like you did everything right."

He shifted into his professional voice, but in a friendly way, and brushed the snow from his shoulders.

"Hard to see by flashlight in this snow," he continued. "But looks like two V-shaped scorch marks on the bleed air tube—hairline cracks probably. Bunch of fried wires all around it. I would guess you got a bunch of gauge fluctuations, and maybe some irregular warning lights. Lucky you shut it off when you did. No telling what it could have burned through next."

"Yeah," said the pilot. "Lucky."

The copilot looked at him sharply. "*Luck*," she thought, "*had nothing to do with it.*"

"What's your next step?" the pilot asked.

"We can button it up and go home tonight," continued the safety officer. "Look at it on the day after Christmas. But bottom line is I'm pretty sure you'll come out clean. A good call in a tough spot."

He turned to go, then turned back again. "It really was nicely done," he said.

The pilot nodded and went back to his work. The other crew members stared after the safety officer disappearing down the stairs, then looked at each other. Then at the pilot.

"*Yes*," each thought to himself. "*Don't try. Do.*"

The crew deck was dark and getting cold. The gauges all rested at zero. The indicator lights were all dark. The cabin was quiet except for the scratching of ball point pens on clipboard and logbook as the pilot and copilot finished the last of the paperwork. Each was lit by a single overhead light. The copilot clicked the pen to retract the point and slipped it into a narrow pocket on the shoulder of her flight suit. She folded the paper in half, then reached up and snapped off the light. As darkness enveloped her side of the instrument panel, she took a deep breath, and tried to look out the wind screen to the front. Snow covered the window completely. There was nothing to see.

"Nice job." It was the pilot. There was no hint of lecture or instruction in his voice. He was speaking like a colleague. Like a friend. Like a teammate.

"That was a little intense for a while. You were very steady. You did fine. Good catch on the throttles. I would be happy to fly with you again."

In the dark, her cheeks burned once more. But this time it was not in shame. This time she was pleased, and she was embarrassed that she was pleased. And yet she knew she deserved the praise. That made it even better.

"Thanks," she said, as casually as she could muster. Yes it had been "very intense for a while." But she had tried her best. She took the ball when it was offered. She took the shot. And she made it. She didn't just try—she did it. Her best turned out to be good enough after all. So this is what it was like to win the big game.

She gathered a few odds and ends into her flight bag, climbed out of the seat, and started down the small hall to the door. Then she turned.

"I'd like to share something with you," she said.

The pilot looked up with interest.

"I know this is a cliché, but you really remind me of my father."

This was an unexpected direction. He nodded his head and smiled politely, unsure of what was coming next.

"He was a NASA engineer," she continued. "Unbelievably smart. Professional. Proficient. High standards for himself and everyone around him. Lived his life to three decimal places—know what I mean? No slack. No compromise. Completely binary—world divided into perfection and failure. Drove himself. Taught me to drive myself."

He was still smiling politely.

"Miserable person to live with. Absolutely miserable. I got out of there the minute I could."

The turn in the story caught him by surprise.

"You're a great pilot. I am lucky to learn from you. But I thought I might mention that story to you before you go home to your kids tonight."

She turned. "Merry Christmas," she said over her shoulder.

The pilot sat quietly for a few minutes, alone with his thoughts. Then he completed his last entry, signed his last document, and snapped off his overhead light. It was quiet, dark, and cold in the pilot's seat. He shivered, rubbed his hands together, and then rubbed his arms. He had sweated through his flight suit, between his legs, under his arms, and across his back. His t-shirt and underwear were both soaked. Now in the chill air it was all uncomfortable against his skin.

The lights were still on in the cargo bay—probably the loadmaster cleaning up. He thought for a moment about calling his wife to tell her that he was back. But then he checked his watch, pressing a button on the side to light the hands and numbers in a green glow. It was late—after midnight. Christmas Eve was over. He had missed reading the kids their

Christmas stories and the excitement of putting them to bed. He had missed wrapping presents for under the tree with his wife. He had missed hot cocoa on the sofa looking out the window together.

But the truth, he knew, was that the course to missing tonight at home had been plotted a year ago when he began to drift away from the family, and wrap himself tighter and tighter into a professional ball. More and more he used competency to substitute for human interaction. Less and less he focused on the people who mattered to him the most. His conversations with them had become more like briefings. His time with them became more like working through the steps of a checklist:

- Supper—check
- Bath—check
- Teeth—check
- Story—check
- Prayers—check
- In bed—check
- Lights out—check
- Switch off.

It was not the right way to treat his children or his wife, and he knew it. He was in a flat spin, and he could not recover. He could not share the burden that was dragging him down, and he could not stay aloft on his own. He needed a helping hand on the control yoke. He didn't know where to get it.

He sighed again and the cloud of steam from this breath rolled across the dials and gauges. No, he would not call his wife now. He was tired. That argument could wait for later.

He started to open the door and descend the ladder to the outside, but was drawn to the crew compartment by the lights. It looked big when it was empty, and the bright white lights lit it all like a hospital emergency room. So he walked to the crew ladder and descended into the hold. As he turned around, he heard a thumping sound and looked down. A bright red liquid splashed across his boots.

The landing had been hard, but not bad given the wind and storm, the limited visibility, and the need to hurry for those bleeding out. Not bad at all. But very hard on the patients clinging to straps, and the nurses trying to stand in the aisles to give IVs.

So as soon as the plane was parked and the engines stopped, he leapt from his seat to see if he could lend a hand. Turning around at the base of the crew ladder, he was stunned at the chaos of the scene unfolding before him.

The floor was littered with equipment. Ventilators, bandages, IV bags, metal and cardboard boxes of every shape and size. Most of the equipment had been latched down, but everything that had been open and in use was in a jumble on the floor.

All twelve patients were in some degree of distress. Those in the red sling seats along the wall were holding their wounds and grimacing. On three stacks of litters, each three high, most of the patients were rocking back and forth while attendants worked on them. Most of them. Some were still.

On several, the IVs had been pulled out and a mixture of army medics and air force medical technicians worked to rig new bags and tubes. One of the bottom litters had come loose from the tie downs on one end, and the patient had spilled part way into the aisle. While he watched, attendants lifted the wounded soldier back on to the bloody litter and tightened the straps that were supposed to hold him in place. The patient was still wearing his battle dress but the trousers ended at the knee. He had no legs.

Directly across from where he stood sat a nurse in the sling seats against the wall of the aircraft. She was holding her left arm with her right. The left arm looked strange beneath the flight suit, and the hand twisted much too far to the side. Something was terribly wrong.

The back ramp was down now, dust swirled everywhere, and people were swarming inside to help. The MCD stood at his side, directing traffic and clean up. Pausing for a moment she turned to look at him.

"Was that a landing or did we crash?" she asked harshly.

He grasped for words. "The storm was really bad," he said weakly. "I tried to . . . uh . . . I tried . . . "

"Don't try," she barked. "People's lives are at stake. Don't just try. Do it right!"

She shifted her attention to four soldiers trying to lift a top litter down from its brackets. One stumbled and the litter sagged suddenly toward the corner he was holding. The patient said nothing. He was unconscious—lifeless. But the pool of blood he was lying in surged down the length of the litter and toward the sagging corner. The bright red liquid poured over the side and cascaded to the ground. It splashed directly on the pilot's boot, soaked the leg of his flight suit, and splashed across the floor. The pilot jumped back, his eyes round with horror.

The bright red fluid cascaded to the ground. It splashed directly on the pilot's boot, soaked the leg of his flight suit, and splashed across the floor. The pilot jumped back, his eyes round with horror.

"Oh geez, sir. I'm so sorry." It was the loadmaster. He held a quart can of red hydraulic fluid in his hands. It was mostly empty.

The pilot looked down to see his boots and the lower legs of his flight suit covered in a dark, wet red. He looked up at the loadmaster again, then down at this boots trying to take it all in.

"Let me get a cloth," said the loadmaster. "I'll wipe that right up. I'm so sorry."

CHAPTER 18: INTO THE DARKNESS

The pilot struggled for a moment to recover his composure. "No, no," he said. "It's all right."

He backed to the ladder, felt it with his hand, and turned to climb. He paused to look back at the airman. "Merry Christmas, Ben," he said. "Merry Christmas."

Quickly the pilot walked the length of the short passage to the door, opened it into the blowing snow, and closed it behind himself as he started down the ladder.

At the bottom he stopped, clinging to a rung with the hand that also held his helmet bag as he steadied himself. Snow was wetting his shoulders but he didn't notice. He felt sick. He lifted his free hand to cover his face for a moment. But his hand was red with hydraulic fluid, left on the ladder by his boots. He stared for a moment, then wiped it on his chest. Then he turned and fled into the dark and the falling snow, toward the parking lot and his truck.

His boots made a deep impression in the snow, which was now building to a depth of several inches. At the bottom of each footprint was a red stain from the hydraulic fluid. Bright red on the pure white snow, the red marks chased him into the darkness and toward home.

CHAPTER 11

CENTERLINE

0100 hours 25 December: Little Rock AFB

The beams from the headlights bounced back from the curtain of heavy snow in a glare so bright that it nearly blinded the driver. The flakes were not big and soft and lacey this time. Instead they were small and hard and mean—the kind that made it nearly as much an ice storm as a snow storm. They swarmed against the windshield like angry bees. The wipers pounded at the highest rate—*tic, tic, tic*—but their only effect was to carve out a semicircular clearing in the middle of each window. The view opened by each swipe was nearly obscured before the next high speed wipe of the blade. It was nature against man and his technology tonight. The victory was going to man . . . but just barely.

Mike Middleton was late getting home. Again.

The snow and slush were several inches deep when the truck navigated the sharp *S* around the concrete barriers, switched to its parking lights, and rolled to a stop at the guard post. There were no other tracks on the street tonight. Perhaps the snow had covered them. More likely, everyone else was at home. The driver slid the window down with the press of a button, and the ice bees poured in. Outside they made a crackling noise, almost like hard sand, as they stacked up on every surface.

The floodlights on the new fallen snow set the scene in stark contrast. The whites were nearly as brilliant as sun light. The shadows dark as the darkest night. It was hard for the eye to balance in between.

The guard bounded out of the warm protective hut as if glad for the momentary company. He had grown to know the truck and its driver, but they had to go through the formalities.

"Merry Christmas, Captain! ID please."

As always the driver clicked on the inside light, then handed out the plastic card, giving the guard a clear view of the inside of the vehicle, the driver, and his identification. He kept both hands on the top of the steering wheel where they could be seen. It was a professional courtesy born of routine.

"Merry Christmas, sir," Middleton responded tiredly. "So you drew the duty tonight?"

"Yes, sir," answered the guard. He examined the front of the card, then flipped it over to examine the back. As he took a step to hand it through the window, his foot slipped on the compacted ice. His arm flailed for just a moment before he caught himself on the side of the truck.

"Hard to keep your balance in this storm" observed the driver.

"Right you are," replied the guard. "Gotta find something to hang on to."

"I'll be okay," advised Captain Middleton. "I'm headed home."

He retrieved his card, returned the guard's salute, and slipped the truck back into gear, raising the window as he pulled away from the gate. The metallic clicking sound of the tiny ice balls crashing on to the snowpack was replaced by the crystal sound of the ice bees striking the windshield. The cab was quiet and warm, like a little home in the storm. But it wasn't home.

Home was still a few blocks away. Tonight those blocks looked strange and wild, with every familiar landmark obscured by the drifting snow.

The high beams caught the letters *Flo* in their glare. The rest of the street name was obscured.

Captain Middleton turned the corner, then pulled the truck to the side of the street and stopped. He rested his head on the steering wheel. He was sick. Not sick to his stomach. Sick at heart.

He wanted to go home to his wife and his children and his Christmas and the way it used to be. He was tired of the separation and the things that were driving them further apart. He was tired of the memories that kept pushing up past the barriers he had erected to separate his life from his work, and tired of worrying about what might happen if he ever relaxed those barriers even for a moment. He was tired of being afraid of the thing that used to give him the greatest joy in life: his wife's voice.

"*In Flight Emergency*," he thought. Except with this emergency he had no one to call. No flight center to flash with his location. No tower to clear the approach. No crew to talk to or exchange ideas with. The snow in his headlights isolated him from everything. There were no reference points anywhere. Just indifferent sky above and cold, hard ground below. He was all alone.

He maneuvered between the cars, and headed down what he hoped was the center of the street. The first wave of wet, heavy show had covered the centerline, and now the curbs had disappeared as well. As the center of the storm moved over the base, the wind smoothed and leveled the subsequent layers until the surface was uniform and trackless, from the dark houses on one side of the street to the other. There were no lights to brighten the way this time. It was late—past midnight and into Christmas Day. The holiday lights were out, the holiday celebrations were over, and the holiday celebrants were in bed.

Except for one house far down the street, where a single strand of colored lights graced a small artificial tree balanced precariously on a table before the living room window. Like a tiny beacon it marked the end of his journey, and he guided the pickup truck carefully down what he hoped was the road, and into a carport lit by the multicolored glow.

He parked the truck, killed the lights, and set the brake. Then he sat for a moment looking at the tired little tree in the window. The effect of the solitary lights and the oversized star was curious. It was sad in a way—such a small little glow set against the fierceness of the storm. The inhabitants deserved better than this. But it was also warm—a tiny little sign of hope and family at the end of a long, dark road.

Gathering bags and packages in his arms, he swung the door open against the icy wind. He crunched his way through the deep, crusty snow to the back door, where he set down his load and returned to the truck. From the bed he lifted a real tree—a spruce, round and full and taller than his head—and carried it lightly to the door. Then he returned to the cab to recover a steaming cup that he sheltered protectively against the wind.

The snow had drifted against the door as if determined to get in. Trying not to make a sound, he opened first the screen, then the wooden door, and stepped softly on to a rug in the kitchen. He stomped his boots off quietly, then shook them free of his feet. Standing in tan woolen socks, he leaned back outside to recover the packages, then leveraged the tree carefully through the door. The small light over the stove snapped on, bathing the dark kitchen in a soft glow. His wife stood at the door that led to the dining room.

"I'm so sorry," he said apologetically. "I didn't want to wake you." His voice was wary, his posture protective. He didn't want to fight.

"I wasn't going to bed," she replied warmly. "I knew you would try to get home tonight. I just didn't know if you could make it in."

"I brought mocha," he said carefully. "Just in case. But I know it keeps you up. . . . "

"Great!" she said brightly. "I wasn't planning to go to sleep for a while. Maybe to bed but not to sleep." She accepted the cup gratefully and took a sip.

"Where did you find a coffee shop still open? And a Christmas tree? Good grief, what's open at this time of night on Christmas Eve?"

She was being very pleasant. Unusually so. *"Oh my God,"* he thought. He remembered what the navigator said and his blood ran cold. *"She wants a divorce."*

He stood silently—undecided what to say next.

"Mike?" she asked again. "Where did you find something open?"

He looked at her carefully. Slowly he realized that she was expecting him to answer.

"Um . . . the 24 hour Shoppette," he replied. Then he stopped. He turned to the bags on the floor. "I have lights."

She stepped across the room and looked in the bag. "Goodness!" she exclaimed. "I guess you do. Two, four, six strings of lights? We'll have planes guiding on us instead of the runway!"

Then she paused. "Expensive," she said.

"Not so much," he replied, a bit too defensively. She hadn't challenged him. The comment was actually more like a compliment.

"Everything was half-priced," he recovered. "After-Christmas sale."

"After Christmas?" She turned her head sideways, like a curious puppy, and pursed her lips. He loved that look—it was so sweet. He had not seen it in a long time.

"It's after midnight," he explained. "After Christmas."

She laughed gently, as if they were sharing a joke. In fact, they *were* sharing a joke. Something was wrong here. Or at least different. Something was very different.

"Shall we set up the tree?" She picked up the bag with the lights, turned and walked through the small dining room with its two booster seats at the table, and on to the living room. She was wearing short Christmas socks—red, white, and green, cut below the ankle, with a fuzzy red ball on the back of the heel. It was feminine. And cute.

"Bring the tree," she called back invitingly. She unplugged the lights to the small tree, and slid the table holding it away from the window. Then she swept aside a number of brightly wrapped packages clustered on the floor, making room for the larger tree.

He carried it in and set it dead center before the window, then moved it off to the side. "I like being able to look out at the storm," he said. "It makes it feel warm in here."

She smiled again and began to open the bags from the shoppette and unwrap the lights. Detaching the single strand of old lights from the extension cord, she plugged in the new lights and held the glowing ball of tiny bulbs in her hands. The colors lit her face warmly. She smiled again. She was beautiful when she smiled. He had forgotten.

"Do you want to check the kids while I get started?"

He padded quietly down the hall in his socks and paused before a door festooned with pages from a coloring book. Santa. Reindeer. Frosty. A snowman made from paper plates, buttons, and pipe cleaners. A chain of red and green construction paper. The door swung open quietly. He could see the bunk beds from across the room and made his way to them carefully, without turning on the lights.

The boy in the top bunk had twisted his covers around his torso and legs. His father unwrapped them slowly and drew the covers back. The boy was wearing pajamas—a Superman top and a Spiderman bottom.

"Dressed yourself, huh champ?" the father said quietly. He shook the sheet to free it, then spread it evenly over the sleeping form. A small hand was grasping an airplane—a gray model of a C-130. The propeller was off on the Number 1 engine. He picked it up and gently snapped it back on the empty hub, then tapped the blades with his finger. The propeller spun freely.

Bending low, the father found the tiny figure in the lower bunk curled in a ball and without any covers at all. Both arms were wrapped around a soft oblong pillow about eighteen inches tall. It was a "Daddy Doll"—a pillow in the shape of a person, with a full length image of her daddy in his pilot's garb imprinted on the front. When you pressed a button on the side, it told a story that he had recorded before his last deployment. It was supposed to help children remember a face and voice during long absences. He wondered if it worked.

Carefully he pulled the sheet and blanket up around her neck. She snuggled the doll closer and sighed.

Backing off two steps, he took a long look at both children. "*They deserve more than I'm giving them,*" he thought. He felt guilty. Again. With a heavy heart he turned to the door.

"What else is in the bags?" his wife asked cheerily when he returned to the living room. She was winding a third strand of lights about the tree and it was beginning to show its multicolored shape.

"The live tree smells great," she said. She stopped when she saw his face. "What's the matter?" she asked.

"Nothing," he lied. Then, "It just made me sad to see them and know I missed reading to them on Christmas Eve. I'm sorry, Joy. I really am." He really meant it.

She nodded while she continued unwrapping lights. "I know you are. But I know it was an important trip. I talked to Martin Jefferson's wife this evening. He called her just before you left San Antonio, and she called me."

"Really?" He was surprised. "How do you know her?"

"Bible Study," she replied. "I go on Tuesday mornings, after Brett and Bryn get off to school."

He was struck again by how little he really knew about her life while he was gone. And how much of that life she spent alone.

"She said it was a really important mission. She said you were carrying wounded who were badly hurt. Said you might have saved their lives by getting them to Ft. Sam in a hurry."

"Well, I hope so," he said. His voice was light and non-committal. He glanced in her direction and found that she was standing still, staring at him—waiting for him to continue.

He paused. Then he took a deep breath.

"The truth is, I just don't know Jo-Jo. They were all burned up. Maybe we helped. Maybe we just prolonged their agony for a couple of days. I just don't know."

He closed his eyes and wiped them tiredly.

"I'm sorry, Mike. I really am," she said. And she really meant it. "Do you want to talk about it?"

He shook his head no. She waited, then went on.

"What's in the big bag?" Her voice said she was trying to change the subject. And the mood.

"Horses," he grinned. "Horses and Power Pilots. All the way from the Scott Base Exchange."

"Oh, I'm so glad!" she enthused, returning to the lights. She had carried a stool in from the kitchen and was on the top step, trimming the top of the tree. It was glowing brightly now—600 tiny glowing lights. It was almost done.

"Did you think I would forget?" he asked.

"I knew you would do your best," she answered carefully. "I'm glad you were able to get them. But if you weren't, we would have survived. The kids have gifts from your parents and my parents under the tree, and some things from my sister. It would have been all right."

She did not look up from stringing lights. Something was really different.

"Joy?" he asked. He was measuring every word carefully. "Did I do something right that I don't know about?"

She smiled to herself, but didn't answer. Instead she climbed down, crossed over to the small dark artificial tree, removed the oversized star from the top, and climbed back on the kitchen stool. She balanced the star carefully on the top of the new tree, and plugged it in. It was the perfect size for the bigger tree. She climbed down, and moved the stool to the side, slid the packages under the glowing branches, and sat down on the couch across from the window to admire her work.

She picked up the mocha from an end table and sipped it. It was cooling but she pretended not to notice. Then she looked at her husband.

"Would you like to open your present?" she asked. Setting down the cup, she knelt next to the tree, then disappeared under the branches, reaching way in the back. She emerged with a small box, six inches square, wrapped in red and green. Smiling a little self-consciously, she returned to the couch.

Her husband reached to press the button on a CD player, then made his way to the couch as the low sound of Christmas carols filled the room. Sitting down next to her, he took the box.

"Well," he began. "You are sitting next to me so I am guessing it isn't going to explode."

It was kind of a joke, but also a bit of a reminder from their last conversation. She looked pained.

He unzipped a leg pocket of his jumpsuit, and pulled out a pocket knife. Snapping it open with the flick of a thumb, he slid the blade deftly along the edges of the paper, cutting the tape without harming the wrapping. They weren't poor, but money was tight every month. The paper could be used again. Setting aside the red and green, he removed the lid of a plain white box and discovered a flashlight, four inches long, with a flat black metallic finish and various batteries, lenses and attachments. *Surefire Aviator* it said on the side.

"Oh yes!" he exclaimed. "This is excellent!" He held it inverted in his fist, and thumbed a button on the back. A bright green dot appeared on the floor. Rotating his wrist quickly, he flashed the light around the room, pausing to focus on the watch on his other wrist. Then he clicked the light off. The watch glowed brightly in the dark.

"This will work with my night vision goggles!" he said. "Some of the other guys had lights like this in the sandbox. This is great! How did you know about this?"

He was working his way through the box with excitement, fingering an attachment, pausing to pick up a colored lens, snapping the button on the back on and off.

"I talked to Rusty's wife," she said. "She bought him one for his last deployment, and he told her you really liked it."

"These are so great!" he answered. "You can clip it on your wrist, you can clip it on your knee board, you can clip it on your hat . . . " He paused. "Hey, this is expensive. You didn't try to squeeze this out of the household money, did you?" There was real concern in his voice. The thought that the kids or the kitchen might have been shorted to pay for his gift bothered him greatly.

"No, no," she smiled quietly. "I did some babysitting. Usually I just swap off with the other wives, but Zoey has a part-time job, and sometimes she comes up short on a sitter. She is getting paid, so she pays me."

Oh. Something else he did not know about when he left the family behind. When he was gone, which was a lot, he knew that she had hardly a minute to herself, watching the children from waking until going to sleep. And she had taken on watching other children for many hours to buy this expensive gift. Suddenly, it meant a great deal to him.

"Okay," he said. "Your turn." From behind a different zipper on his flight suit he extracted a small box, wrapped in shiny gold paper. No ribbons. No bows. But the gold paper flashed beautifully in the light from the tree.

She was more eager than he had expected, and tore quickly at the paper. He smiled. Inside was a small white box and inside that a black velvet pouch. "Feels heavy!" she said. And so it did—quite heavy for such a small package.

She pulled the ribbon that closed the mouth of the pouch, turned it up with one hand, and poured the contents into the other. A heavy gold chain tumbled out, attached to a gold rectangle, the length of the last two joints on her little finger.

"This is a heavy chain!" she said. "And what is this? A watch tower?"

"It's the tower for a beacon light at an airport. See, the top is a light. It has lenses—two emeralds and a diamond. Like the two green beams and a white that mark a military airport." He held the gold tower close for her to see.

"I had it made on my last deployment. I've been holding it for nearly a year."

She was very pleased. "Will you put it on?" she asked. She bent her head forward and held up her hair while he looped it around her neck and fastened the latch. The back of her neck was very attractive. He leaned forward and kissed it softly. She lifted her head and smiled. Then frowned.

"Mike, this is really expensive. Where did you get the money?" It was not an ungrateful question. She was genuinely concerned.

"A year without lunch," he joked. "I needed to lose the weight!" Except it wasn't a joke.

She fingered the tower, hanging now below her chin. The three jewels flashed in the light of the Christmas tree.

"It's a homing beacon," he said. "When a pilot is lost in the dark it shows him how to find his way home."

Her mouth crinkled, and she fought back tears. The change was very quick and unexpected. She fought her emotions for a moment before gaining the upper hand. Then she cleared her throat.

"Mike," she said, looking away from him and toward the tree. "Why didn't you reply to my texts? Why didn't you call me when you got in tonight?"

She turned to look directly into her husband's eyes—searching.

"I thought you would be asleep," he lied. "I didn't want to wake you."

"Mike," she said levelly. "You were in the air in a bad storm with a broken airplane and every airport for a hundred miles in any direction was closed. Did you really think I would go to sleep?"

He paused, looked out the window, then looked her in the eye again. "I thought you would be mad," he said. "I didn't want to fight when I was away, or on Christmas Eve."

She leaned over to hug him. He leaned her way, but he didn't hug back.

"You're damp!" she said in surprise.

"Sorry," he responded. "I sweated through my flight suit."

It took a moment for the enormity of the comment to take shape in her mind. He had just wrestled home a crippled airplane with five people on board through a howling storm. Things had been so tense that in a frigid blizzard, he sweated through everything he was wearing. It must have been terrible. Their lives were on the line. And when he returned successfully, instead of calling to share his relief or celebrate his return, he was afraid to talk to her. He was afraid to hear her voice.

Her face crumpled and she fought back tears again.

"What?" he asked. "What is it?" Whatever it was he was supposed to say, he had done it wrong again.

"Oh Mike, you must think I'm a horrible wife."

They were really off course now, and he had no map. He put his arms around her.

"What are you talking about?" he said. "I'm the one who's never here! You take care of the kids, the house . . . I'm the one who can't keep a promise." Then he paused.

"How did you know we had a problem on the airplane?"

"I was worried about the storm, and when the TV said they closed

CHAPTER 11: CENTERLINE 271

the city airport, I called Mary Jefferson again. He called her soon as you touched down.

"He said it was really bad, but he knew you would get them home. She said everybody knew you were the best pilot in the squadron—maybe the best in the wing—and she always thought it would be okay if her husband was flying with you. She said everybody has faith in you."

She wiped her eyes with the back of her hand.

"Everybody but me I guess."

She took two shaky breaths, and looked out the window. Then she turned to look at him.

"Mike, I am so sorry about the way I sent you out of here. After I talked to her, and then you didn't call and you didn't text. And you didn't come home . . . I thought maybe you were going somewhere else tonight. I thought maybe I had lost you." She was breathing rapidly now.

He smiled and shook his head, and gave her a little squeeze. "No chance," he said. "I was just trying to keep some promises before I headed home."

They were both quiet for a long time.

"Joy," he began tentatively. "Do you really think I'm nuts?"

She sat up and looked at him. Her jaw dropped. She looked shocked.

"You said I needed help," he continued. "You said I need to talk to somebody."

She looked puzzled, then breathed a huge sigh of relief.

"Is that what this is all about?" she asked. "I meant you needed to talk with *me*, you big ninny!"

She took another deep breath and leaned on him. He put his arms around her.

After a moment she said, "But Mike. Why won't you talk to me about this stuff?"

She leaned closer.

"Look Mike, I get it now. I have to trust you more. That's where I've been letting you down. I know you're trying. I've decided I have to trust your judgment. You don't have to get everything right every time. Just keep trying and that will be good enough for me. I promise.

"But Mike . . . you have to trust me, too."

"I know I wasn't there tonight. I know I wasn't there in Iraq. I know I don't understand everything you are saying or feeling. But I am willing to listen. I am willing to try. Can't you meet me halfway?"

He stiffened and sat up straight. He removed his arms from around her and placed his hands on his knees. Now he was the one breathing rapidly. He felt trapped. He looked past her and out the window.

"I don't know, Joy. I just don't know. I just don't know how to talk to you about some of what I have seen. What I have done. I just don't know where to start."

She spent a minute taking that in, then reached out for his hand.

"Try me, Mike. You don't have to be perfect. Just try."

His eyes were troubled. He was looking past the tree, past the window, far out into the storm. Into the past.

"Mike," she said carefully. "This is a pretty important moment for us. We had a great marriage. Then about a year ago something happened. I don't know what it was—you did something, or you saw something, or something happened to you. I don't know what. But you stopped talking to me. You just lost yourself in work. We got completely off course—completely out of balance.

"And instead of trusting you, and helping you and encouraging you, I began pushing you and nagging you. And the harder I pushed, the further you withdrew. I see that now. I want to fix it—to get us back on center. You do the best you can, and I'll be satisfied with that. Promise.

"But I can't do this alone, Mike. Our little team can't survive together unless we talk. You have to share, too."

"I . . . um." His voice was halting. "I . . . um"

He grimaced and shook his head.

"I can't do this," he said. "I can't talk about this."

Her face fell. She closed her eyes, wrapped her arms around him, and pressed her head against his chest. Softly she began to cry.

For a long minute he was completely still; completely quiet. He took two deep breaths. Then softly, evenly, he began to speak.

"One night last tour I was carrying a load of wounded guys into Balad," he said. "Maybe a dozen. I don't know how many. They were all shot up. We were coming back from another mission when we heard a call. They asked for anybody in the area—said the guys were bleeding out. So the loadmasters started re-rigging and we vectored over there. Picked them up on a remote strip. Landed with no lights. It was hot as hell—sand blowing everywhere...."

He was sitting stock still, staring out the window, but trembling slightly. She stopped crying and hugged him tightly.

"On the way back I talked to the tower. They said a big dust storm was blowing up. It was going to be a footrace to get back before they closed the runway. We were thinking about diverting to somewhere else when this nurse came up front... said we had to hurry... said she was out of blood and these guys had to get to Balad and the hospital if they were going to make it. So I decided to give it a try."

He paused again, still looking out the window where the snow was small and fine and hard, pelting the house like sand.

In his ears he could hear the radio and the intercom. Calls for help. Pleas to hurry. Warnings about the weather.

She hugged him more tightly, holding on as if the howling wind were trying to tear him away. He started to speak again.

The storm was still fierce.

But it looked like it was starting to break.

EPILOGUE

EN ROUTE

1600 hours 22 December 2011: Somewhere else

In some ways, all deserts are alike. Hot, dry, godforsaken spots like the back side of the moon. Yet all worth killing for and dying for to someone.

Each desert is also different. Deserts in Iraq, for example, produce sand storms consisting mostly of dust that resembles nothing quite so much as tan talcum power. In Afghanistan, the atmosphere is filled with something more akin to fine dirt—more yellow-brown and ominous.

On this day, the dark Afghan dirt hung in the air and depressed the soul. The radio calls were equally ominous.

"Any rider this net, any rider this net—this is Full House. Request immediate assistance. I have four critically wounded and my medevac was diverted for maintenance."

Rifles cracked in the background of the transmission, punctuated by heavy machine-gun fire. The voice was high pitched and urgent.

"Any rider this net—I am at FOB J-bad—Is there anyone who can meet me on the south side of the runway? I'm gonna lose these guys out here!"

"Out here" was a remote part of the country. The soldiers were bleeding out. There were no aircraft in a position to respond. Except one.

The command pilot's instructions over the intercom were crisp and professional.

"Co, relay through Pyramid to Ops that we will take this mission.

"Nav, get me a heading for J-bad and an elevation for the runway.

"Eng, help me keep an eye on the Turbine Inlet Temperature on Number 4—seems to be running a little hot.

"Load, start breaking down the back half of the aircraft. No seats–rig for litters.

"I have the aircraft."

The pilot took two deep breaths. Using her thumb, Captain JT Williams switched from the intercom button on the control yoke to the radio button.

"Full House," she broadcast coolly. "This is Flash 97. En route your location."

The huge aircraft thundered across the desert with its throttles wide open at barely 100 feet above the ground. Behind, the turboprop engines threw up a dust storm of their own. Ahead, somebody in the family needed help. Flash 97 was en route.

As the C-130 roared into the murky haze, the pilot raised the nose and dropped the left wing to turn. The right wing lifted high as if to wave, and the gray skin flashed once as it reflected the sun through the dirty air. Then it slid rapidly to the left, toward the next mission, and was gone.

ABOUT THE AUTHOR

Dave McIntyre graduated from West Point and spent thirty years in the United States Army, retiring as a Colonel. His time was divided between duty with airborne and armored reconnaissance units, and writing and teaching strategy at the national level. He also taught English at West Point. He retired as the Dean of Faculty and Academics at the National War College. For two years after 9/11 he was deputy director of a national think tank on homeland security, and for four years director of a graduate program in homeland security at Texas A&M. He has also taught national and homeland security at George Washington University, the University of Texas, and the National Graduate School.

He is presently a Distinguished Visiting Fellow at the *Homeland Security Studies and Analysis Institute*, and at the *Bipartisan WMD Terrorism Research Center*, both in Washington, DC. Dr. McIntyre has: a BS in Engineering from the United States Military Academy; an MA in English and American Literature from Auburn University; a PhD in Political Science from the University of Maryland.

Dave spent the last 25 years writing, teaching and speaking on national and homeland security issues. *CENTERLINE* is his debut novel.

Made in the USA
Lexington, KY
11 April 2015